Misery & Company

ANGIE DANIELS

— THE COMPANY SERIES —

Caramel Kisses Publishing

THE COMPANY SERIES

In the Company of My Sistahs

Trouble Loves Company

Careful of the Company You Keep

Misery & Company

ANGIE DANIELS

— THE COMPANY SERIES —

Caramel Kisses
Publishing

ISBN-13: 978-1-941342-27-5

Copyright © 2017 by Angie Daniels

All rights reserved. Except for use in any review, the reproduction or utilization of this work in whole or in part in any form by any electronic, mechanical or other means, now know or hereafter invented, including xerography, photocopying and recording, or in any information storage or retrieval system, is forbidden without the written permission of the author.

This is a work of fiction. Names, characters, places and incidents are either the product of the author's imagination or are used fictitiously, and any resemblance to actual persons, living or dead, business establishments, events or locales is entirely coincidental.

For questions and comments about the book please contact angie@angiedaniels.com.

Caramel Kisses Ink

DEDICATION

This book is dedicated to Sharon Blount of Building Relationships Around Books (BRAB) for repeatedly asking for a sequel. If it hadn't been for her persistence, it might have been years before I got around to writing this installment.

To Mark Kelly, Ashlie Kelly, and Evan Smith for being the best children in the world. I'm proud and I love you.

To my sistahs, Tonya Houston, Kim Ashcraft, Norma Rhodes, and Arlynda Rae Johnson for all the years of crazy secrets and laughter. Without these women, this series would not be possible.

To my husband Todd Christopher Wilson, I could not imagine life without you. I appreciate all your patience while I was working feverishly to complete this book. Love you much, babe!

To all my loyal readers, thank you so much for the love and support over the last fifteen years. Happy Reading!

1
Renee

I sauntered into the room and was well aware all eyes were on me. Tonight, I was going to be the baddest bitch up in this place, and the jealous looks on the faces around me made it clear that most of them wished they were me.

That's right!

The bitch is back!

As I swayed my hips to the beat of the music, it took everything I had not to laugh. I looked good and everyone knew it. I had gone to a great deal of trouble making sure I had found the perfect black sequin gown, guaranteed to turn heads. It was off the shoulders and the mermaid style fit my new body like a glove.

Yep, that's right. I had new 36C breasts and a flat stomach, courtesy of my plastic surgeon.

As I moved across the ballroom floor in rhinestone studded stilettos, I saw haters' mouths drop and tongue wagging in disbelief. I knew what was on all their minds. I knew what they were thinking.

I thought that ho was dead.

No bitches. I'm still alive and kicking better than ever.

Five years ago, I had gotten shot in the face by some dumb wench who thought I was fucking her man. Now mind you, I used to have a bad habit of dipping and dabbing with shit I had no business messing with. You know the saying, karma is a bitch. Well, she had finally caught up with my ass with a nine-millimeter. After temporary paralysis in my face and arm, and years of physical therapy and surgery, I was brand spanking new. What mothafuckas tend to forget is that a bitch is rich, and with money anything is possible even if you had to fly all the way to Latin America to have surgeries performed you can't get in the states. I knew I had to do what I had to do to keep this body of mine as tight as possible.

Yes, the bitch is back!

As I sauntered across the room feeling like girls run the world, small-minded folks whispered and stared. Go ahead! Check me out! Smooth caramel skin, hazel eyes, and shoulder-length, golden-brown sister locs. I looked damn good!

Fuck them!

I spotted my girls sitting at a table close to the dance floor watching my grand entrance. Danielle Cambridge rolled her eyes, and Kayla Whitlow shook her head, while Nadine Hill was laughing. They know how I do, so I don't know why they even try to act surprised.

"What's up, heffas!" I exclaimed once I reached them.

"About damn time," Danielle mumbled.

"Hey, girl," Nadine chimed in.

"Hey, mama." Leaning down, I kissed her cheek, then allowed my eyes to travel around the table as I was greeted by all the rest. Danielle was sitting with her husband Calvin. Nadine was with her wife Jordan. And Kayla was holding hands with Jermaine. There were two empty seats. I sat my ass in one and put my purse on the other. Unlike the rest of them, I had yet to find a man willing to put up with me.

"What I missed?" I asked.

"Not a damn thing," Danielle muttered, and I could tell she was bored. Good thing I had arrived.

"I figured I wasn't gonna miss shit. I decided to take a long hot bath and the water felt too good I didn't want to get out." I reached for a dinner roll, broke it and took a bite. "When you're not getting any dick, you gotta take what you can get."

Kayla was rolling her greenish-brown eyes and mumbling, "You're ridiculous," under her breath.

I didn't give a shit.

"All you missed was a bunch of boring-ass introductions and ceremonial bullshit." Nadine waved her hand, clearly annoyed. "Dinner is about to be served and then it's on to the dancing."

With a sigh, I allowed my eyes to travel around the room. Everyone seemed to be booed up tonight. What the fuck! Hopefully, there was someone dying to put his hands on me. "Where's all the single men? Calvin... Jermaine, I know y'all got some friends."

They both looked uncomfortable, especially Calvin. Probably because I used to ride that chocolate dick long before he'd hooked up with Danielle. He knew firsthand my ass was a straight freak.

"Calvin, I thought some of your boys from the squadron were coming?" Danielle asked.

The university police officer cleared his throat. "I think there are a few of them around here somewhere."

I found it funny that he was looking everywhere but at me.

I wouldn't never say this to Danielle, but after all these years I still think Calvin is attracted to me. Back in the day I would have used that knowledge to my advantage and done some scandalous shit, but not anymore. Those days were behind me. But that didn't stop me from admiring him. He's fine. Tall, dark and sexy, with eyes a woman could stare into for hours, and the icing on top was his slick bald head. Unfortunately, he had turned out to be just a tad bit too needy for my taste, so our relationship had been short-lived. Now he was in love with Danielle and had stood by her when she needed him the most, and for that I would never get in the way of that shit.

Trust me. I had changed a lot. And now I really wanted to find my own man because I was afraid of growing old alone. But men seemed to be intimidated by a strong black independent female, and until I found a man who was up for the challenge, I would just have to get used to being by myself.

"We have exciting news," I heard Jermaine say and noticed Kayla looking up at him self-consciously.

"What?" I asked.

"My wife was just promoted to Executive Associate to the Dean."

My eyes lit up. "Congratulations."

"Thank you." Kayla blushed, which is easy considering her complexion is so beige she could pass for white if it wasn't for her nappy-ass head. Kayla had been working at the University of Missouri-Columbia Medical School since forever. It was about damn time she'd gotten a promotion.

Congratulations went around and then dinner was being served. I stared at the three couples sitting around the table and then started wondering why I was even back here. Hell, I knew why. After being gone five years, I wanted everyone in Columbia to know I was better than ever. And what better opportunity than while attending the Black & White Ball to let the city know just how far you've come.

After I'd recovered from the gunshot wound, I moved away, deciding I needed a change of scenery. One of my writer friends lived in Hampton, Virginia. She'd raved about the place so much, and once I visited the east coast, I was hooked. It was a military area and getting some dick was never a problem. At first it was exciting and buck-wild, but after a while it had lost its initial thrill. My ass wasn't getting older, just wiser, and I had reached a stage of my life where I was interested in finding something with a tad bit more stability. It's funny because at one point a man was the last thing I needed. Now I wanted what everyone else at the table had. Even Nadine and her partner, Jordan, were happy. If a lesbian couple can find happiness, hell, why couldn't I?

During dinner, I glanced around the room and noticed the women looking my way and sneering up their noses. Others were glaring at their men, daring them to even think about looking over in my direction. I found the shit hilarious because even after the accident and now having limited mobility in my left arm, niggas were still salivating.

What can I say? I was a force to be reckoned with. People either liked me or couldn't stand my caramel ass. Seldom was there any in-between. Not that I really gave a flying fuck. Most of them had their own reasons for hating me. Hell, all the shit I'd done over the years, I couldn't blame them, and the others, were simply haters.

After dinner, I rose to mingle with friends I hadn't seen in forever, determined to enjoy the Black & White Ball.

The three-day event, which also included a barbecue in the park, was a kind of family reunion for high school graduates and former residents who came home once every three years to socialize. You were guaranteed to see people you hadn't seen in forever, brag about your life and show off your new man. I mingled with former classmates, laughed, acted fake and then took photographs. Nothing had really changed. I'm serious. It was as if time had stood still. Mothafuckas were still doing the same shit they had been doing five years ago.

The ball was turning out to be a couple's night. I'll never tell them ho's this, but I envied what my friends had, hell even Nadine. I'm strictly dickly, but it didn't stop me from yearning for the fire I saw blazing in her eyes every time she looked at Jordan. What I would give for a man to look that way at me. While they all bumped and grinded on the dance floor, I made my way over to the bar where there was a cute muscle-bound Hispanic guy serving drinks.

"What would you like, pretty lady?"

"You keep talking like that and you can have me." I knew I was flirting, but shit I'm single. I can do that. But the way he looked flustered, I knew he was not at all expecting that. Yeah, I know. I come across a little aggressive at times, but I'm never going to stop doing me. "I'll take a vodka and pineapple."

"Coming right up," he said, winked, and went off to make my drink.

"You need to leave that little boy alone."

At the sound of the deep, sexy voice, I swung around and my eyes widened at the sight of my favorite police officer. He wasn't the fake-ass campus police like Calvin. He was the real deal. David was short and cute as hell.

"Hey, David!" I said and gave him a big hug. When I tried to pull back, he tightened his arm around my waist.

"Hey, beautiful. When did you get in town?"

"This afternoon." I arrived in St. Louis last night and spent some time with my brother Andre and his family. And then got up and hit the mall for the perfect dress before driving to Columbia.

"Damn, you look good!" He was staring like he wanted to lick me up and down. It was a consideration. David and I had history, and I'd even given him some, but the problem was I wasn't looking for anymore drama in this town. The last time had gotten my ass shot.

"Where's your wife?"

His hold tightened. "We're divorced."

I gave him an exaggerated eyebrow raise. "Does she know that? Because some women just don't know how the fuck to let go."

"Yeah, she's already married and moved to Kansas City."

I felt myself getting excited about getting to spend my evening with Columbia's finest down between my thighs.

"What about you? You get remarried?"

"Hell no," I snorted rudely.

After my ex-husband decided he preferred dick to pussy, I spent the last five years trying to figure out who Renee was and what I wanted in my life, so I could be a better woman when I did find Mr. Right. I knew in my heart David could never be the one, but for tonight, I could settle for Mr. Right Now.

He finally loosened his hold enough for me to wiggle away and get my drink from the bar.

"Who you here with?" he asked.

"Danielle, Nadine, and Kayla."

He smiled knowingly as he paid the bartender. I took a sip and was pleased to see he was still the gentleman.

"How about saving me a dance?"

"I can do that." I took that as my cue to leave and headed back across the room, swaying my hips suggestively. All eyes were on me again. I looked to the left, right, and did a double-take. *Oh shit!* It took everything I had not to laugh as I made my way back to the table and took a seat.

"Kayla, is that your cousin and his wife over to the right staring at me?" I already knew the answer, but I waited until she followed the direction of my eyes and groaned a response.

"Ugh, yes, and I'm never going to hear the end of it."

Danielle met my eyes and we shared a look.

Kenny Johnson and his wife Reese. They had been engaged

back when he and I were fucking.

I'm a *USA Today* Best-selling author who has written several books that were keeping my pockets fat. When I was messing around with Kenny, I had been working on a new book. Somehow during all that sucking and fucking, too many details about him and his fiancée ended up in the story. A lot more than I'd realized. Once the book was released, the town's reaction had been like an excerpt from the movie *The Help*. I kid you not. Jaws dropped and tongues started wagging. Damn, I know I'm a good writer, but I hadn't realized just how well I was able to describe members of our community until someone started identifying similarities to the main characters. I personally thought the shit was funny. Let's be honest. I write fiction. Therefore, no one would have known I had been writing about Reese's ass if she hadn't told anyone.

"Wait a minute. *He's the one you wrote about in your book?*" Nadine asked incredulously. She was the one who hooked me up with Kenny in the first place. He was her personal mechanic.

"Hell yeah! I thought you knew that?" It was Danielle's turn to laugh.

I gave a rude snort and acted confused. "What are you talking about? I don't remember seeing him or his wife's name referenced anywhere in my book." I would have said something more if everyone else at the table wasn't giving me the side-eye.

I decided to change the subject. "How come you didn't tell me David Lavell was single?"

Danielle shrugged. "I didn't think you would care."

"David?" Calvin said and then frowned.

I was ready to say something smart about David being a real police officer, but the music changed and he and Danielle got up and hit the dance floor again. Kayla and her husband followed. Jordan excused herself and went to the bathroom, leaving me and Nadine alone.

"I love your new hairdo," I said pointing up at her low-cropped fade. She had it cut so low she might as well have been bald, but Nadine had the right shaped head to pull off the look.

"Thanks, I got sick of worrying about my hair."

I'd decided the same thing when I first started locking my hair.

"You want to go to the boat after this?"

I could see the excitement in Nadine's eyes. I couldn't understand why folks were so excited about going to the casino. But I guess when there is nothing else to do, what do you expect? "Sure, why not."

David came and took my hand and led me out onto the floor. I pulled him close and knew haters were watching. I didn't give a fuck. Bitches, keep your man close because everyone knows I'm liable to steal him! At least that was the way I used to be, but folks weren't going to believe I changed. So, what was the point of trying to explain? All they saw was a beautiful rich bitch with a history of man-stealing.

"How long you here for?"

"Long enough," I retorted.

"Can I occupy your time?" David was licking his lips, all sexy and shit.

"Maybe." There were no guarantees.

I had always been attracted to David, but we've both changed in one way or another. Danielle was dancing beside us, and I caught Calvin looking over with disapproval. I didn't give a fuck. I still remember the day Danielle walked in on him, eating my damn pussy.

I made it back to our table in time to see my son, Quinton, walking into the ballroom. I grinned. He's a heart-breaker. Tall, six-three, dark-skinned with way too many tattoos, but apparently that was what everyone was doing to their bodies these days.

"Is that Soledad?" Kayla whispered, and pointed.

I noticed the woman walking beside Quinton and frowned. What the fuck was he doing with that bitch? Soledad Dibaba was three years younger than me, but looked years older.

"Nae-Nae, you didn't know Q was fucking her?"

Danielle thought that shit was funny. My son was just about to turn twenty-five, so you know I was not feeling that shit at all. It was bad enough he had a son he barely spent two seconds with.

"Q called me last week around two in the morning."

I whipped around, eyes wide. "For what?"

Kayla sucked her teeth. "Q was like, 'Aunt Kayla can I get twenty dollars until payday?'"

I groaned. My son could be so damn embarrassing. "I hope you cussed his ass out for calling you."

"I hung up, but I met him at the mall the next day and gave it to him."

Danielle gave a rude snort. "Well, he still owes me the twenty-five I gave him last month. He's been dodging me ever since."

I would have to remember to give them back their money before I returned home, otherwise, I'd never hear the end of it. "That's your fault. Y'all need to stop giving him money."

Kayla sighed. "You're right, especially since Asia says Q was high as a kite when she last saw him. Eyes all red and slurring."

I hated listening to them talk about my son. Didn't he know he had to represent? I couldn't have him running around begging and asking for money. That shit made me look bad.

He finally made his way over with his old Ethiopian bitch beside him. Quinton came around the table, dimples flashing. He was a mama's boy. I loved his ass, but he knows I have no problem cussing him out if needed.

"Hey, Mom. I was wondering if you'd made it." He was grinning and looking like the little boy I had adored. I rose, smiling and gave him a big hug. Immediately I noticed he stunk of weed. Some other scent I couldn't identify was all over his clothes.

"Q, you stink," I mumbled as I kissed his cheek. He tried to look offended, but I wasn't paying attention. My eyes were on Soledad. We'd gone to high school together. As I was going out, she was coming in. Three years. When I was eighteen, I'd even been to her house and met her parents, who were both from Ethiopia. What the fuck was she doing with Quinton? "Hello Soledad." I didn't even try to hide the fact that I didn't approve.

"Hey, Renee."

Hey, Renee? I figure anyone who could call me by my first name was too damn old.

"Hello, Soledad," Danielle called and was grinning and shit. She was a retired cougar, so the two had a lot in common.

I can see dating someone a few years older, but we're talking about more than a fifteen-year difference. The fact she knew I was Quinton's mother should have been enough for her to have said not no, but, hell no. As far as I was concerned, the only women who messed with men that young had self-esteem issues. As for my son… he was just looking for another mama.

I looked from her to him. "I didn't know you were coming tonight." *And bringing this old bitch.*

"Yeah, I tried to hit you up earlier and tell you I was coming through. Mom, let me holla at you a sec." Quinton took my hand and led me away from the table. I already knew what he wanted before the words left his mouth.

"You think you can help me out?"

I decided to play dumb. "With what?"

"I need to help Soledad with her rent. She's short a hundred."

I knew his ass was lying. He ain't never been in the habit of helping some female with bills. In fact. The second she asked for a dime was the day Quinton was going to pack up his shit and move out.

I was going to have to give his father a call and see what the hell had been going on because the last time Mario and I talked, he'd said Quinton was doing good.

"I guess. Call me tomorrow."

"Thanks, Mom." You should have seen the way his face lit up, like I had promised to buy his ass a new car.

I went back to the table while he and Soledad moved to sit over with her large family. I just stared over there at all those wide foreheads surrounding their table and wondered where the hell did I go wrong? My son should have been graduating from college. Not working at the bookstore riding a forklift. I know it was honest work, but when you have a child with so much potential, you expect greatness. Tamara was getting ready to graduate with a degree in elementary education. That's the shit I was talking about. High expectations for your kids.

"What the fuck?" I mumbled under my breath.

Nadine was laughing. "I can't believe Q is screwing her old ass."

I wanted to snap back, "At least my son liked pussy," since her son was gay. When she first told me about Jay, I fell out laughing. Nadine was married to a female, and her son was dating a man. It runs in the family.

"I'm going over to say something to her."

Danielle shook her head. "Uh-uh. Hell nah!"

"I'm serious. What the hell is a grown-ass woman doing with someone practically the same age as her daughter?"

Nadine started laughing. "Do I have to spell it out to you?"

Even Kayla was getting a kick out of my misery. I didn't see shit funny.

"Fuck y'all."

"Seriously, you need to chill," Kayla said as if she had any control over the way I behaved.

"I wanted to know what he sees in her," Nadine said, and I knew her ass was instigating because it didn't take much to set me off.

"Because he's always trying to find someone who reminds him of his damn mama." I was heated.

"I don't know why," Kayla muttered. "One of you is more than enough."

"No this bitch didn't," I retorted.

I guess Calvin knew I was two seconds away from going-to-fuck-off because he rose and signaled for Jermaine to join him. "Man, I need a drink."

Danielle waited until they were both gone before she glared and hissed, "Leave the shit alone."

"Ain't happening. Did you see the way she was smiling all up in my face as if to say, 'Yeah bitch, I'm with your son, now what?'"

Nadine chuckled. "I thought I was the only one who saw that shit." Jordan nudged her in the arm and mouthed for her to be quiet, but it was too late for that.

Danielle was trying her best to contain the situation. "Girl, just ask Q what the deal is before you get all bent outta shape."

"I'ma ask his dumb ass, but in the meantime, I plan on

talking to Soledad, woman-to-woman." I was up out of my seat and strutting across the ballroom. I didn't even have to look over my shoulder to know Danielle was following. Kayla, too. I think I had overheard Jordan telling Nadine to sit her ass back down. We all knew who wore the pants in that house.

"Bitch, where the fuck you going?" Danielle called after me.

"Come see." I didn't even break stride.

I kept on strutting. Some light-skinned dude tried to holla at me, but I smelled his breath before he could even get the words out. I gave him a dismissive wave and didn't miss a beat. I stepped out into the hall, looked left, then right and glanced Soledad's anorexic ass stepping into the ladies' room.

"Renee, stop!" Danielle grabbed my arm, but I jerked free of her hold.

"I'm just gonna talk to her."

I took off, burst through the door, and stepped inside.

2
Danielle

I hurried down the hall and rounded the corner.
I'm so tired of Renee's bullshit.
Glancing over my shoulder, I rolled my eyes at Kayla. "This bitch…" I mumbled while shaking my head.
Renee was crazy. There was really no other way to describe her. Her mother was either bipolar or schizophrenic, and after all these years it had become evident she, too, was cuckoo for Cocoa Puffs. We all knew it, and despite her unstable behavior, I'd been her friend for more than thirty years. But after all that time, her wild sporadic behavior was starting to wear on my nerves.
I hurried after Renee, wishing for the umpteenth time I hadn't worn the red-bottom shoes. *Christian Louboutin my ass.* They were killing my toes. I'd been better off wearing the crystal embellished BCBG pumps instead.
Renee pushed into the bathroom. Kayla was next, then I followed. Soledad stepped out the bathroom stall, straightening the white and black pinstriped dress. As soon as Soledad spotted us, she looked up, surprised. I guess the three of us barging in was a bit overwhelming.
"Y'all enjoying the ball this year?" Soledad asked and headed over to the sink. "The barbecue yesterday was really good."
"It's cool," Kayla replied.
"Yeah, it's all good, girl," I said and moved to stand in front of the mirror to check my hair and makeup. "Oh damn! How come y'all didn't tell me I had lettuce in my teeth?" I squawked,

then glared over at Renee, who was leaned against the counter, staring down at Soledad's strappy patent leather heels. The moment she tossed the paper towel in the trash, Renee took a step closer.

Oh shit, here we go!

"I need to ask you a question," she began and before the poor chick could answer, Renee started in. "Why are you dating my son?" she asked with a bite to her tone.

It had gotten so quiet, I could hear the water dripping on the granite counter. Soledad looked so embarrassed.

I picked my teeth and tried to pretend I wasn't listening.

"I gotta pee," Kayla muttered cowardly and stepped into the first stall.

Soledad said nothing, but after a few moments, Renee's voice raised an octave. "I asked you a question."

"Oh God." I don't know why my ass hadn't just stayed at the table with my husband. This was why he didn't care that much for my girl. Renee was loud and obnoxious. There were other reasons, but I tried not to think about those.

Soledad finally shrugged. I guess she figured out Renee was serious. "Q and I enjoy each other's company. What's wrong with that?"

"Everything," Renee emphasized with a sharp tone. "That's *my* son. My *twenty-four-year-old* son. You are way too old to be playing house with him."

She had this incredulous look on her face as she replied, "Who's playing house?"

"Yeah Nae-Nae. They're just fucking," I egged on. I knew it was wrong, but I couldn't resist the opportunity to throw shade. Shit, Renee does it all the time. Only, she didn't seem the least bit amused.

"Danielle, shut the hell up! I'm trying to find out what's really going on here."

"You need to talk to your son," Soledad said while fluffing her weave.

"No, I'm talking to you woman to woman. Although it appears I'm the only one who's acting my age."

"Why? 'Cause I'm dating a younger man? Women do it all

the time."

"Not with my mothafuckin' son they don't."

"Can we all just get along?" Kayla yelled from the stall.

"Kayla, you worry about wiping your ass and let me handle this!" Renee cried.

Kayla had always been the quiet one of the bunch although lately she'd become more and more opinionated.

"I wanna know how you can date a boy almost the same age as your daughter."

"My daughter and your son don't have a problem with it, so, why should you?" Soledad retorted boldly.

Renee got all up in her face as she hissed, "Because I see what's happening here. I'm no longer around and Q is looking for a mother, and guess what? He found you."

Soledad smirked "There is nothing maternal going on between us."

Oh shit! I jumped between them just in time to save Soledad from Renee snatching the weave from her head.

"Chill," I warned, unable to understand why Renee was trippin' so hard.

Renee struggled to get free, pointing a finger at her. "Don't fuck with me! Not when it comes to my kids. I'm not one to be fucked with."

Soledad had sense enough to back away several feet. "Listen...I really rather not have this conversation with you."

"Then you should have thought about that before you started fucking with my son!"

Kayla stepped out the stall so fast, the door swung back and hit the wall. On her face was that all too familiar look of disappointment. "Renee, leave her alone. If Q doesn't have an issue with age, why should you?"

"Because I can and you need to mind your own business! What you need to be worried about is that single-ply toilet paper stuck to the bottom of your shoe."

My eyes lowered to the tiled floor at the stream of tissue, and I exploded with laughter. Kayla reached down and pulled it off with attitude.

Soledad didn't dare crack a smile. "Renee, I really care about your son. I don't know what he sees in me, but I'm glad he sees it. We really do have a great relationship." She was practically begging for Renee to understand.

"I don't care how great the relationship is. Q needs to focus on his son and getting his life together, not messing with some old bitch."

Staring through the glass, I saw the way Soledad flinched at the harsh words. Renee could be such a bitch.

"I'm not going to continue this conversation with you."

"Then don't! I'll be letting Q know how I feel because I don't see it." Renee was talking with her hands.

"Nae-Nae, really, you're not supposed to see it." I chuckled. She couldn't be serious. "Can you mind your business, so we can get back to the ball?"

"Ain't nobody stopping you," Renee snorted.

"Uh-uh, ho, you're going with us." I might let Renee think she's running things, but not today. I was out with my husband, and this was an important event for the community. I was not about to sit back and let this crazy heifer ruin it for everyone. "Soledad, you enjoy the rest of your evening. Renee, let's go." I took her arm and yanked her toward the door. Kayla opened it, and we steered her out into the hall.

"Y'all heffas think you're slick!" Renee whipped around, facing us with a glare.

"You were being mean, damn!" Kayla insisted.

She pushed away. "Why, because I wanted an answer?"

Kayla shook her head. "She's a cougar. What more is there to know?"

"Leave that woman alone." I had my finger all up in Renee's face because I needed her to know I was serious as shit about this.

She rolled her eyes.

"Let's get back to the party," Kayla insisted and surprisingly Renee followed. The crazed look in her eyes let me know she was already thinking about her next move. I just hoped it happened when I wasn't around.

I turned away from her and cussed. Damn. Straight ahead was Reese and some chick I'd never seen before heading their wide behinds our way. "Don't even think about it," I muttered under my breath.

Kayla followed the direction of my gaze and hissed under her breath, "Dang."

Renee placed a finger between her lips and pretended to give my warning some thought. "What could you possibly mean?" She, then turned and sauntered off ahead of us.

"What the hell is wrong with her?"

I shook my head. "I don't know. Nae-Nae probably just needs some dick." I hurried to join her, just in case one of them decided to get froggy and swing at Renee. I didn't always agree with the way my best friend handled things, but there was no way in hell I would ever leave her hanging.

Reese and the chick, who had an oddly-shaped body, tried to block Renee from walking past. Did they not get the memo? Renee's ass was relentless.

"Um, excuse me." She bobbed to the left, and they moved to the right. "Y'all bitches would want to get outta my way," Renee warned.

"*Bitches*? I heard about that book you wrote, and I want you to get it off the shelf!" Reese snarled.

"Why?"

"You know why," barked the short chick standing beside her.

Renee leaned toward them and I noticed how they both took a step back. "No, I don't know, so why don't you tell me."

Reese brought a hand to her thick waist and then tossed her friend a look, clearly too embarrassed to speak. Her friend tried to come to her rescue.

"Don't play, you know you wrote all that stuff about Reese in your book."

"I write fiction, you know, make believe, so I don't know what the hell you're talking about," Renee blurted out in characteristic fashion. A hand was planted at her small waist. Her head was bobbing so hard I was afraid she'd get a crook in her neck.

"This is ridiculous." Kayla must have felt the need to say something since this was her cousin's wife. She would have been better off just staying quiet.

"Nah Kayla!" said her instigating friend. "This bitch here had everyone laughing at my girl."

"*Bitch*? I got your bitch," Renee sneered before returning her gaze to Reese. "All I did was create a character. Nowhere in that book did I mention your name. So, you tell me how in the world would anyone think that was you unless you told them all your trifling secrets?" Renee was getting way too much pleasure out of this.

Now their necks were moving and hands twisting like they were dancers in a Beyoncé video.

"You think you're slick with that chicken wing you call an arm," Reese blurted and she and her friend started snickering.

"Uh-oh," Danielle warned.

Renee stepped closer and pressed a finger against Reese's forehead and that chick's head snapped back. "Chicken wing? I bet you I can flap this mothafucka and knock you in your damn mouth."

Reese looked like she'd been popped in the lips as her eyes snapped toward her friend, wide with disbelief. "No she didn't."

Kayla tried to be the voice of reason. "Donna, Reese, y'all need to just let it go."

"Let it go? Ain't that some shit." Donna egged on, and it became clear that this had been her idea in the first place.

Fist clenched, Renee took a step closer. "I don't even know who the fuck you are, so why you in it anyway? What you need to do is take Kayla's advice and get the fuck outta my face."

Donna hissed, then rolled her eyes at Renee. "Reese, there ain't no way in the world I would let her put her hand on me like that. Matter of fact, if someone wrote a book about me, I would have been done something!" she shouted angrily.

"Then do something," Renee closed the distance, putting her new tits all in their faces, but Kayla reached out and yanked her back. You should have seen how scared those two looked.

Reese made the mistake of mumbling, "One of these days," under her breath and Renee went off.

"Bitch, try me and see!" she hissed. Her head was moving

again. "Like I told you before, the problem you have is with your man, not me. I can't help it if I fucked him so well he started telling all your business."

My mouth hung open. I couldn't understand why these two would want to start some shit tonight.

Reese cut her eyes to her left. "Kayla you're supposed to be family, so I don't understand why you in this."

"I'm not. I'm just here to make sure nothing goes down. I think we need to just let this go and move on."

"Shit, that's easy for you to say, other than talking about you and that dead preacher, she didn't dog you out in her book." She tossed me a nasty look. "And Danielle, you ain't no better."

"Go on now, Reese. Don't put me in this shit," I warned, even though I sure as hell didn't care what either of them thought.

She sucked her teeth, then returned her focus to Renee who was standing there laughing as if the shit was funny. Well, I guess it was in a way.

Reese pointed a finger at her and snarled, "I see why you got shot in the face. You really think you're hot shit."

Shaking her head, Renee chuckled. "Nah, boo. I'm just good at *everything* I do. Ask your husband."

Angrily, Reese made a show of waving her ring finger in the air. "I don't need to ask him anything because I'm the one he married, not you. And he's just as pissed as I am."

"Really? Your man called me last week, so he can't be that upset," Renee announced while batting her fake eyelashes.

"What?" Reese looked to her friend.

"She's lying!" Donna said, instigating. "You better than me, because I would have kicked her ass." Reese looked as if she wished her friend would shut the fuck up.

"You're her best friend, so then why don't you kick my ass for her?" Renee shot her a devilish look, but Donna backed down right away.

Scary-asses.

"What's going on here?"

I breathed a sigh of relief. Thank goodness David was walking our way. A little police presence was what we needed.

"Nothing worth ruining the evening over," Reese murmured and signaled for Donna to follow her toward the bathroom.

"I'm going back to the table with my husband," I replied.

"Me, too." Kayla chimed in, and we walked off, leaving Renee standing there with David.

"Where's Renee?" Nadine asked when we reached the table.

I eased down on the chair and mumbled, "Starting shit as usual."

"Are you serious?"

"What else is new?" Kayla looked, clearly disappointed.

Nadine shrugged. "Renee has always been that way, so why start complaining now?"

Now that was one statement I couldn't argue.

3
Renee

I rode with David out to the Isle of Capri Casino in Boonville. After the ball, we all decided to go, then quickly got caught up in the energy at the casino. The place had been remodeled since my last visit, with new carpet and gaming tables. None of us were much of a gambler except for Nadine. Her lucky ass used to have a bit of a problem. I don't know what it is, but she is one of those who can be walking past a slot machine, decide to drop a quarter into the slot and win the damn jackpot. I tried my luck at craps and after I lost thirty dollars, I was done. Fuck that. I love my money too much to be giving it away on some shit that had been designed to fail. Besides, David was on me like stink on shit, determined to make sure I didn't get away from him. I hadn't had any dick in almost two months, so I was looking forward to the familiar ride on his seven-inch dick.

Nadine was at the blackjack table and we all stood around cheering her along. She was sitting with a shit load of chips in front of her.

"Damn, bitch, can I get a loan?"

"Exactly," Danielle chimed in.

It was Nadine's turn and she already had ten points in her hand. "Hit me." She tapped her finger and was dealt an Ace.

"Oh shit!"

We were all screaming and clapping. I couldn't believe she'd gotten twenty-one again. Nadine's ass was a beast at the blackjack table.

"Damn, when did she get so good at this game?"

Danielle shrugged and watched as Nadine pushed half her chips onto the table. My eyes were glued as we watched the dealer pass out the cards. Damn, when did Nadine get balls of steel? She was up fifteen hundred and just put close to half back on the table. A bitch like me would have said, "Thank you very much" and left with my money. But then I have never been one for gambling. I liked my money too much. I rather blow five hundred on a pair of shoes than throw it onto a table at a casino.

I stared down at the ten in her hand and watched as she tapped the table for the dealer to give her another card. It was a Jack of hearts. With twenty in her hands I figured her ass was done, but when she tapped again and was dealt another fucking ace, I was floored. Damn, she had won again.

"What the fuck!'

All of us were laughing and clapping and getting caught up in the moment.

"She's good." David kept whispering in my ear.

"Jordan, your wife has some mad skills!" I yelled across the table.

The look on the peanut-butter brown face was far from pleased. In fact, she looked pissed-the-fuck-off.

A crowd had gathered and it was easy to see that going to the boat had become the after-party in the area. My eyes scanned the floor of all the others still dressed in their gowns from the ball. We were all laughing, talking and having a good time. Damn. I would never admit it, but it felt good to be home with my friends.

I stood there watching Nadine win a couple more hundred and suddenly felt bold enough to jump into the game.

"You sure about that?" Danielle had the nerve to ask. I saw the smirk on Calvin's face as he tried to keep a straight face.

"Hell yeah, I'm feeling bold." It was only twenty bucks. I think I could survive without it.

I waited for some old crusty man to get up from his chair and then I slid onto the seat.

David had returned from the men's room and his eyes lit up when he saw me. "Watch out now."

I just rolled my eyes and waited for her to hand my chips

and I placed them on the table. It was a five dollars minimum hand. I glanced over enviously at Nadine. Her eyes were all glossed over like some fucking crackhead. *Damn, was this shit that addictive?*

I got my cards and looked down and tapped the table until I was up nineteen and decided to stop.

"Hit me," Nadine said.

"Fuck," I mumbled under my breath when she hit twenty, and the dealer got twenty-three. Danielle and Kayla was laughing.

"Fuck both of y'all. This is supposed to be just for fun."

"It is, but it's nice to see your ass lose at something," Kayla teased.

I glared up at her and her husband, Jermaine, who looked like he didn't even want to be here tonight. He was staring off into space.

"I can't be perfect at everything," I reminded as I put the last ten on the table. Even when I went to Las Vegas, if I spent fifty dollars on gambling, then it had just been a good day for that.

In a matter of seconds, I lost my ten dollars and for some odd reason, I was a bit pissed. Probably because Nadine's big-titty ass had won again.

"What the fuck!"

"She's lucky when it comes to them damn tables. That's why I hate coming here with her," Danielle mentioned as I got up to let someone else have a seat.

Everyone seemed to be enjoying themselves but Jordan. She was reared back in the chair with her arms crossed beneath her breasts. "Nadine, that's enough. How about we quit while you're ahead?" she insisted.

"Just one more," Nadine said and was already tossing another five-hundred-dollars-worth of chips onto the table.

I turned away. "I'm going over to the bar and spend my money on something worthwhile."

"Me, too. Let's go get a drink." Danielle took Calvin's hand and dragged him toward the bar, and I allowed David to lead the way. I noticed that his walk was cockier than usual. *What is that all about?* I wondered before deciding it had to be all about me.

I figured the haters who were watching had already figured out David was going home with me. Mind your damn business! I'm single and he's single, which means we can do whatever the fuck we wanted to do.

Danielle and I took a seat. The men decided to stand. David was beside me. I crossed my shapely legs, allowing the dress to ride up above my knees.

The guys ordered a round of drinks and started chatting. They had known each other for years. Being that they were both police officers—if that's what you wanted to call Calvin—their cases sometimes crossed over into each other's jurisdictions. I reached for my cell phone and saw I had a text from my son.

Mom really?

He even had the nerve to add a few emojis to emphasize how he felt about me questioning Soledad. Whatever. I have a right to voice my own opinion.

Danielle gave me a curious look. "Who's that?"

"Q. He's pissed at me."

"He should be. That was none of your business."

I gave her a dismissive wave. "My son will always be my business."

"What're you frowning about?" David asked.

I lightly tapped his arm and said, "Check this out. My son is dating Soledad Dibaba."

"No shit!" His dark eyes widened and then he started laughing. "Damn, is he looking for a mama?"

"That's what I'm saying!"

Danielle turned up her noise. "I don't see nothing wrong with it. If that's what he likes, then that's what he likes. All these silly-ass young chicks out here twerking and shit for free, I don't blame my nephew."

She started imitating and I was laughing. "I know that's right. If you're gonna be a ho, at least get paid for it." We cackled and gave each other a high-five. The men just stood there shaking their heads.

"What are y'all talking about?" asked Kayla. She and Jermaine had come over to join us.

I waved her over. "You arrived just in time. C'mon and have a seat."

Danielle jumped in. "We're discussing cougar women."

Kayla rolled her eyes because she immediately knew who we were talking about.

David shrugged and brought the bottle of beer to his lips. "I don't see anything wrong with it. I lost my virginity to my babysitter."

"I just bet you did," I said with a saucy grin.

"Me either," Jermaine agreed.

Kayla twirled around on the stool and frowned. "So, if Asia starts dating a man who is almost forty, then that's okay?"

"Hell no!" he bellowed. "Let some forty-year-old man knock at my door and I'm going to jail."

Danielle screamed with laughter before saying, "So it's okay for a man to date a younger woman, but it's not for a woman to date a younger man."

"No, that's not completely true. It all depends on what age we're talking about," David commented.

Calvin decided to join in. "And ain't nothing wrong with an older woman teaching a young cat some tricks."

Danielle shook her head. "Really?"

"You don't seem to have any complaints," Calvin challenged. "That move I showed you the other night, that you liked so much... My best friend's mama taught me that when I was in college."

"Y'all are so nasty," Kayla commented with a smile, then looked at me. "Renee, you married a man who was eleven years older than you."

"That's different. I was already a grown-ass woman. If I had been Asia's age and dating a twenty-eight year old, you'd have a fit."

Kayla gave a disapproving look. "If she dated someone twenty-one, I'd have a fit." I could tell by the look on her face she was keeping Asia on lockdown. She had done the same thing with Kenya, and the second her oldest daughter had turned eighteen, she had left the house and never came back.

Another round of drinks arrived, and Jermaine went and

ordered a glass of wine for the two of them. Everyone started talking and laughing at the same time. It felt good being with my friends. This here was the only thing I hated about moving away. I couldn't be in the company of my sistahs.

"Don't forget the Columbia Law Enforcement Association is hosting a Christmas Ball. We have finally secured the banquet room at Stephen's College. All we need to do is finalize the logistical details and we'll start pimping tickets," said David.

"Hey, we plan on being there!" Kayla announced.

Jermaine agreed. "I'm sure I can pawn off some of those tickets throughout the medical school." He had recently been promoted to Student Recruitment Coordinator at the Dean's Office.

"That's what I like to hear," David said.

I listened as they discussed the details of the event and it sounded almost like something I might be tempted to come back and attend. Only, I wasn't going without a date.

"Yo, Danielle. I heard you started some online dating site," I heard David say.

Calvin cleared his throat.

She and Kayla exchanged a look before I cut in and smoothly changed the subject, "How you going to ask about a dating site with me sitting right beside you?"

David held up his hands in surrender. "Hey, just asking for a buddy of mine. He might be interested in joining."

I seriously fucking doubted that unless…

I lowered from the stool and sauntered away, signaling for him to follow me over to a bar-height table for two, so he would stop asking questions and I could have a few moments alone with him to solidify the rest of my night.

"How you like living in Virginia?"

"It's nice. Definitely a big change from this country-ass place. Black folks are truly living the dream there. Good jobs, nice homes and cars… you really should plan a visit."

"Is that an invitation?"

"Absolutely." My life in Hampton was truly simple and quiet. I hit the clubs every now and then, but at forty-three the club scene just wasn't my thing anymore. I was more interested in one-on-one interactions and had even tried my luck at online dating, but I kept meeting one reject after another until I finally decided it just wasn't worth all the time and energy.

"Are you dating anyone?" I figured he would lie, but I asked anyway.

David reached for his beer and took a sip before answering. "Not at all. I tried dating, but I can honestly say there ain't a woman in this town who turns me on like you."

That I could believe, but that didn't mean he didn't have someone coming over and giving him some when he was in need. Personally, I could care less. I'd just rather know than someone sneak up behind me with a frying pan... or a gun.

"I'm planning to retire soon."

"Has it been twenty years already?"

David nodded. "I think I'm ready to kick back and start enjoying life."

I stared up at him and noticed the gray that had popped up throughout his curly hair. His mustache was nice and neat and there were deep dimples in each of his cheeks. He was a handsome man. Finding someone that had their shit together at our age was a rare find. If I didn't want him, then someone else was going to snatch him up.

We talked, finished our drinks, then went back to join the others. Nadine was still at the blackjack table, while the rest of us laughed and talked about shit from back in the day until my eyelids started to grow heavy.

David brought an arm around me and leaned in close. "You ready to go?"

I had almost forgotten I rode with him to the casino, but was glad that I had. It saved me from driving my rental. I nodded and told my girls I'd see them for breakfast in the morning, then followed him out to his car. I must have fallen asleep on the ride to the hotel because I heard David calling my name.

"Renee, baby. Wake up."

My eyes fluttered open, and I spotted him standing over me. I smiled and was instantly wide awake. I took his hand and allowed him to lead me inside and up to my hotel room on the second floor. Once there, I handed him the key and he let us in.

I don't know who grabbed who first. All I know was my dress was off and we were both naked and rolling around in my bed.

"I can't believe I'm here with you again," I heard him mumble before his lips were all over mine. I had pretty much written David off like a bad check. But here I was in the bed with him and he was sliding on the condom and positioning himself between my thighs. And then he pushed inside of me, and my arms and legs were wrapped around him as I tilted my hips upward, meeting every one of his deep penetrating thrusts. I know he was adding a little extra into it, to put something on my mind and I was impressed that he thought enough of me to want to show off. Not that any of that was required. David was an awesome performer. He kept an erection, which wasn't easy to find at our age. Most of the men I was starting to meet had to pop a pill or needed you to play with his dick until he got an erection. David sprung to the occasion and managed to hold onto it long enough for me to get mine before he finally got his. Afterward I cuddled up beside him as he drifted off to sleep.

The sex had been great, but after all the years of chasing after him, having him wasn't as fulfilling as I had hoped it would have been. In fact, I lay beside him, still feeling empty.

I don't know what it is with me and men, but for some reason I can't seem to get the shit right. I wanna say it started with having a father who never loved me.

In all fairness, he's my stepfather and the only father I know. Being raised by him, nothing I ever did was good enough, and I found myself growing up looking for love in all the wrong places from every Tom, Big Dick and Larry. As I look back now, I find that I had been in love with falling in love more than anything else and thought everybody had the potential of being the one, even before the dust had settled. I had to learn to take off the pink-studded sunglasses.

I got pregnant with Quinton my senior year and married my high school sweetheart. Tamara came along three years later, but by then Mario was popping me upside my dome on a regular basis. I had to take a baseball bat upside his head as the grand finale. After that, I walked away and started fucking something fierce before I ended up being swept off my feet by some army sergeant who married me and promised to show me the world. What he had failed to share was that he already had a wife and child. And after that, there had been numerous others whispering false promises. Before I had a chance to memorize their last names, I was bored and off to the next. And then John had come into my life.

He had been rich and kind and introduced a girl from the streets to a life she had only dreamed about. He had been good to me and my kids, and I wanted to be everything I could be for him because he had saved me from one of the lowest points in my life. I was unemployed and my house was practically in foreclosure when he swept in and offered to be my knight-in-shining-armor. Only his was tarnished. John had never been much to look at, not to mention he was fat. I tried. Lord knows I did and yet I just couldn't ever bring myself to love him the way he deserved to be loved. Unfortunately, my black ass straddled the fence about ending our relationship because I couldn't bring myself to hurt his feelings.

Until I found him fucking another man.

I blamed myself because I should have been paying attention, and yet I was so busy fucking someone else's man, I didn't realize John was doing the same. By the time I discovered what was going on, I was sick to my stomach and got the fuck out of there.

But I think it was him showing up on my doorstep to confess he had HIV and insisting I get tested that changed my life. I had been living dangerously for far too long. Nowadays I got more pleasure from my vibrator than listening to a nigga's bullshit. Now don't get it twisted, I still loved the dick. I was just more cautious and selective about who I shared my coochie with. Which was why a night with David was all the fine-tuning I needed to satisfy me for a spell. I had hoped I would have felt more for him. Instead I think it had been more about the chase. Now that he's available, I'm not so sure I'm interested anymore.

Knowing that made me feel sadder than I'd felt in months.

4
Nadine

I walked into the house through the garage and tossed the keys to my Mercedes in a glass bowl at the center of the island.

"Bae, I still can't believe how lucky I was tonight!"

Jordan didn't say a word. Instead she slipped out of a pair of white high-heel pumps and headed up the stairs towards our bedroom.

Damn, I already knew what kind of night I was going to have, and yet it didn't stop me from following her up the stairs.

"Are you going to be mad at me all night?" I asked as I made my way across our large master suite.

Ignoring me, she tried to reach for the zipper of her black gown, but it was just too high on her back. Apparently, she was too pissed to even ask for my help. I walked over and gave it to her anyway. "Bae, talk to me."

Jordan stepped out of the long gown, then swirled around. "What's there to say? You're gonna do whatever the fuck you wanna do regardless, so what does it really matter?" Her large breasts were heaving. I took a moment to take in her beautiful curves.

"You're overreacting. I won big tonight."

"Yes, for once you won, but what about all the other times you haven't won!"

I can't understand why she kept throwing that crap into my face. "I told you I was done gambling. The only reason why we were even out tonight was because Renee was in town."

She glared at me. "That's bullshit and you know it. Renee was just an excuse you used to get to the casino. You wanna know how I know? Because I asked her when you were in the ladies' room and she told me the whole, 'let's go to the boat after the ball,' was your idea."

Remind me to kick Nae-Nae's ass when I see her. But I guess I couldn't really blame Renee since I hadn't told her to keep it a secret. "Okay, so what? I wanted to go and hang out with my friends at the casino. Are you trying to say you didn't have a good time?"

She drew a long breath. "Yes, I had a great time, but it has to stop! You told me never again."

I walked over and drew her close. "I gave you my word. The gambling would stop. It was just this time, I swear to you."

Jordan gave me a look that said she was having a hard time believing me. I leaned in and pressed my lips against my wife's. I needed her to believe I was done with all the gambling. It was just about fun tonight. Nothing else.

"Promise me again," she whispered against my lips.

"I promise, bae. I'm over all that. It's just fun." I kissed her once more, then drew back and reached down inside my purse. "In fact, you can spend this money anyway you like."

I tossed the cash up into the air, and it was raining money all over our carpet. Jordan started laughing and I breathed a sigh of relief. The argument was over.

"I was thinking of finally buying a new sofa."

That wasn't quite what I had in mind, but I was in no position to argue. "Absolutely. A new couch sounds great." A weekend getaway to Las Vegas would have been better, but after what happened the last time, I could see that was not a topic to bring up for discussion.

Jordan's eyes lit up with excitement over a damn sofa. I'm an attorney with a wallet filled with credit cards. She could have bought a sofa a long time ago. Only Jordan doesn't believe in plastic.

"Can we go and look this weekend? I'd really like to go to St. Louis and make a weekend of it?" She was batting her eyelashes like I needed convincing.

My mind was already spinning with trying to come up with an excuse so that we could hit the casino boat in St. Charles. I guess something in my expression caused Jordan's eyes to darken as she spat, "Don't even think about it."

"What are you talking about?"

"You know damn well what I'm talking about. We're not going to St. Charles. I want to take the twins, and we can't do that hanging out at some boat."

"How about we just buy a couch here?"

"No way. Everyone has the same damn furniture because they shop at the same stores. I want to go somewhere unique and different," she insisted.

There was no point in arguing. I watched her get undressed and felt my nipples hardening.

Jordan was a beautiful woman. I remember the first time I spotted her. Back then I wasn't even sure of my sexuality, but it was Jordan who helped me to finally come out of the closet and accept that I was a lesbian.

"I'm getting ready to jump in the shower. You wanna share the water?" she asked with an adorable smirk on her lips I loved so much.

"Sure." Anything to take her mind off me gambling. For some weird reason, Jordan feared I still had a problem. Okay, so maybe I had overspent, and at times had gotten so wrapped up in the game I forgot my last name, but that was in the past. Now…I could quit any time I wanted.

I stripped and stepped into the shower with her. She covered her shoulder length hair with a shower cap.

"Have I told you today how much I love you?" I loved Jordan with my life. I turned her around and drew her into my arms and brought my lips down over hers, kissing her with all the adrenaline I'd felt over the evening. I pushed her lips apart and slipped my tongue inside, mating my tongue with hers. She moaned and her hand came up to cup my breast. I loved when she touched me there. She always made me aroused and turned on by her simple touch. My hands traveled down to her hips. She had gotten thick since the birth of the twins and I loved all her womanly curves. She backed me against the shower wall, and then was down on her knees spreading my thighs and taking my clit into her mouth. I gasped and arched off the wall.

Nothing felt better than her lips and tongue. It was amazing when I think about all the years I had spent dating men before marrying my husband, but I never knew what it felt like to have someone perform oral sex on me until I'd met Jordan. I always heard no one eats pussy like another woman, and whoever said that was speaking the truth. She had me coming in a matter of seconds. My hand gripped her shoulders holding her firmly in place until the last wave passed. I was breathing heavily as Jordan rose to her feet with a wide smirk on her face.

I kissed her hard, then reached for the soap. "As soon as we get to bed, I'll be ready for a snack." We laughed and I lathered her. She was staring into my eyes, and I caught myself dropping my gaze, blushing.

"What?"

"I love you. I don't think I've ever loved anyone as much as I love you."

Have I said how much I loved this woman? I loved her like nobody's business. "Keep talking like that and you won't be getting much sleep tonight," I warned, especially since the twins were at her mother's.

"Don't make promises you can't keep," she purred and then I was dropping the soap and our bodies were pressed against each other, slick with lather and grinding.

I raised my leg on the edge of the tub and brought her between my legs, pressing my pulsing clit against hers. I winded my hips and felt myself get hot down there again. "Rinse off. We're going to bed."

I made sure Jordan was satisfied and sound asleep, then went downstairs to my office. I was a partner at Jacobs, Meyers and Hill, handling mostly divorce and probate cases.

I decided to spend a little time working on a divorce case between two surgeons. I was representing the wife and she wanted everything, including her husband's dirty drawers.

As I looked around, I beamed with pride. We were living near the country club in a thirty-two-hundred square foot home we had built, with more than enough space for two of us and our twins Ava and Evan. They were the apples of our eyes.

Jordan had tried artificial insemination, and when that proved unsuccessful we reluctantly agreed to trying traditional means. We screened candidates until we came across Chance, a man with no intentions of coming back someday demanding parental rights. He was gorgeous with all the qualities we wanted our children to have. Jordan, who'd never been into men, was reluctant at first, but she was the younger of the two of us. I already had a grown son, so there was no way I wanted to be carrying a child. But for Jordan, it was her dream to be a mother.

Eventually she gave in and was willing to have sex with Chance as long as I was present during each of the sessions. I couldn't believe how turned on I had been watching them, and when they suggested I join in on the fun to help ease Jordan's anxiety, I was more than happy to participate. Chance was one hell of a lover and knew how to make a woman come so good, I began to question my sexuality. In fact, it had gotten so bad I started sneaking around with Chance behind Jordan's back and had even started contemplating something more drastic when Renee dropped a bomb. Chance was dating Danielle. Realization hit me and I quickly came to my senses. Thank God Jordan never found out. Now I couldn't even imagine my life with anyone but Jordan. We've been together almost ten years and had a great life together.

I stepped into my office and reached down for my briefcase. I always brought my case files home with me. I logged onto my computer and opened my email and noticed an alert from my bank.

Your account is below fifteen dollars.

What the fuck? My heart started racing. I quickly logged into my bank account when my mouth dropped. I had withdrawn three thousand dollars. I remember going to the ATM and withdrawing money and then going back again. Had I really withdrawn that much out of my account? Not to mention, I already had several hundred in my wallet. Damn. I started beating myself up. I still had a mortgage payment and Jordan's car payment to clear. I logged into our joint savings account and transferred money into my own account. Now that Jordan had a purse full of money, she would never notice, but I'd make sure to put the money back as soon as I was paid.

Pushing the problem aside, I reached down for my file.

I needed billable hours quickly, fast, and in a hurry.

5
Kayla

As soon as we got home, I hurried into the shower. I wanted to freshen up and make sure everything was smelling good for Jermaine. I then climbed out and sprayed my favorite body spray, *Coochie*. I was a Pure Romance consultant. It was like selling Avon, only it was adult toys and products that still made me blush.

I moved in front of the mirror over the double sinks and grinned. I had joined a gym and was starting to see progress. At my age, it was harder to keep my weight under control, but I was determined to do it. It wasn't where I wanted to be, but promising. I just hoped it was enough. Ever since last week, my husband didn't seem that interested in me, sexually that is. It seemed like whatever I tried to do for his attention, it just wasn't there like it used to be.

Mind you, I was a big girl — size twenty-two to be exact — when we first got together. And yet he couldn't keep his hands off all this light-skinned goodness. Now that I'm a size eighteen, his desire for me seemed to have diminished and that crap scared me. It took a lot to get that man and I was not about to risk losing him.

Maybe I was being paranoid. That was nothing new for me. I spent years battling low self-esteem and dealing with men who were selfish and shallow. I worked at the medical school with Jermaine and never thought I'd have a chance of him noticing me. And when he did, my dumb behind had been stuck on stupid. Reverend Leroy Brown, who had been married, had simply been using me with no intentions of leaving his wife. When he ended up murdered, I was framed for something I had nothing to do with. Jermaine stood by me, and I knew at that exact moment he was the one.

We had been through a lot, so there was no way I was losing him.

With that said, I slipped into a cute black nightie I had found at Torrid and took one final look. Not bad. I just hoped Jermaine was also in the mood because I desperately needed my husband to put out the fire burning between my thighs.

I sauntered slowly into our master bedroom. Jermaine was sitting in his La-Z-Boy chair, flipping through channels.

"See something you like?" I said and noticed my husband's eyes follow me around the room.

"Wow! You look—"

"Hot?" I finished the sentence for him and hoped I was right.

"No, I was going to say slim. Are you losing more weight?"

"You're just noticing?" I was pleased he'd noticed or at least I was before I saw him frown.

"Are you sick?"

No he didn't. I stopped and brought a hand to my hip. "No, I'm not sick. I've been cutting back on my portions and walking during lunch with Maureen." Dang, he was a mood killer. Where the hell had he been the last several months when I was spending hours at the gym? Somewhere with his head stuck in the refrigerator. "You sure know how to make me feel good about myself."

Remorse was etched in his brown eyes. "I'm sorry. C'mere." He reached out and yanked me down onto his lap. "You look beautiful, baby. Really you do. Just don't get too skinny. I love having something to hold on to."

I looked up, admiring my husband's golden-brown face and curly hair. Jermaine grinned, showing his beautiful teeth, then he was kissing me and I started shuddering with excitement. Oral sex had better be on the agenda tonight. He caressed my breasts. "Please don't lose these," he whispered.

"Never." I knew how much he loved them. Jermaine reached down between my thighs and started stroking me there. He got me all hot and bothered. I took a long shaky breath, then shifted off his lap and slid down onto my knees. I reached down and squeezed his crotch.

He put his hand over mine. "Whoa, babe. What are you doing?"

"What does it feel like? Tonight, I'm going to please my husband."

"Nah, it's all about you."

"It's been about me for the last week. Your fingers are wonderful and so is your tongue, but tonight, I want you to make love to me," I said and then waited for an answer.

Sadly, he shook his head. "Sorry, babe, but I'm going to have to take a rain check. I think I ate something that's got my stomach upset."

Suddenly I was back on his lap, looking at him with concern. "You need to go to the emergency room?"

"No. I'm sure it's nothing a few Tums won't cure." He lifted me off his lap and was up out of his chair with a hand pressed to his stomach. "I'll be back." He was gone before I could stop him.

After I watched Jermaine head to the kitchen, I went over and laid across the bed. Was my weight loss that unattractive? I heard about women having excess skin and men being turned off. Was that the reason, and he just didn't have the heart to tell me? I was too embarrassed to ask.

I spent my entire life being ridiculed by my own mother. There were the jokes and the nickname she had given me: Ms. Piggy. And then there were the men, and even my daughters Asia and Kenya's father, telling me I was fat and repulsive at the mere sight of my naked body. Too many years I battled weight issues, praying for change and when I'm finally starting to lose weight and feel good about my progress, I find out my husband's unhappy with the way I looked. Why?

I had every intention of asking. Unfortunately, I'd dozed off long before Jermaine had made it back to bed.

6
Danielle

I sauntered into the building in a black pencil skirt, white sheer blouse and my red-bottom pumps. The evening support groups would begin shortly, and I planned on finishing up a few things that couldn't wait until Monday, then head home. I needed to pick up my granddaughter and then meet Renee at Chuck E. Cheese's around six.

Camille had a **Do Not Disturb** sign on her door that indicated she was having a one-on-one counseling session. There was a separate entrance into her suite, allowing her clients privacy and the ability to avoid the daily flow of members that frequented the spot.

I went back to my office to read emails and review the files my assistant had put on my desk. We had five new members to my on-line dating services. It was rare when I met one-on-one. The whole point of the site was to ensure identities remained anonymous, but someone was insistent on meeting me, and was arriving in about ten minutes. I grabbed a bottle of water from the small dorm-size refrigerator in my office.

I moved behind my desk and took a seat, crossing my bare legs. A quick glance up and I was looking at a photo of me and Calvin on our wedding day. I was smiling as if I hadn't a worry in the world and wearing an off-the-shoulder cream gown. In my hands was a bouquet of petunias and lilies. Calvin was holding me protectively. I frowned, because even now he made sure I didn't want for anything. He catered to me and most women would kill for a man like that, but for me it had gotten sort of annoying.

Lord forgive me.

I did not know why I felt that way. Probably because I wanted less predictably and more excitement and spice. I missed being with a thug.

There was a soft rap at my office door. I looked up and stalled.

Shane Michaux was about six-five and should have been somewhere playing basketball, instead of bugging me. But he'd once confessed a motorcycle accident killed that dream. Those big chocolate-chip colored eyes were pretty enough to make even a virgin wanna drop her panties. And those lips, the way he kept licking them had me fantasize about how they tasted.

Why in the world was he here?

"Hey, Danny." He smiled and didn't bother to wait for an invitation before he walked in, invading my space.

"I asked you not to call me that," I repeated for the umpteenth time and forced a frown that I wasn't at all feeling.

Shane gave me a knowing smile as if he knew something I didn't. Like we were friends. That was not how I would ever consider our relationship. In fact, I couldn't even consider him a colleague, not since I'd severed our working relationship.

"Shane, what do you want?" I said and rolled my eyes in an attempt not to look at him. He was just that gorgeous, that he made a woman want to salivate. I gave up drooling a long damn time ago.

"I came to see you. I'm your appointment."

I brought a hand to my desk and pushed up into a standing position. "Listen. As I told you, I can no longer do business with you."

"Yes, you made yourself clear, although I still can't understand why you fired me."

"You know damn well why I terminated our contract. Because you propositioned me!"

He stared as if he was thinking about what I had just blurted out loud enough for anyone paying attention to hear. Luckily, no one was left in the building but Camille and me.

"I didn't proposition you. I said I didn't think your husband was satisfying you the way you deserved."

There was this way he rolled his tongue when he said the

world *satisfied* that always made my pussy purr. Damn, why did he have to be so fine? "I told you, it's none of your business what goes on in *my* bed with *my* husband."

"My bad for stepping outta line, but I'm not taking back what I said. If it ain't true, then why you so salty?"

"I'm not *salty* and it doesn't matter anymore. I've hired a new web designer to handle Positive Connections."

I expected my announcement to wipe the smirk from his face, but instead he appeared amused. "That's too bad. I could have taken your online dating service to new levels. I hope you didn't hire Dickens Web Solutions."

I tried to keep a straight face. "Maybe, not that it's any of your business."

"Do you know they have been publicly known to represent clients that bash the LGBT community?"

Damn. I had no idea. "I'm using a St. Louis-based company," I lied. "But thank you for stopping by… Goodbye."

Calmly, Shane shook his head. "That's not why I'm here."

I was almost too scared to ask. "What can I do for you?" I said impatiently, hoping he would get the hint and leave me alone.

"I'm your four o'clock appointment." He gave me his signature smile. It took me a moment before I realized I had almost fallen for that shit.

"My four o'clock appointment is interested in my online services."

"Yes, and that person would be me." Shane lowered onto the chair in front of me and then passed me his application and the membership fee.

"You're joking, right?"

"No, I'm serious. I know what I want, and this is the only place I can get it."

His words sent images flooding my mind of exactly what it was he was hoping to get. As fine as Shane was, finding a woman shouldn't be a problem for him—at all. Hell, I noticed the first time I spotted him walk into my office, and continued to notice every time we met to discuss the design of a new website. All that ended when he started to get a bit too personal.

"Well, if that's the case, then we have a bit of a problem." I slid down onto my seat and watched as my words removed the smug look on his face.

"And what would that be?"

"To be a client of my dating services, you have to have been diagnosed with HIV."

I waited for his comeback, but when he finally spoke, his response was not at all the one I had been expecting.

"Seven years."

It was a good thing I had been sitting down.

"What?"

Three years ago, I gave up nursing and started Positive Embrace Counseling Center, a nonprofit, peer-led support group for men and women living with HIV, that had since grown to a partnership that was integrated at clinics across the area. As I listened to the meaningful discussions of our members, and heard how hard it was to find love, I decided to start an online dating service for people living with HIV. A place where people could meet others and not have to worry about saying, "Hey guess what? I have HIV," because the diagnosis was a membership requirement. One person told another and then another and before long Positive Connections with the "You're not alone" slogan had one hundred members, and that number had grown to over ten thousand in the last two years. With Shane's help, I had hoped for the site to continue growing to become one of the largest anonymous HIV dating sites. Members' profiles were password-protected and private and were only revealed once they allowed a potential candidate access. I was pretty proud of myself. God had given me a second chance and a chance to help others living with HIV... Like me.

"How come you never told me?"

Shane shrugged. "You never asked. Although, how else did you think I knew so much about the virus?"

I shook my head. "I figured you had done your research."

"Then obviously you hadn't done any of your own, or you would have known or, better yet, have asked."

I was stunned into silence. This gorgeous man had the virus.

He was a true testament that you never knew a person's status just by looking at them. Shane was tall and gorgeous in what appeared to be almost perfect physical health. Not at all the stereotypes that folks used to believe of patients being frail and sickly.

"Wow! Please forgive me." I still had a hard time believing it.

"Of course, but I prefer we do it over lunch tomorrow."

He was back at it again.

"I already made my position clear." I tried to harden my tone. "Now, if you'd really like me to hook you up, I can. Although you can just join the membership and do it on your own."

"You could help me, but you'd be wasting your time."

"Why is that?"

"Because the only woman I'm interested in getting to know better is the one sitting across this desk from me." He was really laying it on with smooth melted butter. That adorable dimple at his cheek wasn't helping either. "Give me a chance and I can show you what you've been missing."

Despite how tempting that offer sounded, Shane was back to disrespecting me. "Missing? I'm not missing anything. My husband takes damn good care of me." If I could just stay strong and not give anything away, I might actually survive his interrogation.

"Really?" There was a challenge gleaming in his eyes that made me feel suddenly very afraid. "I bet you he doesn't even go down on you anymore."

Damn, how did he know?

"The beautiful thing about dating a man with HIV is I can lick all over that clit."

"He would lick over it. I just won't let him."

"It's because you're a good person and you don't want to take that risk. But there's nothing more boring than restricted sex. I like it wild and spontaneous. When my woman least expects, I'm spreading her legs and burying my dick deep."

I was almost tempted to swipe my arm across the desk, knocking everything onto the floor just to get him to provide a sneak preview.

I cleared my throat. "I prefer giving than receiving, even though my husband gives me plenty."

"I just bet he does. You probably have sex and then he holds you in his arms… your cheek resting against his chest." Shane chuckled.

How did he know? Avoiding eye contact, I flipped over the form. "Getting down to business… let's take a look at what you're looking for in a woman."

He smiled playfully. "What I'm looking for is you. Let's not make any mistakes about that."

I ignored the way my pussy was pulsing and glared up at him. "The mistake is I'm not available, so you can either let me help you find someone else or we are done with this conversation."

"You sure don't take no prisoners, do you?"

I grinned, because my brother used to say that about me all the time. "Not in this lifetime." I smirked. "So, let's see. You're looking for someone tall and slender with a great personality." Yes, that would be me and dozens of other women. "What about children?" I reached for my pen and was prepared to take notes.

"I have no problem dating a woman with children, especially since I will probably never have any more of my own." He was giving me that smirk again.

"You have a child?"

Shane nodded. "A twenty-year-old son who lives in Florida with his mom."

I caught myself watching those beautiful lips of his as he spoke and was wondering what they would feel like brushing against my pussy.

"At any rate, I have a few women in mind who would love to meet you."

"What about you? If we had met under different circumstances would you have been interested?"

Damn right. He was too fucking fine to have passed up. Shane was the type of man who stepped into a room and his presence alone demanded attention.

Why did I have to be so weak when it came to him? Ever since I got married, I'd often fantasized about being with another man, but not once had I ever been tempted to go through with it. Until now.

I threw my hand in the air in an effort to shake off the mesmerizing visual effects.

"I think I'm going to have to ask you to leave." I made a show of ripping up his application and then rose and walked around the desk, hoping to pull open the door and show him I was serious. But as soon as I was close enough, Shane reached out and grabbed my arm. Then he was up out of the chair. I stumbled back against the wall with his body flush against mine. Every cell in my body heated on contact.

"Let me go!"

"You don't mean it," he challenged. "I can see it in your eyes, you're bored and desperate for variety in your life."

"That's where you're wrong. I'm happily married with a man who adores me."

He was laughing at me. "That sounds boring as hell, and you know it."

Before I could push him away, Shane's mouth landed over mine. And when my lips parted in surprise, he used that opportunity to his advantage and slipped his tongue inside. Instantly, we were moving at a feverish rhythm. The kiss was none of that gentle shit I got at home day after day from Calvin. Instead it was rough and relentless. I danced with him, trying to outdo him, but the man had talent. I mean mad talent, like he had invented tongue kissing. I felt guilty and tried to push against him just to show that I had at least tried to resist, but Shane took my hands and pinned them to the wall and leaned in even closer. He was aroused, his penis moving against my stomach. If he hadn't been holding my hands I might have been tempted to reach down and see if what he had was worth the risk. But I already had a strong feeling it was and that he knew exactly how to use it to bring a woman whimpering underneath him, begging him never to stop.

I made the mistake of opening my eyes and caught the framed photograph of Calvin and I on our honeymoon perched on the shelf. That was just what I needed to give me the strength to stop what we were doing before it had gotten so far there was no coming back. I pushed him away.

"How dare you!" I exclaimed with very little conviction. Anyone watching would have known I was full of shit. I guess he did, too, because Shane smirked.

"What's wrong? Feel good to you?"

God, why did he have to be so sexy? If he wasn't, maybe resisting wouldn't be so damn hard. "No, not at all."

"Liar." He had the nerve to laugh at me again, a deep hearty chuckle that made my nipples tingle.

I stalked over to the door, but had to pull myself together before I swung around. "Get out."

I guess something on my face or maybe it was the tone of my voice that told him I was really serious. "Just hear me out."

"There's nothing for us to talk about."

"I think there is. I think you're curious to hear everything I have to say. You're just too ashamed to admit it."

I rolled my eyes. I was happily married. There was nothing he could say that would make me think otherwise. Only the longer I was around him, the harder it was to remember that.

"I'm not trying to bring any drama to your life. Not at all. I'm just so attracted to you, I can't pretend anymore."

I made the mistake of looking into his eyes again, and there was no mistaking the desire. Was this shit really happening?

"All I wanna do is touch you."

I swallowed. "That's all?"

Shane winked. "I wanna fuck you, but that's gotta be your call."

"I'm married." I think I repeated that more for myself than for him.

"And I respect that."

I shook my head. "No you don't, because if you did you wouldn't be trying to disrespect my husband. Now please leave."

He walked toward the door, but instead of leaving Shane pushed it shut and turned around. "Answer one question and then I'll leave if you still want me to."

Damn! I was suddenly very afraid.

"Don't you miss having your pussy licked?"

No he didn't just ask me that.

"Tell me now, and I'll walk out that door."

I couldn't do that because he would have immediately saw through my lies.

"All I want is one night with you, and a nigga won't bother you again."

"You won't?"

He shook his head. "No, I won't have to 'cause you *will* contact me wanting more."

Shit, what was wrong with me? The closer Shane moved toward me, the more I was considering his proposition.

"And this is about being with me for just one night?" I don't know why, but I was pissed. Probably because I secretly wanted this to be about a lot more than carving a notch in his headboard.

"It about rediscovering what you've been missing."

I shook my head at the thought. I had a nervous feeling Shane had the ability to show me I'd been missing a whole helluva lot.

"HIV changed my life so I know it changed yours too. But it don't have to. I live life cautiously to the fullest. I love to fuck, and don't feel like I have to go without because I'm a carrier of the virus." Shane was staring at me.

I was staring back.

I had given up a lot in the bedroom, but it had nothing to do with HIV and everything to do with my sex life with Calvin.

The fact of the matter was our sex was vanilla, and yet, it was the way it would have to be. Having an affair came at a price. One too high for me to pay. My sex life might be boring, but my marriage had so many other things to offer. Unfortunately, now, I couldn't remember any of them.

Shane looked way too sure of himself.

My office phone rang and I startled, then hurried around him to answer it. "Positive Embrace Counseling Center, may I help you?"

"Hey, baby. How's your afternoon?"

Shit! It was Calvin. "Hey, you," I said into the phone as I moved around and took a seat in my chair.

"How much longer before you get home? I'm planning on throwing a couple of steaks on the grill."

I swallowed. His attempt at a romantic evening made me feel guilty as hell, especially since I was planning to have pizza with Renee and the grandbabies. "That sounds wonderful, babe. We are just wrapping up, and I should be heading home in a few minutes."

"Drive carefully. I'll see you in a few."

I hung up the phone to see Shane over at my bookshelf, staring at framed family photographs. Even his profile was sexy.

This was maddening.

For weeks, I've been staring and fantasizing about him, gorgeous and chocolate with muscles and much swag.

Shit! I had to get rid of him fast.

"I need to get home so if you're through trying to mess with my head, I would appreciate it if you'd leave."

Turning around, he winked. "The fact that you just admitted I was in your head means I'm getting to you."

I grabbed my purse from my bottom drawer and glared at him. "No, it means I'm tired of this ridiculous conversation." I strutted across my office and out the door as I reminded myself I had a good man at home waiting for me.

Shane fell in step beside me and then insisted he walk me to my car. By the time I climbed inside and pulled away, I realized just how weak I was when it came to him.

It was just a matter of time.

7
Renee

Have I told you I'm a grandma? Well, I am, and damn proud of it.

Quinton started messing around with some hot-ass girl who was still in high school and got her ass pregnant. When I had first found out I was pissed as hell, mostly at my ex-husband for not telling me, and second, because I had to find out on Facebook. Really? I called Quinton and got all in his and his daddy's ass, then demanded the girl's number so I could call and see where her head was. Diamond was so stuck-on-stupid when it came to my son, I couldn't talk any sense into her. Like so many young girls today, they think by getting pregnant, that's the way to try and trap a nigga. Wrong answer. They're still going to do whatever the fuck they wanted to do.

Sure enough, he dumped her gullible ass before the baby was even born and was back to shacking up with some old desperate bitch.

Danielle had to get her daughter Portia to keep me abreast of Diamond's progress and as soon as I heard she had gone into labor, I had flown back to Missouri to be there to see my grandson for myself. A mother knows if it's her son's baby or not. The feet always give it away.

She asked me to come into the delivery room but I wasn't at all interested in seeing some other female's stretched out pussy, so I waited in the lobby and once the delivery was over, I came into the room and walked over to the warmer. I peeked underneath the sheet and looked down at them big-ass Flintstones toes and immediately knew that little boy was my grandson! I had to call Quinton and make him bring his ass to the hospital. He was so damn high, I kicked him out Diamond's room and told him if he didn't get his shit together, he better not ever ask me for shit. I stuck around long enough to shower my grandson with everything he would need that his mother hadn't already bought him. After that, I flew down every chance I got to spend time with him.

Since I was catching a plane home tomorrow, I'd made arrangements with Diamond to spend time with Quinton, Jr. She was more than happy to hand him over, along with a list of things he needed. That wench thought I was fucking Santa Claus. But there wasn't anything I wouldn't do for my grandson, and she knew it.

"Gigi, look!" Quinton, Jr. cried out from the jungle gym.

What? Did you really think I would have allowed him to call me grandma? Hell-to-the-no. I am too fabulous for all that. Gigi stands for gorgeous grandma and that was definitely me.

We had been at Chuck E. Cheese's about a half hour and already that three-year-old was wearing me out. I texted Quinton again and told him to hurry the hell up. It made no sense I had to reach out to his mother to see my grandson when his father should be doing all that. But as usual the two of them were at it again.

I ordered a pizza, mozzarella sticks, and two orders of wings. Danielle was supposed to grab her granddaughter and join us. I was playing Skee-ball with Quinton, Jr. when she finally arrived, looking cute in skinny jeans, pumps and an off-the-shoulder green blouse.

"Hey, girl!" She sounded all out of breath and shit. I looked down beside her at Etienne. She was such a cute little girl with chinky little eyes like her grandmother and soft delicate features. Her hair was in two ponytails that hung halfway down her back.

"Ya-Ya." I gave her a big hug, but Etienne was more interested in playing with Quinton, Jr., which was fine by me. "Here, keep these." I stuffed the pockets of her blue jean shorts with tokens and signaled Danielle to follow me over to the table that was close enough for us to keep my eye on them two.

"Where's Portia at? I was hoping to see her before I left."

"She has clinical today. They got her working at some trifling nursing home in Jefferson City."

"Yeah, but at least she's getting her license as a practical nurse. That is so good."

Danielle couldn't hide the pride from her face. It had been a long haul and yet her daughter was finally turning her life around. She was a good little mama.

"She's been looking at an apartment, but I told her she really should just stay with her grandmother and wait until she gets done with school."

Now that her father had passed away, her mother was all alone in that big house by herself. "I'm sure she loves having Portia's company."

"And she is a big help with Etienne. Between the dating service, Calvin, and my appointments with my doctors, I really don't have time to be babysitting every day."

"I know that's right." We joked a lot, but we'd already raised our kids and paid our dues. Wasn't nobody trying to raise somebody else's child.

"Danny, how is the online service going?"

"Girl, it's going damn good. I am making so much money, Calvin can't believe it! The in-house counseling sessions and support groups are growing as well."

I shook my head in awe, because who would have ever believed Danielle would have become an entrepreneur.

"This dude came into the office this morning…" she started, fanning herself.

"He was that fine?"

She nodded.

"And he has…"

Danielle nodded again.

Damn. That's why you couldn't trust sexy mothafuckas anymore. Their dicks were all tainted and shit.

"This guy was hood and sexy as shit."

I could already see the wheels turning. "Uh-uh. What's going on in your head?"

She had the nerve to try and look all innocent. "There's

nothing going on in my head."

"You're a damn lie." I leaned over the table. "Don't tell me you're thinking about getting some of that." She hesitated too damn long. "Oh shit! You are." I shook my head. The whole point of her online dating services was so people with HIV could meet others with the same thing, although I heard there were different strands of the virus so you could still infect each other. It all sounded nasty to me, but then who was I to judge? Hell, Danielle probably wouldn't have ever known she had the virus if I hadn't dragged her ass down to the clinic with me to get tested after my bitch-ass ex-husband contracted it from the down-low sex. As it turned out, my results were negative, but Danielle hadn't been so lucky, due to some thug. He infected her along with a dozen other females before his beaten body was found floating in the river. Danielle will never admit, but I think her brother, Kee had something to do with that.

With a sigh, Danielle said, "I miss thug passion."

"Bitch, that's a drink."

She laughed. "It's also the way I've been feeling lately."

I shook my head. "Hold that thought." I rushed over to help Etienne and Quinton, Jr onto a small merry-go-around, and trotted back over to the table just as the food arrived. I filled our cups with drinks and came back over to the table. Danielle was texting on her phone. "I hope you're not texting your thug passion."

She laughed. "No, ho, I'm texting my husband."

I pointed a mozzarella stick at her. "I knew you were going to get tired of that boring-ass sex with Calvin. Like I've said before, if he ain't buck-wild before you married him, what's going to change it after?"

She gave me a knowing look. "You know why I married him."

"Then, that should be good enough."

"You got a lot of nerve. You were married to John for how long? And your ass was fucking fifty heading north."

"Yeah, but I don't have—" Shit. I stopped suddenly.

"You don't have what? HIV? So, because I have it, I have to stop living?"

"I didn't say that." I hate when people put words into my mouth. "Calvin isn't my favorite person in the world, however, he's a great guy for you. You almost lost him once before 'because you wanted a thug in your life. Do you really want to take that chance again?"

She got quiet, because Danielle knows I'm right.

"Danny, look, I'm your girl and you know I will ride and die with yo ass, but I wouldn't be a friend if I didn't say you better be sure that's what you wanna do." I leaned back on the chair, grinning. "I know what it's like to want some good dick. David tried to blow my back out."

"What?" she barked and gave me a high-five.

"I needed that. It's a shame I have to come back to this country-ass town just to get fucked."

"Hey, we got the best wings and the best dick."

She wasn't lying. CJ Wings was one of my all-time favorites and as soon as I dropped Quinton, Jr. back home, I was heading over to meet Kayla before I headed to St. Louis for my flight in the morning. Columbia's a wonderful place to visit, but I didn't want to live there anymore.

I was giving her a play-by-play of my night with David when I spotted Quinton walking into the restaurant. He was dressed in a fitted cap, a red and blue polo shirt, jeans, and a fresh pair of red Chuck Taylor's.

"Whassup Mom," he said and slid on the bench beside me.

I immediately noticed how red his eyes were. "Are you high?"

"Nah, just was up late last night."

"Doing what?" Danielle's eyes were sparkling with curiosity.

He had the nerve to get loud. "I'm out here trying to hold it down. You don't see me asking my mom for money."

"That's because you're asking everyone else." Danielle sputtered with laughter.

"I just needed some money that day. I had to give Diamond her child support. I told her I didn't get paid until Friday, but she wanted it now."

"Uh-huh." He knew I didn't believe shit he said. Besides,

he'd failed to mention I had given him two hundred dollars this morning.

"Mom." He reached inside his pocket and pulled out this glass bottle from his pocket.

"Q, put that shit away!" Danielle said and looked around to make sure no one was watching.

He took his time putting the liquid back into his pocket.

"What the hell is that?" I asked.

"That's that wet," he said softly.

"That what?"

Danielle rolled her eyes and I glared over at him. Quinton, Jr. was crying and I pointed. "Go handle that." Quinton jumped out his seat and went over to see what he wanted. Immediately, I looked over at Danielle. "What the hell was that shit?"

She leaned across the table, then glanced over her shoulder to make sure Quinton wasn't listening. "That's wet."

"Wet?" I was confused.

"It's like embalming fluid. They roll up weed and dip it in that formaldehyde and sell it. I heard it has mothafuckas going crazy."

"You're lying?"

"Girl no, and when they smoke it that shit smells terrible."

I shook my head. "They put embalming fluid in dead people, why the fuck would anyone want to smoke that." I just don't understand these stupid young folks and the shit they do with their bodies. I have never been a smoker. Not cigarettes and definitely not weed. I tried it in high school and just was not interested.

"And that shit ain't cheap," Danielle added and bit into a slice of pizza.

"That's why he doesn't have money for anything else. And regardless of what he says, he looks like he's using his own product." I had a feeling that's where my money had gone.

I was ready to tear into his ass, but he was heading toward the table with two hungry kids. I watch my mouth in front of my grandson. After we all ate, the kids played a little longer until it was time to go. I told my son he was riding with me to take Quinton, Jr. back home. I kissed and hugged my little man, gave his mom the bags from our afternoon shopping spree and we left.

As soon as we were around the corner, I lit into his ass. "What the fuck are you doing with that wet bullshit?"

"What?" He had the nerve to try and play dumb.

"You heard me. I raised you better than that. Why can't you get out there and do something positive with your life?"

"Man... you left me."

"Mothafucka, I'm not your man. And I didn't leave you nowhere. You're the one who wanted to stay in Missouri. I left you with your father. I wanted him to finish teaching you how to be a man. Not be out in the street doing and selling drugs."

"This is easy money." He pulled out the bottle and held it up.

"Are you fucking stupid?" He had this look of pride on his face that made me feel sick to my stomach. I tried to snatch it from his hand, but he jerked back out of my reach.

"If God ain't my witness, if you don't put that bullshit away I'm going to put yo ass out my mothafuckin' car."

He scowled, but knew better than to respond.

"I love you, but you need to get your shit together. When you do, let me know, then I will send you a one-way plane ticket to join me in Virginia. The rate you're going, you're going to find your ass in jail, and when you do, don't call me."

I dropped him back off at his car with a bad feeling gnawing at my chest that things were not going to end well.

8
Kayla

I looked up at the sign guy putting my name on the door.

Kayla Whitlow, Executive Associate, Dean's Office.

It was still hard to believe after all the years I spent working in this department. I remembered when I was just a file clerk. Look at me now.

"All done."

I smiled at Grayson and noticed the way he was looking at me. Often, I had seen him staring a little too long to be deemed appropriate. But I'd been caught doing the same thing. I figure there's nothing wrong with looking if you don't touch.

Since I'd first began losing the weight, I'd been receiving quite a bit more male attention than I was used to. Don't be mistaken, I've always had a pretty face. I just had a large round body that I'd been ashamed of claiming as mine.

"Congratulations on your new position," he said and I had the feeling he was stalling in my doorway like he wanted to ask me something.

I tried to think of something to say and finally settled on just simply saying, "Thank you." I gazed at my name on the glass again and started laughing with joy. It really was still too hard to believe.

Grayson must have read my mind. "It's not often you find a black woman with a good job in this place."

And not have to suck her way to the top is what he was implying because that was the rumor around the hospital.

"If you ever need anything, please don't hesitate to contact me."

"I will." I came out from behind my desk and was leaning against the edge striking a pose. Goodness, I was starting to act like Renee. "Tell Lolita I said hello."

He scratched his chin. "We aren't together anymore."

"Oh, what a shame?" What fool would let all that dark chocolate go?

His wife, Lolita worked in housekeeping. That and food service were the departments many of the African-Americans worked throughout the medical facility.

"And how has Mr. Whitlow been?" Grayson was fishing. There was no mistaking the interest sparkling in his gorgeous eyes.

Lord, forgive me. I was committed and never once thought about cheating. But temptation was right smack there: all two-hundred-and-something hard physique, in front of me.

"My husband is fine. In fact…" Speak of the devil, my voice trailed off as I looked up and caught sight of Jermaine stepping out of his office. My front was glass-encased so I could see the entire length of the Dean's Office. At the very end, I spotted my husband talking to the chairman, or in this case, chairwoman of the Endocrinology Department. Dr. Melinda Barber, aka, Black Barbie.

She was a Beyoncé wannabe with long bone-straight weave, bronze skin and a body that said, POW! every time she moved. She was beautiful and successful and the worst part, she was single.

Grayson was still talking, but I didn't hear a single world. I was too busy focusing on my husband. He was bending close to hear something Black Barbie was saying.

"You planning on attending?" I heard Grayson say. "Jazz night on Thursday. It's a new thing."

"I'm not sure," I mumbled and wished he'd just leave. The only reason why I hadn't kicked him out of my office was because his being there gave me an excuse for standing and looking in that direction. Grayson's back was turned so he thought I was looking at him, only I was looking over his shoulder at my husband with that hussy.

My pulse began to race when I spotted her putting a hand on my husband's arm. But what got my heart racing was when I saw the two walk out the door into the atrium. It was time for me to go remind that homewrecker who Jermaine was married to.

"I was thinking—"

I held up a hand stopping him. "Excuse me." Grayson was still talking when I bolted through my door and across the Berber-carpeted floor. My assistant tried to get my attention, but I held up my hand halting her mid-sentence. Now was not the time. Here I was wasting time allowing Grayson to flirt that wouldn't have ever amounted to anything. And in the meantime, I'd left my handsome husband unattended.

That buzzard was sniffing around for fresh meat.

I was almost across the office when a voice stopped me in my tracks.

"Kayla, there you are."

Shit. It was Dean Gary Fox.

"Good morning, Dr. Fox." I smiled up at the distinguished, attractive man. Silver Fox was his nickname around medical school.

"Are the brochures ready for the symposium on Thursday?"

My eyes strayed outside the door. I panicked when I noticed neither my husband or Melinda were in sight.

"Yes, they're ready. I put one in your inbox."

"Excellent." He had on a lab coat, which meant he'd just finished rounds at the hospital.

"I would like to go over my slides. You have time?" I noticed him look over his shoulder following the direction of my eyes.

"Oh sure. Can you give me a few minutes? I was just on my way to the ladies' room."

"I'll be in my office, waiting."

I hurried out, shifting my gaze and panicked. My husband and that homewrecker were gone.

I bolted through the door and looked toward the auditorium, the winding staircase, and swept the space. I hurried over to peek through the auditorium doors and they weren't there, then turned the corridor. There were a few people walking the halls, but not a tall man in a dark suit. The longer I searched, the angrier I got.

Dammit, where were they!

Walking back to my office, I stepped through the side door and hoped Dean Fox wouldn't see me. But at the sound of my two-inch pumps, he stuck his head out the door of his room.

"Grab a pen."

I had no choice but to join him.

The whole time we were reviewing the presentation, I was wondering where the hell my husband was.

The devil is a lie!

Her husband was faithful and committed. Jermaine didn't give me any reason to make me think he was cheating. So why now?

A lack of sex will do that to you.

It had been going on two weeks. I had even planned a romantic evening for us, hoping that would spark the mood. And yet nothing. He had fallen asleep while I was changing into something more comfortable. I had been pissed for days until he had a bouquet of roses delivered to the office. Everyone envied my marriage with him, and at one time I'd felt like the luckiest woman of all.

By the time I'd reached the last office on the left of the receptionist area, Jermaine's door was open and he was seated behind his desk. I walked right in and shut the door with a click. As soon as my husband spotted me, he put down the phone.

"Hey, sweetheart. I was just calling you." he smiled.

"What about?" I asked suspiciously.

Jermaine gave me a weird look. "To see if you wanted to walk to the student union for lunch."

I didn't want to talk about that. "Where were you and Dr. Barbie?"

"Melinda?"

I saw the look he gave, but I wasn't in the mood. "Oh, so she's Melinda now. When did you start calling her by her first name?"

"I always have when students aren't around." He shook his head and gave me a weird look.

"I saw the two of you disappear," I accused, walking toward him.

"What… you're spying on me now?"

"You forget I have a direct view from my office out into the entire suite."

Jermaine hesitated for a moment. "We went down to the lab to see the students dissecting rats." He was talking about the Summer Enrichment Program. High school students had an opportunity to live on campus for four weeks and study math and science while being paid a stipend. I was aware of the donors. I was the one who wrote the grant each year to renew funding.

"You jealous?"

"No, I'm not jealous!" I barked.

He smirked. "Yes, you are. It's written all over your face. You come barging into my office looking like you're ready to kick someone's ass."

"Did I really look that bad?"

"Yes." He reached out and pulled me down onto his lap so fast, I squealed and couldn't resist a smile. "Sweetheart, I don't want anyone but you. All I talk about is my beautiful wife."

Then, why wasn't I getting any. Hell, that's what I wanted to know.

Jermaine kissed me and asked, "Are we on for lunch?"

"I rather run home for a quickie."

You would have thought someone had pulled down the shades the way his face darkened. "Why lately does everything always have to be about sex with you?"

I mumbled rudely. "Probably because I can't remember the last time I've had any."

"I told you. I haven't been in the mood lately."

"When are you going to be?" I asked and gave him an evil look.

"If all our relationship is based on is sex, what will we have left when we get old?"

Sex. I hope. I released a sigh and pushed off his lap. "Just forget it."

"Listen, how about we set up some private time and maybe

go to Kansas City for the weekend."
"Really?" I said, feeling hopeful.
"Yes, Kayla. A romantic getaway."
I was so looking forward to it.

9
Renee

I was folding clothes and watching HGTV in my bedroom when I received a call. One quick glance down at my cell phone identified it as a Missouri number. I didn't recognize the number, but I figured it was either someone I didn't know or one of my trifling family members calling to beg for some money. Either way I was bored so I decided to answer.

"Hello?"

"Renee?"

I didn't recognize the voice. "Yeah, who's speaking?"

"This is Soledad. Your son's girlfriend."

No, this old bitch wasn't calling my damn phone. And she was trying to be slick by reminding me she was fucking Quinton.

I went back to folding towels. "What can I do for you?"

"Well… Q just walked into my shop and he's acting strange."

"What do you mean strange?"

"I mean he has this spaced-out look in his eyes, and there's blood on his t-shirt."

The blood caused me to drop the towel I was folding. "What do you mean blood?"

"There's just a few spots. I tried to ask him about it, but he walked in and headed straight for the restroom."

"What the fuck…" I was pissed. "Put my son on the phone!" I didn't mean to snap, but how the hell are you gonna call someone's mother and mention blood without having an answer?

"Quinton, your mom wants to talk to you!" I heard her knocking on the door and him mumbling something. After a few seconds, Soledad came back onto the phone. "I hear the water running, but he won't come out."

I was quickly losing patience. "What did he say to you when he first came into your shop?"

"Nothing really." There was a pause. "He looks like he's on that stuff."

I rolled my eyes. Stupid-ass mothafucka. I'd just been there two months ago telling him to get his shit together. For the life of me, I don't understand how someone can use the shit they're trying to sell, not that he should be selling it in the first place.

"Have you seen him on that stuff before?" I asked, because inquiring minds wanted to know.

"Yes, and as a matter of fact..." There was a slight hesitation. "He was holding the bottle in his hand when he came in."

I was so ready to hang up the phone. This was some bullshit I didn't want to be a part of. If my son wanted to ruin his life, then that was his choice.

"He took it in the restroom with..." her voice trailed off. "He's coming out. Q, I have your mother on the phone! She wants to talk to you."

Again, I heard him mumble something I couldn't understand, which pissed me off. "Soledad, ask him about the blood."

"Q, where did that blood come from? C'mere." There was another pause. "Lift up your shirt."

"What is it?" I barked.

"I don't know. Q, please, move your hand so I can see." She was talking to him all slow and gentle. "Renee, it's a small hole, like he hopped a fence and got caught on the barbed wire or something. Q, what happened to you?" There was mumbling and then silence. This chick was treating him like a baby and wrecking my nerves.

"Q just went outside, He's still holding that stuff. I don't know what to do. Should I call the police?"

I couldn't believe how timid she sounded. "If you think you should, then call them." Because this was truly a waste of my time. It was obvious I wasn't going to get any answers. "I'm gonna to call his father."

"Okay, I'm going to go and see if I can get him to talk. I have a shop full of customers. Everyone is saying something ain't right."

"That's because he's on that shit!" I groaned. "Let me call his dad. I'll call you back."

This shit was just too much. His father was supposed to be teaching him how to be a man, not letting him hang out on the streets like some freaking thug. I scrolled through my phone for Mario's number, then hit Call. He answered in a low voice.

"Hey, whassup?"

"Whassup is your son is over at Soledad's shop acting weird. She says he's spaced out and he has blood all over his shirt."

"Blood?"

"Yeah like he got caught on a fence or something. Soledad's ready to call the police."

"Then tell her to call. I'm tryna get a payday loan. As soon as I get done with this paperwork, I'll run by there and check on him."

"You do that and then we need to talk. I didn't leave my son there so he could be caught up with a bunch of niggas and start selling drugs on the street."

"Look, Renee, I'm busy. Like I said, when I get done, I'll run by there and see what the hell's goin' on."

Don't you know that mothafucka had the nerve to hang up on me?

I went back to folding clothes and decided to let Mario handle it. Hell, he asked to raise his son, so let him deal with Quinton's sudden desire to get out on the street and act like he was raised in the hood.

I'm the first to admit, urban books are popular, but I don't get the fascination with the hood lifestyle. I blame a lot of that shit on the music videos that glamorize all that gangsta shit. For my son to have been raised in a middle-class family, the need to be knee-deep in that bullshit just didn't make any sense to me. Quinton should have been in college somewhere or had joined the damn army. Instead, he wanted to be dipping weed in embalming fluid and hustling on the streets.

I had put my laundry away by the time my phone rang again. It was Soledad. There was clearly worry in her tone. "Q's still acting strange. I took the bottle away from him. What do you want me to do with it?"

I don't know why the hell she was asking me. The first thing I wanted to say was throw the shit away, but I had to stop myself. If that was a drug, then there was no telling who Quinton had gotten it from and if there was any money associated with it. The last thing I wanted was to cause my son problems by throwing away merchandise.

"Just hide it somewhere. What's he doing?"

"He's playing with the hole at his side. Sticking his finger inside it and staring into space. There's blood on his hands."

"What the hell?" Whatever the fuck was Quinton smoking?

"I think I need to call the police."

"Okay, you're there assessing the situation, not me. Do what you feel you have to do. I called his father. He said —"

"Oh!" she interrupted. "He's pulling up now."

I hung up and went back to letting Mario handle it. I was hungry and had no intentions of cooking tonight. I took a seat on the bed and reached for my iPad and was looking at the menu of a seafood restaurant a few miles away when Mario called me back.

"What the hell is going on?" I spat into the phone, and the words that came out of his mouth stopped me cold.

"He's been shot! My son's been shot!"

I couldn't have heard him right. "*Shot?*"

"That stupid bitch! Anyone can see he's been shot!"

At this point I could tell he was in the car because wind was whipping, and I heard Quinton moaning somewhere close by.

"I'm so fucking pissed, I could hit something! All them standing around looking at him like he's crazy!"

"Shot?" I still couldn't believe it.

"Hell, yeah, shot! That's a got-damn gunshot wound! He's in the car with me. I'm taking him to the emergency room now."

Shot? Oh my God!

"Dad, hurry!" Quinton was moaning and crying out in pain.

I guess that meant he was finally coming down off his high.

"Dad, hurry!" I couldn't bear to hear my son in that kind of pain.

"What..." I couldn't even find the strength to speak.

"I'm pulling up at the hospital. I'll call you later," Mario told me and then the phone went dead.

Shot? My baby had been shot!

I walked around the room in a daze telling myself it couldn't be that bad. He was just at the shop, standing around. There had been very minimal blood. Hell, he had been playing with the wound at his side, so it couldn't possibly be that bad.

I thought about calling my girls back in Missouri to tell them what had happened, but I figured there was no point in worrying them. Everything was going to be alright. I had to believe that.

To take my mind off Quinton, I ordered my food, then drove down to the restaurant to pick it up. I had just stepped up to the counter when I received an unknown call from Missouri.

"Hello?"

"Renee, this is Curtis." His voice trailed off and that allowed the name to register. He was a good friend of the family and a minister.

"Hey, what's going on?" I asked. As he began to speak, I moved the phone away from my mouth while I told the cashier. "I'm here to pick up my food. Renee Moore." I noticed her giving me a strange look. What the hell was she looking at? She was the one with the bad weave job. Her tracks were clearly visible.

"Sorry about that, Curtis. What's going on?" I figured he probably wanted me to do some fundraiser event for the church.

"Renee, how soon can you get here?" There was a long pause and I froze, because I suddenly realized why he was calling.

"I...are you at the hospital?"

Ms. Wack-Weave had the nerve to point to the No Cell Phones sign near the register.

"Can I have my food, please?" I barked and was clearly irritated. "Curtis, are you at the hospital?"

"Yes, I just happened to be here praying with another family when I spotted Mario."

The cashier pointed to the sign again. "Your order is ready, but could you finish your call first."

"Can you just give me my fucking food? This is a family emergency!" I didn't mean to be so loud. The people standing around were looking at me, and I heard Curtis sigh in the phone.

"Renee, are you listening?"

I stepped out of line and moved off to the side while she went to get my food.

"Where is Mario?" I insisted. He was the person I needed to be talking to, not Curtis.

"He punched the wall and went off somewhere to blow off steam." Yep, that sounded like him. "Renee, it doesn't look good." I could hear the worry in his voice. "You gotta get here."

I guess the full force of what he was saying finally hit me. My knees buckled and I had to use the wall to hold me up. "But he was hardly bleeding," I protested.

I heard the cashier trying to get my attention, but I waved my arms silencing her ass so that I could focus on what Curtis was about to say.

"I was standing with Mario when the doctor came out to talk to him. Quinton has internal bleeding. The bullet hit his lung and there's no exit wound."

Internal bleeding.

Oh.

My.

God!

"Ma'am, your food is ready."

"Would you leave me the fuck alone!" I shouted and then turned and bolted out of the restaurant. To hell with my food. There was no way I was going to be able to get anything down.

"They rushed him into surgery. Dr. Wagner just happened to be on duty tonight, and he's one of the best surgeons in the country. He said it's going to be several hours, but if anyone was on call tonight, I'm glad it was him."

Several hours.

"You really need to get here as fast as you can. Mario fell apart at the news. I think his brothers are on their way over, but you need to get here." He sounded so desperate, I cried out and ended the call.

I headed back to my house on autopilot. All this time I didn't even think about it, but there was a possibility my son might not make it. Quinton could die!

"Nooo...Nooo!" I screamed. "Not my baby. Not my son."

He'd had a promising future with a full-ride scholarship to play football for Purdue, that after a semester he fucked up academically. Even after I threatened to cut him off, he still made no effort to act right and eventually he lost his financial backing. To this day, I should have insisted Mario tell him to get his shit together and let him know that he had no home to come back to. But, instead I listened to his decision to return to Columbia and stay with his father, instead of moving to Hampton with me.

"Nooo! Lord, please...Nooo!" I wailed.

Why? I don't understand. I've always done everything I could for my kids. I gave him anything he wanted, so why would he have chosen this life? I grew up poor, so I'd worked hard trying to give them everything I never had as a child, and I guess that's where I had gone wrong as a parent. I made everything too easy for him. After Quinton fucked up school, I should have insisted he join the military. If so, right now he wouldn't be lying on a cold surgical table.

"This can't be happening. It can't be." I was shaking my head in disbelief, refusing to believe that something like that could happen to my child. I just couldn't allow myself to believe it. But it didn't stop the tears.

I went into the house and cried my eyes out, then walked around like a zombie trying to figure out what I was supposed to be doing. My cell phone rang, and I practically dived across the couch to answer it.

"Renee?" It was Danielle. "I just heard what happened to Q!"

I wasn't surprised. In that little-ass town, news traveled fast. "I-I can't believe it."

"I heard he was at Soledad's shop walking around like

nothing was wrong."

I sniffled and wiped tears away. "He was so high I guess he had no idea he'd been shot."

"Or he was in shock."

Just like me. I lowered onto the bed. *Oh my God! My baby's been shot! And I hadn't been there. I would have known. I would have known.*

"I'm driving up. Just as—"

"D-Driving?" Danielle sputtered. "Are you fucking crazy? You are in no position to be trying to drive."

"I want my car."

"Fuck that car! Show off your Range Rover some other time. Get your ass on a plane."

"I...I... you're right."

"Of course, I'm right. Throw some shit in a bag and get to the airport. I'm going online right now to book you a flight."

She was right. What in the hell made me think I would be able to drive? And also, I needed to get there before it was too late. *Bitch, don't even start thinking like that.*

"He has internal bleeding," I told her. "The bullet hit a lung."

"Oh my God," she said in a hushed voice.

Danielle was an LPN. So, if she was frightened, I had even more reason to be scared.

"Portia said no one knew it was a gunshot wound because he was hardly bleeding. Now that explains it."

"Mario knew what it was the second he saw it," I informed her.

"Good for him. Okay, the next flight is scheduled to leave out at six in the morning. Can you get to the airport that early?"

I was crying again. "I doubt my ass will be able to get any sleep tonight."

"That's the soonest flight. You're gonna have a layover in Charlotte."

"Okay."

"I'm booking it right now. You need to start packing."

I couldn't even clear my head long enough to think about what I needed to be taking. "I will in a few minutes. I just need a moment. This feels so unreal."

"I know girl. But it's going to be alright. He's young and strong."

"And stupid! I knew when I saw him something was going to happen. I could just feel it in my bones that this whole drug dealer mentality was going to end badly. Why didn't I insist that he go home with me?" I wailed.

"Because we have to allow them to live their own life. All we can do is try to guide them, but at some point, we have to stop sheltering them and let them go."

"I know. I know. He was such a good kid. How could he have gotten off path?" I was kicking myself in the ass.

Danielle released a long breath. "I blame it on this world. Black men just don't have a chance. We gotta be strong for them."

Yes, I needed to find a way to stay strong and not fall apart. "All I want to do is hug him, then choke the shit outta him!"

"And I'm going to be standing in line behind you. Alright your ticket is bought. I'm sending it to your email right now."

I loved the way Danielle was always there when I needed her, but that didn't stop me from bawling.

"Renee, stop it dammit, before you make me cry!"

"I can't help it. T-that's m-m-my baaaaaaby!" I wailed.

"You know I know. He's like a son to me. But Q's gonna be okay, so stop thinking negatively."

My phone beeped, and my heart took off in a sprint when I noticed it was Mario. "I-I gotta go. Mario's calling."

"Okay, I'll call you later," Danielle said in a rush before I quickly clicked over.

"Mario?" I could barely get the words out. "Is Q okay?"

"He's still in surgery. It's gonna be a long while before anyone comes out." Mario already sounded worn out and tired.

I couldn't even get my body to move. I just sat there frozen, sitting on the edge of my bed. "What did they say?"

"They said if we had waited thirty more minutes he would not have made it." He took a shaky breath. "He's bleeding internally. That's why there was hardly no blood. He was bleeding on the inside." There was a sob in his voice, and the sound ripped at my heart. I couldn't even call him a bitch. And folks know I'm good at doing that. Nope. Not this time. Mario loved him almost as much as I did. I'm sorry, but no one can come close to the love a mother has for her first-born.

A sob caught in my throat and I tried to hold it together. It wasn't easy, but I had to at least try for Mario's sake. "I feel like everything is going to be alright. Thank you for getting my baby there in time." I didn't even want to think about what might have happened if there had been another customer in front of him at the payday loan office. Thirty more minutes and Quinton wouldn't have even had a chance of making it through the surgery.

"Is anyone there with you?" I asked. I hated the thought of him walking through the corridors of the hospital crying. Even worse, just trying to pass the time while waiting for surgery to be over.

"Barry and Freddie are on their way."

"Good." I was glad to hear that. Those were his brothers. I didn't want him to be there all on his own. I suddenly asked. "Did you empty his pockets before Q was admitted?"

"Yeah, he handed me a wad of money and his wallet."

"That's a relief." There was no telling what could have been in his pockets. "Where's your wife at?"

"She's at home with Cammy."

I don't know what possessed his old ass to start a new family, but to each his own.

"She'll be here in the morning after she gets my little girl off to school."

I released a long sigh. "I have a flight in the morning. I'm not sure when I'm supposed to get there, but I'll be there."

I just prayed my son hung on long enough for me.

10
Renee

I managed to pack a bag while I talked to Kayla, and then decided to try and lay down. I was so mentally exhausted and managed to fall asleep before Mario called me again. He was too emotional to talk. The moment I heard the crack in his voice, the surgeon came onto the phone, and I started to cry. If Mario couldn't talk, then it had to be bad.

"He's resting. We repaired as much as we could, but after five hours his body was getting cold and we had to stop."

"But he's going to live, right?"

Dr. Wagner hesitated and I knew he was choosing his words carefully, but I preferred that to lying and giving me false hope. "Only time will tell. He's weak and in a barbiturate-induced coma. He still has the endotracheal intubation. That's a breathing tube that was inserted during surgery through the mouth down into the trachea. It will help him breathe while he's resting. We need him stronger. In a few hours, we'll be able to tell how well he's doing."

"But you got the bullet out?"

"No, it's still in his back, close to his spine. It would have possibly done more damage to try and remove it."

I was trying to grasp everything he was saying, but all I heard was my son might not make it.

"He's young and that's what's going to work to his advantage. But only time will tell."

"Thank you."

"You're welcome. I'll drop by the unit to check on him later."

I hung up the phone and started bawling. My baby was

fighting for his life. I immediately thought about all the things I had done wrong in my life. And all the people I had hurt. Was this karma or God's way of getting my attention?

"I hear you, Lord. I hear you. But not my son. Please, not Quinton."

I remember when he was first born and the nurse put him in my arms. He stared right up at me with those big brown eyes of his and instantly I fell in love. No one could tell me my baby wasn't beautiful, even though now that I look back, he was one homely-looking baby, but it didn't matter. He was mine.

Quinton had been such a good little boy with his big round head and wide nose. He was such a joy and then when Tamara was born, he was so proud to have a little sister. He had grown to be six-three and everyone started looking at me and Mario, wondering how our son was taller than either of us. Folks even whispered that maybe someone else had been dipping in my cookie jar. But I just rolled my eyes at all those haters. My biological father had been six-five. The height just skipped a generation.

I called Uber and on the entire ride to the airport all I could think about was my handsome son. The girls loved him to the point I had to cuss a few of them out for banging on my door at all hours of the night. All the attention just swelled my son's head to the point I had to keep condoms on hand. Not that it done his ass too much good since he'd knocked up Diamond. But I thanked the Lord for that little boy. I gasped because I was going to have to call his baby mama and let her know he'd been shot. Maybe seeing Quinton, Jr. would give him the will he needed to fight for his life.

I hurried into the airport and even boarded the plane in a daze. Before we pulled off I called the nurses' station to check on Quinton. He was stable. His father was sleeping in the chair beside him. I turned off my phone and said a silent prayer that nothing changed while I was in the air. I needed him to just rest until I got there. I always believed that people could hear what you were saying even in a dream state, and with that in mind I was certain that all Quinton needed was to hear my voice.

I settled back against my seat, wearing a pair of designer

sunglasses. I preferred the window and Danielle also knew me well enough to know she'd better book my ass in first class. I hated I had to fly into Kansas City, Missouri, but whatever it took. All that really mattered was that I got to that hospital in time enough to tell my son to fight.

I got settled in and hoped I would get lucky and no one would be seated beside me. Closing my eyes, I said another prayer for Quinton, then left him in God's hands until I could get there and take over.

On the flight into Charlotte, the seat beside me remained empty. Once we landed, some of the passengers got off. I got up and used the bathroom, then settled back onto my seat while I waited for the plane to board again, and closed my eyes. I heard someone open the overhead compartment over my seat and opened one eye and then another to find a tall gorgeous man stuffing a briefcase inside. His dark cocoa arms were raised so I couldn't see his face, but his body was something you could not miss. He was wide and built in a way a woman like me—even in my current mental state—couldn't help but appreciate. I focused my attention on the airline staff outside my window. I rather he'd think I hadn't noticed.

"Hello." His robust voice boomed. "You look so deep in thought I hope I'm not disturbing you."

"If I said yes, would you move to another seat?" I was being a bitch, but I didn't care.

"This is a full flight, so I doubt that's gonna happen."

I couldn't help but smile as I turned to look at him. "You are…" My voice trailed off as we finally made eye contact. It took a moment before it hit me where I knew him from.

"Clayton?"

He gave me a weird look like he was searching that big head of his for where he knew me. "Renee?"

I smiled. "You remembered." I always did have that kind of effect on men.

"Who could forget?" he replied with a chuckle.

He sure knew how to make a girl feel good about herself.

Clayton lowered that beautiful physique of his onto the seat beside me and I made a show of moving over like I was giving him more room.

"Do you mind if I lift the arm rest?"

I love when a man is considerate like that. "No. Not at all."

He was looking at me again.

"What?"

"I can't believe I ran into you again. What's it been five...six years?"

"More like nine."

We had met while the girls and I had been vacationing in Jamaica when my older sister Lisa was still alive. The memory reminded me of Quinton's fight for his life.

The pilot was heard over the PA system and I settled back and fastened my seatbelt. "What are you doing in Charlotte? Promoting another book?"

My eyes widened. "You remember that I was an author?" *Incredible.*

"Of course, I do. I spotted your books in the store. I love seeing successful black women doing their thang."

"Thanks." I nodded. "I actually live in Virginia now. I'm headed back to Missouri. Family emergency."

"Anything you wanna talk about?"

He was being sincere, but I shook my head. "No, not really, but thank you for asking."

"Well, I don't know if you've noticed, but I have wide shoulders to lean on if you need to," he said and smiled.

"Oh, I'd have to be blind not to have noticed." I was batting my eyelashes. I don't know how I was able to flirt considering where my mind was.

"How's Kayla?"

"I was wondering how long it was going to take before you asked about her," I replied, brow raised. "She's happily married."

"I knew she would be." I expected him to look disappointed, but instead he seemed truly happy for her.

"Good for her. What about you? Still married?"

"Nope. I had to let that go. I don't think marriage is meant for me."

"Sure, it is. You just haven't met the right man yet." He

winked.

"I don't know about that. What about you? I remember you were saving yourself for your wedding day."

He scowled at the memory. "I met a school teacher and we were together three years before she woke up one morning and decided she'd made a mistake."

"What? She ever tell you why?"

He shook his head. "Nope, other than she wasn't happy. I'm not going to beg a woman to be with me. I have too much self-respect for that."

Well, at least he was no bitch.

The stewardess came up and took our drink orders. I had vodka and was surprised to see Mr. Celibate order a jack and coke. I could have called him out, but decided to let it go.

"What were you doing in Charlotte?"

I'm a college football recruiter now. I was at the University of North Carolina checking out a student we're trying to recruit."

I shifted comfortably on the seat. "You're no longer playing for the Chiefs?"

"Oh no. I retired about four years ago."

It was great to see he had kept himself in such good shape. "Good for you. I'm still writing and working on starting my own publishing house."

"Really? Tell me more."

While we enjoyed our snacks and drinks, I told him about my plans of stepping out on faith and starting my own publishing house. It was nice to have a man listen without interrupting to talk about himself. Instead, Clayton appeared interested in everything I had to say.

How in the world was a man like that single?

One of the stewardesses did the whole safety brief that I had seen so many times I was able to recite it verbatim and had Clayton chuckling. It felt good being able to put my worries aside for a few moments and laugh. *Thank you, Lord.* Because I knew it was all his doing.

I wasn't religious. Don't get me wrong. I believed in God and his son Jesus Christ, but I had never been much for going to church. Too many hypocrites trying to point their fingers at you when they know they just spent the weekend riding the deacon's dick. I didn't have no time for that. I prayed when I needed to, and after I was shot, I started praying a lot, asking God to give me a chance to finally get it right. I feel like I've been a woman of my word. I stopped sharing dick, especially with men who had in-house pussy and I wasn't so wild and reckless. Blame it on getting older. I was in my forties and it was time to start acting like it. I'll admit living on a leash wasn't easy.

See, back when the girls and I had gone to Jamaica, Clayton had the hots for Kayla. And I'm not going to lie, that shit pissed me off. He'd passed up all this caramel goodness for a bowl of Jell-O. Don't get me wrong. I love me some Kayla, but her ass had been a wide load back then and too damn holy for me, but that was exactly what Clayton had been interested in. She was so busy sniffing behind that fake pastor who was screwing half his congregation, she didn't even notice the poor guy. But I had. And what Kayla had, I wanted. I threw myself at Clayton and the more he resisted, the more I wanted him. I'm not sure why. I think it had a lot to do with being jealous. But no matter how much I tried to throw the pussy at him, he kept reminding me how celibate he was. That was before I cornered him in Kayla's room and once he saw my body, it was a wrap. I was bobbing up and down on that dick so good you would have thought I was on a pogo stick. Unfortunately, Kayla walked in, and it was over before I got mine. Stingy bitch.

After that Clayton wouldn't even hear me out. I know. I was wrong. He had been celibate and I wanted to see if I could be the bitch to break him. Checkmate! I was a scandalous ho back then, but I had changed.

Really, I have.

We talked most of the flight. I got so comfortable, I made the mistake of taking the tinted shades from my eyes and didn't realize it until I saw the look of alarm on his face. "Why are your eyes swollen?"

I dropped my head and was embarrassed at how fast realization came rushing back. Clayton slid over and placed his arm around me.

I wasn't running game. I was truly feeling the weight of my fears and it was just too much. All I kept thinking about was where had I gone wrong?

"I'm okay," I lied. As a mother, I was losing my mind with worry. All I wanted to do was hold my son in my arms and tell him everything was going to be alright, even though I was having such a hard time believing that myself. But I had to believe. All I had right now was faith, and I needed God to hear me.

"My son is in the hospital." I was whispering so the white folks sitting behind us wouldn't be all up in my business. "He was shot."

"Oh snap! Is he okay?"

I shrugged and leaned in closer. Clayton's large warm body was very comforting "I don't know. I really don't know. Last time, I talked to the hospital, he was stable, but only time will tell. I'm just trying to get to him as fast as I can."

"I'm so sorry." He reached for my hand and laced my fingers with his. I knew he was just trying to bring comfort and I appreciated it. "Tell me about your son."

"Handsome and knows it." I began with a smirk. "Looks like a mixture of my ex-husband and me."

"Is his father still in Missouri?"

"Oh yeah, he's the one who took him to the hospital. The surgeon said if they had waited thirty more minutes he…" My voice cracked and I found myself crying. Lord knows I always try to put on a tough exterior, but even King Kong had a weakness.

"Is everything okay?" I looked up to see the Olive Oyl-looking stewardess standing over us. Nosy wench. I saw the way she had been staring at Clayton.

"I'm fine."

"Can we have a box of Kleenex?" Clayton said, ignoring me. I saw her green-eyes wink before she rushed off to retrieve the box.

"I'm fine." I insisted. I just needed a moment. "Talking about my children always hits me like that."

"That's understandable. They're a part of you."

There was something in the tone of his voice that made me look up at him. "You have children?"

He scowled and then nodded. "Yep. I have a three-year-old son."

"Damn." I couldn't even imagine having a toddler at my age. I loved my grandson, but that's because I can give his ass back.

"Joint custody?"

He lifted his left eyebrow and managed to look just as sexy as The Rock when he did it. "Nah, she wasn't having that. She wanted that child support check."

A gold digger after a baller's check. Why wasn't I surprised? "You got yourself one of those?" Despite the tears running down my face, I was laughing. The stewardess returned, and she didn't know what to make of what was happening. "Just give me the box!" I snapped and tore it from her hands. I noticed Clayton trying to keep a straight face.

"You haven't changed much."

I expected a look of disappointment, but instead Clayton seemed to be clearly amused by my antics.

I gave him a sheepish grin. "Actually, I have. I don't curse as much, and I haven't had any dick since August."

The couple sitting to our left looked our way curiously. I leaned forward so I could see around Clayton and asked in the sweetest voice I could manage, "Why you looking at me? Your husband ain't been giving you any either?"

The woman gasped. Clayton put a hand over my mouth and I started laughing.

"Renee, you're too much."

I settled back on the seat and quickly sobered. "Yeah, I know. I have my moments. I just hope the shit with my son isn't God's way of getting back at me."

He shook his head. "Not at all. The Lord doesn't make us go through any more than he thinks we can handle."

"Well, I think I've reached my limit with this one."

11
Nadine

I pulled in front of the day care center where Ms. Gina was waiting to greet the twins, Ava and Evan.

"Mommy, I'm not feeling good," Ava whined.

Dammit, not now. "What's the matter?"

"My stomach hurts."

I did not have time for the dramatics this morning. "Well, let Ms. Gina know."

"Okay."

"My stomach hurts too, Mommy." Leave it to Evan to never be left out.

I was barely paying attention. I went through this with them almost every day because they'd rather stay home than be at school with their friends. Today was one day I didn't have the time or patience. My hands were shaking. I needed to go.

I could already hear the sound of slot machines.

"You'll be fine just as soon as you see your friends," I said impatiently. Through my rearview mirror, I stared back at my two beautiful children. They had smooth peanut-butter-brown complexions just like their mother and eyes like their trifling father Chance.

By Cesarean section, she had given birth to twins and our relationship had been stronger than ever. There was no doubt in my mind I loved Jordan and wanted to spend my life with her. There wasn't a man around who could do for me what Jordan could and that included eating my coochie.

"Good morning, Mrs. Hill," Ms. Gina greeted me as she opened the rear passenger door.

"Morning," I said, then turned on the seat. "I'll see you this afternoon," I called after the twins.

Ava was already crying, but that's what she did best. Evan skipped away and was probably already anticipating recess.

"Should I come in?" I asked and hoped Ms. Gina said no.

"Oh no. Ava will be fine once she sees the new dollhouse we got."

My daughter's eyes lit up. "Oooh! You gotta doll house?" That girl never missed anything.

Ms. Gina shut my car door, waved, and took Ava's hand.

I released a sigh of relief as I watched her dance up to the school. Her ponytail bouncing against her shoulder blades.

I didn't have to be in court until ten, so that gave me three hours. I should have been working on a client's case, but instead I decided to use the time wisely.

I was headed on Highway 70 towards Kansas City when my oldest son called.

"Mom, did you send the money yet for my rent?"

I scowled. What did he think I was some kid he had to keep reminding every few seconds? "Jay, I told you I would send it this evening after I got off work."

"I'm just making sure. My landlord is breathing his halitosis breath all over me."

I laughed at his attempt at humor.

"I will have it to you tonight. I promise."

He was attending college in Indiana, majoring in dentistry. We chatted until I pulled off the highway toward the casino. The closer I drew near, the more my palms began to sweat. It was as if I could hear the tables calling my name.

Nadine. Nadine.

I was so anxious to get started, I parked my car in valet and then hurried inside.

The moment I sat down at the blackjack table, I released a long sigh of contentment. Show time! I had every intention of doubling my money before I rushed off to court.

Two hours later, I was headed back to Columbia in a daze.

How was that even possible? I asked myself for the umpteenth time.

I had been on a winning streak and had been up fifteen

hundred when I decided to bet it all and loss badly. After that, I was certain I could recoup it if I was willing to wait it out long enough. But two thousand dollars later, I hadn't won my money back.

What did I just do?

We were already behind on the bills and on top of that I had gambled away my son's rent. Now I somehow had to come up with a way to get all the money back without Jordan finding out money was missing from our joint account.

What were you thinking?

I was ready to strangle someone. That person being me, myself and I while I drove frantically to family court. I was about to argue a child neglect case and my mind needed to be focused on the problem at hand. Not my own problems, which as far as I was concerned was at a greater magnitude.

How in the world was I going to make Jordan's car note?

I had spent it. Every dime I'd had to pay bills this pay period was gone because the table had been calling my name every single day this week.

Stupid. I should have walked away while I was ahead. Instead I had been greedy, thinking that if I'd stuck it out long enough I would have been able to win it back and win it back big. Instead I had embarrassed myself when I hadn't even enough money to get my car out of valet.

I pulled into the parking lot and reached for my briefcase on the back seat. And since I was a few minutes early, I pushed my personal problems aside and focused on the case in front of me.

A five-year-old child had fallen in the street and gashed his head because his mother had been busy talking on her cell phone and ignored him. The state was in no rush to take a child away from a mother, but there was something about the twenty-something-year-old that rubbed me the wrong way. Maybe it was because she was always on the defensive. I'd wanted so badly to turn down the case, but her father was rich.

And I desperately needed the money. Now more than ever.

12
Kayla

"I don't know how the hell you get up this early every single morning!"

I could feel the temperature of my body rising, but I refused to stop moving even as I glared over at Danielle. "My naked body in front of a full-length mirror is my motivation," I declared and noticed her frown.

"I guess," she muttered.

Skinny heifer.

Weight had never been a problem for her tall and slender behind. Unfortunately, I hadn't been blessed with the same type of genes.

"Couldn't we at least have met in the evening after work," Danielle asked, ponytail swinging.

"That's when I don't have any motivation," I confessed between breaths. "Now be quiet. I'm stressed. I didn't ask you here to whine about getting up so early. I really need someone to talk to."

"Okay," Danielle replied. "But as soon as we are done here I need to run over to the hospital and check on Quinton."

I felt guilty thinking about my problems with Quinton fighting for his own life. When Danielle had called me last night and told me the devastating news about him being shot, I immediately dropped down onto my knees and started praying hard. Renee had done a lot of scandalous things in her life, and I still believed she was partly responsible for the death of Reverend Leroy Brown, but regardless, she didn't deserve this. By the time I had crawled into bed, I was shaking with worry.

"So, get to it. Whadda you want to talk about?" Danielle

asked while huffing and puffing.

Dang, she sure had a way of making me feel like I was inconveniencing her, and yet I was so desperate I didn't have time to care. "I think my husband is messing around."

"What?" Danielle whipped around so fast, she lost her footing, slipped, and fell off the treadmill. "Mothafucka!"

I hit Stop and rushed over to help her.

"You okay?" I was trying not to laugh. When I tried to help her up, Danielle pushed my hand away.

"You better be lucky no one is here to see this!" she declared while her eyes traveled with embarrassment around the gym. The area was relatively empty. There was someone on the stair climber in the corner. She was wearing headphones and too busy watching the television monitor overhead to notice.

I expected Danielle to storm off to the dressing room, but was relieved when she got on the treadmill again. "You better get to talking, because if I fall again I'm leaving!"

I laughed. "No, you're not. Your nosy tail wants to hear what I have to say."

She waved her hand at me. "So, true. Now get to it."

I waited until we were both walking at a moderate pace before I drew a deep breath. "Like I said, I think Jermaine is cheating on me."

"Why do you feel that way?"

I shifted my eyes and decided to broach the subject that had been bothering me. "Because we rarely have sex anymore."

"Have you asked him why?"

I nodded. "He says he just isn't in the mood." I tried to sound calm, but I was a wreck inside.

"Well, maybe he isn't. Some men don't want it quite as much after they reach forty."

I shook my head and it took everything I had not to cry. "He doesn't even get an erection like he used to. I think he's turned off by the weight loss."

"The weight loss? If anything, he should be even more attracted to you," she added with an incredulous look.

"I don't think so. He's made comments about I looked fine the way I was, and why was I trying to lose all this weight? I told him it was more about me being healthy since that diabetic scare."

Danielle was shaking her head in disbelief. "I can't believe him. I would have never imagined Jermaine to be so selfish."

"I don't know what's gotten into him, because he's never been that way before."

"It sounds like there's a lot more going on." She pondered the possibility. "Has he given you any reason to think he's messing around?"

I took a deep breath. I couldn't believe I was confessing all my secrets to her, but I desperately needed to get it off my chest before I went crazy. "Well, there's this doctor. She's always sniffing around his office."

"Doctor, huh?"

"Yeah, she's beautiful, black, and single. He acts all giddy when she's around. I think he's having an affair with her."

"Damn." Danielle's eyes gleamed with anger and I was happy to see that she really cared. My hurt was her hurt.

"One thing you've got to understand, it doesn't matter that he's wearing a ring. There's always going to be some desperate bitch sniffing around."

"I don't think she's desperate."

"She's single *and* beautiful. She's gotta be desperate! And women like that can't be trusted."

"So, what do I do?"

Her eyebrow went up. "Watch her ass and if you see her disrespecting you, then you're gonna have to check her."

"I don't know. She's one of our department chairs. The dean wouldn't be too happy about that." I just got a promotion. I wasn't ready to lose my job.

"I bet if he knew why, he would understand." Danielle must have seen the look of skepticism on my face. "Okay, then wait until the two of you are alone and then tell her to stay the fuck away from Jermaine."

"That might work," I replied although deep down I wasn't so sure.

"In the meantime, you've got to find some ways to spice up the bedroom."

"I've been buying nighties."

"Forget a damn nightie! Use some toys and flavor shit." Her eyes suddenly widened. "Oh my God! You sell all that crazy shit and you don't use your own products?"

I shrugged. "I use some."

"Dammit, you're supposed to be using *all* of them! How can you convince customers to buy products you haven't already tried yourself?"

"I just read the reviews."

Danielle laughed and sped up the treadmill to a slow jog. "Kayla honey, haven't you learned anything from Renee and I?"

More shit than I'd ever admit. "Yes, you two are freaks."

"And you love us to death." That made me laugh because she was right. "You've been living vicariously through us for years."

I would never admit it, but I had. Only I was too much of a Christian woman to do half the things those sluts had. But, after putting faith in a no-good minister and being framed for murder, I wasn't as tightly laced as I had been before. In fact, I had loosened up and was doing things I didn't believe a Christian woman should be doing. Flirting was one of them.

"Okay, so what should I do?" I was desperate.

"Plan a romantic evening," she suggested.

"I already did that. We went to the Lake of the Ozarks for the weekend and he fell asleep."

Her mouth kind of hung open. "And you didn't wake him up?"

"Have you ever seen my husband when he falls asleep?" There was no waking that man.

"No, but I know how to wake a man up. Do I need to show you?"

I turned up my nose. "No way."

Danielle held on to the rail and locked eyes with mine. "Then how about a porno because you're not doing something right if your husband would rather sleep than screw?"

I wasn't sure if that was the case. Back in the beginning he couldn't get enough of me, so there had been something he'd enjoyed. And a lot of it. Sex had been endless until he'd lost interest.

All I know is I had to do something and do it fast before it was too late.

13
Danielle

I still couldn't believe my godson had been shot.
Quit lying!
Shit, okay… yes, I can.
Quinton was wild and reckless, just like his damn mother. Only difference is, his drama involved drugs and guns. I must say, Renee's never been about that life. If anyone got off on the thrill of thug life, it had been me.

As I headed home from the gym, I thought about all the drug dealers, mama's boys and scrubs I had wasted my years with that I let eat up my food, drive my car, spend my money, and you know what's worse? I allowed their trifling asses to run all up inside me without a condom. Hell, I'm surprised I ain't contracted HIV sooner.

Stupid ass.

I went to school, studied to be a licensed practical nurse, knew all about venereal diseases and yet I didn't even have the common sense to practice safe sex. I think that's what hit me the hardest and caused something inside of me to snap. I guess finding out you have the virus that causes AIDS would do that to anybody. Especially when you've been infected by someone you love.

My stupid ass loved Ron with my every breath and had even allowed my feelings for him to come between me and my daughter. Then that nigga shit on me. That mothafucka didn't even bother to tell me he had it. If I hadn't gone with Renee to get tested, I might not have found out in time. Bastard!

While I stopped my Lexus at the light, I smirked. Karma's a

bitch. That's probably why Ron's ass had turned up dead in the river.

After that, I was too stunned to feel anything for anyone, including Calvin. But that didn't stop him. He continued to pursue me. Despite all the bullshit, that man never stopped loving me. A bitch like me didn't deserve him because even after he'd proposed, I still felt nothing. I was operating in shock, going through each day with no memory of what I had done the day before. I knew I needed to start taking care of myself, but I had a difficult time accepting I had it.

My cell phone vibrated. I reached over and spotted a text message from my daughter Portia.

Etienne is asking for you.

I smiled at the mention of my granddaughter. She was my pride and joy. **Tell her I'll be by later.**

I hit Send and pulled away at the green light, thinking about Portia and how good a mother she had turned out to be.

For the longest time, I hadn't even told my daughter I had HIV. All those years, preaching to her about safe sex, and there I was catching the one thing I tried to prevent her hot ass from ever having to deal with. What kind of mother was I? Hell, I had been so afraid she would stop loving me and not allow me to be around Etienne. But I had been dead wrong. The moment I told her, Portia wanted to quit everything and take care of me. She was frightened I was going to die. Why? Because that's the way I had behaved. Therefore, I knew the only way I could get her to believe I was going to live was I had to start believing it myself. No more being angry at the world and blaming others for what had happened to me. I had to come to the realization that I'd been through too damn much in my life to allow HIV to control me.

I found a phenomenal HIV specialist in Kansas City because I refused to take the chance of anyone in Columbia finding out. He immediately started me on a treatment regimen, which included a combination of three or more antiretroviral drugs. With each passing day, I started leaning on the people who were most supportive in my life. I began seeing a therapist who helped me to accept my status and stop blaming myself for having unprotected sex.

Over time, I started to believe I could live just as long as anyone else. I'd detected it early and had started treatment, not to mention I was finally taking care of my health. I was crazy because I'd expected to be sick and suffering, but instead my viral load stayed at under twenty and currently were almost undetectable. Even my CD4, which is how healthy my immune system is, maintains a good range.

I really thought everything would change. But I still laugh. I cry. I eat the same way as before just a little healthier. HIV was not a death sentence.

Only probably, I felt alone.

I wanted—correction—needed someone to talk to who understood what I was going through. Someone with the same status so I didn't have to feel ashamed. I ended up on the Internet looking for chat rooms and communities of people with HIV. I was amazed at the people I found who also were looking for someone to open up with and share. Talking made me feel human again, like I belonged because everyone was just like me. It was about the time I made the decision to quit my job as a nurse and start Positive Embrace Counseling Center.

That was probably the smartest decision this dumb bitch ever made because I sucked at picking out men.

Funny thing is, in the beginning I wasn't even that interested in Calvin.

I met him for the second time about six years ago. At the time, he was just a campus police officer investigating an alleged assault case involving my daughter Portia. We had dated once before even though I had vaguely remembered. He was fine with a physique that was living proof that milk did the body good. I'd always loved a tall man, and Calvin didn't disappoint in that category. Six-four with a mocha-brown complexion and square face with deep dark eyes. The mustache and shaved bald head only added to his handsome good looks. My husband was fine enough to make a woman wanna lick him up and down like an ice cream cone. Only he was as plain as a scoop of vanilla. I wanted swirls, and chips, some wild exotic flavor. Calvin was the type of man you wanted when you grew older. Not now. I wanted thug passion. A nigga that was hard and knew how to beat up the pussy.

It's funny because it was that love of a thug that caused me to be drawn to him in the first place. Ron, the asshole I had been fucking, lay around sucking up my electricity and all my food.

My daughter's little cry-wolf-scheme on a college campus allowed Calvin to ease me into a conversation that had me yearning to get to know him all over again. And suddenly things began to change. I started to really notice him. Mostly because I had been on the rebound. Was desperate and pathetic. Calvin was a good man. Better than I deserved, which is why it was time to start putting my plan into motion.

I stepped into the house, and Calvin was in my dream kitchen. He was just finishing up the dishes.

"Hey, sweetheart." He was smiling with those pearly whites as he came around the island to kiss me on the lips.

I drew back. "No, I'm all sweaty and stinky."

"Do I look like I'm complaining?" he asked, showing me those gorgeous teeth as he looked me up and down.

"Let me get in the shower first," I insisted and reached down and stroked his crotch. I heard his breathing grow heavy.

"Why, when all you're gonna do is get sweaty again."

He did have a point.

We both smiled. I laughed as Calvin lifted me like I was a bag of apples and carried me through our new home. He had bought it for me as a surprise almost a year ago. Four bedrooms, three baths in one of the best neighborhoods in Columbia, I smiled every time I pulled into the driveway. It still felt like a dream.

As soon as we made it to the room, we were stripping off our clothes. I was excited because spontaneity was rare in our relationship, so the hunger in his eyes was an excitement.

Twenty minutes later, my mission was accomplished. I watched as he walked into the bathroom to discard the condom.

I despised them.

They were one of the main reasons why I hated HIV. If I had used them, then maybe I wouldn't be infected. They would always be a painful reminder because now that I had it, I had to use one every time my husband and I decided to have sex. I didn't use them when I was dating, so now I'm forced to use them during my marriage.

How disheartening is that?

"Ooh baby! Damn that was good!" Calvin sat down on the bed beside me. I tilted my head for his delicious French kiss then took his hand and dragged him down on top of me. He was sucking my neck when I said those words that stopped him cold.

"I would like to invite another woman into our bed."

"What?" He practically jumped off me and rolled to the side, so I could see the shock on his face.

"I would like to add another woman to the mix."

"Why in the world would you want to do that?" he looked dumbfounded.

"Because I know you love oral sex, and I hate that you can't do that anymore."

"I could. You won't—"

"Err!" I held up my hands and immediately put an end to that foolishness. "I would never put you at risk like that."

"As I've told you before… we're married. You're my wife. We are in this together."

I shook my head. "Yes, but I draw a line at exchanging body fluids."

To me fluids were fluids and my tainted vaginal secretions on his tongue was just straight up nasty. Even though the risk was low, I refused to take the chance. I appreciated him wanting to show me he was willing to accept the risk, but I was not putting that on anyone. "Ron fucked up my life by infecting me. I would never do that to anyone, *especially* my husband."

He sighed, but didn't bother to comment. I decided to shift the conversation to his needs.

"Don't you miss sex without condoms and having your dick sucked?"

Calvin dropped his head, and I knew he was lying before he'd opened his mouth. "No."

I snorted in disbelief. "What man doesn't?" I know I missed being a freak in the sheets. "I want to find someone, not just you, but for us. We can have her tested, make sure she's disease-free, and let her join us. The rules will be simple—no emotional attachment, just strictly to keep my husband satisfied."

I could tell there was something spinning in his head.

"Are you talking about a threesome?" he finally said, eyes widening.

"Hell no. You know I'm strictly dickly. This is all about you." I smiled. "I want my husband to be satisfied."

"I *am* satisfied," he insisted, but there was still that spark of interest in his eyes.

"No, you're not," I whined and turned onto my side. "Not the way you used to be. I see the look on your face every time you roll on a condom. I really want to do this for you…for us."

Calvin hesitated before saying, "Where are you going to be during all of this…"

I felt the need to reassure him. "I'll be right there, watching and guiding her."

"Guiding?"

I nodded, coaxing him. "I'm going to tell her what she can and can't do. She'll have to say, 'Mother, may I?'"

He laughed nervously and even though he seemed to be afraid to say the wrong thing, I could see he was warming up to the idea, which let me know convincing him was going to be easy.

"I'm willing to do whatever it takes to spice up my marriage and keep my husband happy."

Calvin was studying me, and I could tell he was trying to figure out if I was truly serious or not. If he only knew.

"Do I get to pick her out?" I could hear the excitement in his voice.

"Absolutely."

"Of course, you can share your preferences," he quickly added. "I don't want anyone trying to be you." He was such a smart man.

"So, no skinny, brown skin?"

Calvin turned his chocolate eyes on me. "No, I'm thinking thick and caramel," he said far too eagerly.

I stilled and glared at him. "And honey-blond hair?" I said

with attitude. If he told me he wanted a Renee look-alike, I was going to personally kick his ass.

"With thick long hair and goosebumps for breasts."

"Goosebumps?" I laughed. Okay, I was a member of the itty-bitty titty committee. Renee was before she bought them damn boobs.

"Anything you want, baby," I said, kissing his cheek.

I couldn't believe how easy it had been to get him to buy into the idea. But, then again, he was a man, and after the road I had been down, I put nothing past a man. I was so turned on, I was ready to make love right then and there. I rolled him onto his back, slid on another condom, then I was riding his dick. My pussy was so wet. We were so turned on, it ended quickly. Together we collapsed onto the bed and was silent until our hearts slowed.

"We can talk about it some more later. I need to drop by the hospital before I go into the office. I have a group discussion and a monthly meet-and-greet for new members who are ready to be open about their status."

He raised an eyebrow. "Sounds like the center is growing."

"It is. You should drop by sometime and see us in action. You haven't been by in a while." Part of me thought maybe he was afraid to be seen coming in and out of the center and suspected of having HIV.

Calvin kissed me, then eased back. "I'll have to make an honest effort. Anyway, I better go myself. The organization is meeting this afternoon to finish planning this damn Christmas ball."

I loved to dress up. It was a rare opportunity.

We shared a shower and then I wrapped myself in a large towel while I lathered my body in my favorite Bath & Body Works scented lotion. I saw the way my husband lustfully eyed me while I slipped into a chocolate sweater-dress that reached my ankles and a pair of Gucci knee-length boots. That cost me a month's salary, but the longing in his eyes was worth every dime.

By the time I walked out the house, a smile tilted my lips. That had gone better than I'd planned. My nipples were hard just thinking about all the fun ahead.

14
Renee

The moment the door opened on the plane, I was racing up the ramp toward the airport.

"Renee hold up! You forgot your bag!"

I halted and turned around to find Clayton running up with my rolling Louis Vuitton bag.

"Thank you." I took it from him with one hand, while dialing my ex-husband with the other.

"Is someone meeting you here?" he was asking. I was so focused on the phone ringing that it took me a moment to realize he'd spoken.

"No, I'm getting a rental." I was practically speed-walking. I don't know why I'd decided to wear heels other than I needed to be cute. Damn. My son is fighting for his life, and I waste time to think about keeping it sexy. What the hell was wrong with me?

"Is there anything I could do to help?"

I shook my head and was furious there had been no answer. Mario knew damn well I was going to be anxious to know what was happening. "No, I just need to find the rental car desk."

He pointed to the left. "It's this way."

I tried texting Mario. That fucker had better call me back. Otherwise, I was going to lose my mind before I even made it to the hospital.

We rounded the corner to discover there was a long line at every rental car agency

"Fuck!" I muttered.

Clayton followed the direction of my eyes. "You sure you

don't want my help, because it looks like you're going to be in line all day."

I was in too much of a rush to refuse. "What do you have in mind?"

He pointed over toward the rental exit door where a man was holding a sign.

Clayton.

"I should have known," I muttered and followed him toward the limousine driver. He escorted us outside to a gorgeous white 300C limousine. I climbed into the back and was settling on the butter-soft leather by the time Clayton moved inside.

"Arthur is going to drop me off at home and then take you to Columbia." He sprawled out on the space opposite me.

I sat up straight on the seat. "Are you serious?"

"Of course." He was so humble.

"I really appreciate this."

"Hey, I believe in doing whatever I can for good people."

I relaxed against the leather again and gave him a saucy grin. "Good people, huh? You sure you remember who I am?"

He tossed his head back laughing full-heartedly and caught me off guard when he rose and moved to sit beside me. His presence was comforting. Just what I needed, without even knowing I did.

"Question for you." I heard him say.

I looked up from a text I was sending to Danielle to meet his eyes. "Yeah, what's up?"

"Were you in an accident?"

Damn, he noticed. Clayton was one observant mothafucka.

He was pointing at my face. "I notice your face on that side looks a little different from the other and your arm when you're not using it seems a little limp." He was talking soft, almost cautiously, like he expected me to punch him in the chest. I was almost tempted. Talking about my face was almost as bad as a man asking a woman if she'd picked up weight.

"I was shot five years ago."

"No shit!"

My mouth gaped open with amusement. "You just cussed."

He shrugged. "I do every now and then when it's needed. How did you get shot?"

"By some crazy bitch." I rolled my eyes. Hey? He cussed, so now it's my turn. "She thought I was messing with her man."

"Were you?"

This time I did punch him in the chest. "No, and he wasn't even her man. He was my girlfriend Danielle's man, who is now her husband. That crazy heifer had caught me wearing Calvin's sweatshirt when I hugged him, so she just assumed we were messing around."

Clayton gave me a comical look. "If you were wearing one of my boy's sweatshirts, I would think the same thing."

I waved my hand impatiently. "I wasn't messing with him. Besides it wasn't even her man. She was just some stalker who thought he was." My phone beeped and I looked down. Danielle was returning my text.

I'll meet you at the hospital.

"I'm sure that was a scary moment in your life."

I shrugged and put my phone away. "Not as scary as the one I'm living in now." I returned my eyes to his. "I would give up complete mobility in my arm again and even go back to drooling if it will save my son's life." Shit I was getting teary-eyed. "My kids are supposed to bury me, not the other way around."

"Whoa! Nobody's burying anyone. You're going to get to your son, he's going to hear your voice and that's going to make all the difference."

"I hope so."

Clayton held out his hand. "Give me your phone."

I tossed it to him. "What are you about to do, take some selfies?"

"No way! I don't see how people do that all day long."

"I'm one of those people," I replied with a grunt.

"No, I'm putting my number in your phone and calling myself, so that I can call and check on you and your son later."

I felt a warm feeling at the thought of him wanting to check on me and Quinton. He really was such a nice guy.

"Here ya go." He handed me my phone back and I grinned

when I noticed he'd saved his name. Clay.

"I noticed you already had a Clayton in your phone, so I thought the Clay with KC on the end would remind you which Clayton you were looking for."

"Good looking out. But I like Clay. I think I'll call you that."

"You can call me anything you want," he said trying to sound sexy and trust me, he succeeded.

I smiled. "Now it's my turn to ask a question."

"Go for it."

I turned on the seat so we were facing each other. "Are you still celibate?"

He was laughing again. "No, after I married, I realized what I'd been missing. Now I'm just more selective about my choices. I guess you could say I'm now more of an emotional lover. I know that's supposed to be a female thing, but I need some kinda mental connection before I can be intimate with a woman."

I nodded because I knew exactly how he felt. "I know exactly what you're saying. I've been the same way ever since my husband announced he had HIV."

"What?" His eyes were wide with alarm.

"Yeah, it scared the shit outta me. His gay ass came over making me think he'd got that shit from me. But I got tested and my results were negative, thank God, but it opened up my eyes that I can't just be fucking and sucking just anyone."

I saw that my comment made him grin.

"What?" I asked innocently.

"Fucking and sucking... you know that's a turn-on, right?"

Now it was my turn to laugh. "Sorry, I know I have a nasty mouth. But it's gotten better over the years. I think the change is because of being shot, or I'm just getting older."

"I think life changes us." He was staring at me with this adorable grin and then we were kissing. It was slow, sensual and very controlled. Nothing touching but our lips and tongues.

The car stopping was the only reason why I drew back.

Clayton winked. "This is my stop. I hope everything works out for your son."

I couldn't believe how nervous I felt. "Thank you. My head is such a mess right now I'm not sure what I'm doing. But I really appreciate your help."

"Any time." Leaning over, he planted a soft kiss to my cheek and I wrapped my arms around him, just long enough to give him a hug of gratitude.

"Take care. And I'll be checking on you."

"You do that," I murmured under my breath.

He climbed out and the driver shut the door. I lowered the window and stared out at the beautiful brick mini-mansion in front of me. There was a circle driveway and a long walk to a pair of tall wrought iron doors. It was way too much house for a single man. The driver removed his bags from the rear, then Clayton turned once more and gave me that signature smile of his.

"Bye, Clay."

"Take care, Renee. Keep your head up."

I nodded. When he walked away, I raised the window. Leaning back on the seat, I drew a long breath. Maybe I could get a nap in before I got there, because once I arrived I was not going to be able to sleep until I knew Q was going to pull through.

The window lowered slightly, and I was staring at Arthur through the rearview mirror. "Ma'am, where to?"

"University of Missouri-Columbia Hospital." I told him, then spread out on the seat and closed my eyes. When my cell phone rang, I looked down. The name on the screen caused me to pause, but I decided there was just no way of avoiding it any longer.

"Mama?"

"Hi, Tamara," I said, faking cheer.

"Where are you?" Her voice was low and shaky. There was no disguising the uneasiness.

"I'm in the car." It wasn't a complete lie.

"Mama, I just saw something on Facebook. Is Q okay?"

I sighed. That damn social media. Folks put their entire lives on that thing. In a town as small as Columbia, I should have known news would travel back to my daughter.

"No." I paused because I had to pull myself together. "He's been shot."

"No!" she was whimpering with disbelief. "Please tell me my brother isn't dead."

"No! He isn't dead!" I said and realized I had snapped. I hadn't meant to, but the last thing we wanted to start doing was talking that possibility into existence. "Q is in stable condition. I'm on my way to Columbia now to see him."

"How could this happen?"

I could think of several scenarios, but I wasn't about to start worrying her. Tamara had been away at college, so she had no idea what her brother had been out in them streets doing. Hell, even I didn't know the extent or the reason behind someone shooting him.

"We don't know. Hopefully, the police will figure it out." I doubted that, otherwise Mario would have told me by now if they had.

"This is so crazy! I told him the other day he needed to get out of Columbia."

"The two of you spoke?" They had never been super-close, so I found that odd.

"No, I mean yes, on Facebook."

Fucking Facebook again.

"He had posted some new Air Jordan's he'd bought next to a bag of weed and a gun."

"*A gun?*" Dumbasses. No wonder he got shot.

"I don't know where he got it, but the second I saw it, I sent him a text and told him he shouldn't be posting stuff like that because even if you delete it, it's never really gone."

"Exactly. I told him before to stop flossing in front of everyone." The problem with Quinton is that he'd never been a leader, instead he had always been a follower.

"Mama, he actually asked how I was doing and to stay in school. Said he messed up and wished he'd done the same."

Wow. I was amazed at his confession. Like I said, other than being siblings they really had nothing else holding them together except Mario and me.

"I was worried because a few weeks ago, Portia hit me up

and said I needed to stay away from Q. That he was into some mess I didn't want no part of."

I would have to ask Danielle to speak to her daughter and get some information.

"I want to see him, Mama."

I thought about what she said. If it had been my brother, I would have wanted to be there. Andre and I would never be what one would consider close, but we were blood, even if only half of it was the same.

I shifted my head on the seat. "Let me check on how he's doing, and if you want to take a few days off from school, I'll send you a plane ticket."

"Okay." There was a pause. "Are you doing okay? Is Aunt Danny gonna be with you?"

I was touched at my daughter's concern for me. She wanted to make sure I wasn't going to face what I was about to see all by myself. "Yes, Danny's supposed to meet me at the hospital. Your dad's also there. I'm heading there now from the airport."

"Mama, please call or text me the second you see him!" she begged.

"You know I will." I cleared my throat. "I love you."

"Love you too, Mama."

15
Renee

I felt like I had just fallen asleep when the driver was calling my name. I woke up trying to remember where I was and suddenly jerked upright in alarm. I slid my purse over my arm and climbed out to find Arthur already holding my bag for me.

"Thank you." I reached inside my purse and tried to tip him, but he refused.

"No ma'am! Mr. Clayton pays quite well."

With another nod of thanks, I hurried into the hospital while fumbling in my purse for my phone. I had five missed calls and one had been from Mario.

I moved up to the information desk. "I need to know what floor my son's on." I don't know why I hadn't thought to ask.

"What's your son's name?"

"Quinton J. Martin."

I stood there impatiently waiting for her to type in his name.

"How do you spell that?"

"Q-U-I-N-"

"Can you go slower?"

"Q…U…I—"

"Did you say K?"

"I said Q!" As in your queer-looking ass. "Look, you either find my son in that system or I'm coming over that desk and finding him myself."

She blinked not once, but twice. "Please watch your tone, or I'm going to have to call security."

"Then call them!" Don't challenge me and expect me to take a knee because that shit was not about to happen. I tapped my acrylic nails on the countertop and mean-mugged her nappy-headed ass. She looked like she lived right in the hood and yet didn't even know how to spell Quinton. She was a disappointment to the African-American race.

Lucky for her, my phone rang. It was Danielle.

"Where you at?" I asked and stormed off toward the elevators.

"Fifth floor, ICU."

"I'm on my way up."

That bitch was probably calling security, but I didn't give a fuck. Let them try and stop me from seeing my son and see what happened.

I climbed on the elevator and spotted some guy staring at me.

"I kno—"

"Save it." I held up a hand, cutting him off. I was not in the mood for small talk. As soon as the elevator stopped, I hurried off and moved down the hall. I was shaking so bad, mentally trying to prepare myself for what I was about to see.

I reached the waiting area and it was filled with people. Family, friends, and folks I didn't even know, but I knew they were here for my son. As soon as I made eye contact with Kayla and Danielle, I was ready to fall apart again.

"Hey, girl," Kayla said and pulled me into a tight hold. "I'm so sorry."

"Thanks," I mumbled and released her to be hugged by Danielle as well.

"You seen Mario?" I asked as I glanced around. All eyes were on me.

"He went down to the cafeteria to get something to eat," Danielle said.

I nodded and watched as Mario's wife, Rita, came over to greet me with a hug. Her wig was crooked.

"Renee, I'm so sorry."

I gave her a quick hug, and she pointed at the door. "He's in there. You have to dial the phone to get in."

Folks were calling my name and trying to get my attention. Others were staring and whispering. I ignored all their asses and moved to the door and dialed the nurses' station.

"Yes?"

"I'm here to see Quinton Martin."

"Just a moment."

I rested the phone on my shoulder and pushed my rolling bag over to Danielle. "Can you hang on to this?"

"I got it."

The woman came back onto the phone. "Ma'am, Quinton already has too many visitors."

"*Too many?*" Who the hell was in there? "I don't give a shit, I'm his mother."

There was a slight pause before the door lock was deactivated. I gave everyone staring at me a hard look before I slammed down the phone and stepped inside. Rita was right on my toes.

"He's been having visitors all morning."

"And Mario let them in?" I was so pissed. "Which room is he?" I said dismissively. I would get in their asses later. Right now, I needed to see my son.

I followed her around the bay. Each room was glass encased so that the nurses at the station could see what was going on. The sound of machines and patients breathing gave me an instant chill.

Straight ahead was my son's room. The reason why I knew it was his was because I spotted my cousin Keneshia standing next to the door. *What's up with these crooked wigs?*

I stormed over to the door.

"Hey, cuz."

I gave her a weak smile, stepped inside and then stopped in my tracks. My eyes did a quick sweep. There had to be about six people in his room. Other than Keneshia, I didn't know who any of them were. Three of them were standing over Quinton's bed, staring at him like he was a fucking science project.

When I heard someone whisper, "Who's that?" I snapped.

"Get out of here." I twirled around, glaring at all of them. "Get the hell out of my son's room!"

Keneshia had sense enough to listen. "Y'all, we need to give him some time alone with his mama."

They scurried out, and I moved over closer to the bed where Quinton was lying hooked up to all kinds of machines. The breathing tube was down his throat and bandages were all over his chest along with drainage tubes. A sob rose in my throat.

"The doctor said he's stable."

At the sound of Rita's voice, I whipped around. I thought I told everyone to get the fuck out.

"Why were all those people in his room?" I was angry, and I didn't give a damn if it showed.

Rita hesitated for a second. "I tried to keep them out, but they kept coming."

"What do you mean *tried*? You're his stepmother. Do we have any idea who shot him?" I asked with bite to my tone.

She shook her head.

"Which is why he don't need all those mothafuckas in his room! How do we know one of them wasn't the shooter?"

She started babbling uncontrollably. I ain't have time to be listening to excuses, instead I marched out his room and right up to the nurses' station. A beautiful young brunette was sitting behind the desk.

"May I help you with something?" When our eyes met, the smile on her face slipped away. I guess she saw my wrath.

"My son was shot! How in the world does he have all those visitors?"

She gave me a sympathetic look. "I tried to talk to his father, but he was too upset."

His bitch ass. That's why I divorced him. "That's *my* son in there and nobody, I *mean* nobody, other than me, Renee Moore, and his father, Mario Martin, is allowed in that room without an escort. I also don't want anyone calling up here getting information about him. Everything needs to go through us first. Do I make myself clear?"

She nodded. "We can do that. Let me put it in his file."

Rita stood beside me, flabbergasted. I don't know why? Did she really think I was getting ready to put her name on the list? Hell no. Mario can let her in.

"Now that that's taken care of I'm gonna go and visit with my son, *alone*." I didn't even bother to look her way as I left and went back to Quinton's room. She tried to follow. I shut the door behind me to reiterate I didn't want anyone coming in there.

I walked slowly over to his bed and took several deep breaths. As I gazed over at him, my heart began to beat a nervous rhythm. Tears were teeter-totting but I pushed them bitches back. I had to be strong.

What have you done?

The room was quiet except for the sound of the oxygen machine. I glanced up at his heart rate on the monitor, and it looked strong. There were also no alarms going off, so that was a good sign. Pulling a chair beside him, I took Quinton's hand in mine and stared down at his long fingers. There was a tattoo that ran the length of his arm.

ALICIA.

Dumb ass. I told him not to be putting some chick's name on his body because that shit was for life, but stupid mothafuckas never listen. He and she had been history ever since he left for college and came home to find her knocked up by some other dude.

"I don't know why you're so hard-headed?" I said and dragged in a shaky breath. His eyes were closed. Quinton had a set of long lashes I always wished I had. His goatee was fresh and so was his hair. He never went a week without getting a shape-up done. This was my baby. My big baby and he'd been shot. Even seeing him lying there and it was still hard for me to believe. Not my son.

"What in the world did you get yourself into?" I said aloud because I knew good and damn well he could hear. "Who did you piss off?" Of course, he didn't answer, but that didn't stop me. I just kept on talking to him while I let my private tears roll down my cheeks.

"By the way... when you get up from here, I going to kick your ass because you don't listen," I hissed angrily. "I didn't spend seventeen hours in labor for you to take me through this bullshit."

I dragged in another shaky breath and squeezed his hand. "Q, you can't do this to people who love you. Do you know what I went through mentally trying to get here! I know you think you're grown, but in my eyes, you're always gonna be that big-nose baby I gave birth to." I stopped and smiled. Memories came flooding back. It's amazing the things we never forget. The pain of labor, yes, but seeing your child for the first time, that will never leave your mind.

"I remember when I first saw you, I was thinking your father can't ever say you weren't his son. Try to get me on the *Jerry Springer Show* if he'd wanted to and make a fool of himself." I laughed. "You were so chocolate and cute, I couldn't stop staring at you. Your eyes were open and you were looking at me. I was in love. And the second I stuck my titty in your mouth, it was a wrap. You were hooked." I was laughing again. "You were a straight-up titty baby."

"Did I just hear you right?"

I glanced up at Mario coming through the door and scowled at his short ass.

"I was telling Q how much he loved that titty."

He laughed. "Yeah, he did, and I remembered feeling jealous."

Mario was short, chocolate, and simple. I rolled my eyes. "It ain't like I had much anyway."

He was smiling so hard I could see every tooth in his mouth. Thank goodness, they weren't yellow. "I noticed you have plenty now."

"You better be quiet before Rita walks in."

That took the smile from his face "She said you banned all visitors, including her."

"I didn't *ban* her. I made it clear the only two people who can be in his room without an escort are you and me."

"Same thing."

"No, it isn't. Those nurses don't have time to be remembering the face of every mothafucka that walks onto this floor. When you're here, she can visit with you."

"Renee, you're tripping."

"No, I'm not. We have no idea who shot him, and until we do, I don't want nobody coming in here passing on information about him." I was done with that conversation. "Now what did his doctor say?"

He hates when I change the subject, so I was shocked when he just let it go. Mario walked in closer and stood over our son's bed. "He's stable and strong, those are the two things in his favor. Not to mention lucky."

I had to agree with that.

"Only time will tell. I had members of my congregation drop by and say a prayer for him this morning."

At this point, anything was better than nothing.

"Since you're here, I'm going to go home, shower, and change. I'll come back later, but if anything changes you, call me. I'm serious."

I nodded. "I'll be right here." I didn't plan to leave the hospital until I knew my son was going to be alright.

"I'll walk out with you." I rose and kissed Quinton on the cheek. It was nice and warm. "Get some rest, Q. I'll be back to check on you in a few."

I stepped out the ICU with Mario, and as soon as I walked into the lobby all eyes were on me.

"What the fuck y'all looking at? Yes, ain't nobody allowed to go anywhere near him unless I say you can. Now what?" I brought a hand to my hip and pivoted to the left and then right, waiting for someone to say something.

"She just got here and already starting mess." I heard Kayla mumble under her breath.

"Come sit your ass down." Danielle came over and took me by the arm, dragging me to a couch in the corner near a large window.

"You need to stop." Kayla had the nerve to be shaking her head at me.

I looked up to see Keneshia walking over to me. Damn, my family could be so embarrassing. "Girl, straighten your damn wig."

I didn't mean to embarrass her, but I was already running out of patience. Quickly she reached up and tilted it, like it was a damn halo.

"Thanks for looking out, cuz."

She was wearing spandex and a blouse that left little to the imagination. Probably because she wasn't wearing a bra and everything was sagging.

"I can't believe what happened to Q." She looked like she was about to cry. I ain't have time for this shit.

"Do you know who did this?"

"Cuz, the rumor is Dollar shot him," Keneshia said it as if I knew who the hell that was.

"Dollar, who is that?"

"This dude that hangs out with Shemar," she explained.

"*Who the fuck is Shemar?*" I don't have time for this bullshit.

"This pussy I went to high school with." Keneshia nodded her head. "Yeah, I could see him doing something like that. He can't be trusted. He shot this young dude last year."

My head was spinning with all this ghetto-street bullshit.

She lowered onto a chair across from me and said, "Nae-Nae, Q was at my house when he got a phone call. He told me he was going to meet someone."

"Did you see where he went?"

Keneshia shook her head. "Nah, I was in the bathroom, taking a dump."

Okay, that was too much damn information.

"But somebody told me they saw him sitting in a car at Burger King."

Danielle looked up from her phone. "Portia said someone saw him get into a black SUV."

Keneshia sputtered, "Oh snap! Dollar's girl drives a big black Escalade."

"Has anyone talked to the police?"

"Police?" She frowned like she'd just sniffed a jar of pickled-pig-feet.

Danielle gave a dismissive wave. "You know how folks around here feel about the police."

Yep, the same as other blacks across the country—they didn't trust them.

"Have either of you heard of this dude?" My eyes landed on Kayla and Danielle, but they sadly shook their heads.

"I can ask Portia," Danielle said and reached down for her phone and started texting. It seemed like Portia was the only one with her ear to the streets.

"Why you think he shot Q?" My eyes shifted to my cousin, who was looking at Danielle as if to say, "Should I tell her?"

"Just tell me!" I snapped. Can't they see my nerves were shot?

I guess Keneshia decided since we were family, it was her job to tell me. "Because Q's shit was fire. He got it from the city, and they say Dollar was jealous."

She was wasting my time with speculations. I shooed her away and she walked over to speak to some other chick that was dealing with her own personal tragedy.

Danielle tapped my arm. "Portia said she heard it was Dollar, too, but that's all she knows."

I shook my head. "Don't nobody know what really happened, but Q."

Kayla took my hand. "He'll wake soon enough, and start running his mouth."

"We can only hope." With a weary sigh, I rose and disappeared into the restroom. When I came out the stall to wash my hands, I caught sight of me. I was one to talk. I looked a hot mess. There were bags under my eyes from little sleep, and I didn't have on a stitch of mascara. I pulled my locks up in a neater ponytail, then decided that was all that mattered.

As soon as I stepped out, Soledad came rushing over to me, wrapped her arms around me and started crying. "I'm sorry. I had no idea Quinton had been shot! I thought he had just got stuck with a fence or something."

She sounded stupid and even though I had a problem with her old ass dating my son, she looked a hot mess with mascara running down her cheeks, so I wasn't going to make her feel any worse than she already did. "It's all good. His father got there in time, and now he's in here alive and breathing."

"But if I had known, we could have gotten him here sooner."

I stepped back, folding my arms to regain some of my personal space. "What difference would it have made? He'd still be lying in that bed, fighting for his life." I didn't have time to be dealing with someone else's guilt and grief. I had enough of my own.

"Can I see him?"

I shooed her away. "Later. He's had way too many visitors, and I need to get a handle on this situation."

Her lower lip trembled as she nodded. "I understand. I'm just thankful that you're at least letting me be a part of his life."

I had just turned away and swung back around so fast I watched her flinch.

"Hmmph. Let's get one thing straight. This right here is all about my son and what is best for him. Don't think for a second that I no longer have a problem with you fucking him, because I do. That shit is not gonna change. But we can fight about that later. The only one who should be fighting right now is Q—for his life." Before she could see the tears running down my face, I turned and walked away.

16
Nadine

I got out of court and went to the hospital to sit with Renee. I would have much rather have gone home, but sometimes we can't do what we want to do. Besides I probably needed to stall long enough to figure out what was going on. I had called home and Jordan was acting strange, which meant she was pissed. I had a pretty good idea what it was she wanted to discuss, but I was hoping I was wrong. By the time I'd made it up to the waiting room, Renee was sitting and talking with Danielle and Kayla.

I still couldn't believe Quinton had been shot. I remembered when he was just a sweet little boy playing with his race cars. Now he was out in the street selling drugs and getting shot, or at least that's the story I'd heard. There seemed to be very little evidence and more hearsay than anything else. I just hoped Quinton made it through, so he could clear up all the speculations.

As I rounded the corner and stepped into the room, I spotted Renee's ex-husband Mario sitting on a long couch with his two brothers.

"Whassup Nadine!" Mario's youngest brother, Freddie, was grinning in my direction. His legs were short like they were underdeveloped and his belly sat in his lap. He had always been too damn silly for any decent woman to take him serious.

I waved, then nodded over at the oldest. "Hey, Barry."

He was slouched down on the couch, squeezing his crotch. "Whassup, Nadine! When you gonna give a brotha like me a chance?" He was licking his big lips like he'd just finished sucking on a rib.

The others started laughing and adding their own two cents. I rolled my eyes. "You ain't got what it takes."

"I know that's right." Kayla laughed.

"Unless you got some titties hidden up underneath your shirt you don't have a chance in hell," Danielle offered.

The group roared with laughter, and I took a seat. Renee was just finishing up a phone call. She looked worn out, but I wouldn't dare tell her that. She walked over and I gave her a huge hug.

"How's Q doing?"

"About the same. He's stable, so that's all that matters right now. The longer he rests, the better." She flopped down on the chair, smiling, and I sat beside her.

"What's got you smiling?" I asked. I noticed the way her eyes traveled over all of us before they landed on me again.

"I was just talking to Clayton."

"Clayton?" I wasn't following.

A satisfied grin crept up on her face and that always meant she was up to something. "You know…we met him in Jamaica."

Kayla leaned forward. "Are you talking about *my* Clayton?" She had this incredulous look on her face.

I guess I wasn't following. "Who is this again?" I asked and noticed even Kayla looked stunned.

Renee started laughing. "Remember when we went to Jamaica… the Kansas City Chiefs football player that was interested in Kayla, but she was too busy sniffing behind Reverend Brown's ass."

And then it hit me. The gorgeous dude who'd been into Kayla. I also remembered what had happened next. My mouth dropped. "You're shitting me?"

She sent her locs swinging as she shook her head. "Nope. We shared a plane on the way to Kansas City. And he had his limo driver bring me here."

"Damn, bitch!"

"What a minute, who is Clayton?"

I was more than happy to share the particulars with Danielle, who had been unable to go to Jamaica with us. It was the trip when I met a female who helped me to finally come out the closet. "Clayton was this fine-ass—"

"He *still* is a fine-ass. I think he's even better looking, now that he's gotten older," Renee added.

I waved my hand impatiently at her for interrupting. "Anyway, he was gorgeous, rich and celibate and he was all into Kayla, but she was in love with the reverend at the time."

"I think I remember Renee telling me about him." Danielle gaped at Kayla. "I can't believe you passed up a baller for that tired-ass mothafucka?"

Kayla had a look on her face, like she wanted to cuss her out.

"What's wrong, Kayla?" I asked. I was wrong for being an instigator, but I couldn't resist.

She shrugged her shoulders. "Nothing's wrong. That was in the past. I'm so over all that."

I shrugged, turned my back and finished my story. Danielle was waiting eagerly for me to dish even more. "Anyhoo, Renee's conniving ass was determined to get his attention, and before long we walked in to find her riding his dick."

"What?" Danielle's eyes were wide. "Why the hell didn't nobody tell me about this?"

"Because it wasn't worth telling," Kayla mumbled.

"Says who?" Danielle replied and started laughing. Renee and I both struggled to keep a straight face, but then we were laughing as well.

"I did tell you. You just don't remember," Renee told her.

"Kayla lighten up." I coaxed because her high-yellow self was red as hell.

"I don't know what you're talking about. I could care less about him. I'm happily married. Why would I care if Renee saw him at the airport?"

I knew she was lying. We all did. You could see it in the way she was swinging her leg.

"I don't know what you're tripping about. It's not like I'm fucking the dude. All he did was help a sistah in need."

"We know all about your needs," Danielle mumbled under her voice.

My eyebrows inched up. "Clayton could have been Kayla's

husband."

"She was too busy sniffing after that dusty-ass reverend." Renee started laughing and Danielle joined in. Those two always were like two peas in a pod.

Kayla glared at us for a long few seconds before saying, "Would y'all quit talking about me as if I'm not here. Why in the world would I be thinking about some ex-football player that Renee screwed?"

Danielle gave a rude snort. "I wish I could have been there to see that. I mean... not your naked ass... but the drama that unfolded on that trip."

I sighed and was glad to be wrapped up in someone else's drama for once. Anything was better than what was possibly waiting for me at home.

I slapped my palms together, eager to change the subject. "So, what's the word on the street?"

Danielle was the first to speak. "Everyone thinks some thug named Dollar shot him."

I nodded. "I've heard the same."

Renee didn't look convinced. "I don't think anyone knows what really happened, but Q."

I just hoped he pulled through so he could tell us.

***

You know how you step into the house and know something is wrong? Well, when I walked through the side door from the garage, it was so quiet I expected Jordan to jump out at any second swinging a bat. It wasn't even seven o'clock, but the house was quiet, which meant the twins had been put down for bed early. I had a feeling it was because she didn't want an audience.

I made it into the kitchen, where I reached inside the refrigerator for a bottle of White Zinfandel. I poured myself a glass and took a sip before I heard soft footsteps headed toward the rear of the house.

Here we go.

"What took you so long?"

I swung around and put on a fake smile. Jordan was wearing

shorts and a Mizzou sweatshirt. "After court, I went to the hospital to check on Quinton. You want a glass?" I said, tilting mine.

Jordan gave me a dismissive wave. "Any changes?"

I shook my head. "No, he's resting, but he's still alive, so that's a good sign."

She gave a slow nod. "I'm glad to hear that. Please let Renee know she and her son are in my prayers."

"Will do." I walked over and tried to kiss her cheek, but she jerked away. "What's wrong?" I braced myself for the fallout.

Without taking her eyes off me, Jordan reached inside her pocket and waved a sheet of paper at me.

"Where's all my money?"

"What do you mean *your money?*"

"Dammit, you know what I mean! Where is the money? I went to the bank today and discovered five thousand dollars was missing from our savings account!"

There you have it. Jordan found out. My hope had been to put the money back before she'd noticed, but I should have known I couldn't hide anything from her for long.

With mixed emotions, she gazed at me and I felt my heart drop to my stomach. "What did you do with the money, Nadine?"

"Someone borrowed it. I—"

She cut me off with a little attitude. "Borrowed?"

"Kayla and Jermaine are having some financial problems and asked for a loan so I gave it to them. She's planning to give it back at the end of the month, so I didn't bother to tell you," I lied. Guilt tried to creep in, but I pushed it away.

There was a brief second when I was unsure Jordan was going to believe me before I saw her shoulders sag in relief. "You should have told me."

"You're right, sweetheart, I should have." I placed my glass down on the counter and drew her into my arms. I parted her lips with my tongue and slipped inside in a deep kiss. The problem was Jordan was a good woman. She may be a little suspicious and watching my every move lately, but I know she loves me and the last thing I wanted to ever do was to hurt her.

"You want some cake?"

"Cake?" My eyes widened, and a big smile spread across my face.

"The twins and I baked it."

I watched her sway her lush hips over to the counter and cut a slice. While I sipped my glass, I tried to push the worry from my mind, while I watched my sexy wife saunter over to me.

"Open up," she ordered.

I parted my lips and took a forkful. The rich chocolate melted on my tongue. "Ooh, that's good! I don't know how you do it." She shoveled another bite into my mouth, and sure enough, the cake was delicious as always.

"Now you know that's a secret. If I tell ya, I might have to kill you." Jordan was always good to me like that. Doing little things when I least expected. Planning romantic evenings, buying small gifts. I married her within days after gay marriage had been legalized in Missouri, at the courthouse in front of a few of our friends.

Jordan moved close enough for her breasts to rub up against mine. "The babies are sleep," she cooed close to my ear. Grinning, she took my hand and led me toward the bedroom.

Talent, beauty, and she loved me and our children. What more could I ask for? If only I had thought about that a few months ago. If only I could go back and do it all over again.

"Sweetheart, let me take a quick shower first," I told her.

"Okay, but don't be too long." Jordan had that look in her eyes indicating it was on and popping.

I rushed into the ensuite, started the shower and began pulling off my clothes when she reappeared.

"Oh, and baby?"

I swung around. "Yeah?"

She raised an eyebrow. "Kayla better have my money back by the end of the month, otherwise I'm going over to that medical school and showing my ass." Before I could respond, she continued. "Then I'm going to take the twins and leave, and you'll never find us." The look in her eyes scared me.

And then, just like that, the yearning was back in her eyes. "Now hurry up because mama is ready for some good loving."

I waited until she was gone before I dared to breathe.

Damn.

I just needed to make sure to get that money back before that ever happened. If Jordan ever found out I'd lost all of it gambling, I would lose her and the twins forever.

17
Danielle

By the time I left the hospital and made it to Positive Embrace, a support group meeting was about to begin. Members were eating snacks and mingling. Mindy, an HIV advocate and marketing assistant, facilitated the meetings.

"We have forty-five new members," she whispered in my ear as I brushed past. And she wasn't talking about the peer-support session. She was referring to my online dating service. That was where the real money was at.

I glanced across the room of members, shook hands with a few, welcoming them, and my eyes landed on Shane. Sexy bastard. The moment our eyes made contact I rolled mine and headed to my office at the rear. I had just pushed the door shut when it was flung open, and my head whipped around.

"Shane, what the fuck—"

I barely got the words out before he was pushing me against the wall and shutting the door with a click. "I don't like the way you looked at me."

"How would you like me to look at you?" I said, barely above a whisper, as he brought his hand up to palm my breasts.

"I want you to look at me like you're happy to see me," he growled while his hands were rolling up my dress.

"If I do, I'd be lying."

"Now you're really lying." He yanked my panties down

with a start, and then I heard him unfastening his pants, followed by the sound of his zipper.

"I can't." I protested.

"Yes, you can." He pulled my ass back and plunged deep inside of me.

I released a sigh of pleasure. "Shane."

"You like this dick... Tell me you like this," he said rather arrogantly.

"Oh, God!" Like was an understatement. I hadn't felt anything that had come remotely close in a long time.

"Quit running and bring that pussy to me."

I met his strokes. "Like this?"

"Hell yeah, just like that," he hissed. "Just like that."

As I'd said before, I loved me a thug. And Shane was fucking the shit outta me.

For weeks, I tried to ignore Shane's advances, but after a while I realized there was no point in avoiding the inevitable, especially when I was yearning for something my husband couldn't give me. I wanted to live my life the way I wanted to and not settle for less than I felt I deserved. If there was one thing HIV had stolen from me, it was my sexual freedom. So many of my online members had found theirs again. Now I wanted mine back as well. Which was where I had come up with the idea of allowing Calvin to have a little pleasure of his own. It was only fair.

"Have you been giving my pussy away?"

For a second I thought maybe he had somehow installed hidden cameras inside my house and knew I had broken Calvin off a little bit this afternoon. I let out a long moan. "No. It's all yours."

I knew what he was talking about. Raw dog, and giving me that good-good. This was why I had started my on-line service. To give members a chance to reconnect sexually, without having to worry about sexual limitations due to status.

Every stroke was bringing me closer to an orgasm. He gripped my butt cheeks and spread them wide as he lifted me up to the tip of my toes. "That's it. Oooh, baby!" All I needed was for him to hit my spot and I was going to explode. "Come on, Shane. I wanna feel you come deep inside me."

What my husband didn't know was that once I got him in bed with another woman, I planned on asking him if I could have someone for me, who was also HIV positive. And that person would be Shane.

When I finally exploded, my entire body shook. I cried out in a combination of laughter and ecstasy.

This had been too easy. My carefully-laid plan was underway.

18
Kayla

I was sitting behind my desk getting ready for a year-end budget meeting when I looked up to see Black Barbie standing in my doorway.

She sure knew how to ruin my almost perfect day.

"Hello, Kayla, you got a minute?" I don't know why she bothered to ask since she'd already walked into my office. Although, I noticed she'd shut it behind her.

I looked at her skeptically. "Is there something you want?"

"Actually, there is." She strutted her skinny behind over toward my desk. "I was talking to one of my research assistants, Camilla."

"Carmela," I corrected.

"Yeah, whatever." She waved a perfectly manicured hand through the air.

Damn, she didn't even know her name.

"Anyway, I overheard her telling someone you sell Pure Romance products." She gave me a look like she was having a hard time believing it. Sometimes I had a hard time believing it myself. I had attended a Pure Romance party and the host bragged about how much money she was earning, I immediately asked her to sign me up. I hoped by being a consultant it would help me develop more confidence with my personal life.

"Oh, is that all." I reached down inside my top drawer and removed my new fall catalog. "Here ya go."

I could see her eyes sparkle. "Yes, this is exactly what I needed. Um, is there anyway if I gave you my order today, you could have it to me by Friday?"

"Yes, I keep a pretty good inventory in stock."

She clapped her hands together. "That's good! Because I have a date Friday, and I don't want to disappoint."

There was that sneaky look again.

"Do tell. Anyone I know?"

I swear I saw her look guilty before she dropped her head. She shrugged and mumbled, "I'm pretty sure you do." Her eyes were looking out my window as if she was waiting for someone before she swung her eyes back in my direction. "Can I email you my list?"

"That would be fine."

She gave me one of those two-finger waves that annoyed me. I glared at her and was envious of the gray dress beneath a lab coat with a V-neck that verified her breasts were still round and perky. With two girls who both had spent six-months a piece on my breasts, I couldn't say the same. It took a push-up bra to pull off the same look. Especially with the recent weight loss, my breasts sagged even more.

I watched her leave and made sure she headed left, instead of right toward Jermaine's office. I was relieved when she did not, but I didn't trust that slut any further than I could see her.

After that, I tried to focus on work, but it was useless. Instead, I kept thinking about my husband and wondering what had happened to the snap, crackle, and pop.

A few hours later, I walked into the house and found Jermaine in his man cave. I stood in the doorway, staring at him wearing a pair of gray sweatpants that hung low on his hips. A white t-shirt allowed the world to know my husband was still in good shape. Another reason why I was killing myself at the gym.

"Hey."

"Hi, sweetheart." Jermaine barely looked up from the computer.

"What are you doing?"

"Gaming."

I don't know why I was so jealous. I knew he was into all that dungeons and dragon crap when I first moved in with him, and it had gotten worse with modern technology. In fact, most of the time it seemed he'd rather spend time in his virtual world than in the one he had with me. As long as he wasn't with Black Barbie, I didn't care.

"What would you like for dinner?" I waited. "Do you hear me?"

"Uh yeah, I already had a sandwich."

I drew a breath and then turned and headed toward the staircase.

I took a moment to admire my beautiful home with dark wood flooring and the modern furnishings my husband and I upgraded to a few months ago. I had custom blinds and drapes on every window. My life was almost perfect. The only thing missing was the affection of my husband.

"Hey, Mom."

I looked up to see my sixteen-year-old daughter coming down the stairs followed by three of her friends who all greeted me with a wave.

"Where are you going?" I asked because a good mother kept track of her daughter's whereabouts. I can't always say I've been there for my girls, but ever since I married Jermaine I made family a priority.

Asia swung a small purse over her shoulder. "We are headed to Jeff City. We're playing them tonight."

I knew she was talking about football because her boyfriend played on the team.

"Don't be out all night," I reminded her.

"We won't." The girls chorused. I noticed they were all dolled up and wearing Kewpie mascot t-shirts and skinny jeans.

Kimmie had a car since I refused to get Asia one until she started improving on her grades. She had been a straight-A student before Brad had come into her life. She was beautiful and outgoing with confidence and was so much different than I had been at her age. Even my oldest, Kenya, who was away at college, had so much going for her. She wanted to be a lawyer and had the ability to be anything she wanted to be. Only she was no longer interested in being in my life.

Bump that! I was going to get my husband back in my bed.

A few minutes later, I had Barbie's list and was going through my inventory in the back of my walk-in closet. Flavored lubricant, handcuffs, and a slinky negligee that I didn't have the curves for.

Or did I?

If Melinda planned on wearing this outfit for my husband, then I was going to wear it for him first. I reached inside for the same negligee—but in a larger size—and held it up to me. Danielle said I needed to learn to live a little and she was right. If I wanted to save my marriage, I really needed to start trying to do something different.

I climbed into the shower and lathered myself with Bath & Body Works and decided to trim it up. Maybe a bald vagina was what it took to get his attention. I reached for Jermaine's razor and my shaving cream, then went to town. I ended up reaching for a pair of scissors for a nice clean look. I oiled up, slid the nightie over my body, and smirked. It looked good. I'd never been a centerfold model, but I could give a plus-size model a run for her money.

I packed all the items Barbie needed in a bag and prepared her invoice. Usually I gave a ten percent discount, but not in her case. That homewrecker can pay full price. I reached for the manual *Tickle his Pickle* and read through the first three chapters. By the time I heard Jermaine putting dishes in the kitchen, I had mustered up enough guts to walk down the stair and struck a pose. He was inside the refrigerator with his back turned to mine.

"Hey, you."

He turned around, and I loved the way his eyes lit up. "Hey, sexy. What's your name?" My husband sure knew how to make me feel good.

"I don't know. How about you come over here and find out?"

Jermaine put the bottle of beer down and closed the distance. He met my lips in a hard kiss that was full of so much fire and desire, I was ready for him to just go ahead and take me right there.

I untied his sweatpants and slid them down to his knees, and before he could stop me, I had his penis in my mouth, working it like it was a lollipop. I really didn't know I had it in me, but I had him leaned back against the wall, guiding my strokes with his hands.

"This one is called the polishing." I fisted his cock.

"Oh shit! I like that one." He was moaning and groaning loud.

"And this one is the intimidator," I cooed.

"Ooh, I could get use to that."

"And me stroking your balls is called hands in motion."

"Ooh, damn!" Jermaine was rocking into my mouth and I was sucking and stroking away. His chest was heaving. His enjoyment just fueled my confidence, and I worked overtime. I wanted him to know I was the only woman he would ever need. I could satisfy him in every way. And for a moment there he had me almost believing that that was possible. His hands were holding onto my head and controlling the motions and the intensity. It was more intense than I was used to, but I refused to stop because that was what he wanted. I started feeling hopeful and that I had a chance to get my husband back where I needed him when I drew back. It took Jermaine a few minutes to realize my lips were no longer wrapped around his cock.

"Kayla, why you stop?" Jermaine looked pissed, like he'd been seconds from an orgasm. Both we both know that wasn't true.

I glared up at him. "Why isn't your penis getting hard?"

He looked confused, then glanced down at his crotch and looked away.

"The whole time I'm down there doing my best work and you haven't gotten hard, not once." I rose and stepped away, but I didn't take my eyes off him, because I wanted to see if he tried to lie to me.

"I guess I'm just under a lot of stress." His voice was calm and nonchalant, unlike mine.

"Stress! What kind of stress do you have as a recruiter?"

"*Are you serious*? The Dean has been coming down on me about our low numbers. I don't know if you've noticed, but recruitment is down." He smoothed a hand across his hair, then reached down and pulled his sweats back up over his behind.

I sighed. My man had been holding the weight of the world on his shoulders all by himself. "Why didn't you tell me?"

"Because I didn't want to worry you."

"We are a team or did you forget that? If you have a problem, I have a problem." I reached out and took his hand in mine. "We are in this together, but you've got to stop shutting me out."

He smirked and slid his arm around me. "You know you're something else."

"I am and don't you forget it."

"Never that." He kissed me once more and went to retrieve his beer.

"How about we go away this weekend?" I suggested. "I was thinking of the two of us driving up to St. Louis for the evening. I hear they have this new jazz club."

"Sounds like a date."

I squealed with delight. "Great. We can head down as soon as we get off work on Friday."

Jermaine tried to drop his gaze, but wasn't fast enough. "What's wrong?"

He hesitated, and immediately I knew I wasn't going to like what he was about to say.

"I can't Friday. I have to attend a science fair in Kansas City."

I took a deep breath, rolling my eyes at him. "Really? How come this is the first time you've mentioned it?"

"Because it slipped my mind until now. I need to meet with some potential medical students." He took a swig of his beer and dismissed the conversation. "You wanna watch a movie?"

"I'd rather we get back to what we were doing." I pouted.

I tried to reach for the waistband of his sweats, but he stopped me. And he didn't dare look up to meet my eyes. "I'm no longer in the mood."

"What man isn't in the mood for sex?" I said with a shade of disappointment.

He scowled and top a long sip from the bottle before he answered, "This one. I said I just got a lot on my mind."

He must think I'm stupid. Dr. Barbie had a date on Friday,

and I bet all the money I've been saving for a tummy tuck, that man was my husband. I looked at him, waiting for the guilt to manifest across his face. I was certain the truth was about to be revealed. But after a few awkwardly quiet moments, I realized it just wasn't going to be that easy. I walked over and stood all in his face. "Are you having an affair?" There. I said it. Folding my arms, I waited. Obviously, that was not at all what he'd expected to hear from me.

"What?" He looked confused. "Where in the world would you get a crazy idea like that?"

"It probably has something to do with my husband no longer being attracted to me." My lower lip quivered, but I refused to let him see me cry.

"Kayla, you are my wife, and I am very attracted to you. Get that thought out your head." Jermaine pressed a kiss to my lips. "I love you."

"I love you, too." I waited, hoping he would say more, but instead he stepped away.

I don't care what he says, there was something going on, and I planned to find out what that was.

19
Renee

I woke up to find my son was still breathing. That alone was enough to be thankful for. Last night I'd slept on the couch beside him that was far from comfortable, but it was a small sacrifice. If he had taken a turn for the worse, I wanted to be there.

I went into the bathroom to clean myself up the best that I could, then made my way down to the hospital cafeteria. It's amazing, when it comes to your kids, you don't give a fuck about hygiene and Starbucks, because all you're focused on is them.

By the time I made it back up onto the floor, with a cup of coffee in my hand, Mario was standing near the waiting area, pacing. The moment he spotted me, he came charging over to me.

"What the fuck is she doing here?"

I followed his eyes to see who he was referring to. Soledad was sitting in the corner of the waiting room with her sister. Did I really have to spell it out to him?

"I assume she's here to see Q." I thought that was obvious.

"I don't want that mothafucka anywhere near him! If I hadn't gotten there when I did, he would have been dead!"

I grabbed his crazy ass by the arm. "Keep your voice down," I ordered through gritted teeth. "You think she doesn't already know that? Give her a break." Now if Quinton had died, then I would have been all over that stupid bitch, but thank God, that wasn't the case.

I brushed past him and walked over to the door and called the nurses' station. Soledad spotted me and jumped up from her chair.

"Renee, can I please see Q?" Her eyes were practically pleading with me. I nodded and once someone buzzed the door, we walked back to his room.

"How is he?" she asked nervously.

"He's alive to see another day. Doctor said he just needs to rest and get stronger."

I noticed the way her shoulders sagged with relief. I stepped into his room and took a seat while she walked over and kissed his cheek and then started crying.

"I feel so bad. How could I not have known that was a gunshot wound? He just seemed so normal!"

"You mean high."

I noticed the way her eyebrow inched up. "Yeah, he was really high."

"I think part of that may have been shock."

She dropped her head and nodded. "You're probably right, but I could smell it on him."

"Smell what?"

She waved her hand. "That mess he likes to smoke. It has the worst smell to it, and I never let him come around me when he was fizzing out like that."

"Are you talking about that wet?" A bitch like me needs clarity.

Soledad nodded. "He knew he wasn't allowed to bring that mess in my house, and he couldn't smoke around me either. But I could always tell, just by looking at his eyes."

"So, when he came into your shop, what exactly did he say because I really need to piece together this puzzle?"

"Nothing. He just went straight to the restroom. By then, I had called you."

"Do you have any idea where he was that day?"

"He was at his cousin Keneshia's. Last we talked, he was about to take a quick nap and he'd be by the shop later."

I sat there sipping coffee, trying to take all this shit in and stared over at Quinton, wondering what had happened to the innocent little boy I had raised. That was what made things so damn confusing. What would possess Quinton to want to be a part of that lifestyle when I'd always been willing to give him whatever he wanted?

The nurse came in to give him a sponge bath and I immediately rose. "The last thing I want to see is my son's naked ass."

Soledad's cougar ass just grinned. I'm sure she had a different opinion all together.

I left her in there and went back out into the lobby. Mario immediately signaled me over. He was standing next to this big linebacker-looking dude.

"Renee, this here is Meechie. He wants to talk to us about something."

"So, you're Meechie."

He nodded. "Yes, ma'am. That would be me."

I smirked. "Nice to finally meet you."

Meechie was Quinton's closest friend. I never met him, but I'd heard Quinton mention him so much you would think I had.

We moved over to the corner near the window, so we could talk in private. Mario sat beside me on the couch while Meechie took up the chair across from us.

Before he could even get started I asked, "Do you have any idea what happened to Q?"

"Q was with me and then I dropped him off at his cousin's on Forrest Avenue. I had to go and see my mom, but I told him I'll scoop him up on my way back. He knows he ain't supposed to make a move without me. I don't know what he was thinking. We supposed to always roll together!" Meechie was slamming his hand in his fist, spittle flying from between his lips. He was so fired up, I leaned back against my seat.

"So, what do you think happened after you left him?"

"I think Dollar asked Q to meet him, and then that nigga tried to rob him."

I exchanged looks with Mario before meeting Meechie's eyes. "Someone told me he was picked up at Burger King, possibly a black Escalade."

He nodded. "That's Dollar's girl's ride. She's always in it with her smoker mama."

I had a sick feeling, just thinking about someone pulling a

gun out on my son. If he shot him, did that mean he refused to give up his stash?

"Check this out…" Meechie turned and made sure no one was listening, then he leaned forward with his elbows resting on his knees as he whispered, "I heard that nigga's been hiding out at this motel and is planning to show his face at the football game Friday night." He started rubbing his palms together. "I can handle this anyway y'all want me to handle it."

"Handle?" I looked to Mario and he looked as confused as I was. "What are you saying?"

He raised an eyebrow. "I mean I'm going in strapped. Shit, my baby mama was murdered a few months ago. Now I don't give a fuck what happens to me."

"So, what are you saying?" *Because inquiring minds wanted to know.*

Meechie's eyes were wide, and he was talking with his hands. "Y'all just need to let me know how you want me to handle this. You give me the word and it's done. I'm ready to walk into that party ready for retaliation."

His message was crystal clear, not that I hadn't figured out sooner what he had been hinting at, but I needed to make sure.

I stared at Mario, and he looked at me before shaking his head and saying, "We don't want to have no part of that."

As much as I wanted Meechie to cash Dollar in for some change, I didn't need any drama. "He's right. Leave us out of it. Now, however *you* feel like you need to handle things for your boy, then you do whatever it is you have to do, but leave my name out of it."

"Mine, too."

The last thing I needed was for Meechie to get arrested and say I told him to do it. Hell to the no!

He had this look on his face like he was ready to cry and I would have lost it if that big mothafucka started bawling.

"It's all good." Was all he said, then Meechie nodded. He rose and walked over to talk to some shady-looking dude who kept mean-mugging us.

"Who the hell is that?"

Mario shook his head. "I have no idea."

I placed a hand over my mouth, so they wouldn't be able to see what I was talking about. "Did he really say what I thought he said?"

Mario nodded. "Yep, and I would love to be there to see that shit go down."

So, would I.

* * *

Visitors came through all day long. Mario didn't have any vacation time left. He went to work. I was the gatekeeper so I sent every one of them away. My son was not a fucking science exhibit.

It was after lunch and Danielle and I were sitting in the waiting area when she looked up at the girl stepping into the room and frowned. She had to be in her late twenties, brown-skin, thick and pretty. Her hair was in two-strand twists that hung down her back.

"Who is that girl that keeps coming up here to see Q?" Danielle asked.

I looked over and shook my head. "One of his many hoochies I'm sure. I sent her home yesterday, so I don't know why she keeps coming back."

"Let me handle this." Danielle rose and walked over. "Baby, what's your name?"

"Laquela."

"Well Laquela, I don't know why you're here, but nobody's going in to see him."

She brought her hands up to palm the sides of her face. "But I need to see him."

"Well, it's not gonna happen today. He needs his rest." Danielle managed with more patience than I would have.

She looked on the verge of tears before she nodded and finally left.

Danielle waited until she was gone before she said, "What the hell is my godson pumping into them chicks?"

"Who the hell knows."

She gyrated her hips. "I guess Q got that fire stick."

I didn't not want to think about the size of my son's dick.

Danielle dropped down on the seat beside me and whispered. "I don't get it with all these chicks coming up here to see him." She nudged me in the shoulder. "Then look at Soledad's ass, just sitting over there pretending she don't know what's going on."

I looked over near the vending machines where Soledad sat, knitting a scarf. I barely understood it myself. When it came to looks, she couldn't hold a torch to any of the chicks who'd been seen swaying their wide asses into the waiting room. Now those were the women I was used to seeing with Q. Not someone simple and meek. But Soledad had a car and a roof over her head, and that was more than I could say about most of them young chicks.

"Why does my nephew always end up living with them old bitches?"

"I don't know what it is. Searching for his mama, I guess. Although I told him you can't duplicate perfection."

Danielle laughed, and I struggled to keep a straight face.

She crossed her legs. "If he had all these women, then why was he always staying at your cousin's place?"

I gave a rude snort. "Because that's his security blanket. As soon as a chick starts asking him to pay bills, Q goes ghost on their asses. I'm serious. I had one call me to complain. I told her a boss chick would have had her hand out before he stepped through her door."

Danielle was high-fiving me, but she was one to talk. She'd spent too many years letting thugs run up in her for free. Having her lights and cable cut off. One thing about me, I could care less what he was working with if his pockets were light.

"Is that your cousin?"

I followed the direction of her finger down the corridor toward the elevator. Danielle knew damn well that was Keneshia getting off that elevator. That was why she started laughing. Keneshia was heading our way with some crackhead-looking chick. And today she had on a new wig.

"Are my eyes playing a trick on me, or is her wig blue?"

"It's blue." Not to mention she had on leggings, a t-shirt with no bra underneath, and house slippers on her feet. "My family is so fucking embarrassing," I mumbled under my breath, while managing to keep a straight face.

"Hey, cuz." Keneshia sounded so winded. "This here is Jewel."

I looked up at the tall, dark, chick with short hair that required either a perm or a pick.

"Hello."

When she smiled, I noticed she was missing a few teeth. Danielle and I jerked back on our seats, like Ice Cube and Chris Tucker in the movie *Friday* and said, "Damn!"

The chick didn't even realize we were talking about her. "Q told me a lot about you. You're a writer, right?"

"Yes." And I couldn't wait to write about her.

"He's my dawg. We hang out together, and he'd been talking about moving to Virginia Beach. I've been talking about moving that way and going to school." She shook her head. "He did not deserve this."

"What do you think happened to him?" I asked, crossing my arms.

"I think Dollar shot him. I saw that nigga yesterday, and he tried to say he didn't have anything to do with it, but I asked him if that was the case, then why was he hiding?"

"Where is he?" Danielle asked.

"He's staying over at that extended stay on Providence. He was with that high-yellow bitch he's fucking."

My brow rose. "The one who drives a black Escalade?"

She nodded. "Yeah, that's her." She looked toward Keneshia and then hesitated before asking me. "Can I see him?"

I nodded and rose. How could I say no? Jewel might prove to be useful.

"I better get to work." Danielle stood, and we hugged before she departed.

As soon as the nurse buzzed me in, they followed me into the intensive care. When we reached Quinton's room, Jewel moved in close and I noticed the animated way her lower lip began to quiver.

"Damn, Quinton! How did you let yourself get so caught up?"

Keneshia shook her head. "I tried to talk to cuz." I noticed half of my cousin's gut peeking out the bottom of her t-shirt.

Jewel cried out, "We had a plan! You and me, against the world!" She started clapping her hands, like Celie in *The Color Purple*.

These two were a ghetto hot mess.

She grabbed his hand. "Q! I need you to wake up and talk to me. I have to hear your voice."

What's with all these women?

I signaled for Keneshia to come talk to me.

"Was Q fucking that one, too?"

She shrugged. "Jewel said they were. Q said they weren't. I just know they hung out at her hotel smoking."

"There's been this one chick coming by here to see Q. Her name is Laquela."

"Laquela?" Jewel whipped around. I should have known she was ear-hustling. "Is she tall, dark, with nappy braids?"

The way her head looked, she had a lot of nerve. "Yep, that's her."

She sucked air between her missing teeth. "That's his baby mama."

"Who's baby mama?" I hoped like hell she wasn't talking about Quinton!

They both turned and looked at each other before Keneshia said something that practically stopped my heart.

"She Dollar's baby mama."

What the fuck?

I was still reeling from that information when a call from the nursing station informed me the police were here to speak with me.

I stepped out into the waiting area and grinned when I spotted David standing there, looking gorgeous in his uniform. I approached and slowly slid my hand along his chest.

"Hey, sexy," I said. He drew me close in a warm comforting hug.

"I heard about your son and thought I'd come and see how you were holding up." His eyes were full of concern.

"Is that the only reason why?" My brow lifted.

David wore a crooked grin and brought a hand gingerly to the side of my face. "I was also looking for an excuse to come and see you, too."

"I've been kinda busy." I pulled away from him.

"Understood. You wanna go down to the cafe and have lunch?"

"I'd like that." I fell into step beside him down the corridor of the hospital. Mario, who worked in hospital's supply distribution center, was just coming up off the elevator.

"Any changes?" he asked, and I saw the way he was looking at David before he reached out and gave him dap.

I needed to tell him about Dollar's girlfriend, but I'd tell him later. I boarded the car and shook my head. "No. Keneshia's visiting with him."

He nodded. "I'll just come back on my next break." Mario got back on the elevator. "Where y'all headed?"

"To get some lunch."

He looked at David, then me. "You mind if I—"

"Yes, I do," I blurted, because I already knew what he was up to. "Where's Rita? She coming to the hospital later?"

Mario shook his head. "Probably not. She has class tonight."

"Tell her I said hello." The elevator stopped on the ground floor, and I got off, along with David. "I'll see you later." I didn't even bother to look over my shoulder at him.

David gave me a smirk, but I just shrugged. "I can't deal with my ex's bullshit right now."

We walked to the cafeteria and grabbed some food. I hadn't had much of an appetite since I'd arrived, but the smell of French fries made my stomach growl, so I put that on my tray with a diet coke. We found a table away from everyone else and took a seat.

"I assume your son is still sedated," he asked in a low, sympathetic voice.

"Yes, until the doctor feels he's strong enough for them to remove the breathing tube," I said, gazing at him.

David bit into his sandwich and said casually, "We really need to talk to him."

Nodding, I bit into a fry. "I'll let him know, but you know

how these young folks are. He's not gonna talk to you."

"We already have a pretty good idea who did this. I just need Quinton to confirm."

I doubted that. "Really? And who would that be, because inquiring minds wanna know?" I said half-jokingly.

David chuckled and took a bite of his sandwich. "Now you know I can't do that."

"Then neither can I. And if that's the reason why you invited me to lunch, then you're wasting your time."

"I just wanted an excuse to see you," he drawled between bites.

I chuckled and pointed a fry at him. "I don't believe that either, because I haven't heard a word from you since the Black & White Ball. What is this? Outta sight, outta mind?"

His voice deepened. "I didn't think you wanted me to call you."

What's up with all these weak-ass men? "I like a man who doesn't give a fuck what I want and instead does what he wants. You feel me?"

There was a hint of pleasure in the teasing smile he gave me. "No, but I would love to feel all over you later."

I don't know what it was, but David suddenly came across as thirsty. Maybe it was that bad haircut or the fact he shaved off his mustache. I don't know what it was, but when he hinted at coming back over to the hospital after he got off duty to hang out with me, I declined. I didn't at all feel comfortable about his nosy ass hanging around me, just trying to get information.

After lunch, I went back up onto the ICU floor. As I exited the elevator, my phone rang. The number was unfamiliar.

"Hello?"

"Hey, Renee. How's it going?"

I smiled at the sound of a booming voice that made a woman want to drop her panties. "I'm good, Clay. Just heading back in to check on my son."

"Any change?"

"No, but no news is good news." I really needed to believe that.

"Then that's a good thing."

"Yeah, it is." I stopped walking and took a seat on the window ledge.

"I put you on my prayer list at church, but I have a feeling that everything is gonna be okay."

"I sure hope you're right. I want this to be over. I want my son to get up out of that bed and ask me to make him some baked macaroni and cheese."

"And he will. Maybe in time for Thanksgiving," he assured me.

"I really want to believe that." I felt the threat of tears and changed the subject. "How did your recruiting go?"

"I think I might have the player locked in."

"Oh, that's great!" I could almost see his sexy grin.

"Yep, I hope so. These kids nowadays want the sun and the moon. Me, I was just glad to have enough money to buy my mama a car."

I chuckled. "Really?"

Clayton gave a husky little laugh that made my pulse quicken. "Yep. She'd had the same beat up Chevy Nova for so long. Seats were duct taped together. Hole in the floor so big her feet touched the ground like Fred Flintstones." I was cracking up as he described a car that even the cruddiest junkyard wouldn't take.

"Anyway, once I signed my first NFL contract, I headed straight to the dealership and bought my mom a beautiful white Mercedes."

"Ooh, I need a son like you." I gasped when I realized what I said. There was a pause.

"You will. Just wait and see."

All I could do was hope.

"I'll call you later," Clayton said.

I breathed into the phone, "Okay."

"And you better answer." He sounded so sexy when he said that.

I laughed. "I guess you'll find out."

"Don't have me come there and bend you over my knee," he teased.

"Ooh, I might like that," I cooed.

"Knowing you, Renee, you're probably right."

20
Danielle

"Are you sure she's coming?"

It took everything I had not to laugh. My husband was so eager, it was getting to be comical.

Reaching over, I squeezed Calvin's shoulder. "Relax. Joiee's coming. She even called to confirm." I went back to eating wings, with buffalo sauce sliding down my fingers.

"Okay." He looked almost hopeful.

Calvin had no idea, but for weeks—long before I had even mentioned it to him—I'd been screening candidates who had responded to an anonymous ad for a woman interested in assisting me with keeping my husband sexually satisfied. After shifting through all the sluts, I had found a woman I thought would be perfect. Joiee Tennison. A single mother of a five-year-old boy. She worked part-time as a dental hygienist while taking night college courses. After a bad divorce and with her busy schedule, she wasn't looking for anything more than great sex and a few extra dollars to supplement her income. Damn right it was prostitution, but I figured as long as Calvin knew I was in control, I didn't have to worry about him taking things too seriously.

Joiee was all about the hustle and I had mad respect for her. We'd talked extensively to her on the phone, and I found her to be professional, funny, and most importantly not a native of Missouri. The last thing I needed was someone I grew up with finding out what was going on in my bedroom. Columbia was too damn small for that bullshit. Joiee was hoping we could all be friends and I agreed. That way whenever I wanted to sneak off and spend time with Shane. I could call and ask her to keep Calvin company.

As I bit into another wing, I couldn't help but smile. Life was going to be too good to be true.

My phone vibrated, and I glanced down at the screen. "Oh good! She sent a text. Her babysitter was late."

I noticed Calvin's broad shoulders sag with relief. "Why do I feel like I'm going out on my first date?"

"Because in a way you are. This is going to be a new experience for you." I held up my mug and made a toast. He tapped his bottle of beer against mine.

Calvin kept watching the door. He was so nervous it was almost sexy. "C'mon, how many of your boys could say their women would allow them the same?"

"None that I know," he confirmed, and I was pleased.

If I even thought about telling my girls what I was about to do, they'd probably say I was crazy as hell, allowing another woman in bed with my husband. Especially Renee, after that swingers shit she used to do with her husband. But I guess I was more focused on what I was going to gain from the experience. I would be happy. My husband would be happy, and it would only strengthen our marriage.

We were on our second round of beers when I looked toward the door to see a woman walk in and the glass in my hand stalled. Even before our eyes met and her glossy plum-colored lips curled upward in acknowledgment, I knew it was her.

Joiee sauntered over to us in black stiletto booties and skinny jeans that been designed for her body type. Tall and statuesque with endless long legs that were made to be wrapped around a man's waist. Her hair was dark, long and straight and swayed side to side along the center of her back with each step. A pink cashmere sweater dipped dangerously low in the front, displaying generous cleavage and round perky breasts. By the time she had reached our table, I was already trying to think of a way to get rid of her ass.

"Danielle," she said, greeting me with brown eyes that were sparkling warm and genuine.

"You must be Joiee."

"I am." She was so giddy that if the situation had been different it would have been easy to have liked her. Only I already couldn't stand the bitch.

"And this is my husband, Calvin."

You should have seen the look on his face, like he'd just won the fucking lottery. If my shoes weren't expensive, I would have tossed one at his head.

"Hello, Calvin," Joiee said and there was no doubt in my mind she liked what she saw. Calvin rose to his full height, and I watched the way they were looking at each other, hungrily ready to rip off each other's clothes and get busy on the table.

"It's a pleasure to finally meet you."

Too bad I couldn't say the same.

While he took his seat, I focused on Joiee. I said we wanted different, and we definitely got that. I just hadn't realized just how different.

As Calvin motioned her to take the seat to his left, I glared out the corner of my eyes. Nowhere in any of our conversations had she ever mentioned the most important thing.

Leaning across the table, I blurted out, "Joiee, how come you didn't tell me you were white?"

She had the nerve to look like I'd been the one hiding my identity. "I'm sorry. I didn't think it mattered."

"Well it does." I didn't even bother to hide the attitude.

Nervously, her eyes shifted from me to my husband and then back to me. "Did you ever mention your race?"

"I didn't have to. I'm a sistah who grew up hangin' in the hood, and that rings in my voice every time I speak. You on the other hand, sound like a white chick who's spent her life riding black dick."

"Danielle." Calvin nudged me under the table.

"What?" I was just keeping it real.

Joiee cleared her throat and combed French-tipped fingernails through her hair. "I'll admit I prefer black men, and I'm sorry if I didn't tell you I was white, but unless Calvin is against the idea, I don't see what the problem is."

I was ready to jump out my chair and tear into her, but Calvin brought a hand to my arm.

"No, we don't have a problem with it." He looked at me. His eyes were asking what the problem was. I rolled my eyes. "My wife believes in being truthful. Relationships built on lies never last."

I smirked at Joiee and guilt flooded her face.

"You're right. I should have been honest. I apologize. I just, for once, wanted to be judged based on who I am, instead of the color of my skin. I'm so sorry."

She was batting her eyelashes and looking so guilty. I didn't believe it for a moment, but Calvin looked happy. Suddenly, I remembered that was what this was supposed to be about. Calvin. Not me. Joiee's job was to keep him occupied, so that I had time to spend with Shane. Therefore, what did it matter who my husband slept with?

But even with that said, something about Joiee bothered me. If she lied about her ethnicity, then what else had she lied about?

"How about we start over?" Joiee stuck her hand out. "Hi, I'm Joiee Tennison, and I'm a white girl."

Calvin laughed and changed the subject. "Joiee, what would you like to eat?"

"Wings would be great."

They laughed some more, but I just sat there with my brow raised suspiciously. I didn't see shit that was funny.

Stay calm, girl. Don't let this fake bitch get to you.

Calvin ordered a round of drinks, and I watched as the two of them interacted as if they'd known each other forever. Despite the deception, the connection was better than I'd imagined.

My bladder was full, so I figured it was as good a time as any to dash off to pee. That would be a good time to give Shane a call and let him know how well things were working out.

"I gotta empty my bladder," I said. My words fell on deaf ears because they were so engrossed in a conversation, my comment was ignored. I rolled my eyes and sauntered off, with attitude, then reminded myself that this was what I had wanted.

Bitch you can't have it both ways.

I had to giggle because it was crazy, but true.

I had barely stepped into the stall and I was dialing Shane's number, anxious to let him know "game on." I lowered my panties to my ankles and was squatting when Shane picked up.

"What's up baby?" He sounded happy to be hearing from me. Imagine the things that did for my ego.

"It's happening!" I said. He could probably hear me emptying my bladder, but I didn't care. "I'm here at the restaurant. You should see Calvin's face. He's so into this shit." I went on to explain.

"That's good. So that means you can sneak away and bring them goodies over here?"

"You are nasty."

"Say you don't like it."

I laughed. "I'd be lying if I did."

"You coming to see me or what?"

I was wiping my pussy and had to grab another two-ply of toilet paper. That nigga was making me wet. "Shane, baby, I'll see what I can do."

"You need to do better than see. I'm sitting here in my recliner, horny as a mothafucka."

I can't believe I was squatting over a public toilet, rubbing my pussy and grinning like a damn fool. "Shane, if I bring this good pussy over there, what are you gonna give me if I do?"

"I got some premium D over here waiting for you."

I was laughing and yanking my panties back up over my hips with one hand. "Some premium D huh? I like the sound of that. Let me see if I can get this white girl to entertain Calvin while I step out."

"*White girl?*" he sputtered. "What the fuck you talking about?"

I wondered if he'd heard me. "Yeah, she's white, and I'll tell you all about that later. Let me get back before I'm missed. Although the way they were looking at each other, they probably already snuck off somewhere to fuck." Even as I said the words that idea pissed me off. Calvin better not even think about disrespecting me that way! Yeah, I was being a hypocrite, but I didn't care.

"I'll call you back in a few." I ended the call and exited the stall and screamed when I rounded the corner.

Joiee was leaning back against the sink, arms crossed, but it was the smirk on her lips that gave me a sick feeling.

"Joiee, I didn't know you were in here."

"I know. You were talking pretty loud." She arched a perfectly-scissored brow.

I was two seconds from knocking that smirk off her face. I was panicky and wondering just how much she'd heard. "That was my girlfriend trying to bribe me to come over and see some bad-ass shoes she just bought."

"Really?" She knew I was lying.

"Did you come in here to eavesdrop on my conversation or to use the toilet?" I snapped, trying to sound in control.

"Actually, I came in here to wash my hands. Hearing you on the phone was just a delightful surprise."

"Delightful, how?" I was almost afraid to ask.

She crossed her arms beneath her breasts. "It sounds like we'll both get what we want." Joiee winked, which pissed me off even more.

"Which is?"

"C'mon. I can tell you're bored with your husband. Why else would you hook him up online with another woman unless, of course, you can't—"

"There ain't shit wrong with me!" I said with straight attitude.

"Good, I didn't think so."

My HIV status was none of her damn business.

"Then I think you've found the right woman."

I sucked my teeth. "How so?"

She ignored my lack of enthusiasm and kept talking. "I'm horny for some black dick, and you're craving new dick. How perfect is that?"

Joiee was one smart bitch.'

"I'll keep Calvin occupied," she said with quotation marks in the air. I guess she had overheard more than I thought. "And you go explore."

I stared in her face for a few seconds, and I could feel her sincerity. I let out a grateful sigh. "It's a deal." I held out my hand, but instead of shaking it, she frowned down at it.

"You might wanna wash that first."

Laughing, she sauntered toward the door. "Go see those shoes, and I'll keep your husband entertained. I promise." She walked away, looking every bit as confident as she had when she entered the restaurant.

I washed my hands, and for a moment thought again this was a bad idea. I was preparing to give "Becky with the good hair" the boot, but my phone chimed and I saw the text from Shane. I opened it and my jaw dropped. He was lying back naked on the bed with his dick in his hand.

"On second thought…"

With my excuse ready, I went back to the table with a smile.

21
Renee

I was sitting in the Man Street Cafe in the hospital's lobby when I noticed a blocked number calling my phone. Usually I don't answer those, but for some reason with everything that had happened with Quinton, I felt I needed to.

"Hello?"

"Is this a Renee?"

I didn't recognize the voice. "Yeah, this is me. Who is this?"

"I'm Adrianna. I'm a good friend of Mario. I'm also friends with your son."

I wasn't quite sure why she was calling me or how she had gotten my number, but I figured I'd play along.

"Please don't tell anyone this, but I think I was the last person to see Q before he was shot."

"What?" Adrianna had my full attention now. "Who did you say you were again?"

"Uh… I'm a friend of the family. Q calls and we spend time talking about his… Ummm, problems."

I couldn't help but wonder how old this one was as well, because I already had a sneaking feeling she was another one Quinton had been knocking off.

"So, when did you see him exactly?"

"Well, he called me to come over and pick him up from his cousin's house."

His lazy ass couldn't even walk three blocks. That sounded like him. "And where did you take him?"

"I drove him down to Burger King. We got something to eat, then sat there in my car and talked until this black Escalade pulled up, and then he got out."

I now had a confirmation to the black SUV. My heart was pounding so heavily I could barely get the words out. "Did you see who was driving?"

"I saw a female behind the wheel when she pulled in, but the windows were heavily-tinted, so I couldn't make her out. Q jumped in the back seat."

I blew out another shaky breath. The woman had to have been Dollar's girlfriend. But that much I already knew.

"Did he tell you who he was meeting or what he was about to do?"

"No," Adrianna hesitated before continuing. "I assumed someone was getting ready to make a buy. Q had that crap with him. He kept pulling the bottle out of his pocket and holding it up proudly, like it was a diamond ring."

Dumb ass. Dammit! I was no closer to finding out what happened to my son.

"He really is a good kid, but I could see he was into some stuff he didn't need to be doing. I tried to talk to him, but he seemed to be kinda lost."

Kid? I had been right. Another old bitch.

"Anyway, don't say anything to his dad about this. Mario and I work together, and I really don't want any issues, but I felt I should at least let you know I saw him."

I hung up and stared out the window, watching an ambulance pull into the circle drive and stop in front of the ER. How in the world did my life end up here?

I looked up to see Danielle sauntering into the restaurant, looking fabulous in skinny jeans, black ankle-length boots, and a red long-sleeved polo shirt. "How's Q?"

I shrugged. "Alive and stronger. The nurse was in doing vitals, so I decided to come down and get something to eat."

"Let me grab a cup of coffee, and I'll have a seat with you." While she walked over to the counter, I looked down at my phone and noticed a text message.

How's things going?

I had my first smile of the day. It was Clayton.

It's going. Thanks for checking.

Any time beautiful. Keep me posted.
"What're you smiling about?"
Danielle was back and staring all in my face.
"No reason." I muttered. I wasn't ready for all the questions.
"Hey, Danny, check this out. Do you know a chick by the name of Adrianna? I guess she works in supply distribution with Mario."
"Yeah." She nodded and had a look like she was waiting to see where this conversation was going. I decided to make her wait. I took a sip from my coffee first before continuing. "Anyway, she just called me a few minutes ago and told me she was the one who drove Q to Burger King."
"Adrianna did?" Danielle had this incredulous look on her face.
I nodded and took another sip. "Yep...said they were good friends. Friends, meaning they were probably fucking, by the tone of her voice. I just don't get it with my son and these old bitches."
Danielle was grinning, like she knew something I didn't. "Are we talking about the same Adrianna I'm thinking about?"
"Hell, I don't know. She said she was good friends with Mario's family."
"No, she's *good* friends with Mario."
"You've lost me."
Her brow rose. "I mean, the two of them have been..." what she was implying started to finally click.
"*You're lying*? Mr. Deacon is fucking around on his wife?"
She started nodding. "I guess so. I heard from Veronica that it's been going on for some time. In fact, they've been seen slipping off to that raggedy-ass van of hers at lunch."
"Oh shit!" I was giggling. I couldn't even imagine, but then I didn't put anything past a man. "So then what's her connection with my son?"
It was Danielle's turn to sip and shrug. "Hell, if I know. They might have both been knocking her dusty-ass off."
I was laughing again. "Do I know this chick?"
"You would if you saw her. She used to be married to this crazy dude who would lock her in the closet on weekends. She

finally escaped and left his ass."

"Wow!"

I looked up and spotted Keneshia and her skinny friend moving across the hospital lobby toward the elevators. I sighed and was tempted to pretend I didn't see them, but that would have been rude. I waved my hands and they headed my way. I was pleased to see she had at least put on some jeans and a sweater that actually fit. Jewel was wearing thigh-high chocolate boots and a sweater dress.

"Where does your cousin buy them damn wigs?" Danielle muttered under her breath.

I shook my head. "I don't know, but somebody needs to tell her to give them shits back."

She gave a sputter of laughter, and I tried to hold it together. Keneshia walked into the restaurant and stood in front of me. "Hey, cuz."

"What's going on?" I gave a head nod to her friend Jewel.

"How's Q doing?" Keneshia asked.

"He's the same, but getting stronger."

With a solemn face, Jewel stared up at the ceiling and said, "Praise the Lord. I've been on my knees ever since I saw him."

With all that dry white crusty shit, around her mouth I didn't know if she meant she'd been praying or sucking dick.

"Jewel has something she wanted to tell you." Keneshia nodded her head, urging her to speak. I signaled for the two of them to take a seat at the table with us.

"Well, I talked to Dollar again yesterday."

My hand tightened around the glass.

"He came to my room at the hotel. It was him and his girl. He said he's been laying low because everyone was accusing him of shooting Q, and he didn't have nothing to do with that."

"Then, why is he hiding?" Danielle snapped.

"'Cause he's afraid for his life. He knows Meechie is going to shoot him on sight."

"Do you believe him?" I asked between sips.

Jewel hesitated, then shook her head. "No. Not really. Because he kept saying, 'If I did shoot him, it's because that nigga owes me money.'"

I looked at Danielle and then at Keneshia. She looked like she was seconds away from crying.

"His girlfriend Laila said Q got in her car and sold some wet to her and her mother, but then she let him out near Fourth Street and she don't know where he went after that."

It was frustrating, but at least I was starting to get a timeline. Quinton had been at Keneshia's, who had been on the toilet taking a shit when he received a phone call. He'd had Adrianna come and pick him up. They went to Burger King, got something to eat and then sat in the parking lot until the black Escalade with Laila and her mama had arrived. And according to them, he sold them some wet, and they had dropped him off on Fourth Street, which was about a half a mile from Soledad's shop. So, what happened next? I looked to Danielle, whose expression told me she was as confused as I was.

Jewel went to the register to buy herself a cup a coffee. I slid down low on the seat. This shit was crazier by the second, and yet, I still didn't have answers.

"Fuck! I just wish I could unlock his phone. I'm sure it would help me to put together a timeline."

"Jewel can unlock it."

I looked at Keneshia side-eyed.

She was nodding and looking serious. "Cuz, she is a whiz with the computer. She can do things I can't."

My cousin didn't even have her GED, so that wasn't saying much.

"Kee, that chick looks like she is one crack pipe away from an overdose."

She frowned. "I'm serious. Jewel used to have a good job with the government, working with computers."

I looked at Danielle with skepticism. She shrugged. "Nae-Nae, what do you have to lose?"

I still wasn't convinced. She might try to pawn the phone. "I just know. If we type in the password too many times, you can never unlock the phone."

Keneshia stepped all in my personal space. "I would try her, cuz."

I wanted to tell her to shut the hell up. Jewel came around

the corner, heading our way, and by the time she'd reached us, I had decided to give her a chance.

"Hey, Jewel, I heard you're good with computers."

She shrugged. "Yeah, I'm okay."

"You think you can unlock Q's phone for me?"

"What kind?"

I reached into my purse and pulled it out. Mario had given it to me this morning. "It's a Galaxy."

Jewel held out her hand and I gave it to her. Before I had a chance to tell her not to try too many times or the phone would lock, she handed it back to me. "Piece of cake. It's 1113."

I looked down at the screen saver of some bitch's big wide ass. "How the hell you do that?"

Jewel shrugged. "Easy. I learned it while I was at MIT."

"M...I...T? What the hell are you doing here?" Danielle gawked.

"It's a long story." Was all she said and busied herself pouring sugar into her coffee.

I decided to focus on Quinton's phone and find out Jewel's story later.

The two of them walked off to talk to some pregnant chick they spotted walking across the lobby. I went to work before the phone locked again, although now I knew it was my grandson's birthday.

"Let me see." Danielle came around and took a seat beside me on the bench as we scrolled through his phone. "Oh, hell nah!"

Nothing but straight titties and ass. "Don't these women have any shame?"

"Ho, we were just like them at their age." We chuckled at the memories.

"Yeah, but damn."

I didn't want to see that freaky shit, either, so I focused on the last text message which was to his baby mama, telling her he would have her child support. The last phone call was from an unknown number.

We went back upstairs and I gave Jewel and Keneshia a chance to go in and visit with Quinton. I started to stay in the room with them, but when Jewel started hooping and hollering and laying hands, I got the hell outta there and let them have at it.

Danielle and I took a seat in the waiting room. *The Real* was on so we watched that bullshit.

"Mama!"

I looked up to see my daughter, Tamara, rushing into the waiting room followed by Mario. I rose and gave her a big hug. She was the spitting image of that man. Dark, slender, and short, with a thick afro. She had that Pam Grier thing going on.

"How was your flight?"

"It was good. Hey, Aunt Danny." Tamara moved over to talk to Danielle while I signaled for Mario to come closer.

"You got a moment?"

"Sure." He followed me out into the corridor, away from prying ears.

"Your side-chick called me today."

"My side-chick?" Mario had the nerve to try and laugh it off.

"Yeah, Adrianna." That wiped the smirk from his lips.

"Whadda she want?" he asked and suddenly looked nervous as hell.

"I don't know how she got my number, but she wanted to let me know she was the last person seen with Q before he hopped into the black Cadillac Escalade."

"No shit?" I could see the wheels turning in his head.

"That's what she said, but explain something to me... why do I get the impression the two of them were more than just friends? You and your son got some choo-choo train action going on that I need to know about?"

Mario had this angry look on his face, but I didn't give a fuck. My days of being afraid of him ended decades ago. "Hell, nah! I don't know what the deal was between the two of them, but I told her before I didn't like her hanging around with my son."

"And what did Q have to say about it?"

"He said wasn't nothing going on between them, that she was always reaching out to him. But that's why I'm not speaking to her now, because I think she's up to something."

"Does this something have to do with Q getting shot?"

He dismissed that possibility with a scowl. "No, I think it has to do with someone calling my house and hanging up on my wife."

"Sounds like you got yourself some drama." His wife wasn't a bad bitch like me, but Rita wasn't one to take no mess either. "Are you planning to tell the police about her being the last one to see him?"

I could tell by his hesitation he wasn't feeling that idea. Probably afraid Rita would catch wind of the story and start connecting the dots.

"Nah, I'ma have a talk with Adrianna and see what's up. Hopefully, Q wakes up soon, then he can tell us what happened himself."

Yes, that was what I was praying for.

He took Tamara in to see Quinton, and I returned to my seat beside Danielle.

"Did you tell him you spoke to Adrianna?" she asked.

"Yeah he's not too happy about her relationship with his son. I think he also suspects Q was knocking off his woman."

"Hey, good dick is hard to find."

I started laughing with her. "That is true. And if Q is slinging anything remotely close to what his father was working with, I can truly understand."

Danielle howled with laughter and so did I. Damn, it felt good to laugh.

"Hey, speaking of good dick…" She purposely allowed her voice to travel off. I sobered quickly and gave her a side-eye.

"You're getting ready to confess some shit, aren't you?"

She nodded.

I swiveled on the chair. "Then get to it, because inquiring minds wanna know."

She reached down for her phone, tapped an app and then tilted the phone so I could see. I stared down at this gorgeous Idris Elba lookalike.

"Daaayum! Who is that?"

She released a shaky breath, then put her phone away. "That's Shane Michaux."

Damn, even his name was sexy. Pronounced Me-show. I'd

have to remember to use that name as a character in one of my books.

"And what's the story?"

"I've been fucking him since a week after the Black & White Ball," she blurted out in a rush.

"You slut!" I shook my head. "Thug passion."

"Hell, yeah."

I gave her a knowing look. "I told you yo ass was gonna miss being fucked properly."

She looked like she wanted to cry before she pushed those tears away. "I know. You warned me."

Back when she had first told me she was going to marry Calvin, I had asked her if she was sure that was what she wanted. I don't care what her ass says, Calvin was her rebound man. One of those nice guys who would do anything for you... that women never seem to want until they have been dogged out at least a dozen times before. To this day, I think the only reason why she decided to settle down with him was because she found out she had contracted HIV, and was afraid of being alone.

"Does he know you have..."

She nodded. "He has it, too."

I almost slid off the chair. "No shit? How the hell that happen?"

"I met him at the center. He's handling all of the web design and internet marketing for my online dating service."

I was too stunned to speak.

"Nae-Nae, it's almost too perfect. I'm able to get fucked by him without the limitations I have at home."

The two of them were free-flowing and not worrying about being infected by HIV because they both already had it. It sounded clever and nasty at the same time.

"You were dying to suck a dick that bad?" My brow rose.

"I was dying to get dick without a dry-ass condom."

I was too through with her ass. That's how she had gotten into this mess in the first place. I love me some Danielle. Always have, but right now she sounded stuck on stupid.

"Did I read somewhere or maybe I heard this shit on Oprah's

old talk show, but isn't there different strands of HIV?"

Danielle was looking at everything, but me, when she shrugged her shoulders and said, "Yeah, but HIV is HIV."

I slapped her on the arm, drawing her attention. "And there is also AIDS! Danielle, you were a nurse. You couldn't possibly be that damn naive."

She waved her hand at me. "What does it matter how many strands of HIV I get? It's still not gonna change the fact that I have it," she spat defensively.

I could see I was arguing a moot point. "And what about Calvin during all of this? What are you going to do when he finds out?"

"Well, I have a plan."

"I'm listening."

She started talking about the ad she had set up and the woman she and Calvin met for lunch the day before.

"*You hooked your husband up with a white woman?*" This story was getting crazier by the second.

"Yes, that wasn't the plan, but once I met her I decided she was just what he needed to help him pass the time. She's supposed to fax me her lab results this afternoon, and once I know she is disease-free, it's on and popping." She had it all planned.

"I see. And where will you be while all this is going on?"

"While they are doing their thing, I'll be with Shane." She shifted her gaze to a full-figured woman walking past us.

This was a *Lifetime* Movie waiting for me to capture on paper. And people ask me where I get the material to write about. Life! I live and breathe this drama every day.

I reached out and gently took hold of her wrist. "Danny, you remember what happened with my marriage, with all that swinging and ménage shit me and John were doing."

Danielle pulled away and fanned a heavily-jeweled hand through the air. "Girl, puhleeze. That's different. John's ass was on the down low. Shane isn't, and neither is Calvin."

"Yeah, but what if this Joiee chick is, and this is her way of sliding in. Hell, she might invite you to join them and turn your ass out."

Danielle turned up her nose. "Now you know good and damn well, I'm strictly dickly."

"Okay...okay...Nadine said the same thing and you see how Jordan turned her ass out," I reminded her.

She laughed. "Now you're talking stupid. I love Shane's dick way too much for that."

"Love?" I frowned because I hoped like hell that wasn't where this was headed. "You got feelings for this dude?"

"I just crave spending time with him. Girl, he's cocky and confident. He's done time, grew up in the hood. But since he got out of prison, he educated himself."

Just the way she liked them.

She was beaming with pride. "Now he builds websites and handles marketing. Shane's done pretty good for himself."

"And he has HIV," I added, just in case she forgot.

"We *both* have HIV."

"Why don't you just divorce Calvin and be with this dude. It sounds like a marriage made in heaven." I ain't one to talk, but we were just getting too old for this shit.

"Because I love my husband, and we have a great life together. I'm not about to give that up."

This bitch really thought it was just that easy. "Then why take the risk?"

She had this big grin on her face, like she had it all figured out. "What you don't understand is once I get Calvin to have sex with Joiee, I plan on asking him for the same."

"The same?" I wasn't quite following.

Danielle looked around as if someone might hear our conversation. "The same privileges. I'm going to ask him if I can have sex with someone with HIV without the limits that he and I have, because I don't want to take the chance of him contracting it."

"You know that is the dumbest shit I have ever heard, and yet, it makes sense."

"Of course, it does."

She had lost her damn mind. "And knowing Calvin, he will fall for that shit."

Danielle grinned and was just a little too sure of herself. "I think so, too. And once he does, we'll both have the best of both worlds. Everyone should be happy."

Maybe, but I had a feeling even the most carefully laid-out plans ran the risk of backfiring.

22
Nadine

I got out of my meeting with the senior partners and made my way to my office.

"Nadine, you have a few phone messages."

I took the pink slips from the receptionist desk. As I flipped through them, my stomach did a nervous roll. The bank was calling about the payment on Jordan's BMW.

I drew a long breath and went back to my office and took a seat behind the desk. I was two months behind and didn't see any way I was going to get that caught up any time soon. Jay had been calling me about his rent. My credit cards were all maxed out and payday was two weeks away. After the last incident, Jordan was keeping a tight watch on the joint account, so if I even thought about take fifty cents out, she would know and be asking why.

"Dammit."

I searched my brain, trying to think of an answer and even considered asking Renee for a loan. But that bitch was going to want to know every detail before she handed me any money, and l just wasn't sure I wanted to hear her mouth. I logged onto my bank account and decided it was probably time to cash in one of my money-market accounts. There would be a penalty of course, but it was better than taking a risk of Jordan's car being repossessed.

As soon as I opened the account, my heart jumped. I was overdrawn again. How in the world was that even possible? I wondered. I quickly scrolled through all the transactions.

"Oh no!"

The quarterly insurance premium had come out of my account. I had completely forgotten. As a result, my monthly tuition payment for my son's education had bounced.

"This can't be happening." I was so over my head and drowning in debt, I wasn't sure how I was going to fix this. Even after I cashed in the money market, there was barely going to be enough to pay both that and Jordan's car payment. I went ahead and processed the transaction anyway and took what little I had left in my own personal savings into my checking to get it out of the red. I was going to have to come up with a quick solution or I was in a world of trouble.

My phone rang and I looked down to see it was Jordan.

"Hey, baby."

"Hey, you," she cooed. "How's your day?"

"It's good," I lied. "Can't complain. I'm going to try and get out of here a little early and then run by the hospital for a little moral support."

"That's why I was calling. This morning the twins wanted pancakes and bacon for dinner tonight, so I wanna plan dinner around the time you're going to be home, so we can eat as a family for a change."

"I would like that. I'll call you after I pick up the twins and I'm on my way. We should be home by six."

"I'll see you then."

I hung up and thought about how much I loved my wife and our children. There was nothing I wouldn't do for any of them, which was why I had to find a way to get myself out of the mess I had gotten us into. At this point I was willing to do just about anything…except ask Renee. I didn't want to hear her mouth and because she had more than enough on her mind with Quinton getting shot and trying to figure out who was responsible.

I picked up the phone and dialed a number that was on one of the pink slips. He'd been calling me all week. I had been avoiding him for obvious reasons, but I couldn't any longer. In the past, I had the upper hand. Now I needed him.

"About damn time you called me back!"

"I'll be there in a few." Before he could say anything further,

I hung up and expelled a long breath. How in the world did I allow myself to get in such a mess?

Now, I had to make a deal with the devil.

An hour later, I pulled up at a house on Worley Street. I left my purse under the seat and walked up to the front door of the house. Immediately, it opened and some big beefy black dude with long dreadlocks was standing at the door mean-mugging me.

"I'm here to see Turk."

"Who the fuck is you?" he barked.

I was more afraid of my wife than I was of this big dude in front of me. "His attorney. You going to let me see him or not?" I shot him a don't-fuck-with-me look and he moved out of my way.

I walked into a small cluttered house that smelled like old fish grease and found Turk lounging across a couch. He was playing video games with two other niggas. All three of them had controllers in their hands. Some kind of gang war was playing on a seventy-inch television screen.

"Nadine, take a seat."

"I rather stand." I folded my arms beneath my breasts. "I asked you not to call me at work." Everything I did for him was paid under the table.

"Shee-it! Then answer yo got-damn phone."

"I'm busy."

He stopped playing and glared over at me. "You saying you too busy for my money?"

How I wish that was true. "I'm saying I've got a heavy client load. And just haven't had the time to call you back. But I'm here now, so what's going on?"

"I need you to handle those charges for me." He pointed to an envelope on the table.

I stared down at it like it was the plague before I picked it up. Quickly I scanned the contents. "What is this, a warrant for your arrest?"

"Yeah, so what?"

He pushed a briefcase across the table. I took a deep breath before opening it and looking side. The answer to my financial problems was inside. All in twenty dollar bills.

"What are the charges this time?"

"Domestic abuse and battery," he said like it was no big deal. There had been a warrant out for his arrest since last week.

I had to swallow. "Is there anything you need to tell me?"

"No. I just need you to do your job." He gave me a long hard look with those dark beady eyes of his that always made me feel uncomfortable.

"First thing in the morning, I need you to turn yourself in, and I'll have you out on bail by lunch."

"Don't be fucking late," he warned, then went back to playing his game.

I rushed back to my car and drove away with the taste of bile in my throat.

What in the hell did I do? Especially after I swore I would never ever represent him again.

As soon as I was far enough away from his house, I pulled out my iPad and logged into the city government database, pulling up the case file and the evidence the prosecution had against Turk.

As I read the file, I shook my head.

I had two beautiful babies and no matter how much Jordan and I disagreed, I could never dream of causing her any physical or emotional harm.

Swelling to the brain. Broken ribs.

How was I supposed to defend someone who treated women that way?

No longer able to hold it together, I hurried out of the car, rushed over to the bush and puked out the bacon and eggs Jordan had made me that morning. Along with the two cups of Gevalia dark roast coffee.

I leaned over, with my palms resting on my knees of my designer slacks and dry-heaved until the tears started rolling down my cheeks. This was not the career I wanted. I had joined that particular law firm to be in control of the types of cases that I took on so I could fight for what I believed in. Not this. Not this. Instead, I was being controlled by a gambling addiction that had caused me and one of the most crooked real estate investors/drug dealers in the area to cross paths.

It was about six months ago that I found myself winning big at blackjack. I was up ten thousand and should have cashed in my chips and taken my black ass home, but instead I had gotten greedy hoping to double my money. I had been smelling myself, if you let the young folks tell it. I had been so high on that adrenaline rush I felt each and every time I was within ten miles of the flashing lights, that I had no control whatsoever of what I was doing. An hour later, I walked away from the table in a daze and flat broke.

I had been on my way out the door when I had felt a tap at my shoulder. I turned around and there was this black man with a big white smile and scary dark eyes. He offered to buy me a drink and if I had been in my right mind, I would have refused. But he had also offered an opportunity to get my money back with plenty more where that came from. And I was like a dog following a big-ass milk bone.

One drink led to dinner and a proposition. All I had to do was help him find his wife, who had run off with his son. I was reeled in by the story of his love for his child and the envelope of cash, five thousand now, and another he planned to give me once I found her.

A private investigator located his wife and child in less than a month. She accused him of assault and battery. Afraid for her life, she'd ran. But Turk claimed she was a drama queen who'd do anything to keep his son from him. But during discovery, I found out so much more. Years of emergency room visits, broken bones. Being chained to the bed for days at a time. To this day, I regret painting a picture of a grieving father yearning to be a part of his son's life. It had been more than I could have ever stomached, and yet because of a previous drug habit, Turk was granted joint custody. After that I vowed to never represent him again.

But, here I was once again desperate for money and Turk was now being charged with the exact things his wife had claimed would happen.

Beatings.
Broken bones.

There was no way I could represent him again. But what choice did I have?

I hit the highway and instead of heading east, I headed south with determination on the brain. My palm was itching and that was always a good sign. I felt lucky. I wouldn't stay long, I told myself. Just long enough to win what I needed, so that tomorrow I could give Turk his money back, then I would be able to hold up my head. I glanced down at the clock. I had plenty of time before I needed to pick up the twins.

I reached for my cell phone and called my assistant, lying that I had to run to the courthouse and wouldn't be back in the office until morning. I then tapped the briefcase lying on the seat beside me and headed toward Boonville.

* * *

"Answer me Nadine! What the hell happened?"

Jordan had been going off on me for the last fifteen minutes and with good reason. I felt a splitting headache coming on.

"Nothing happened. I told you I lost track of time."

She glared at me. "*Time*? Do you know how embarrassing that was?"

I could barely look her in the eyes. "I said I was sorry."

"Sorry, yeah you're sorry alright," Jordan snapped back as she paced a path in our bedroom. "Who forgets to pick up their children from daycare?"

My heart skipped a beat. It was just as bad as if sounded. "I didn't forget. The time just got away from me. That's all."

"Where the hell were you? I'm *not* gonna ask you again." Before I could reply she added, "And don't say the office because I spoke with your assistant."

So much for that. "I was at the hospital with Renee. Things weren't looking good for Quinton."

Please forgive me for lying. Nevertheless, that took some of the fire out of her rage.

"Oh no! He's not going to die, is he?" Jordan questioned. Immediately I felt guilty at the look of panic in her eyes.

I shook my head rapidly and lowered onto the bed. "Oh no. His oxygen levels dropped. Now don't quote me on this, but his sats levels were low, meaning he wasn't getting enough oxygen to the brain. The monitors started beeping like crazy, alerting the staff. When Renee called me, she was screaming. I rushed over there."

She took a seat beside me. "That's so sad. I don't know how she's able to sit in that hospital day after day, waiting for him to open his eyes. If it were one of our children, I would have lost my mind."

I hesitated before saying, "Renee has always been a trooper."

"I don't care what you say, nobody is that strong all the time!" she snapped.

Jordan was right. The first time I ever recall seeing Renee fall apart was when her sister lost her battle with cancer.

Lisa and I had been best of friends. The rock who kept all of us crazy women together. Her death had hit us all. But for Renee, she had fallen apart because her sister was really the only family she had ever been able to depend on, other than us girls.

Feeling overwhelming guilt for the lie I told, I drew Jordan into my arms and pressed my lips to hers. "I'm sorry. You know I would never do anything to hurt our babies." I slid my tongue inside her mouth and kissed her with all the pent-up frustration I was feeling and tried not to think about the mess I had gotten myself into. While she lowered the zipper on my pants, I went to work unbuttoning her blouse. Making love would momentarily make me forget my problems. They had only gotten bigger the second I'd placed those chips down onto the table. Once again, I had lost big, and at the rate I was going, I risked losing even more.

23
Kayla

On Friday, I was up early in the kitchen fixing breakfast when Jermaine finally made his way down. He looked gorgeous in his black and gold Mizzou polo and black slacks.

"Man! What you got cooking up in here smelling all good!"

I ignored the overnight bag he sat on the floor beside him and tilted my head for his kiss.

"I've made all your favorites, scrambled eggs, cheese grits, country ham, and biscuits."

"Lord have mercy! You tryna make me fat," he said jokingly.

"Nope just trying to make sure I keep my man satisfied."

"I'm very satisfied."

I shuddered and wished those words were true.

Last night, I moved to chapter five in the blow job how-to, and there was still very little success. Jermaine ended up flipping me onto my back and eating me out until I was screaming at the top of my lungs. Asia banging on the wall, meant she'd heard. I tried to explain to her sex was something married couples enjoyed, but she got grossed out, said she already knew about sex and didn't need me to try and explain. I was more embarrassed than she was.

"C'mon and have a seat." I steered Jermaine over to the kitchen table and wasted no time putting a plate of food in front of him. I grabbed us both a cup of coffee and took the seat across from him.

"When will you be back home?" I made it my business to know his whereabouts.

"Tomorrow afternoon. There's a reception going on tonight

that I want to attend."

I noticed he was looking down at his plate as he spoke.

"Sounds like fun."

"It goes with the job." He took a bite of his ham and finally leveled his gaze on mine. "What are you planning to do while I'm away?"

"Hang out mostly at the hospital with Renee. I'm hoping Q wakes up soon."

"I hope so, too."

"Asia is going to a football game and some after party tonight for a local rapper. I wasn't feeling the idea, but I know I have to stop treating her like a child." Jermaine had been instrumental in that change. He knew how strict I had been with Kenya that my daughter barely spoke to me anymore. She'd rather get a job and spend the summer gone than home with me. I had been on the verge of making the same mistake with Asia before my husband set me down and talked some sense in my head. I couldn't treat my girls that way. I guess after having a mother who barely paid me any attention, I wanted to shelter my own girls at all costs. Well, it had cost me one daughter. I couldn't survive losing another. As a result, Asia had a relaxed curfew and could do a lot of things her older sister never could, which had been another reason why Kenya hated me so much.

"I'll call you when I get in. I'm going to be trying to meet with as many students as I can, encouraging them to attend our medical school." He stopped chewing and his brown eyes grew serious. "With recruitment down, I really need to get some strong candidates interested in applying to our program."

"Sweetheart, I understand." And I did and felt bad for thinking he was planning to spend the weekend with Black Barbie. My husband had never given me a reason to suspect him for cheating, so why was I feeling that way now?

Yesterday, I had dropped off the bag of goodies to her office. Unfortunately, Melinda hadn't been around for me to pick her brain. However, just to be one hundred percent sure, I was going to drop by again this afternoon and see if I could get any idea of who she was planning to spend her evening with.

"Next weekend we will do something special. We can still go to St. Louis if you'd like?"

He knew exactly what I needed to hear. "That would be a wonderful idea."

After breakfast, I hurried to get ready for work. Jermaine followed me out and kissed me hard enough to solidify his love. I watched through my rearview mirror, making sure I saw him get on the highway heading west before I made a left onto Providence Road.

I don't know why I was getting myself all stressed out about him being away for the night. Jermaine loved me. I was a full-figured woman and yet he still loved me. That should count for something.

By the time I walked into the Dean's office, I was feeling confident that everything was going to be alright. I greeted the other staff, then headed into my office and made myself a cup of coffee. I wasted no time logging in and working on a budget report I needed to turn into the finance office by close of business. My assistant had completed the minutes for last week's staff meeting and I still needed to approve those, so she could distribute them to the board today.

My morning had been flowing perfectly when I looked up to see Joyce Dumas standing in my door. She was a budget analyst for the Department of Urology.

"Hey, girl! How's it going?" she asked.

She was one of those sell-out sistahs who would throw you under the bus to advance her own career.

"It's been good, as you can see." I swept my arms, making a show of my new office.

"Congratulations. Definitely well-deserved." She sauntered in, looking impeccable in a navy pantsuit. Her mahogany bob haircut looked perfect as always against her light-brown face.

"What can I do for you?" I wanted to tell her if she was sniffing around looking for Jermaine, she was wasting her time. No, I'm not tripping. Before my husband and I had started dating, Joyce had been one of the many sluts who'd been sniffing around his office.

"I was wondering if I could get a copy of labels for all of the department chairs, as well as their assistants."

"Sure, but you could have emailed me that request." I was suddenly suspicious.

She smirked. "Actually, I saw the goodie bag you gave Dr. Barbie, and I was hoping you could hook me up as well."

"Sure." I reached inside the side pocket of my briefcase and removed another catalog. "Actually, I was just going to come down at lunch and ask her if she had received her bag. I had dropped it off on my way out yesterday."

"I know, she was swinging it on her way out. That's how I got a chance to see inside." Joyce giggled and licked her lips. "I need a little excitement in my life."

I smiled at her. "Sure, just let me know what you want and email it to the address on back and I'll get it for you. Some of the stuff I can get to you right away, but with the demand I've had lately, I might need to place another order. If you decide to have a party, I will give you a twenty-five percent discount."

"Cool. Thanks."

"Let me get that list for you." I was more than happy to hand her a set of preprinted labels. "Here ya go."

"Thanks again. Maybe if you have time, we can have lunch next week. I've been dying for a slice of Shakespeare's pizza." Her offer seemed sincere enough.

"Ooh, you and me both, but I'm watching my weight." Shakespeare's was one of my weaknesses.

"I noticed, and it's look really good."

I was surprised to hear a compliment coming for her mouth, but I let it go to my head anyway. Joyce headed to the door and I took in her slender frame. She could eat an entire pizza, and it wouldn't have made a difference.

I noticed she stopped just as she was about to exit my office. "Oh, by the way, if you're looking for Dr. Barbie she's not here. She took the day off."

I felt as if my chair had been yanked out beneath me. "What did you say?"

"I said she's off. She'd been planning it for weeks. Said she had something special planned. I figured that's why she asked for the bag of goodies. Anyway, I'll give you a call."

All I could manage was a mechanical head nod, and even that was no easy feat.

Melinda wasn't at work, and neither was my husband. It could have just been a coincidence, or could it? After all my husband was attending a recruitment fair in Kansas City…or so he said. I tried to tell myself Dr. Barbie taking the day off didn't mean anything at all. People took off on Friday all the time, and yet I could get my mind to accept that theory at all.

Lunch-time rolled around, and I practically bolted out the door and down the hall to see a coworker of mine. Maria Sanchez. She was a beautiful Puerto Rican woman.

Her lips softened when she spotted me. "Hey, girl, long time no hear. What's up with ya?" Her attempt to be hip was always amusing.

"I've been good, but I need a favor."

She flipped her long black ponytail. "Sure, what can I do for you?"

"My car won't start and triple-A can't come for another hour. Can I borrow yours? I need to run to my house." Lord, please forgive me for lying.

"Sure, absolutely." She rumbled inside a huge purse while I waited impatiently for her to find the keys to her Subaru. "You feel like hitting the mall this weekend? Macy's is having a sale."

"Sure," I replied and closed my fingers around the set of keys. "I'll be back shortly."

I was practically shaking as I made my way down to the parking lot and slid behind the wheel of her vehicle. Before I had left my office, I had looked up the address I needed. I made my way to Providence Road and then headed to Nifong Road and took a right. Before long, I was where I needed to be.

Dr. Barbie's house.

Taking a deep breath, I slowly drove down the road, looking at house numbers, which wasn't easy. The houses were far from the road and all the mailboxes weren't labeled. However, when I noticed activity on a house in front of me, I stalled.

There she was.

The UPS driver was on the porch and must have rang the bell, catching her by surprise. She had come to her door with her hair all over the place, but it was what she was wearing that caused me to have a mini-heart-attack.

A black and gold Mizzou recruitment polo shirt. The same one my husband had been wearing when he'd walked out the house. Her legs were bare, so were her feet. I bet the slut didn't have any panties on underneath. The way the driver was smiling, he had the same suspicions. Dr. Barbie finally went back inside.

Please Lord, Nooo!

My eyes frantically traveled up and down the street, but there was no trace of my husband's SUV. Dr. Barbie had a three-car garage and the door was down, so there was no way of knowing if his vehicle was parked inside.

I was so close to crying, I didn't know what to do except pick up my phone and call Jermaine. But when he didn't answer, the first tear slipped from my eye, followed by the others. For once I wished I could have been like my friends and been bold enough to go up and bang on Black Barbie's door, but I would never be that crazy. One wrong move and I would be sitting in front of the Dean with my job in jeopardy.

When I returned to the office, I tried to act normal, but it wasn't easy. My text messages to Jermaine went unanswered and he had yet to return my phone call. *You bastard! How could you treat me this way? After all that I have done you step on my heart this way.* I loved him more than I have loved any man before. The pastor had been stupid love and my baby daddies had been desperation. But what I had with Jermaine was different... or so I thought, because in the end he had turned out to be just like all the rest.

By the end of the day I was a nervous wreck and was tempted to go by Dr. Barbie's house again, only I was certain she would have recognized my car or even worse my husband would have spotted it from the bedroom window. Instead, I headed to the hospital, hoping Renee and Danielle could help me come up with a plan of action. But when I arrived at the unit and spotted someone familiar standing there, I practically lost it.

24
Renee

"Who is that?"

We all whipped around and stared down the hospital corridor where a tall gorgeous man with so much swag was headed our way.

"Who the hell is that?" Nadine muttered.

"Got-damn! I don't know, but he's fine as hell," Danielle replied. "You think he's here to see Q?"

I smirked. "Nope. He's here to see me."

They both turned and looked at me inquisitively, but my eyes were focused on the man moving toward me with a smile so bright, I couldn't do anything but smile back. He was wearing faded jeans, a Kansas City Chiefs long-sleeved jersey and fresh white sneakers on his feet.

"Is that who I think it is?" Nadine gasped and then reared back on the seat. "Oh, my God! It is!"

"Nadine, who is that?" Danielle asked impatiently.

"That's Clayton, the former NFL football player."

As soon as he realized he had an audience, Clayton grinned and said, "Whassup ladies!"

I rose and stepped forward just as he wrapped his large arms around me and lifted me off the floor. I knew the others were watching and hating.

"What are you doing here?" I asked when he finally lowered me back to my feet.

"What I tell you? Ignore my call and I'm personally coming down here to spank that behind."

I laughed because I just never thought he'd seriously do it.

"You remember Nadine."

Reaching out, he shook her head. "Yes, good to see you again."

"The same here."

"And this is my girl, Danielle."

He brought her hand to his lips and you should have seen the star-struck look on her face. That fool was probably coming in her panties.

"Nice to meet you Clayton. I've heard quite a bit about you."

He chuckled. "I hope it was good things."

"All good," she purred and my brow cocked at the way she responded.

We were all sitting, talking and laughing when Kayla arrived. The second she recognized Clayton, the color drained from her high-yellow face.

"Clayton?"

He looked up and grinned. "Hey, Kayla." He rose and even gave her a big hug. Not as big as mine, but enough to show that he was happy to see her. I wish I could say the same about her. I don't think I ever saw her look that distraught.

"What's wrong?" Danielle asked her.

"Nothing," Kayla replied in a far-off voice, then took a seat. Her eyes shifted back to Clayton "What brings you to Columbia?" Like she really had to ask.

"I thought I would come and check on Renee and see how her son was doing. Congratulations, she told me you're married."

"I just bet she couldn't wait to share that info," Kayla muttered it low enough that he probably didn't hear, but I had and so did Nadine because she was struggling to keep a straight face.

"What's wrong with you?"

"Why would you invite him here?"

"Excuse me?"

"Why would you invite him here? We've all come together to show our love and support while Quinton is in there fighting for his life, and you decide to invite dick into the mix."

"What?" Danielle's jaw dropped.

"Oh shit!" Even Nadine was surprised.

I was stunned because I ain't never heard Kayla talk like that.

"Whoa, I didn't come to cause any trouble." Clayton started to get up.

"Sit back down," I ordered. "There's no reason for us to be rude, now is there Kayla? Or are you just jealous because he's here to see me?" She did not want to go there with me.

"I could care less who he's here to see, because you've never cared about anyone except for yourself."

"Whoa, wait a moment!" Danielle waved her hands in the air. "Where the hell is all this coming from?"

Clayton was up out of his seat before I could stop him. "Look, I can see y'all got a lot to sort out. I'm going to run downstairs and make a few phone calls. I have an aunt in the area. I'll see if she's at home. I'll come back and check on you in a little bit."

This time I didn't even protest when he got up and headed back in the direction of the elevators.

I twirled around and glared. "What the hell is wrong with you?"

"You're the problem!" she screamed.

We all ducked and looked around to see who was listening to our conversation. Kayla had everyone's attention in the waiting room, including the white people.

"Women like you are always trying to have something that doesn't belong to you! You can't ever be happy, but gotta take what someone else has."

I was two seconds away from punching her, but something in her eyes told me something else was possibly going on. "Is this about me or is something else going on…like, with you and Jermaine?"

Kayla got quiet and dropped her head. I don't know what the hell was going on with her, but she had better say something, because I was seconds away from coming out of my chair. How the fuck she going to try and embarrass me like that?

Danielle moved over beside Kayla, and I noticed the tears streaming down her cheeks.

"Is this about Jermaine?" she asked.

Kayla nodded her head, and it took me a moment to feel sorry for her.

It was Danielle who explained. "Kayla thinks Jermaine is having an affair."

"What?" Nadine moved beside Kayla and reached for her hand. "What makes you think that?"

"Because we don't have sex anymore," she said softly.

"Yep. That would do it."

"But I told you to bring it, if he doesn't," Danielle said, which meant this was a conversation I hadn't been privy to.

"I tried all that, even started using my products, but he doesn't seem aroused by me."

"Maybe he needs Viagra." Danielle rolled her eyes in my direction. "What, I'm not trying to be funny. He ain't twenty-one anymore. Men get older, their dicks don't work the way they used to. Hell, I bet that old-ass preacher couldn't get it up every time he wanted."

"Renee, shut up," Nadine demanded.

"What? I'm just being honest. Just because he can't get it up doesn't mean he's fucking around."

"Maybe," Kayla mumbled, and then she had this look like maybe she might have misjudged him.

Oh, hell no! "Bitch, what else you got, because if you ran off Clayton for some suspect bullshit, I'm going to personally fuck you up!"

Nadine groaned and muttered something under her breath about leaving to go have dinner with Jordan.

Bye.

Danielle kicked out her boot and aimed at my shin. "Can you keep it down? We aren't the only ones in the waiting room."

I glanced around at the people sitting and staring at us. "Fuck them! They don't like it, they can move to the family lounge."

"You are ridiculous," Kayla muttered.

"No, you are for going off and embarrassing me in front of Clayton."

"Renee, I said shut the hell up," Danielle growled between her teeth.

"Whatever." They were not going to ruin my mood. I've been on edge for days worrying about Quinton. I finally had a moment when I—for that brief few seconds—had put my problems aside, and these bitches wanted to spoil it for me.

"Jermaine told me he was going to a recruitment fair in Kansas today, but I think he's over at this house."

"Oh damn." Now we were getting somewhere.

"Are you talking about the same doctor?" Danielle said, and I could tell Kayla had been having these suspicions for a while.

"I went over to her house, and I saw her coming out onto the porch in the same shirt I had ironed for Jermaine this morning."

"Oh snap!" I didn't mean to laugh, but I did. "How long have you been suspecting these two were messing around?"

"For a few months now."

I was so disappointed in her. "How many times have I told you, trust, but verify. You should have nipped this shit long before she got your husband in her bed. Now he's pretending to be recruiting, but he's fucking instead."

"Would you keep it down?" Nadine ordered with a wave of the hand.

"What? It's not like those women don't know what fucking is." I swirled around and stared at the four women sitting nearby. "Isn't that right, ladies? Especially since you're spending more time with your eyes all in my mouth instead of on that television screen."

"Oh God," Nadine mumbled and then felt she needed to apologize for me. "Ladies, please excuse her. She's worried about her son."

They nodded like they understood what I was going through. Hell, maybe they did. Sitting there meant they also had someone in the ICU.

Danielle rolled her eyes and returned her attention to Kayla. "What did she say when you confronted her?"

"Well, I didn't confront her exactly. I just drove slowly by her house as she was stepping out onto the porch to get the mail."

"Damn, and you say it was Jermaine's shirt she had on?"

She was struggling not to cry. "Yes. It was one of his

recruitment polos he wears all the time."

"Wait a minute, haven't I seen you wearing one of them?" I said, trying to show that it could have been a coincidence.

"Yes, because I got it from Jermaine."

"Okay, and couldn't anybody else get one? I mean you do work for the School of Medicine."

Kayla looked like she was thinking about what Nadine said before she shook her head. "No. I mean maybe. But I tried to call Jermaine, and he didn't answer."

Danielle shrugged. "Maybe he was busy."

"Or maybe he was inside Black Barbie's house?" She got all loud and shit. I couldn't believe it. Like I said, I was not used to this Kayla. But a woman scorned is not one to be fucked with. I just had no idea Kayla had it in her.

"Damn, Black Barbie." I'd heard it all.

Nadine was soothingly rubbing her arm. "Was his car out front?"

"No, but neither was hers. They were probably in the three-car garage of hers."

"Three-car? Where does she live?" I asked curiously.

"In Huntington Estates."

"Damn, I always wanted a house there." With that half a million-dollar price tag, I never could see being house-poor, no matter how much I love to floss in front of all the haters in this town. "Sounds like Jermaine found him a rich bitch."

They all rolled their eyes in my direction.

I gave them the finger. "Listen, Kayla, it doesn't matter what she does, remember you have one thing that she does not."

"And what's that?" she asked with tears running down her face.

"His last name." Why is it I have to always school these three?

"As long as you're his wife, you're in charge. Think about the scandal that would buzz around the medical center. He doesn't want that and I know she doesn't. She probably isn't even tenured yet. An affair would be career suicide for her."

"Renee is right." Nadine chimed in.

Of course, I am.

"So, what should I do?"

"Either do nothing or confront him. That's a choice you have to make for yourself."

"Renee, what would you do?" Kayla asked and her eyes were pleading for me to tell her how to proceed.

"Uh-uh. Don't ask that heifer that," Nadine said.

"Don't hate because I know my way with men. But then...I guess that's something you don't know much about." I smirked because Nadine knew I was right. Damn, I felt good!

"Fuck you Renee."

I was laughing. "Whatever, you know I'm right. And I thought you had to go meet your wife for dinner," I reminded her.

"I'll leave in a few."

That wench was afraid she might miss something.

I turned and faced Kayla with a hand propped at my waist. "I would have walked up those steps behind the UPS driver, went inside and found my husband lying in the bitch's bed. Photograph the shit!" They all might try and act brand-new, but they remembered the photographs I had taken of my ex-husband when I caught him dicking another dude in his ass. "I think you need to let them both know you know, and blackmail their asses."

"Don't listen to her! You need proof. Never confront someone unless you got concrete proof," Danielle insisted.

"I couldn't bear to see any more than I had." Kayla went on to tell us about the days leading up to his disappearing act, and Barbie also taking the day off. It sounded obvious to me, but I've learned that things aren't always the way they seem. And even though she pissed me the fuck off, I never wished any hurt to her. I wanted Kayla's relationship to work, so that I could truly believe there were a few successful marriages in the world.

"Kayla, I think you need to go home and talk to your husband," Danielle told her.

"He won't be home until tomorrow morning."

"Have you called him?" she asked.

She nodded. "We spoke when he arrived in Kansas."

It was my turn to ask the questions. "Have you contacted the hotel where he is staying?"

"No."

Dummy. "That's the first thing you should have done was see if he checked in."

"I guess you're right." I could tell she was hesitant because she took forever to reach inside her purse for her phone. "He's staying at the Hyatt."

Kayla was such a chicken. I was already reaching for my phone and doing a voice search. "Hyatt. Kansas City, Missouri." I waited for Siri to connect the phone. It took all of two seconds. "Hi, can you connect me to Jermaine Whitlow's room."

"One moment."

While I waited, all eyes were on me. Kayla was practically holding her breath.

"Ma'am, there is no answer in his room."

"But he has checked in, correct?"

"Yes, he has."

I made a show of nodding for everyone to see. "I'll call back later. Thank you." I ended the there. "There, see, now was that so hard?"

Danielle squeezed her hand. "See, all that worrying for nothing."

I was getting ready to tell her just because he checked in didn't mean shit. He could have that bitch up in his room with him or be down the hall in hers. But I didn't want to make her feel any worse than she already did.

"Just call him later." I rose. "Well, come on, let's go in so y'all can see Q because I need to go find Clayton. That man came all this way to see me and I'm being rude."

They nodded and agreed and we filed into my son's room. All of us stood over his bed, staring down at him. "He's doing better. Getting stronger every day. That's all that matters."

"Praise the Lord," Kayla whispered.

Danielle was shaking her head. "My nephew is such a good-looking kid. I don't know why he insists on doing dumb shit."

"They all do. My son has finally come out of the closet and

admitted he's gay." Nadine admitted.

"What?" Kayla's eyes were wide with horror.

I gave a rude snort. "I don't know why you're surprised. I knew his little ass was gay all along."

Danielle chuckled. "Yeah, it was kind of obvious."

Nadine glared at me. "Fuck both of you."

"What's the big deal? You're a lesbian and your son is gay. I don't see anything wrong with that picture."

"I do," she grumbled.

"Why? It's okay for you to be gay, but unacceptable for him? Where is the irony in all that?" Danielle asked incredulously.

"I guess I never expected him to turn out like me."

"And?" I shrugged. "Get over it. He needs you to accept him the same way he's accepted you."

Some people are just stuck on stupid. Mind you, it took me awhile to accept that Nadine was gay. I used to call her all kinds of mean names like, carpet muncher and dyke, but I've learned over the years to just accept people for who they are. They didn't choose to be that way, it just happens and that doesn't make me any better than them. There was already enough hatred in the world, so Nadine didn't need it from me.

"I guess you're right," Nadine finally admitted.

Kayla pointed. "You know. Q might be in a coma, but I bet you he's listening to everything we are saying."

"Well if he is, he's cracking up at what you just said about Jay."

By the time we made it back out, Clayton was standing there talking to some female who was batting her eyes. He spotted me and headed our way carrying a familiar bag.

"What you got?" We all were intrigued.

"Drinks. I made my way down to this bar up the street called Tropical Liquors and found out you can take drinks to go. I got all of you frozen Long Island ice teas."

God, I could get used to this.

I took the small box and looked inside. The heavenly smell of liquor fluttered to my nose. "How the hell you manage to walk out with four drinks?"

"Yeah, and it's even in a box." Danielle added with a huge

appreciative grin on her lips.

He winked. "I have my ways."

We each took a Styrofoam cup. "Thank you," we said one after the other.

I signaled for Clayton to walk over to the windows and sit on the ledge with me. "Sorry about earlier."

"It's all good, baby."

I sucked in a breath at the endearment.

"I'm sure y'all had something deep to discuss amongst girlfriends."

I stole a glance in Kayla's direction. She was busy sipping through her straw and staring off at nothing. "She's upset about her husband. He told her he went to a recruitment fair at the University of Kansas City this weekend, and she doesn't believe him."

His brows lifted. "The university huh…"

I swung around. "What?"

Clayton turned so his back was toward my girls. "The recruitment fair was two weeks ago. The reason why I know, I was there talking to a science major who's the starting quarterback."

Damn. Wait until I tell Kayla that. I had jumped to my feet before he could stop me.

25
Danielle

Renee is always acting extra.

When she had that crazed look in her eyes, I knew her ass was about to do something cray-cray. I should have left with Nadine when I'd had the chance.

"Where the hell are we going Nae-Nae?"

"Where the hell you think?" she said and expected me to get with the program.

Kayla was sitting with her hands folded on her lap, staring straight ahead.

"Uh, would someone care to tell me what is going on?"

My eyes shifted to Clayton. I forget he was even there, which was retarded because we were riding in his Hummer.

"We about to handle some business," Renee said between sips.

The crazy bitch still had that drink in her hand. I wish I could blame her spontaneous bullshit on liquor, but I couldn't even lie. She was always ready for some ridiculous do-or-die bullshit. Don't get me wrong. We appreciated the way she always has our backs and her relentless need to avenge her sistahs, but at forty, this shit was getting ridiculous.

"Jermaine's been lying to Kayla and we're about to go to that bitch's house and see if he's there," Renee explained. I couldn't believe she was acting like this with Clayton in the car.

"And then what... shoot the place up?" Clayton asked jokingly.

Renee yelled over the seat. "One of y'all got a gun in your purse?"

"Oh, hell no!" he swerved and Renee started laughing.

"Clayton, I thought you didn't cuss."

He pointed a finger at her. "You always seem to bring it out in me."

"Wonder why?" Kayla said with a rude snort.

"We're gonna go confront Black Barbie," Renee confirmed. "Kayla, give Clayton the address."

Kayla gave her the address, then looked over at me and mouthed, "Danny, please stop her crazy ass."

I don't understand why the fuck she had even given up the address. "Renee, Kayla does not want to go over there!"

That crazy wench swung around on the seat with the straw still between her lips. Lush ass.

"Don't you want to know the truth?" she insisted.

I noticed Kayla couldn't even look Renee in the eyes as she mumbled, "I guess."

"Of course, you do," she urged.

"Nae-Nae, we're not about to embarrass her!" I warned her.

"Whatever!" Renee gave us a dismissive wave and swung back around on the seat.

"Do y'all do this often?" Clayton asked. He was looking at me in the rearview mirror.

I shook my head regrettably. "Hell, yeah. All the damn time, back in the day."

"Hell, I needed something to do. I'm tired of sitting and waiting for Quinton to get stronger. He's like a watched clock that never moves."

"Maybe, but what you're planning to do is childish and fucking retarded," I muttered then looked up and met his eyes. "Clayton, I hope you know what you have gotten yourself in to. You bounced the first time you met her, so why the hell would you be running around with her crazy ass now?"

"That's a good question. Not sure if I have an answer yet."

"Hopefully, you won't regret your decision," Kayla mumbled, and I wasn't sure if she was talking about Jamaica or what was about to go down.

"Relax," Renee managed between sips. "If there's nothing going on, then you can go back home with a big Kool-Aid smile on your face and live happily ever after." If Renee really believed that was a possibility, she wouldn't have come over here.

Kayla pointed. "Stop! That's her house over there."

"That's where she lives?" I asked incredulously.

"Yep, that's it." She sighed. "I came over at lunch and spotted her coming out of that house."

Renee was out of her seat before I could stop her. Quickly, I jumped out the Hummer and hurried over beside Renee before that crazy bitch did something stupid.

"Nae-Nae wait! What the hell are you getting ready to do?"

"I'm gonna peek in the garage and see if Jermaine's vehicle is in there."

There was no stopping her, so I signaled for Kayla to join us and didn't even bother to wait to see if she'd gotten out. Knowing her scary ass, probably not, but if I let Renee out of my sight, there was no telling what she was liable to do.

"Let's go this way," I suggested and we scurried around and into the next-door neighbor's backyard. There was no way in hell we were going to walk up the driveway of that woman's house.

"Damn these shits are nice." I was admiring a massive brick house that was closer to a cool million than not, and something Calvin and I would never be able to obtain on our own.

"They're living the mothafuckin' dream," Renee chimed in.

The three-car garage was on the side of the house. We walked across the yard, which even though it didn't have a fence, it was nice as shit with a gazebo, concrete pavers, and a wraparound deck that was made of some special red composite material. Damn, I was jealous because this was the life I wanted. The life I damn well was going to have. All it took was for my online business to elevate to the next level. I was hoping with Shane's help, this was how I was going to be living.

"Shit, if I had known this little-ass town has houses like these, I might have stuck around a little longer. Hell, maybe I need to look at buying a second home."

Rich bitch. I love my girl, really, I do, but there are times when I wish she'd help the little people.

"Buy a second home? Bitch I'm still waiting for you to pay

me back for that first-class ticket I bought you. Remember some of us ain't got it like that."

Renee slapped her forehead like she should have had a V8. "Oh damn! You should have said something. I'll write you a check on the way back to the hospital."

I felt a little guilty for asking. I don't know why since it's my damn money. "We can worry about that later." I heard movement coming up behind and swung around fast, fist balled.

"Whoa! It's me," Kayla said, throwing up her hands.

"You almost got yo head knocked off. I thought you were the owner of this here house," I told her.

"You told me to come on," she replied timidly. "So, I got out, even though you know I'm not interested in this crap."

"As usual, Renee was being ridiculous." We tried to whisper, but our words were overheard.

Renee turned and rolled her eyes. "Keep it moving, before someone calls the police," she warned.

We walked to the end of the yard, then I watched how crazy she was acting, looking both ways before darting across the driveway and along the side of the house. I probably looked like an idiot myself, doing the same thing, and Kayla followed.

"Now what?" I asked since Renee seemed to have all the answers.

"I'm going to look inside the windows and see if I can see Calvin's Navigator."

We all tried to look inside the garage, but the windows were covered with dark curtains and it was impossible to see around them.

"Damn, now what are we gonna do?" I blew out a dramatic breath.

"I guess we better go." Kayla suggested and started to back away.

Renee totally ignored us. "Look, there's a small window up there." She pointed to a small window that I couldn't reach even in a pair of stilettos.

"How the hell do you expect us to reach that?" I asked.

"Easy. Y'all going to lift me up," Renee announced.

"The hell we are!" I snapped.

Kayla started shooing us.

"I would lift you up, but my arm is too weak. So, instead of you falling on your wide ass, you and Kayla can lift me," Renee explained. She had an answer for everything.

I looked from Renee to Kayla, who looked ready to bolt out of there at any second. Damn, I wished she would grow some balls.

"Fine," I said since it didn't seem we had much of a choice.

We both held out our hands and Renee raised up. "Damn, bitch you got your stank pussy all in my face."

"Fuck you. Even my shit smells like a floral arrangement."

I leaned most her weight against the side of the garage. "Hurry up! You're heavy."

"Then, hold still."

"Shush, would y'all be quiet!" Kayla urged in a panic.

I tried to steady my hold on Renee, but it wasn't easy, not with all that ass she had.

"What do you see?" Kayla asked anxiously.

"There's a dark SUV in there."

"I knew it!" Kayla wailed loudly. "My husband is in there."

She was jumping to conclusions. "It's too dark to be able to tell the make and model."

"She owns a white Mercedes."

"Yep, now that I can see."

To my horror, I heard someone turning the lock on the door and before Renee could get down, the door flung open and there stood a beautiful woman. In our surprise, Kayla jerked back and Renee landed on the ground onto her ass.

"What the fuck!"

"Who's out there?" the woman demanded and had the bold audacity to step out onto the porch.

Kayla ducked around the house, so she wouldn't be seen.

I stood there, frozen. She had been right. Black Barbie was beautiful with bronze skin and hair that was too long and wavy to be anything but fake. She had a curvaceous shape women yearned to have. I bet she didn't have any kids.

"Shit," I muttered.

She flicked on the porch light, but by then Kayla had darted across the yard. I followed, but not Renee. Her crazy ass got up from the ground and stepped out from the shadows.

"Excuse me for being in your yard, but I'm looking for my dog. Have you seen him?"

"Are you fucking kidding me?" I muttered under my breath.

Kayla was livid. "What in the world is she doing?" She started walking forward, but I grabbed her arm and stopped her.

"Don't! She's gonna see you."

"Well, let's at least move closer, so I can hear what she is saying," Kayla insisted to my surprise.

"No, I haven't seen a dog." I heard the woman say.

"Hmmm, I think he's under your deck." Renee made a show of stooping down low. "I think he's stuck. Can someone go under there and get him? Is your husband home?"

This girl was a trip.

"Can you see him?" Barbie asked.

Renee shook her head. "No, but I saw him run over here."

Kayla and I watched with curiosity while Renee made a show of walking around to the other side of the porch. Barbie stood there in the t-shirt without shame. I would have too if I had a body like hers.

"Riley, C'mere sweetie!"

I don't know why Renee never considered becoming an actress, because she was a natural. Crazy chick had me almost believing she had lost her dog.

"I don't understand, he's usually not one to run off. Riley! Where are you?"

"Riley!" Even the doctor was now calling out for the imaginary animal.

"Would you happen to have a flashlight?" Renee asked. "I want to make sure he isn't trapped under there."

"She's ridiculous," Kayla whispered and shook her head.

I waited until Barbie went inside before I rushed over. "Renee come on! Let's get out of here.

"No way. Not until we find what we came for."

She was now peeking through the windows of the rear of the

house.

Kayla tossed her hands in the air and headed back toward the Hummer.

The French doors opened and Barbie came out. I quickly ducked around the house before she could see me.

"Okay, here you go," she said and handed Renee the flashlight.

Renee made a show of pointing it under the deck. She was taking all damn day, and I was ready to get the hell out of there. It was getting dark, and this whole thing was starting to feel creepy.

I was also ready to go back to the Hummer. Maybe I could convince Clayton to put his foot on the gas and leave her ass behind.

All of a sudden, I heard Renee let out a high-pitched scream that caused me to startle. In a panic, I came racing around the house in one direction, and spotted Kayla coming from the other.

Renee darted across the yard like a maniac.

"What's wrong?" I asked. She was making me freak out.

"There. Under there! He's was staring right at me!"

Dr. Barbie was standing on the porch, eyes large with horror.

Clayton came running around the house calling Renee's name. "Are you okay?"

Wow, at least he wasn't a punk.

"Renee...who was staring at you?" I asked.

"A possum! A nasty, beady-eyed-ass possum!" she cried.

What the fuck!

My head whipped around toward Kayla. All that over a fucking possum. I could not believe my ears. But my surprise was nothing compared to the look on Kayla's face.

"Are you okay?" I heard Clayton say, but I was no longer interested in what had my best friend spooked. My gaze had followed the direction of Kayla's eyes to the porch, where a man had come running out the French doors in nothing but a pair of boxers.

"Oh shit," I mumbled under my breath and shook my head at the familiar sight.

Renee must have also seen the look of alarm on Kayla's face, because she stopped talking about that damn possum and looked toward the deck as well.

"Is that him?" Clayton whispered.

By that time, Kayla had stormed over to confront the two of them. They looked like they'd been caught stealing.

"Kayla...what are you doing here?" Dr. Barbie asked.

"Be quiet." Kayla held up her hand, silencing her. Her attention was on the man beside her. "How could you?"

Renee was looking from me to Kayla and then back onto the deck. My mouth was open. I was completely floored.

"Who is that?" she whispered.

Dr. Barbie wasn't having an affair with Jermaine.

"That is Gary Fox. The dean of the medical school."

"Ain't that a bitch." Renee was laughing when that possum came out from under the deck. It darted across the yard and had her screaming and running out toward the street. Now it was my turn to laugh. She had always been terrified of them. I just never realized how much.

While Clayton followed her back to his vehicle, I listened to Dean Fox trying to bribe Kayla to stay quiet. I remember him from when I worked at the hospital.

Suddenly, I started giggling uncontrollably. Why did the crazy shit always happen when Renee was in town?

My phone rang. I reached down inside my pocket and noticed it was Portia. I started walking toward the Hummer as I answered it. There was a lot of background noise. "Hello?"

"Mama!"

Something in my daughter's voice frightened me. "Portia, what's wrong?"

"Mama!" she cried. "There's been a shooting at the football game! I think somebody might be dead!"

26
Nadine

Ever since Jordan found out I had been cyphering money out of our accounts, things had been shaky at home, so I decided we needed a night away from the twins. Just she and I alone together, so we could talk.

I took her to her favorite restaurant. CC Broiler's was a small quaint spot and one of the best places in town to get a steak. I knew she loved their Chicago Rib-eyes. They were blackened and seasoned so good. The flavor made your toes curl in your shoes they were that good.

Jordan looked beautiful in a pair of gray slacks and a black V-neck sweater that showcased her generous breasts. Her hair was hanging loose and large curls bounced around her face every time she turned her head. We had just finished our salads when Jordan made an announcement I was not ready to hear.

"I'm thinking about going back to work."

"Why?"

She cleared her throat. "Because we need the money."

When we first decided to have children, we agreed Jordan would stay home and raise our family. Later she decided she wanted to go back to school, and I agreed just as long as she worked it around the twins' schedule. Now she was trying to change the rules and I wasn't having it. As far as I was concerned, her going back to work signified I had failed as the provider.

"We don't need the money," I insisted.

The look she gave said she didn't believe shit I was telling her. "I just want to take some of the burden off you. You work so hard. If I could just help you carry some of the load, I think it would make all the difference." I guess she meant the difference between our current situation and the poor house.

I reached over and covered her slender hand with mine. "Look at me." I said because I didn't want there to be any misunderstanding of what I was about to say. "You are my wife and I vowed to take care of you and the twins. Nothing about that has changed. Sure, we've had some rough spots, but we're going to get through it. Like we do everything else. I have a few new clients and been billing like crazy lately, so we're going to be fine. Trust me."

I noticed her shoulders relax and she seemed somewhat relieved.

"I trust you."

That meant a lot coming from her. "In fact, I was thinking maybe we can take the kids to Florida during the Christmas holiday." I smiled at her.

"Oh, baby! That would be great." Her chuckle was soft.

It was so easy to please her. Jordan had never asked for much. She was simple. That was one of the things I loved most about her. She was a great homemaker and knew how to do more with less. Lately she'd been having to do a lot of that, but I was confident all of that was about to change.

"Nadine?" she said softly.

"Yeah?" My gaze locked with hers.

"I hope you know I love you with all my heart. I've made a lot of mistakes in my life, but marrying you was not one of them."

"And I love you. You sacrifice so much for me and the twins and I want to spend the rest of my life showing you just how much that means to me." She smiled and so did I.

I really felt like things were finally starting to return to normal. We enjoyed our dinner. I ordered some drinks and when Jordan insisted on dessert I ordered the crème brûlée. I was already thinking about making love when I felt a large presence. Looking up, I found a familiar black man dressed in thug gear standing over our table.

I glared up at him and noticed my wife looking uncomfortable.

"Nadine, who's that?"

That's what I wanted to know. "Can I help you?"

He had the nerve to smirk at me. "Turk wants to talk to you." He tilted his head in the direction behind me, and I suddenly remembered this was the same dude who'd be standing guard at Turk's house. I looked over my shoulder, and sure enough Turk was sitting in the corner. Damn!

"What's going on?" Jordan asked, and I could see she was annoyed that I had avoided the question. What was there to say? Anything that would come out of my mouth would only make matters worse.

"Babe, that's one of my clients." I explained and with a sigh I rose from the chair. "Ask the waitress for the bill and I'll be right back."

I glared at Turk's messenger, dropped my napkin onto the table and walked toward his table. He had the nerve to be sitting there eating a steak without a worry in the world. I muttered a curse and was ready to tear into him for ruining my evening.

"You want something?" I said and had straight attitude.

Turk didn't even bother to look up. Instead he pointed his knife to the chair across from him and said, "Sit."

At first, I thought about objecting, but that big black man pulled out the chair.

I lowered onto the chair and leaned across the table. "What is so important you interrupt dinner with my wife?"

"She's a beautiful woman. If she ever decides she wants a man in her life, I'd be happy to lay some pipe."

The big dude started chuckling, and I was ready to come across the table and punch him in the mouth. But that would not end well.

"Turk, what do you want?"

He was chewing, so it took him a moment to reply. "I think

we have a problem."

"What's that?"

"I received a package in the mail this morning."

I swallowed. After the incident at the casino, I had cashed in another money market account and a few of my CDs. The bank penalized the shit out of me, but it was better than being married to Turk. It was a risky move, but instead of taking the money back to him, I put it in a box and mailed it Express mail.

"I changed my mind," I tried to explain, hoping that would make the difference.

"And you think you can just mail me my money and it's a done deal?" His eyes were laughing at me. "Cheddar can you believe this shit?"

"Nah, Turk," the big dude said and laughed.

"I can't represent you on that case," I said soft and low, wishing Cheddar would take his big ass somewhere else.

"It's a little late for that. I already retained your services."

"And I changed my mind."

His nostrils flared. His gaze bored into mine. "There's no changing your mind. You're my lawyer."

I leaned in close so no one else could overhear what we were talking about. "Listen, I read the charges, and I can't get involved."

"You're already involved. I've bailed your ass out one too many times, and now yo mothafuckin' dyke ass is gonna get me off."

Cheddar moved in close.

Turk pinned me with his stare. "If not... I would hate to see something happen to wifey." His eyes shifted over to my table. I stole a glance and saw the uneasiness in Jordan's eyes as she tried to pretend she wasn't watching. For her benefit, I faked a smile, even though I was feeling sick to my stomach.

"Now reach under the table and grab that bag."

I looked under and there was the identical bag I had mailed to him. I already knew what was inside.

"Go ahead and take it. I don't have all day."

I couldn't believe this shit was happening me. Cheddar reached down and picked up the bag, then swung the strap over my shoulder.

"I expect a call tomorrow to discuss my case."

What other choice did I have except to nod?

I think that was the longest walk I ever took, back to the table. Jordan was frowning, and I could see she was not at all happy.

"What was that all about?" she asked with her arms crossed. I guess she figured out it wasn't anything good. "We are supposed to be having a romantic evening out, and instead, you're conducting business."

I slid back onto my seat. "I'm sorry about that, but that is one of my biggest clients."

"And what's in the bag?"

"Some items he needs me to look at to strengthen his case. And that's all I can really say," I added quickly before she asked to see what was inside the bag. "Now all I want to do is go home and make love to you." I said hoping to get the mood back.

"Ma'am, excuse me."

I looked up to see our waitress standing over us.

"Yeah?" I said hoping she had our bill ready.

"I'm sorry, but your credit card has been declined."

"Credit card?" She must have us confused.

"What? *Declined*?" Jordan glared over at me.

"What are you talking about? You haven't even given us the bill yet," I snipped in response.

"While you were over there talking…" Jordan tossed quotation marks in the air, "…I gave them the Visa."

I was so embarrassed with the two of them staring at me. I slowly slid the bag off my shoulder and into my lap. "Oh yeah. I forgot that's the card I canceled." I was lying, and the waiter clearly didn't believe me, but I didn't give a shit. As long as he got his money, that was all that mattered. "Give us a minute. I'll just pay in cash."

He walked off, but I had a feeling he wasn't going to be far away, in fear Jordan and I were going to try and sneak out.

Jordan crooked a brow. "What is going on? First the bank account and now the credit cards. I need to know what the hell is happening to us."

"We will discuss it later. Right now, I have a bill to pay." Discreetly, so Jordan couldn't see me, I slid back the zipper of the bag, reached inside and removed a stack of bills. Underneath the table, I peeled off a few. I already knew Turk had paid me with twenties. I set the money on the table.

"I'll just pay in cash, and we can sort this out when we get home."

Jordan leaned across the table to whisper. "We have a three-thousand-dollar limit. Are you telling me the card has been maxed out?"

I shook my head, mortified at the intensely awkward moment. "No, I think I might have forgot to mail the payment. I'll take care of it when I get home." I just prayed she didn't call the number on the back of the card to confirm. "Come on, let's go."

As soon as we rose, I looked over my shoulder and shot a look at Turk who was eating his dinner as if he didn't have a worry in the world. Reluctantly, I slid the bag back over my shoulder and headed toward the door. There was no turning back.

27
Renee

This was like a fucking bad dream.

"Oh shit! The high school is that way!"

While Clayton turned the Hummer at the corner and followed my directions, all of three of us whipped out our cell phones.

"I can't reach Asia!" Kayla cried.

And I couldn't reach Tamara. I didn't even have to call to know she was at that football game. It was the first home game of the season against their rival, Fulton High School.

"What's Portia saying?" I asked and looked over into the back seat.

Danielle's brow furrowed. "She's saying there are people everywhere!"

That was not what I wanted to hear. "Damn. They probably won't let us anywhere near the football field."

"Just let them try and stop me! I need to find my daughter." Kayla was practically hysterical. "What have I done? I was so busy trying to find out what my husband was doing that I had taken my eyes off my daughter." There were sobs in her voice.

"She's gonna be okay," I assured her. "Q is already laid up in a hospital bed. Lord knows we can't handle another one."

"I hope so. I sure hope so," she moaned.

Danielle was texting in the backseat. I tried texting Tamara as well, since these kids nowadays didn't know how to do much else.

"Turn right there!" Kayla screamed and Clayton made a sharp turn at the corner.

The road into the school was closed, so I pointed to the lot across the street. "Right there."

He barely brought the Hummer to a complete stop before we were all jumping out and racing across the street. The police were everywhere, trying to keep the crowd back, so we moved over and joined the others that were standing around the school's student parking lot.

"This is some bullshit!" I heard some female say.

"Hey, Rosie, girl what's going on?"

I should have known Danielle would know her.

She sucked her teeth. "Hell if I know, but my son is on that team. Y'all mothafuckas better tell us something!" she yelled across the parking lot.

I pulled my sweater tighter around me and looked down at my phone again. Nothing. Where the fuck was Tamara?

"Anybody know what the hell happened here?" I said aloud.

They looked as clueless as we did.

"My son said shots were fired in the bleachers." I heard someone yell.

"What the fuck!" Danielle murmured.

Kayla was on the phone, talking to someone and freaking out. I looked over at the crowd and saw Jewel and Keneshia, who lived directly across the street. I rushed over to them. Keneshia had a pink do-rag on her head.

"Cuz, he got him!" she announced.

I stared at her with wide eyes. "What…what are you talking about?"

Danielle hurried over. "You seen Portia?"

Keneshia who knew her, nodded and said, "Yeah, she's somewhere over there talking to the police. They're tryna find out what everyone saw."

I held up a hand. "Wait a minute, get back to what you were saying."

Danielle fixed her attention on me. "Saying about who? What did I miss?"

Keneshia blew out a breath and lifted her hands. "Dollar. I think that's him laid out on the ground."

"What?" Oh shit.

"Hell to the naw!" Danielle bellowed.

I couldn't believe what I was hearing. "What happened?"

It was Jewel's turn to speak. "I saw Dollar the moment he stepped out onto the bleachers and I could tell by the way he kept looking over his shoulder, something was about to go down."

"She's right, cuz. My ass got the hell away from him." Keneshia shook her head. "I don't even think Dollar saw it coming."

Jewel nodded and brought a hand to her bony waist. "I bet you Meechie did it! I knew that nigga was up to something the way he wouldn't sit down."

Meechie. I couldn't believe he had been a man of his word.

I could barely find the breath to say, "Did you see him shoot him?"

They both shook their heads before Keneshia said, "It happened so fast, I don't think anybody saw it coming. But, I saw the two of them talking, right before the shit went down."

"Damn," was all I could muster.

"That was some Vin Diesel type shit. It was so crazy, because it took everyone a few seconds to realize what had just happened. After that, everyone was screaming and stepping over folk and trying to get the hell off out the bleachers."

"Have you seen Tamara?"

Keneshia tipped her chin. "Yeah, she was with this tall girl with long hair."

I turned. "Kayla, I think that sounds like—"

"Mama!"

We all whipped around to the sound of Asia's voice. She came sprinting across the lot.

"Oh, thank you, Jesus!" Kayla was crying and waving her arms acting a damn fool. I stood there and watched the two of them and was happy Asia was okay.

"Oh shit! Here comes Portia." It was Danielle's turn to hurry over to embrace her daughter, who collapsed against her as her mother held her close.

I gave them a moment before I stepped forward and asked, "You seen Tamara?"

Portia looked to her right and left. "Yeah, I saw her somewhere around here."

"Portia, what happened?" I asked and didn't mean to sound so impatient.

She shook her head. "I don't know what happened. I saw Dollar and after what had happened to Q, I knew there was gonna be something goin' down. I think he knew it, too, because he kept looking and moving around. I saw him talking to this one dude and then the next thing I know Meechie stepped up to him, and before I knew it, we were ducking and bullets started flying!"

Damn, this was some crazy shit.

Danielle hugged her daughter close again. "I'm just glad you're okay."

"Hey, is everything okay over here?"

I swung around to find Clayton rushing over to us. His eyes were wide in disbelief while he muttered, "Damn, it's always the small town."

"We're not so small anymore, but this place has been a melting pot to a lot of bullshit over the last few years, which is part of the reason why I had gotten the hell up outta here," I told him.

"I'ma start making you give me a dollar every time you cuss," he whispered close to my ear.

"Then yo ass better get ready to retire early 'cause if I don't find my daughter in the next sixty seconds, I promise you I'm about to act a damn fool!"

He chuckled with laughter and draped an arm across my shoulders. His touch was warm and comforting, to say the least. "It's a good thing I got here when I did."

"Why is that?"

"Because I can see Ms. Nae-Nae needs someone to look after her."

I started to smart off that I didn't need anyone to look after me. I was an independent black woman who'd been taking care of herself for a long time, but I wasn't feeling that liberated now.

His phone rang and while Clayton answered a call, I allowed my eyes to travel over the crowd of people, looking for any familiar faces. My heart was beating so fast I could barely think straight. Was all this crying and chaos a result of retaliation for my son? I just prayed it hadn't been at the expense of someone else's life. I don't know what I would do if…

And then, over near a bike rack, I spotted a group of girls with their arms wrapped around each other. The one on the end in faded distressed skinny jeans and an over-sized sweatshirt was Tamara. She spotted me at the same time and relief swept through my veins. My baby was safe!

"I see my daughter," I murmured and walked off, not even sure or caring if Clayton had heard me. Instead I was crying and laughing while I moved in her direction. I made my way through the crowd of spectators who were being more nosy than concerned when movement caught the corner of my eye. When I recognized the man wearing all black coming my way, my breathing stopped. It was Meechie. He was moving with wide cautious strides. We were just about to cross paths when he slowly raised his head and our eyes met. As soon as he was certain he had my attention, Meechie gave me a head nod. I swallowed, understanding the meaning and continued walking.

He had been a man of his word. The job had been done.

Up ahead, I saw a stretcher being rolled away from an ambulance and into the thick of the crowd. The sight made me suddenly anxious to get back to the hospital with Quinton.

By the time Mario arrived to pick up Tamara and had taken her home with him and Rita, the body was being taken away.

According to Tamara, shots were fired and all hell broke loose. People were running and screaming. My daughter had fallen while trying to rush off the bleachers and had banged up her knees. But she was alive, and that's all that mattered. As soon as I told Mario who had allegedly been murdered, he gave me a look trying to read my eyes. When Tamara wasn't looking, I simply nodded.

They left and I was headed back to join the others when David stepped in my line of vision. I could tell by the tension at his neck and shoulders, he was all about business.

"What are you doing here?" He had the nerve to give me the side-eye.

I placed my hands on my hips and stared him straight in the eyes without flinching. "My daughter was at the game, so you best believe I was going to be here."

He cupped my cheek. "Relax. I'm just showing concern."

I relaxed a little. "Who got shot?"

He smirked. "You don't know?"

I shook my head.

"C'mon, Renee. It was Damon Banks, aka, Dollar."

My heart lurched at the confirmation. "The name doesn't sound familiar."

David laughed and drew me near and whispered in my ear. "Between you and I, we both know he's the guy responsible for shooting your son."

"What!" I could have won an Academy Award for my performance. If he thought he was getting anything from me, he was wrong.

"Now if that was true, then why haven't you arrested him?"

"I was planning to bring him in for questioning, but it seems someone had other more permanent plans for him."

"Hmmm, I wouldn't know anything about that," I said and refused to give him any satisfaction. "If he did have anything to do with my son getting shot, then good ridden to him. Somebody just saved the taxpayers of this town a lot of money."

David called after me, but I had already given him my back.

I made it over to the others. Danielle gave me a two-finger-wave. "I got a ride."

"With who?" I asked.

"Shane," she said close to my ear. "Portia's just left with her girl Alanna so I'm gonna get out of here as well."

Clayton took us back to the hospital. Kayla and Asia got out and went to her car while I sat with him in the circular driveway of the hospital.

"What do you think happened to that guy tonight?"

"I don't know." I wouldn't dare admit the truth, no matter how much I was feeling Clayton. Tomorrow wasn't guaranteed to any of us. What happened to Dollar, I planned on taking that shit to my grave.

Tamara was going to have problems sleeping tonight. I would call her as soon as I made it back up to the ICU.

Clayton reached out and laced his fingers through mine. "You know you're more than welcome to come and spend the night with me in my hotel room. I'm sure you could use a good night sleep."

The offer was tempting. "I'm not gonna be able to sleep until I can smile in my son's eyes. But thanks for offering."

Clayton gave me a long look. "You remind me of my mother."

"You better be kidding."

"Yo chill. I just gave you a compliment," he said with a dangerously sexy smile.

"I can't tell."

"A real mother will die for her children. I see that in you. Your kids are your life. My mom was the same way."

"I brought them into this cruel world, and I always said the only person who has permission to take them out is me."

"My mom used to say the same thing." He chuckled.

"Is she still around?"

He stopped laughing, then leaned back on the seat. I noticed he had put the car in Park and didn't seem in any rush to leave. "Nah, she passed away two years ago."

"I'm so sorry."

"She had a good life. I made sure of that. She just decided she wanted to do some cosmetic surgery that a doctor tried to convince her not to do and she ended up having a heart attack on the table."

"Oh, that's terrible!"

"I guarantee my mother is up in heaven saying 'well, at least I died with a perfect set of tits.'"

Was he joking? I sure in the hell wasn't sure and I didn't know if I should laugh. But when Clayton chuckled I broke a smile and caught myself giggling along with him.

"My mother had been a special woman just like you. She'd had a mouth on her. Cuss like a sailor."

Playfully I slugged him in the chest. "And you're always

talking about me."

"Because I couldn't get my mother to stop no matter how much I complained. Her response was always, 'Son I'm grown.'"

"Sounds like the two of you were close."

He sighed. "Yeah, we were very close."

Clayton leaned over and the next thing I knew we were kissing. And I was holding on to him as if I didn't ever want this moment to end and reality to set in again.

"Here." I looked down as he put a card in my hand.

"That's the key to my room. If you change your mind, come on over and slip under the covers with me. If not, just come on by in the morning to shower and change. Either way, my casa is your casa." He placed another key in my hand.

"What's that?"

Clayton smirked. "A rental parked on the top level of the garage. I thought you might need one."

I was grinning like a damn fool. "That's mighty nice of you."

He winked. "For you, I think I would be willing to do just about anything."

"I like the sound of that." It was nice to know that even at my age I still had that whip appeal. What was even better, I hadn't given him the goodies in nine years, and yet Clayton was still willing to do just about anything.

I kissed him once more, then went back inside the hospital. Soledad was camped out in the waiting room.

"Go home," I told her.

"Renee, I—"

"Soledad, go home before I go off on your crusty ass! If anything happens I will give you a call. Only one of us can be in his room, so there's no point in you spending the night on this hard-ass couch."

"But—"

I held up a hand, silencing her. "Listen, you hanging out here every single night, waiting for my son to get better is starting to get on my damn nerves." I didn't give a damn that I sounded mean. I was tired of Soledad hanging around and Mario mean-mugging her every morning when he arrived to find her there.

"Okay, I understand. I just need to see him and let him know 'I'm sorry.'"

"Trust me, he knows you didn't know. Hell, if his ass hadn't been so fucked up on that wet shit he would have been able to tell you himself. Now go!"

I turned and went over to the phone and got buzzed into the unit and closed the door behind me. I made it to his room and over to Q, lying there peacefully breathing. His oxygen level had increased. His color was good and his body was warm. He was going to pull through. I could feel it in my heart. My son was going to make it.

"Q, they got him. Meechie got Dollar for you," I whispered against his cheek. "Your boy is a true soldier. Now I just need you to get better and then come home with me." I kissed his cheek and was certain Quinton had heard every word.

28
Danielle

"I can't believe they were shooting at the football game!" Shane cried incredulously.

"This town has gone to shit."

We had just pulled away from the curb. After all that shit went down, I had Shane come and pick me up and we went to Smoke & Fire to eat some barbecue. I loved their burnt ends.

"My daughter was down there, so I was freaking the fuck out but she was fine. Some guy got murdered. We think it was Dollar. That's the dude I was telling you about who shot my nephew." I explained as I leaned back on the seat.

"No shit!"

I nodded. "I know, right. I think his boy, Meechie decided to retaliate. Anyway, it was chaos by the time we finally got out of there."

Shane shook his hand. "Columbia is starting to be off the chain."

"Ain't that the truth." I still couldn't believe the type of evening I was having. First sneaking around at a doctor's house and then to a crime scene at the high school. It's crazy but stuff only happens like this when Renee's around. Of course, she didn't have shit to do with the shooting, but I think it's just that kind of vibe that crazy chick seemed to generate.

"You wanna go have a drink or something?" he asked as he stopped at the light. "That bar on Hwy 63 is open late."

I love when a man is thoughtful enough to ask. Unfortunately, hanging out with Shane suddenly felt more like a date than a fuck and that thought made me feel a little uneasy, because I wanted to keep things strictly about my business and sexual pleasure. Getting to know each other on any other level you ran the risk of feelings getting involved, and that was not where I was going with this.

We were heading east and I looked over at Tropical Liquors. With the kind of day I had been having, I was suddenly craving another Long Island iced tea.

"Hey turn over…" My voice trailed off at what I saw.

"Turn where?" Shane took his eyes away from the road and followed the direction of my voice. "What's wrong?"

I was sure the color had drained from my golden-brown face. "No the fuck he didn't." I heard of downright disrespect but this truly took the cake.

"Hey, babe, isn't that your husband?"

Not only was that Calvin going inside Tropical Liquors, but he was with Joiee.

"Oh snap! Is that the white girl you were talking about? She's fine as hell! Titties and a big Kardashian booty!" Shane was cracking up, but I personally didn't see anything funny. Those two were walking side-by-side, laughing and talking as if they didn't give a fuck who saw them together. That was not part of the deal! That thirsty bitch was staring up at him, and the smile on her face hinted to the whole damn town there was a helluva lot more shit going on than casual conversation.

Neither of them saw me riding by the bar with my head out the window, and that was a good thing. The last thing I wanted was for Calvin to think I was spying on him, or even worse, to think I was jealous. Because I wasn't. I was just pissed he was being open about his side chick, in public.

"Did you want to stop?"

"Hell no! Keep fucking driving!" I snapped.

"What's the fuck wrong with you?" He was laughing again.

"Nothing," I muttered. "I'm just anxious to spend some time with you." That was a weak lie, but with pussy on his mind he didn't seem to notice.

The entire ride I had all kinds of thoughts running through my head. When we got to Shane's place and went inside I was no longer in the mood for sex, but my car was still at the hospital. I was already there, so I might as well get the shit over with. Beside I'd be damned if I'd be sitting at home waiting on Calvin to return. Let him wonder where the hell I was at. But the longer I thought about it, I realized he would just think I was still at the hospital with Renee.

Damn.

"C'mon up so I can show you some of the upgrades I added to the site. I even finished creating an app that members can start downloading."

I followed him up to the loft, but stopped halfway up the stairs to shoot a quick text message.

I'll be home in the next hour

I hit Send, put my phone away and walked up to his desk.

Shane went on to explain the techno shit that I didn't care shit about. Hell, that's what I paid him for. Next weekend was a free offer for interested viewers to explore the site and meet members. After the three-day trial, they needed to sign up to fully utilize the services.

"Uh-huh...it looks great," I muttered impatiently. I was still thinking about seeing Calvin and that slut at the bar. What was worse, my husband had yet to hit me back.

"Hey, what's on your mind?"

"Nothing," I replied and forced a smile.

"You're lying." He gave me a devilish look, and I found myself focusing just on how sexy he was.

Shane came over and gave me a long, wet kiss that I must admit took my mind momentarily off Calvin. He took my hand and led me to his room and I didn't object. Maybe sex was just what I needed to get my head right.

He pulled my shirt over my head, while I unbuckled his jeans and lowered the zipper. As soon as he dropped his boxers, I went to work slobbering all over his dick.

"Damn, boo," he was moaning so loud I looked up at him staring down at me. I loved that lustful gaze that always seemed to take over whenever I gave him a blow job. I was all into it until he brought a hand down and grabbed a fistful of hair.

"Uh-uh. What I tell you?" Nothing made me stop faster than a man touching my hair. So much for that.

I rose and he tried to laugh it off, but I rolled my eyes.

With one push, he had me down on the bed and was yanking my jeans, followed by my panties down to my ankles. Shane went to town between my thighs. I heard my cell phone chime and a grin curled my lips. Calvin had responded and would be home when I got there. Knowing that he would be there waiting for me, I was able to clear my head and focus on what Shane was doing that had me moaning in every kind of way. This was what I had missed with Calvin. Other than penetration, there was nothing that beat having my pussy licked.

In a few short moments Shane had me gripping his head and calling out his name. He definitely had that head game to a science.

I dragged him up on top of me and grabbed hold of his dick and guided it where I needed to feel it most. Shane was pumping like he'd just been paroled, and I was his first taste of pussy. Those strokes were long, hard, and deep.

"Damn, girl, this shit is fire!" he moaned near my ear. That was one thing I liked about Shane. He knew how to express himself. Calvin used to do the same thing, but that was before we had limitations. He said it didn't matter, but I could tell that the level of enthusiasm was nowhere near what Shane was displaying.

It wasn't until after we were finished and lying there beside each other that a thought caused me to bolt upright on the bed.

"What's wrong?"

"I gotta get my ass home." I rolled over, grabbed my clothes and moved into the bathroom so I could take a quick shower before I had him take me to my car. I didn't want to go home smelling like soap, but I didn't want to smell like another nigga either.

I retrieved my cell phone, and I had been right. There was a message. It was from Calvin's phone, but the message wasn't from him.

Take your time. He's in good hands.

My heart started pounding all crazy. What in the world was that slut doing texting me from my husband's phone? By the time I was standing under the water, a scary thought had occurred.

I was going to lose my husband. There was no other way to explain it. The lack of excitement was a clear indication I had been losing him for some time. No wonder he had been so quick to jump on the "Becky bandwagon." "No he fucking didn't."

I had played right into his hands and gave him what he'd been yearning for. There was no other way to explain it.

I had been played.

* * *

I couldn't get home fast enough. When I pulled into my driveway, I noticed there was a gorgeous blue Lexus parked in front of my house. I also noticed lights were on in the master bedroom upstairs.

"No, the fuck he didn't," I muttered. I was too angry. I didn't even have time to put the car in the garage. I just kicked it in Park, ripped the keys from the ignition and jumped out. Carefully, I opened the side door, because I didn't want to give Calvin any warning I was coming into the house.

I went inside and drew in a long breath when I spotted Joiee in my house. Calvin was sitting on the couch beside her with that smug look on his face. That mothafucka was truly feeling himself.

He had the nerve to say, "Hey, baby."

"*Hey, baby*? What the fuck is going on in here?" I stepped in and slammed the door so hard, if it had been glass it would have shattered.

Stunned, he jumped up from the couch. "We were just sitting here talking."

"Talking? Is that what we call it now?" I eyed the Tropical Liquor cups that were sitting on my glass coffee table without coasters underneath.

Joiee crossed her legs and behaved totally oblivious to what was going on. "Your husband is sitting here telling me about the first time he laid eyes on you." She smirked her lips. "Love at first sight, huh? That's amazing!"

Her words caused me to pause. I looked from one to the other. "Did you text me from my husband's phone?"

She smiled and then even had the nerve to try and giggle.

"Oh yes. I just wanted to let you know that he and I were together, and there was no reason for you to rush."

"I didn't ask you…" I let my voice trail off. What in the world was she doing? There was no way in hell I was going to let them see just how jealous I felt, especially when I'd asked for this.

"Whatever. Y'all do you." I turned and moved upstairs to my bedroom. The first thing I did was walk over to our bed to inspect the sheets for wet stains. For his sake, the bed was just the way I had left it that morning. Unmade, with my hair scarf lying on top of my pillow.

I was kicking my shoes off when I heard a car door open. By the time Joiee was pulling off, Calvin was taking the stairs two at a time. Immediately, I pushed my feelings back and swirled around.

"Danny, baby, are you alright?"

I nodded my head and took a long shaky breath. "Yes, I'm so sorry. I shouldna reacted that way, but when I came home and saw her car in front of the house and the lights on in our bedroom… well, I jumped to conclusions."

He took my hand and led me over to the bed. Calvin lowered me onto his lap. "Baby, I don't know what the hell I was thinking bringing her to the house, but I swear she did not come up to our bedroom. I must have left it on when I ran upstairs to grab our wedding album."

I considered his eyes, and it only took a second to know he was telling the truth. His eyes didn't lie.

"We met for drinks at Tropical Liquors, but there were too many people there, and I decided we didn't need an audience to get to know each other, so I invited her back here to sit and talk."

"Well, I wished you had told me!" I snapped and then felt guilty. "But I'm sorry for overreacting. I really don't mind her coming over." Just as long as it wasn't in my bed. That way I could keep track of them.

"And, I'm sorry for that." Leaning forward, he kissed my cheeks. "You forgive me?"

"Of course, I do. I want you to have fun and enjoy yourself. Just not too much fun, okay?" I added with a grin.

"Never that." He laughed and then he kissed me long and hard. Next thing I knew we were like two wild animals, clawing at each other. We removed our clothes and were under the cover, kissing and suckling. Thank God, I had taken a shower before I had come home. It was crazy, but I was so fucking horny. Maybe it was seeing my husband with another woman, I don't know except I wanted him inside of me.

"Hurry, Calvin."

"Okay, hold up." And he was reaching over for a condom from the nightstand, and it ruined the moment because it reminded me that foil package would always be between us. He entered me with one push, and then he was moving at a feverish pace. I hadn't seen my husband this way in years. It was quick, hard, and explosive.

Damn, I had the best of both worlds.

Afterwards, we lay there together. "When are you going to see Joiee again?"

"Tomorrow evening."

I had a feeling he was going to say that. "I see how happy you are."

"I am. I didn't realize just how much I missed those things until now."

I sat up on the bed. "Miss what things?"

"Foreplay."

I practically jackknifed upright on the bed. "You've already had sex?"

"No, not yet, just foreplay."

All the air got sucked out of me momentarily at the mention of the two of them being intimate. "She's sucked your dick?"

The guilt on his face said it all. "Yes. But in the car, not in our home," he added in a rush.

I know I didn't have any right to be pissed off. But I was. Maybe because I didn't expect him to do it so soon. "Oh."

He sat up on the bed beside me. "I thought this was what you wanted?"

"It was. I mean it is. This is exactly what I wanted. Nothing means more to me than for my husband to be happy."

"I'm glad to hear you want me to be happy." He grinned.

"Remember, this was your idea. Just don't forget the only woman I love is you."

"Do you really mean that?" I asked, searching his eyes. No matter what, I had to stay number one.

"I do. I want you and only you," he said, stroking my cheek.

I kissed him, then searched his eyes with a false look of uncertainty. "I want what you have. That look you now have in your eyes. I want that, too."

He was kissing me on my neck, breathing in my scent as he said, "What can I do to make my wife happy?"

Before I realized it, I heard myself saying the words aloud, "I want sex and foreplay without boundaries as well."

Calvin drew back and gave me a long, hard look as if he was considering the possibility. Men can be so damn territorial. "What do you have in mind?"

"What if I was to find someone with the same status as me?"

"The same status? Like that online service you have? You're kidding, right?"

I shrugged. "It was just a thought. If someone had the same status I wouldn't have to worry about infecting someone."

He grew quiet.

I pouted. "Just forget it! It was just an idea, but I can see you're not feeling it, so don't worry about it." I kissed him and then rolled over. "I'm just glad you're happy."

I closed my eyes and he cuddled close, wrapping his arms around me.

"Tell me about your time with Joiee and what you enjoyed most tonight?" While he talked I lay there and pretended to listen with enthusiasm and interest. Eventually we both dropped off to sleep. It wasn't until the following morning that Calvin approached me while I was in the bathroom brushing my teeth.

"Hey, you got a minute?"

I rinsed out my mouth, then turned and looked his way. "Sure, what's up?"

"I thought about what you said last night and you're right, why should I be the only one having all the fun?"

It took everything I had to hold it together. "What are you

saying?"

"I'm saying if you want to find someone... then I'm okay with that."

His words practically broke my heart. Here it is. I wanted this, or better I thought I did, but I guess I expected him to be more resistant and not be so eager to agree. "Okay, well, I'm going to have to give it some more thought, but I appreciate you giving me the green light."

"It's only fair. I appreciate you giving me a gift."

"A gift?" I snapped and was ready to bite his head off. "Is that what you consider that chick to be, is a gift?"

"I guess I said that wrong."

"Then you better clean it up, because I am not gonna have my husband enjoying being with someone more than he enjoys being with me. If that's the case, we can end that right now."

I didn't like the look of momentary panic on his face. She sucked his dick and already he was ready for another round. "Not at all."

"Good." I leaned in and kissed him long and hard, then reached for the zipper on his pants and began to ease it down. "I think I need to remind you who's boss."

Twenty minutes later, he left for work and I was stepping out the shower. I purposely waited until he was gone before I pulled out my favorite gray dress. Then I paid close attention to my makeup and hair. I was meeting Shane for lunch and I wanted to make sure he couldn't keep his eyes off me.

You got what you wanted.

It was still hard to believe our relationship had come to this. Calvin with Joiee and me with Shane. It was nutty and not at all the way I'd planned my marriage to be. I had hoped to have been with one man for the rest of my life, and instead I was sleeping with two different men who satisfied different needs. I guess we must learn to play the cards that we're dealt.

I hurried inside the hotel, stopping at the desk to pick up the key he had left for me and then up to the room. Before I could turn the knob, it was flung open, and I was yanked inside into Shane's waiting arms.

"What took you so long?"

I grinned up at him. "I had a little delay this morning, but it's all good."

We were kissing and hugging and then I drew back. I didn't spend all that time looking beautiful for everything to be pulled off before he'd had a chance to truly appreciate it. Besides, after all the sex I had engaged in in the last twelve hours, I was starting to feel a little dirty.

I pushed away from him. "I'm hungry."

He pointed to the table. "Breakfast is ready, so let's sit and eat."

I sauntered over to the table and loved the way he stood there salivating with each step.

"Damn, your ass looks good in that dress."

That was exactly the response I had been hoping for. He took a seat across from me, and I reached for my breakfast with waffles, scrambled eggs, sausage and fresh fruit.

While we ate, I rubbed my toes along his legs.

"I got home to find my husband's new little white girl in my damn living room." I went on to tell him about the welcome wagon that had been waiting for me and the aftermath. "And guess what?"

He sipped his juice. "I'm listening."

"I spoke to Calvin this morning and he agreed to the arrangement."

Shane smirked. "Are you saying what I think you're saying?"

"I'm saying we won't have to sneak around for too much longer."

Smiling, Shane lifted me up off the floor and swung me around.

The only problem was now that I had what I wanted, I wasn't so sure it was what I really wanted after all.

29
Renee

I spent another night on the makeshift bed beside Quinton's, but this time I woke up with a damn crook in my neck. Mario walked in making way too much noise and pissed me off even more. I rolled over to find him and his wife walking into the room.

"Good morning." Rita was smiling and sounded way too damn chipper this early in the morning.

"Hey." I sat up on the chair and combed my fingers through my hair. Even just waking up, I was still cuter than her.

"Has the doctor been in yet?" Mario asked.

I shook my head. "Nope. Not yet. I'm gonna shower, so call me and let me know what he says."

He nodded and then Rita jumped in. "We will call you the moment he leaves," she assured me.

"Where's Tamara?"

Rita took a seat on a plastic chair. "Still sleeping. She was up most of the night on the phone talking to her friends about what happened."

My daughter probably had the shit posted all over Facebook.

"I left her the keys to my car, so when she wakes up she can come over." Her country ass was a bona-fide Susie Homemaker. Luckily my kids liked her.

As I made my way to the exit, I turned and signaled for Mario. "Let me holla at you for a moment." In other words, what I needed to say needed to be in private.

He followed me outside the room, and I waited until we had moved away from the nurses' station. "David confirmed that was Dollar who was killed last night."

He nodded and looked to make sure nobody was standing behind him before he said, "You think Meechie did it?"

"Yep." I nodded. "I saw him right before I found Tamara. He just gave me this look that pretty much told me he did it."

Mario shrugged. "Hey, that was good looking out. That's all I got to say."

"I have to agree." When it came to revenge, I was the master of an eye for an eye.

"I'm just wondering if there were any witnesses to that shit."

I shrugged. "I guess time will tell. I just hope it doesn't come back to point at Q."

"Exactly."

I had reached the door, so I pushed on it as I said, "I'll be back later. Call me if you need me."

I didn't stop walking until I had made it through the hospital and was relieved not to run into anyone. I stepped into the parking garage. When I reached the top, I chirped the remote and the lights of a brand new black Volvo winked at me.

"Oh, Clayton, what are you trying to do to me?" I murmured. He sure knew how to get my attention. In fact, I thought about him the entire fifteen-minute drive to the hotel.

I grabbed my Louis Vuitton bag out the trunk and rolled it up through the lobby like I owned the damn place. Some skinny chick had just returned to her post behind the desk when she spotted me.

"Good morning, can I help you?"

"No, you cannot," I answered and sauntered my ass through the lobby and over to the elevators. I had been at the Hilton enough times that I knew my way around.

I made it up to his suite and slid the key card into the slot. I could have knocked, but why? If Clayton had something to hide, then he shouldn't have given me access.

Unfortunately, he wasn't there when I entered the room. Probably for the best. I was feeling grimy and looking forward to a nice long, hot shower.

I stepped into his bathroom. It was large with a huge shower, double sinks, and a round, jetted tub. Within minutes, I was under the spray of the water thinking about everything that had happened the last few days since Quinton had been shot, and once again tried to connect the dots.

My son had been at my cousin's when he had received a phone call for a buy. He called Adrianna, Mario's side chick, and asked her for a ride a few blocks up the street to Burger King. And then she sat with him, talking in the parking lot until a black Escalade pulled into the parking lot. A woman had been behind the wheel of the car. Quinton climbed in back, and they pulled away. It was assumed that Dollar had also been in the SUV. He was dead, so there was no way anyone could question him. But that didn't mean I couldn't try and track down his girl.

I heard a door close and wiped the water from my face.

"Renee, you in here?"

I smiled at the sound of his voice. "Yes, I'm in here."

I opened the frosted shower door slightly, just as Clayton filled the doorway. He was wearing a Raiders' t-shirt that clung to his sweaty body and black sweat pants that hung low on his waist. Damn, he was fucking sexy.

"You came."

I was holding the door against my body so that all he could see of me was my head, neck, and shoulders. "I decided to take you up on your offer and come and steal some of your hot water."

He crossed his arms. "That's why I gave you the key. How's your son?"

I love the way he thought of someone other than himself. "He's stronger."

Clayton nodded.

"You been working out?" I asked and decided to take that time to stare him up and down.

"Yeah, I try to get in a two-mile run every morning. This old guy has got to keep his body in shape."

"I think you're doing a pretty good job."

He chuckled and I grinned, loving the sound, and the way his beautiful eyes lit up.

"Mind if I join you?" Something mischievous danced over his features.

He was already pulling the shirt over his head, so I don't know why he'd even bothered to ask. I watched him undress.

My brow rose. "You sure we should be showering together?"

"Yes, unless you have a problem with it?"

My eyes lowered down to his dick. It was waving at me. "No, not at all."

Clayton grinned. "Good." I moved out of the way to give him room, and he stepped inside. I noticed the way he was staring. He swallowed heavily.

"Damn, I forgot how beautiful you were."

I don't know how that was even possible, but I was just glad he noticed. I rubbed the bar of soap along his chest and then rubbed past his navel, but when I'd reached his groin, Clayton grabbed my hand and drew me toward him. We started kissing and rubbing all over each other. His touch had my body on fire, and I wanted him like I hadn't wanted a man in a long time.

"Hold on a moment," he whispered and then he was gone and back with a condom rolled over his erection. Clayton lifted me off my feet. "Wrap your legs around me."

I brought my hands to his waist, and he leaned me back against the shower wall. I wrapped my legs around his hips. Clayton positioned himself then guided his dick inside me. I sighed with pleasure the second I felt his warm flesh surrounding me.

"Ohhh," I moaned near his ear, driving him to deepen his thrusts.

"I like the way you feel," he whispered.

"Make me come," I begged. "I need to come!"

Clayton was stroking me again and again, and then he was pounding me so thoroughly with his dick until I practically lost it. Over and over, relentlessly, until an orgasm hit me so fast, I screamed and my body shook. He came with me. Laughing and completely spent, Clayton sagged back against the wall of the shower. He set me on my feet, and I leaned against him until my heart slowed.

"Now, that was worth the visit," I murmured, causing him to laugh some more.

I stepped back under the direct spray of the water, taking him with me, and we showered, soaping each other. We started kissing, and it wasn't long before he was hard again and carrying me out the shower and over to the bed. I couldn't think of a better way to start the morning.

I had fallen asleep in his arms. When I woke up, the clock on the nightstand read eleven o'clock.

"I better get back to the hospital."

"As much as I hate to see you leave, I understand," he murmured against my lips. "I'm going to run by and see my aunt this afternoon. Make sure you call me later."

I got dressed and headed down to the lobby and had just stepped off the elevator when I stopped. "No fucking way," I muttered then hurried my steps out the hotel's sliding doors. "Danielle!"

She swung around and you should have seen how big her eyes got. That little bitch! What the hell was she up to? Her hot ass was strutting out the hotel toward her car in a tight dress that stopped just below her ass.

"What are you doing in a hotel in the middle of the day?"

She had the nerve to look me up and down. "I should be asking you that."

I brought a hand to my hip. "I'm grown and single. I can fuck in a different room every day of the week if I wanted to. Now I asked your hot ass a question."

Danielle dropped her eyes briefly. "I met Shane for breakfast."

"You little slut!" I hissed and then started laughing. "You sure there wasn't some pussy on the menu this morning?"

"Whatever." She took a deep breath and rolled her eyes. "I talked to Calvin and he agreed to my proposition. But that's after I found his little white chick at my house."

I waved my hand. "Errr, okay, back that shit up! I don't have a clue what you're talking about, so start at the beginning."

"Get in." Danielle signaled for me to climb into her vehicle, and I took a seat in front and turned on the seat.

"Now start that shit over and don't leave nothing out."

She went on to tell me the hookup turned out to be white

and how yesterday she had come home to find that bitch lying on her couch like she'd financed the shit. The fact that Calvin was enjoying the arrangement a bit too much was an immediate red flag to me.

"Listen, I truly understand the hunt for some good dick, but Calvin is a good man. Do you really want to risk losing him just for the same orgasm you can get with some toys? Hell, call Kayla! I'm sure she'll give you the wholesale rate on whatever it is you want. It ain't like she's using the shit."

She laughed and was clearly taking this whole situation too lightly. "It's nothing serious. They're having fun. The same as me and Shane. It's just that now I can see Shane whenever I want without worrying about getting caught."

"I don't have a good feeling about this."

"Why? It's not like I'm sneaking around behind Calvin's back." Danielle was feeling herself a tad too much.

"Yes, but how do you know he isn't sneaking around behind your back? You said you came home and this chick was in your house. Fuck that! A bitch ain't coming in my house until I say she can."

Danielle looked over at me with skepticism. "Yeah, it did kinda piss me off."

"*Kinda*? Bitch please. That was straight disrespect on Calvin's part! I'm not tryna start anything, but there ain't no way in hell he should be bringing that bitch to your home."

She shrugged as if it were no big deal. "Calvin figured there was nothing to hide. He wants me to know when they're together."

This bitch sounded stupider by the second. Was this really my best friend sitting beside me? Because if it was, she hadn't learned shit from me over the years. "Be honest, Danny…how did you feel seeing your husband with that woman?"

Her face said it long before she did. "It was a little awkward."

"Girl, you're gonna mess around and that man is gonna decide he likes what she has a lot more than you," I said with a sigh.

Danielle had the nerve to laugh like I didn't know what the

fuck I was talking about. "You're being ridiculous. That's not gonna happen," she said, though her tone left me unconvinced.

"Yeah you keep thinking your shit don't stink." I could tell she didn't want to listen, but I wouldn't be much of a friend if I didn't at least try to talk her stupid ass into some sense. After that, if she still decided to continue with that bullshit, I had every right in the world to tell her, "I told you so, dumb ass."

"Have you forgotten you're HIV positive? Calvin married you and loves you despite that."

"So what? Now I owe his ass something?" she said defensively.

"Okay, maybe I didn't say that right," I said apologetically because I could see she was hurt by my response. Geesh, what is up with these sensitive ass people acting all brand new? I have never been one to pull back punches. Ain't shit about to change. "Your husband loves you despite your status. That's not easy to find. I just hope this Shane dude is worth taking that risk."

"I don't know. Ever since I found out I had HIV I just don't give a damn anymore. I don't know what's wrong with me."

"I don't know either. But, whatever it is, you need to figure it out quick and get that bitch away from your husband. Seriously, Danny, it's not a good move."

I could see from the look on her face she knew I was right. "I don't know if it's gonna be that easy. I already got Joiee involved in our life."

I shot Danielle a warning glance. "Well you better figure it out quick because I got a feeling this shit is going to backfire. My life should be proof positive you can't have your cake and eat it, too."

Her silence caused me to shake my head.

I put a hand on her shoulder. "I love you, girl, but I just can't let you go out like that. Fix that shit. Tell him you changed your mind. Tell Becky bye!"

"It's Joiee."

"Bitch, you know what I mean!" I got out the car, slammed the door and leaned inside the window. "Tell the white girl to go find her own Mandingo."

"Okay…okay…you're probably right." This time her voice shook when she spoke.

I was glad to hear that at least she was thinking about it.

"Call me later." I shot her a grin, then I waved goodbye and sauntered over to my rental. As I put the key into the lock, my cell phone rang and I looked down. It was Mario. Quickly, I answered it. "Hey, Mario. What did the doc—"

"Get your ass to the hospital, ASAP!"

30
Kayla

I was sitting in the living room waiting when Jermaine finally returned home. He must have expected me to be upstairs because as soon as he saw me sitting on the couch, he jumped. Good. He needed to be scared, although I'm certain he'd never be as frightened as I was.

"Sweetheart, what are you doing?"

"Waiting on you." I had my arms crossed at my chest and hoped he couldn't see that I was shaking. "I've been calling your phone, but haven't gotten an answer."

He slapped his forehead. "Yeah, about that. You're not going to believe this. I dropped my phone in the toilet."

"No, I don't believe it." That wiped the smirk from his lips. "In fact, I even tried calling your hotel room and got no answer." Jermaine looked confused or maybe he just wasn't used to me being so thorough. *Well guess what, I have girl friends who are!*

"Are you checking up on me now?" He had the nerve to crack a smile.

"I don't know, should I? Because apparently you see something wrong with me wanting to hear my husband's voice." *Didn't he understand, my heart hurt?*

"Not at all, but I told you I would be busy all weekend."

He tried to give me a look as if he was disappointed. He couldn't be anywhere near as disappointed as I was. I never thought I'd see the day my husband would lie to me.

"I ran into an old friend at the hospital who's now a recruiter for UMKC. He told me he was at the University of Kansas two weeks ago and guess what he was doing? Scouting out students at the science fair."

You should have seen the way his jaw dropped. I was so hurt I started crying. Lord, Jesus, please give me the strength. "Who were you with all weekend? I know you're having an affair." I blurted with major attitude.

"An affair?" Jermaine frowned up at me like I was the one who had done something wrong. "Why do you keep accusing me of that?"

"Because it's true!" It hurt me to nod. "At first I thought you were having an affair with Dr. Barbie. I was so adamant I went over to her house and made a fool of myself. Now I don't know how I'm going to hold up my head. I would be surprised if I still had a job."

"*You thought I was having an affair with Dr. Barbie?*" Jermaine had this incredulous look on his face.

"Yes, but it's Dean Fox she's sleeping with."

"Melinda is having an affair with the dean?" he gawked, then he dropped down on the couch. "What in the world…" His voice trailed off. I didn't know if his surprise was disgust or disappointment that Dr. Barbie hadn't chosen him instead.

"Do I even want to know what possessed you to go to her house?"

I shook my head. "No, it's not important."

Jermaine turned resting his elbows on his knees. "Sweetheart, what made you think I was having an affair?"

My eyes were watering and the last thing I wanted was to appear weak, but I have never been good at hiding my emotions. "We rarely make love. You don't seem to get aroused anymore. What else am I supposed to think?"

Jermaine slid over closer beside me. "I'm so sorry."

I searched his eyes. "How could you do that to me?"

He shook his head. "You got it all wrong."

"Then set things straight," I insisted with a sob.

"I made a big mess of things, didn't I?" He brought a hand to my chin and tilted my head so I had no choice but to look at him. I was sure I looked a mess. My eyes were all red and puffy. I had been so miserable I had given Asia permission to spend the weekend with her girlfriend, just so I could have the liberty of crying my eyes out without an audience.

"Kayla, honey, look at me."

I glared up at him.

"I'm sorry for all the pain I put you through."

"You already said that." Mentally I was counting to ten so I wouldn't go off or start crying again. "Do you have any idea how hard it's been for me, wondering why my husband doesn't want to have sex with me anymore?"

"I—"

"Wait! I'm not finished." I held up a hand silencing him. He'd made me wait this long, then he could do the same for me. "At first, I thought it was because I was fat, then I thought maybe it was my recent weight loss."

"No honey, I love you just the way you are."

Tears blurred my vision. "If that's the case, then why? Why wasn't I good enough, pretty enough, skinny enough?"

He cupped my chin. "Kayla, you are all those things."

I jerked away from his grasp. "If that is the truth, then tell me why are you having an affair?" I was damn near yelling at him.

Jermaine smirked and then I don't know what came over me. I reached for the lamp and slammed it down over his head.

"What the..."

"I'm tired of being used and abused! That's the way it's been my entire life... but no more!" I said bluntly, then got up and started toward the door.

"Where the hell do you think you're going?" he barked.

"Outta here!"

"Sit your ass down!" Jermaine caught my wrist and yanked me down onto the couch beside him. I was too stunned to reply. While he rubbed the top of his head, his eyes were large and blazing with anger. "Don't say a word until I finish."

Leaning back on the couch, I started to cry again. "Why? All you're doing is driving the blade deeper into my heart. Please, just spare me the apologies and just let me go." I went on and on until I noticed the blood trickling down his face.

"Oh my God! You're bleeding!" My eyes widened with

alarm. He didn't try to stop me as I scrambled to get a towel from the kitchen. I came back and pressed it gingerly to his head. *Lawd*! I'd already been arrested for attempted murder once in my life. I didn't want to go through that again.

"I'm sorry. I didn't mean to hit you so hard," I explained as I applied pressure.

"Kayla..., I'm not having an affair," Calvin said and looked so sad. "The only woman I want to spend my life with is you."

"So why—"

He pressed a finger to my lips, then removed my hand from his head and brought it down onto his lap. I stared and waited until he finally said, "I have prostate cancer."

My jaw dropped. "What? When?"

"I found out a few months ago."

My whole body seemed to deflate and the tears started again. "And you're just telling me now?"

"I didn't want to worry you."

I wagged a finger in his face. "I'm your wife. I'm supposed to be worried about you!"

"I just didn't know how to tell you. I wanted to get a second opinion first."

"And did you?" My heart was suddenly beating too fast. This man had my head spinning.

He nodded. "I lied to you. I didn't go to a recruitment fair. I went to one of those private cancer treatment centers for a second opinion." I didn't know if I should be mad or overjoyed. The stricken look on his face put a halt on my celebration. "They confirmed Dr. Horsham's diagnosis."

I hugged him close and was so afraid of letting him go. Not my husband. Not this amazing man who had brought so much joy into my life.

"We are going to fight this." I couldn't bear it if he said no.

Jermaine nodded. "I'm going to see my physician again on Monday to look at my options."

"Then I'm going with you." Jermaine squeezed my hand and for the first time I saw fear.

31
Danielle

I had already been thinking that maybe the whole "you got yours and I got mine was a bad idea." But, if Renee wants to take all the credit and think she's responsible for my uncertainty, then so be it. I knew after last night that messing around with Shane had pretty much run its course. Things just weren't as exciting at it had been in the beginning. It had never been about more than sex, but I guess seeing my husband with someone else just shined a different light on the situation at hand. Instead of heading to the center, I decided to go by the university police department and see Calvin. Parking on campus was always a bitch, so it took me awhile to find a meter saving me from having to go to the parking garage.

I strutted in and remembered I was wearing my husband's favorite dress and probably smelling like another man even though I had made sure to shower.

The receptionist waved at me and I stopped long enough to look at new pictures of her grandbaby before I was able to escape and headed toward my husband's office. Captain Calvin Cambridge. My lips curved with pride. Last year he had been promoted, and I had been right there by his side. I knocked once and then pushed the door open.

What I saw was like an arrow to my heart. "What the hell?"

Joiee was sitting on the end of my husband's desk with her legs crossed like she was the queen bee. As soon as Calvin saw me, he sprung up from his chair. His eyes were like a deer caught in headlights.

"Hey, babe."

"*Hey, babe?* What the fuck is this wench doing here?"

"I beg your pardon?" she blurted out in disbelief.

"You heard me." I got all up in her face and almost laughed at the way Joiee leaped off the desk. "Get the hell outta here!"

She wasted no time grabbing her purse and headed toward the door. "Calvin, I'll call you later."

"If you do, I will come after you and yank every hair outta your head!" I called and slammed the door behind her.

"Danielle, what the hell?" Calvin was glaring at me. "I'm confused. I thought this was okay with you?"

"It is. I mean it was…but I changed my mind." I sputtered like an idiot.

"What?" His eyes narrowed. "What changed since yesterday?"

"I no longer think it's a good idea."

"So, you're saying you don't want me seeing Joiee no more?"

Don't you know this mothafucka had the nerve to look upset? I decided that was my fault. A woman should have never dangled an opportunity for new pussy in front of her man's face.

"Yes, that's exactly what I'm saying. Is that a problem?" The truth was I loved my husband, and I was willing to do whatever it took.

He huffed a sigh. "No, there's no problem. This was your idea not mine, remember?"

"Yes, but after seeing her with you, I decided I didn't want anyone else touching my husband. You were right all along. It's not a good idea."

Calvin stared blankly at me before speaking. Maybe I had pushed him too far. I prayed I hadn't. "Okay. So now what?"

"Now we go back to what we had," I said, hoping that he agreed.

"Which is what, exactly?" he asked suspiciously.

I fluttered my eyelashes. "Marriage and commitment. Just you and me."

His eyes locked with mine, and I didn't like the uncertainty. "This morning you were interested in meeting someone on your dating site. Now you're not?"

"Hell, no. I just said that to see how you'd react." I was making this shit up as we spoke. "I was hoping when I'd said that you would have refused and I would have told you then how I felt. Only, you didn't bite. But after having breakfast with Renee, I decided I better hurry up and set the record straight... I don't want that wench anywhere near my husband."

He gave a skeptical look. "So, this bullshit is over then, right?"

"Yes, baby," I managed in a baby voice that always got a smile from him. Seeing the corner of his lip tipped upward confirmed that I had hit it on the nail.

"Okay. I don't want to hear any more about it, agreed?"

I nodded and then leaned over and wrapped my arms around his solid frame.

Calvin gave me a kiss, then glanced down at his watch. "Look sweetheart I have a meeting downtown. How about we go to dinner tonight?"

"That sounds wonderful."

I waited and walked out with him and I noticed the entire time his cell phone was buzzing in his pocket.

"Are you going to answer that?"

"Nah. I'm with my wife," he emphasized. "Whoever is calling me can wait."

That probably would have sounded good to someone else, but not me. When you run game, you know when it's standing right in front of you.

We walked out onto the parking lot. I waited until my husband pulled off and reached inside my purse for my phone. It took no time to scroll through my phone history. I blocked my number before making the call.

"Hello?"

"This is Danielle," I told her. "Your services are no long needed."

I expected Joiee to be caught off guard. What I wasn't expecting was the eerie laughter.

"Really? Does your Calvin also feel that way?"

No this wench didn't. "Of course, he does."

"Hmmm, that's funny because that's not the impression I got

when he called and asked me to come over to his office. Matter of fact, he sounded excited about the two of us spending more time together."

I listened in stunned silence. Instantly, I wanted to cuss her out, but there was no way I was going to let her know her words had gotten to me. "That's neither here nor there. We don't need you now."

"What about Shane? Does he know his services are no longer needed?"

My heart churned. How in the world did she know about Shane? And then it hit me as I remembered her coming into the bathroom while I had been on the phone with him.

"What about him?" I said as if it were no big deal.

"I would hate for Calvin to find out about you and him," she stately flatly.

My head was spinning with possibilities, but I would never let her know that. "Not that it's any of your business, but there's no Shane and me."

I could tell by her chuckle she didn't believe me. "Whatever you say."

"Just stay the hell away from my husband."

"I can do that. The question is can your husband stay away from me?" Joiee had the nerve to laugh in my ear.

"I don't think that will be a problem." I forced my voice to sound confident.

"Maybe. Although…the way he was begging to lick my cunt again… the problem won't be me, it will be him."

"What the—"

The phone went dead.

Lick her cunt? I swallowed as my head began to swirl. She was lying. I was certain of it. Joiee was just pissed off because I ended things before he'd gotten a taste. There was no way what she had said was true. When I had walked in on them both at my house and again in his office, both times they'd been fully dressed.

"Lying slut," I muttered under my breath.

I put my car in Drive and moved out onto the street. Reaching down I turned up the radio hoping the sound of

Future and Rihanna singing *Selfish* would take my mind off what Joiee said, but instead all I could see was Calvin down on his knees, between her thighs and his lips sucking hungrily at her clit. I tried to hold back the tears, but I couldn't. I had sent my husband into the hands of another woman and I had no one to blame but myself.

Angrily, I reached down for my phone to call him. But I didn't have a chance to call because my phone vibrated. I reached down and looked at the text message on my screen.

Get yo ass to the hospital.

32
Renee

I rushed to the hospital, and almost had an accident trying to get there. Everyone was moving too slow. When I neared the hospital, I made a quick right, running through a red light and drove sixty-miles an hour up the hill. Within seconds, I parked my car in the emergency lot and rushed through the lobby sprinting, yelling "Get out the way!"

I didn't even bother waiting for the elevator. Instead I took the stairs two at a time, hurrying up five floors. As soon as the nurse buzzed me in, I rushed down to my son's room and I almost passed out when I found him sitting up on the bed.

"Q!" I rushed into the room and pushed passed Rita to get close enough to kiss him. His eyes lit up with happiness at seeing me.

"Slow down. He's still out of it," Mario complained.

"Be quiet and mind your damn business." I rolled my eyes. "Hey, baby. How are you feeling?"

Quinton blinked his eyes and cupped his neck with his hand. My stomach churned with fear. "What the hell is wrong with my son? Why can't he speak?" *Lord, I know I said please give me my baby back but I meant in one piece.*

"I was trying to tell you, he can't speak yet. It's because he had that feeding tube down his throat."

I released a sigh of relief. "Oh, thank God."

"He'd just came out from under anesthesia, so he's going to be a little out of it."

"What happened after I was gone? I thought you promised to call me when the doctor came in." I barked. You better believe I had attitude.

"His doctor felt he was strong enough to start waking him up, so he ordered the nurses to discontinue whatever it was that kept him asleep," Mario explained.

"He's right," Rita chimed in. "I was getting ready to call you, but the next thing I knew Quinton's eyes were open and he was staring at us."

I was feeling some kinda way because I wanted my face to be the first one my son had seen. The fact that it had been this crooked-wig-wearing chick had me slightly salty. One thing I never liked, sharing was my kids.

Ignoring them, I focused my attention on my son. He was slumped on the bed and looked like a stroke victim, not my charismatic son. "Q, how are you feeling?"

He shook his head, indicating he wasn't feeling that good.

"Save your strength. There's no need to rush," I explained. "Mama ain't going nowhere."

Rita was tucking the covers in around him. "The nurse just gave him something for pain, so he'll probably fall back to sleep."

"Oh, okay." Well, that explained it. "I'm just glad to see those beautiful eyes again." I had every intention of questioning him, but now was not the time. Right now, I was just thankful for God bringing my son back to the living.

"Well, we're gonna go and get something to eat. We'll be back later." Mario walked over and kissed Q's forehead. "Love you, son. I'll be back." He looked like he was ready to break down. I sure the hell hoped not. I would also lose it if he did.

I took Quinton's hand in mine and had a seat. Tamara came into the room, wearing a college sweatshirt and jeans.

"Hey, Q, Daddy said you were awake!" She walked over to the bed, looking almost afraid to see him.

I gave her a sober look. "Yeah, he's a little out of it, so he's fading in and out."

"I'm just glad he's going to be okay." There was a sob in her voice. I looked away before I started crying myself.

"How'd you sleep?" I asked after I had gotten myself together.

She took the seat on the chair beside me. "I tossed and turned for a bit. I still can't believe Meechie killed that boy."

"Hush, girl. You can't be talking like that!" I scolded. "There's no telling if the police got this room bugged." I gave her a firm look, because she should know better than that.

"My bad."

I noticed Quinton was wailing around in the bed, his eyes all wide and agitated.

"What's wrong?" I asked and then it hit me. "Oh damn! He heard you mention Meechie's name.' Quinton nodded his head in confirmation. "Meechie is fine so don't you worry about all that. We'll talk later." I needed to assure him, but he was still moving restlessly. Quinton grabbed my arm like he was trying to tell me something, but a small Asian nurse walked into the room, interrupting.

"I see someone is up and about," she said with a warm smile.

"Yes, but he seems a little agitated," I told her.

"We figured as much, considering all he has gone through. Let me give him another push of Demerol and he should be sleep shortly."

Quinton looked at me with this look of panic. I reached up and rubbed his cheek soothingly. "It's gonna be okay. You're safe and have nothing to worry about. Not on my watch."

* * *

I called Soledad to let her know Quinton was awake and she practically shattered my eardrum. I left permission for her to go up and see him while I was gone.

Tamara and I went to the mall while he slept. She needed a new coat before heading back to school, and then we headed to Old Navy so she could get a couple of sweaters. I never cared much for their clothes, so I hung out in front while she shopped. Clayton texted and I decided to call him instead.

"Hey, you." He sounded happy to hear from me. That made me feel all warm inside.

"Guess what?" I said.

"What?"

"My son's awake!" I squealed.

I heard the sigh of relief in his voice. "Oh, baby... that's great news."

I just loved the way he called me that.

Tears were clouding my eyes, but I was laughing. "Yeah, it's pretty exciting."

"Have you had a chance to talk to him about what happened?" Clayton asked.

"No, his voice is raw from that tube in his throat, and he's still on painkillers. I hope to speak with him once he's ready."

"Well, all that matter is that he's okay. Maybe now you can get some rest."

"Yes, but only if I get to spend time with you before you leave." Clayton was planning to head back home the day after tomorrow. Tamara was leaving in the morning. After that I wanted to spend as much time with him as I could.

"I'm going to have dinner with one of my cousin's this evening. She's making me a pot of black-eyed peas and ham, but you got the key. I'll see you tonight."

My stomach fluttered with anticipation. "I'll be there." I ended the call then went to find my daughter.

Tamara and I finished our shopping, then I dropped her off with one of her girlfriends. They were going to see a movie. When I made it back to the hospital, Soledad was coming out the ICU with her eyes red. My heart began to pound.

"What's wrong?"

She shook her head, then threw her arms into the air. "Nothing. Everything is right! Praise the Lord!"

I rolled my eyes and brushed past her. I should have fucked her dumb ass up for scaring me like that.

"He's awake," she called after me.

"Yeah, okay," I mumbled and didn't even bother to look her way until I had picked up the phone and called the desk. By then I saw a big, handsome six-foot-five presence come up behind Soledad. Meechie's eyes met mine. Goodness! I was staring into the eyes of a killer.

"May I help you?" The voice on the other end of the phone startled me. I had almost forgotten I had called the ICU.

"Renee Moore to see my son, Quinton."

She buzzed and I signaled with my hand for Meechie to join me.

I walked him back to the room so he could see Quinton for himself. I could have let him meet with him alone, but part of me just had this feeling I needed to be there to make sure Quinton wanted to see Meechie since he couldn't speak for himself.

As soon as he saw us walk into his room, his eyes lit up with recognition. Meechie reached out and gave him a fist bump.

Quinton had this look on his face like he wanted to say something. I turned to Meechie. "He probably wants you to confirm about Dollar."

He moved forward. "He's history, man."

I nodded. "Now I don't have to worry about you trying to get back out in them streets, trying to get the guy who shot you."

Quinton looked puzzled, then started frantically shaking his head and doing a writing motion with his hand.

"You want to write something?" I asked.

He nodded.

I looked around for a sheet of paper and found a small pad near the phone. I grabbed a pen from my purse, then reached for a bible to steady it and held it up so Q could write. It took some effort, but he finally wrote one word.

No.

"No?" I glanced up at Meechie who looked equally confused.

"No what?" Meechie asked, then stood stone-faced and quiet while he waited for an answer.

Quinton was wailing around and started getting agitated. I leaned in closer and said, "Are you talking about Dollar?"

When he nodded, I suddenly had this uneasy feeling. I was afraid to ask, but I had to know the truth. We both did. "Q... did Dollar shoot you?"

When he shook his head, I almost collapsed.

Even Meechie sucked under his breath and mumbled, "What the fuck?"

I gave my son a puzzled look. "Quinton, listen to me... did

you just say Dollar didn't shoot you?"

He nodded impatiently and then confirmed it by scribbling, YES.

Holy shit!

"Then who did?"

He lifted the pen again and began writing. With his weak muscles, his penmanship was worse than mine had been after I'd been shot. I stared down at it and couldn't make it out. Meechie practically snatched the paper away.

"Turk did this to you?" he barked.

Quinton nodded.

Instantly, Meechie dropped the paper and practically bolted out the room.

"Q, I'll be right back," I said and raced after him. But by that time, he'd pushed open the door and stepped out into the waiting area. The door popped open like a small explosion and everyone stopped talking and turned to see what was going on. Danielle had arrived and she tried to get my attention, but I held up my hand and hurried down the hall after Meechie.

"Meechie, stop!" I ordered only he blew me off and continued his long strides down the hall. Someone was getting off the elevator. He stepped in, so I climbed aboard with him. I waited until the door was shut so we could speak in private. "Who the hell is Turk?"

His eyes locked on mine. "He runs the streets around here. Me and Quinton had a few run-ins with him because he said we were on his block and he wasn't having that. I told the nigga to do what it do."

All this war on the streets and who was King was aggravating. "So now what are you planning to do?"

"The same thing I had planned to do with Dollar. Smoke his mothafuckin' ass." He let out a disdainful laugh.

"Err! Pump your brakes. Did I just hear you say, *I had planned to do*? Wasn't that you who shot him at the game last night?"

Meechie frowned at me. "Nah, that wasn't me."

I stared blankly at him. Was he playing possum? I couldn't tell. "I saw you at the game. Why did you give me that head nod?" I imitated the move.

"I was just confirming his ass was dead." He leaned in, all in my personal space, with eyes that suddenly looked so scary I reared back slightly as he continued. "Make no mistake, I had every intention of smoking that nigga, but someone got to him before me."

"Ain't this some shit," I said under my breath.

"But, don't worry. Turk… I got that shit handled."

Meechie got off the elevator, and I watched him storm across the hospital lobby until the elevator doors shut again.

33
Danielle

Something was wrong. I knew it the moment Renee came rushing out of the ICU chasing Meechie. The first thing that came to mind was something happened to Quinton. Maybe he'd coded and died, but then Renee would have been hysterical, instead of rushing out the door. Even though I was in a shitty-ass mood, I had come up earlier to see him right after she had texted to let me know he was awake and had even visited with him for a little while. He'd spent most of the time sleeping, so I thought now would have been a better time to come back.

I still hadn't had a chance to talk to Calvin about that disturbing conversation I'd had with Joiee. He had been on an interview board all afternoon. I had picked up my phone and started to text him, but then decided some things were better discussed in person. I wanted to see his eyes. It wouldn't take but a few moments to be able to decide if his ass was lying or not.

I walked down the hall toward the elevators and waited for Renee to return. The second she got off the elevator I could see something was wrong.

"Girl, you are scaring me. What the hell is going on?"

Renee started hyperventilating and I moved her over to a chair where she took a seat.

"This is some crazy shit that I couldn't even begin to write about in my book." Her voice cracked, like she was trying to hold back powerful emotions.

"What happened?" She was scaring me.

She heaved a deep sigh. Her words came out in a rush. "Well, for starters Dollar didn't shoot Q."

"What?" I wasn't sure if I had heard her right. "Dollar didn't do it?"

She shook her head. "No, it was some drug dealer named Turk."

"I've heard of him. Woman-beater that messes with Kim Stevens' youngest daughter. I think he's sent her to the hospital a few times with broken bones."

Renee shrugged. "I don't know him, but that's the name Q wrote on a sheet of paper."

"Damn girl. Then why did... Oh shit!" I gasped, and leaned in close and whispered, "Meechie killed that dude for nothing."

"That's the crazy part. Meechie said he didn't shoot Dollar. Someone else did."

I gave her a puzzled look. "But Tamara and Portia both saw him there."

She nodded. "Yeah, and I even saw him there. Meechie said he planned on it, but someone beat him to it."

"What the fuck! So who shot Dollar?"

Renee shook her head. "Hell if I know. Probably has nothing to do with Quinton, but it's just crazy because now everyone thinks that's the reason why Dollar was killed."

"Damn. So what about Turk?"

"Meechie is ready to retaliate. He went out of here with one thing on his mind and that's taking that nigga out."

It was my turn to shake my head. "This is crazy. As soon as Q is better, you need to get him the hell out of here because Meechie is about to start a war."

"You took the words right out of my mouth."

* * *

I hung around for a while, doing everything I could to keep Renee's spirits up, but it was hard to focus on being a good friend when you have your own problems to deal with.

Mario and Tamara arrived around dinner time. She was heading back to school in the morning and planned on spending the rest of the evening with Renee. I figured she was in good enough company me for me to leave her.

I headed home and stopped along the way for some barbecue. My husband loved *Smoke & Fire* so I decided to get some more burnt ends.

When I pulled up into the driveway, I pushed the remote for the garage and was instantly pissed.

Calvin wasn't home.

"Where the fuck is he at?" I muttered and pulled my car in sideways taking up both parking spaces. I knew it was a childish move, but right now I was in my feelings.

I grabbed the bag of food and went inside the house and immediately reached for my phone and tried calling him and got even angrier when he didn't answer. I tried again and called him everything but a child of God when I heard his voice mail message. I sent him a text.

Angrily, I moved through my spacious home past the living room, and as soon as I eyed the couch, I couldn't help but wonder if that was where she had given him the blow job, or even worse, he had eaten her pussy. I stormed over to it and caught myself inspecting the cushions for sex stains. You better believe I was going shopping for a new couch next week because I'd be damned if I ever sat on that shit again.

I went upstairs and decided to shower and change into something else. My eyes kept shifting back to the bed, and I remembered the light being on when I had come home that evening. Images started dancing before my eyes of the two of them getting their freak on in my bed. Calvin laying on his back and Joiee's head down between his legs, taking his dick deep inside her mouth. It wasn't supposed to have bothered me. But, just the thought of him eating her pink pussy ripped at my insides.

What in the world have I done?

Calvin wasn't at home and he wasn't answering my phone calls or text messages. Was he with Joiee? Something told me he probably was.

I marched over to the bed and immediately started ripping the sheets off the bed, including the pillow cases. One glance at the mattress pad and I ripped that away as well. Thank goodness it had been on the bed, otherwise I'd be buying new mattresses in the morning.

I probably looked like a mad woman hauling all that to the edge of the staircase and tossing it down to the bottom. I stormed back into the room and grabbed the comforter and pillows. I knew it was too much and yet I carried it anyway. When I reached the steps, I reared back and tossed it so hard my feet slipped out from underneath me and I went sliding down the stairs on my ass. I couldn't even stop my fall because I had gotten wrapped head to toe in the blanket like a mummy.

"Dammit!" I hit the hardwood floor with a hard thump. By the time I managed to unwrap myself and got up, I was boiling with rage. I stepped over the bedding and marched upstairs. Grabbing my cellular phone, I called a number in my history log.

"Hello?"

"Put my husband on the phone!" I barked.

"Excuse me?"

"Wench, you hear me! Where is Calvin?"

There was soft laughter before Joiee cooed, "What's wrong? Feeling paranoid?"

No she didn't. I wanted to reach through the phone and strangle her lily-white ass.

"Hold on a moment," she said and the next words out of her mouth caused my pulse to stall. "Hey Calvin... your wife is on the phone."

"What!" I shouted and then the tears started falling. I had been right all along. He was over Joiee's house. Kissing and holding her in his arms the way he held me. I could see it. "Put his ass on the phone now!" I screamed.

There was more laughter. "Danielle, like I said before, Calvin's in good hands," she taunted.

"Bitch, I will fuck you—"

The phone went dead.

"FUCK!" I screamed at the top of my lungs and called her back, but this time she didn't answer. I called her twice more and the phone went directly to voice mail, which meant she had turned it off.

I stormed through the house and went downstairs to the kitchen. As soon as I saw that barbecue, I picked it up and sent it flying across the kitchen. The secret sauce and chunks of smoked meat went flying all over the place. I didn't give a fuck. I just left it there.

He was with her. Calvin was in the arms of another woman. All I could see was images of the two of them together in every sexual position I knew first hand. The tears were falling again. It was my fault. I was the one who'd brought Joiee into his life. Not Calvin. Me. I thought him being with another woman would have been the answer so I could spend all the time I wanted with Shane. I was so determined to get what I wanted, it never once dawn on me that the two might actually be attracted to each other. Now they enjoyed spending time together so much, they were spending every moment they could together.

"Nooo!" I wailed.

I couldn't blame my husband. I mean what man would turn down the opportunity to sample some new pussy if he had his wife's blessings. But the second I spotted her and realized just how much she was interested in getting to know Calvin, I knew I had made a mistake. What in the world made me think I wouldn't have been jealous?

Once again, Renee had been right.

I wiped my eyes and grabbed the bedding and carried it outside and stuffed it inside two trashcans. As I went back inside, I heard my phone ring. It was Calvin. I guess Joiee got off his dick long enough for him to call me.

"Yes?"

There was a pause. "You called me." I didn't miss the attitude in his voice.

"That was over an hour ago." Now I had attitude.

"I told you I had interviews, then a board meeting I had to attend. What's with all of the missed calls and ignorant text messages?"

Being captain of a police department came with a lot of responsibilities, but it also allowed him the liberty to sneak out and goof around.

"Because I needed to talk to you. Where are you now?"

"I just packed up my stuff and getting ready to head home."

He must think I'm stupid. "So if I called you on your office phone you would answer?"

"Well I would have, if I was still there, but I'm already out in the parking lot."

I sucked my teeth. *Yeah right.* "You sure you ain't with Joiee?"

"What? Joiee?"

"Don't play dumb, Calvin! You were at her house. I heard you while I was on the phone with her." Okay, that was a stretch, but he didn't know that.

"What the hell are you talking about?"

"I'm talking about you and Joiee. She's sucking your dick and you're enjoying every second of it. I bet you have her teasing that vein right near the head, the same way you make me do."

There was silence. He didn't even bother to deny it.

"Tell me I'm wrong!"

There was more silence, and saying nothing was like a swift kick to my gut.

"Please say something, dammit!"

"Say what? That you're crazy. This whole thing was your idea. Not mine. I didn't even want to do it. Now you're acting like a damn lunatic."

"Because you said you would stop seeing her!"

"And what make you think that I haven't?"

Calvin was still seeing her. I could feel it. He could deny it all he wanted, but I knew. Even now I could hear Joiee laughing and making fun of me. She was getting a big kick out of my misery. I bet she was bouncing her perky boobs around the house, sticking her flat ass all in his face. What man could resist all that?

"Look, I'm headed home. We're supposed to go have dinner, remember? Let's just go and have a good time." From the tone of his voice I could tell I wasn't the only one who was no longer interested in that.

"No need. I picked up dinner. It's on the wall waiting for

you!" I ended the call and stormed upstairs. I would be sleeping in the guest room tonight because our mattress was going out on the curb.

34
Renee

"Hey, Mom," Quinton said softly when he spotted me walking into his room.

I made eye contact with Soledad and went around to the other side and took a seat on the chair beside him. "I see you're talking this morning. How are you feeling?"

"Better." His voice was low and raspy, but at least he was alive.

Soledad brushed the hair away from her face and looked over at me. "His doctor was by to see him. Says he's doing good."

"The bullet is still in my back, though," Quinton said like I didn't already know.

I nodded. "Yeah I know. It was safer to leave it than risk spinal injury by trying to remove it." My eyes narrowed because I wanted to make sure he knew I was serious. "Q, I hope you understand how lucky you are. Do you know you could be wearing a colostomy bag?" Or even worse, dead.

He nodded and his voice was low when he spoke. "Soledad told me."

Was she his mama now?

I looked over at her. "Can you excuse us? I need to talk to my son about something private?"

Quinton gave her a look and nodded his head in agreement. Ain't that some shit. I could care less if he agreed or not. Get the fuck out!

My eyes followed Soledad out his room, and I waited until she had walked past the glass before I lit into him.

"What the hell happened?"

"Huh?" he really looked confused.

"Don't huh me. I need to know how the hell you got shot!"

He swallowed and I could tell he was about to milk his inability to speak clearly to the max. "I was just riding."

I placed a hand to my knee. "I don't know why you think your mama is stupid. Do you have any idea the hell I've been going through these last few days, wondering if you were going to live or die? If I was gonna have to bury my first born?" My lip quivered, but I'd been damned if I allowed a single tear to fall for his dumb ass. "You put me through so much bullshit, and for what? Not a damn thing. So I'm gonna ask you again. What the hell happened?"

"Someone wanted to get some wet from me." He blew out a breath and tried to bat his eyelashes innocently. That shit was not going to work.

"And?" I glared at him. He was stalling and wasting my time. "You said Dollar didn't do it, so what happened after Adriana picked you up at Burger King?" His eyes grew round. "Oh yeah! I know all about you fucking around with your daddy's girl behind his back."

"I—"

I pointed my finger at him. "Boy, shut the hell up with your lies! I know you and what you like. I still don't understand your obsession for old pussy, but you could have at least left Mario's side bitch alone. Now get back to explaining."

He had that look on his face like he'd been caught in a lie. Like I said don't nobody know a boy better than his mama.

"Dollar's girl and mama wanted some wet, too, so I had Adriana drop me off at Burger King and they scooped me up. One of Turk's boys wanted to holla at me about something, so I told him to meet me there and he hopped in back with me." Quinton was starting to lose his voice and probably was also stalling. He reached over for his glass of water, and I tapped my foot impatiently while I waited for him to get it together.

"I thought he wanted to talk to me about working for Turk, but that nigga tried to rob me."

I sucked my teeth, but kept my mouth shut.

"I punched him in the face and tried to push him out the vehicle. He pulled out this little whack-ass gun and shot me."

"What I tell you about your mouth? Talk like that to them other old bitches, not me." I pointed my finger. "Now the other day you told Meechie Turk shot you."

"Well he did... he's the one who would have told that nigga to shoot me," he said as if it all made sense.

If I had a gun I would have shot his stupid ass again. "You are so dumb. Don't you know Meechie ran out of here yesterday, looking for Turk? Are you trying to get your friend killed?"

"Huh?" Here we go again.

"You heard me."

"What's going on in here?"

My eyes snapped up to see his father coming through the door. It was probably a good thing because I was ready to snatch his ass out that bed.

"You need to talk to your son because he's stuck on stupid right now."

Quinton sucked his teeth. "Why I gotta be stupid?"

"Because you fuck with your own product, meet customers in cars alone, sent your friend to do your dirty work and... oh yeah, you got shot!"

Mario was waving his hands. "Renee, keep it down."

"You don't tell me what to do either! This boy has been sniffing and smoking that shit too much because it's fucked with his brain."

"Mom's tripping."

I lost my composure. "Boy, you ain't seen tripping!" I sprung out of the chair and over to the bed. I was practically in the air when Mario caught me and dragged me.

"Whoa, whoa! Let's just calm down and figure this out."

I yanked free of his grasp and glared over at Quinton. His eyes were wide. He needed to be very afraid. Calming down wasn't at all what I wanted to do, but I rolled my eyes and let Mario take the lead. I explained to him what his dumb son had been up to and even threw in again the part about his side bitch picking Quinton up, hoping that would help him to see that he needed to be on my side with this. The muscle ticking at Mario's neck proved that I finally had his attention.

I lowered back on the chair. "How did you get to Soledad's shop?"

Quinton wouldn't even look at me. "When I saw he had a gun, I tried to jump out the car before he could shoot me. I started walking and didn't even know I had been shot."

This was crazier than any book I'd ever written and I've been known to write some wild shit.

"So now —" I broke off, narrowing my eyes. "Q, what's your plan after you get out of this place. You gonna try and get revenge?"

The corner of his mouth twitched, then he started batting his eyelashes the way he's been doing ever since he was a child. "No. I'm gonna move to Virginia with my mom."

"Now that's what I needed to hear." Maybe there was hope for his dumb ass after all.

***

I was so sick of Quinton and all his excuses. He still didn't know how to take accountability for any of his actions. I really don't know where I went wrong with that one.

I'd had enough for the moment and decided I was going to Cracker Barrel's for breakfast. I texted Nadine as soon as I climbed into the elevator to see if she had time to meet me.

Sorry, on my way to court.

Oh well. I was comfortable in my skin and didn't mind eating breakfast by myself. I would just spend the time outlining the next scene of my book. Now that I knew Quinton was going to be okay, I could go back to focusing my attention on my livelihood.

I made my way across the lobby toward the parking garage and a very unfamiliar female voice called out to me.

"Ms. Moore?"

I turned around and the moment I realized it was Laquela, Dollar's baby mama and my son's stalker, I frowned. She'd been showing up at the hospital almost every day until I told her not to come back.

"Can I see Q?" Her eyes shifted with uncertainty.

Enough was enough! "Little girl, come over here. Let me rap with you for a moment." Tossing a hand in the air, I signaled for her to follow me. I needed to know what the fuck was going on. I took a seat on one of the chairs in the hospital lobby and waited for her to do the same. She turned on the seat, hands in her laps and looked afraid of what I was about to say.

"I need you to start by telling me who you are?"

She looked confused. "Q and I are friends."

See, this is the shit I be talking about. "Really? Who's your baby daddy?"

Her eyes widened. She must have thought I didn't know. Don't ever underestimate me.

She started shaking her head. "I have nothing to do with that. He's my baby's daddy. That's it. My daughter doesn't even hardly know him."

Her eyes looked honest enough. I'd give her that. I've heard enough stories about deadbeat daddies that much rang true.

"Q and I have been friends since high school," she explained.

Okay, enough about the friendship. "What happened to my son?"

She looked confused as if I was accusing her of something and then shrugged. "I don't know what happened to him. Really, I don't. People were saying Dollar did it and next thing I know I heard he got shot."

I watched her clenching her hands and I reared back on the chair. "Do you know who shot Dollar?"

She did an agitated eye roll. "It could have been anyone. To be completely honest, if I had a gun, I woulda shot him a long time ago for the way he neglected his daughter. The last time I saw him, he'd asked me to bring Lydia by. When I pulled up, he and his uncle Kango were in a heated argument about him using his Mama's house as a trap house."

I had no idea what that was, but it sounded like another word for a drug house.

"They were clowning something fierce in the front of the house in broad daylight." She sucked her teeth. "I took my daughter and left. That was the last time I saw him."

"Do you know a man by the name of Turk?"

The fire in her eyes said she did. "Who doesn't know him? He's got most of the blocks in the hood on lockdown. Besides, he and Dollar couldn't stand each other." I could see she wanted to ask me a question, but decided not to push. I would let Quinton fill her in on the gossip.

"I swear to you I ain't got nothing to do with nothing. Me and Q are friends, that's all."

That part was probably true, but I could see it in Laquela's actions the last few days, she wanted more. But as long as he had a fetish for old bitches, she didn't have a chance.

"He's awake."

Her eyes lit up with excitement and then clouded with tears. "Can I see him... please?"

I nodded and shooed her away.

As I watched her hurry to the elevator, it was clear to me she was in love with his dumb ass. He was too caught up to realize she might be a good match for him. Loyalty and commitment was key.

I texted Mario so he'd allow Laquela to see Quinton and to give those two some privacy. This was one time if my ex-husband wanted to keep Soledad away, he would get no push back from me.

35
Nadine

I left the firm and went to pick up the twins from daycare. After what happened the last time, I made sure I left in plenty of time before the daycare closed. Jordan was still pissed about Turk showing up and ruining our dinner and I just didn't need any more drama. Surprisingly, she had been quiet the past two days. Probably because I had taken the money I had gotten from Turk and put it into my account and replenished the others as well. By temporarily getting us out of debt, I was able to keep her off my neck at least for now.

I pulled in front of the center. There were three cars ahead of me. Gloria was there in the yard with all the children. As the daycare student monitor, it was also her job to bring the children out to the parents' cars. And she took that shit seriously. If she didn't know you and you weren't on the approved list, it didn't matter if you were Jesus Christ, you weren't getting any kids under her watch. I appreciated her dedication, but I remember one time I was running late and Jordan had also been unavailable. I called to let the center know Kayla would be swinging by to pick up the twins.

"Is she on the list?" Gloria asked with attitude.

"No, that's why I'm calling, so you'd be aware."

"If she's not on the list, then the children cannot be released to her. That's the policy."

"But I'm all the way in Jefferson City. I can't get back in time!" I cried flabbergasted.

"If you want someone else to pick up your children, then you need to come in and fill out the required documents."

"*Did you not hear what I said*? If I could come in, then there would be no need for someone else to pick them up."

"I'm sorry, but that's the rules."

Liar. That chick didn't sound sorry at all. I was so pissed off I hung up on her. I practically had two car accidents speeding down the interstate, trying to pick them up. The next time I had a chance, I made a list of every possible person who might pick up my children, which ended up being a total of three people.

It was my turn to pull in front of the gate. Gloria came over to the car, smiling. I lowered the window on the passenger's side.

"Good afternoon, Mrs. Hill. You have two sleepyheads on your hands." Bunching up her fat face, Gloria frowned. "I don't think they got much sleep last night. Could be they went to bed with the television on."

"Not at all. My children are in bed by eight o'clock every night." I explained, not that it was any of her business. She had the audacity to look surprised. That's what she gets for thinking.

"Well, nevertheless, they'll be ready for bed early tonight." She clapped her hands. "Evan and Ava, come on you two!"

I followed her violet gaze over near the sandbox where my beautiful five-year-olds were sitting. When they noticed me, they slowly rose. Yep, they were sleepy. Evan was rubbing his eyes. Ava was whining and stumbling all over her feet. She was practically carrying them to the car. I jumped out and came around to open the door.

Gloria was frowning again. "You really should have stayed in the car?" The center preferred we stayed in our vehicles to ensure nothing slowed down the line. I was usually all about following the rules, but I didn't give a fuck today.

I scrunched up my nose. "It's faster if I help."

I guess she agreed because for once Gloria didn't bother to argue. I ignored the other mothers impatiently honking their horns.

"Mommy, I'm sleepy," Ava wailed.

"Me too!" Evan refused to be left out.

"Good, then you should be ready to eat, shower and go to bed." Jordan attended evening classes at Columbia College until nine. If I put them to sleep, I might have some quiet time to prepare for a case I had in the morning.

I got them strapped into their seats, then rushed around and climbed back in. I pulled away and had barely got around the corner when the kids were making way too much noise. I should have put one of their movies in the DVD player.

"Mommy, I'm hungry!" Ava announced.

"Me too," Evan mocked.

I decided I might as well stop and get them something to eat and keep them awake just a little bit longer so they would sleep through the night.

"How about Burger King?"

"Yay!" They sang in unison and were suddenly wide awake.

I headed over to the restaurant. Within minutes they'd gobbled down their food like two hungry puppies and slipped out of their shoes so they could play around in the jungle gym. The more they wore themselves out, the better for me.

While they played, I took a seat, reached for my phone and read some emails. I logged onto my bank account and was relieved to see there were still a little over two-grand in there. I'd had no intentions of depositing that money I had received from Turk, but it had become necessary. Now I was committed to getting the charges dropped. After that, I planned to part ways with him forever.

My phone buzzed, and I looked down and smiled when I saw it was Kayla.

"Hey, girl."

"How's your day going?" I asked, because Danielle had shared the details of Renee convincing them to head over and confront the woman she thought had been having an affair with Jermaine. I never understood how you can allow a woman who's had no luck with men to give anyone relationship advice.

"Nadine, I have to say. It's truly been a miraculous day. Q is awake."

"Oh shit! That's fabulous! That boy is so lucky."

"Luck ain't have nothing to do with it. That is truly a blessing from the Lord. After he gets out the hospital, it's about time Q dedicated his life and find him a good church."

I wasn't all the hung up on religion, but this was one time I had to agree. "Yes indeed."

I looked up and made sure I could still see those two running through the maze overhead. "I'll have to come see him tomorrow. Jordan has class and my kids are running on empty."

"I remember those days." I heard sadness in Kayla's voice that caused me to pause and put my own problems aside. I really hadn't been much of a friend lately.

"Is everything okay with you? Danny said something about you and Jermaine were having problems."

"We were or at least I thought we were. One problem solved, then another manifest." She drew a sigh. "I just praise the Lord for his blessings. We'll have to get to lunch later this week, and I will tell you all about it."

"It's a date. I'll give you a call tomorrow." I would have to pencil her in on my calendar.

"Alright girl. You keep your head up. It's not as bad as it seems."

I stilled and suddenly became suspicious. "What are you talking about?"

"Whatever it is that's bothering you. I can hear it in your voice. It's gonna be okay. I'm certain of it."

"I sure hope so." I wasn't sure how Kayla always knew when I needed to hear some words of inspiration, but her calling had come right on time. I needed to stop stressing because everything was eventually going to work itself out.

When we ended the call, my phone notified me I had a text message. I looked down at the screen and frowned.

I need to see you ASAP

Dammit. It was Turk. I was so damn tired of him. *You're not the boss of me.*

I can't. Got my kids

I should have known he was going to hit me right back.

Come to the casino or I'm coming to your house

My heartbeat palpitated. That was the last thing I needed.

Jordan would be home in a few hours and I couldn't take the risk of Turk showing up on my doorstep. But what scared me the most was, trying to figure out how the hell did he know where I lived?

I'll be there shortly

It was almost seven and getting dark outside.

"C'mon you two, it's time to go."

There was a bunch of whining and even Evan started crying, but I just helped them back into their shoes and out to the car. I figured if they cried on the way over there, they were bound to fall asleep, and I could have them knocked out for bedtime by the time we made it home.

I turned on the movie in the DVD player. *Finding Nemo* was their favorite, so they quickly quieted down. Whoever came up with having a DVD player in the car was God sent, because it was a great babysitter on a long ride.

I jumped onto the interstate and before we were outside the city limits, the twins had gotten very quiet and started to fall asleep. I didn't plan to be at the casino no longer than it took for Turk to come out into the parking lot and tell me what it was that was so important I needed to come and see him. After that I could take my children home to bed. They could take baths in the morning.

By the time I got to the casino, the parking lot was surprisingly empty. Probably because last Friday had been payday, so most folks had already gambled it away and was broke.

I reached inside my phone and dialed Turk's number.

"Speak."

"You asked me to come, so I came. I'm out in the parking lot." I didn't even try to hide my annoyance.

"Come inside."

"Can't. I told you, I got my kids." He acted as if he thought I had been lying.

"Well, I'm in the middle of a game, so I'll send my niece out to babysit."

"Bab—"

Turk ended the call before I could ask him if he'd lost his

damn mind if he thought I was going to leave my children with a stranger. Angrily, I pulled into a handicap parking space near the front of the lot and waited. The movie was still playing, but the twins were fast asleep. Ava was sleeping so hard, she was snoring.

I spotted a young woman, early twenties, strutting down the ramp, long fake ponytail bouncing. She was wearing pumps, leopard-print leggings and a gold blouse. I watched as she brought a phone to her ear and a few seconds later, mine rang. When I didn't recognize the number, I knew it had to be her.

"Yeah?"

"This is Kimmie." She gave an impatient huff. "Where are you? My uncle wants to see you."

I jumped out the car, not to wake my kids up, before I said, "I already told him I'm not going anywhere."

She spotted me, waved, then ended the call, but instead of turning away she continued heading my way. Was she fucking deaf?

"Didn't you hear what I said?" I said as she approached.

"Listen," she began and sucked her teeth. "I don't need no problems with my uncle. He asked me to sit our here with your kids while you ran in, so I'm going to sit here."

"Don't I know you?" I asked because she sure looked familiar.

She nodded. "I saw you this summer at the Johnson family reunion. You were there with Kenya's mama."

"Oh yeah." I breathed a sigh of relief. She was related to one of Kayla's cousins. That chick was related to almost every damn body.

I followed Kimmie's eyes to the rear.

"Oh, my goodness. I love *Finding Nemo*! Do you mind if I watch it while I wait? It probably won't take but a few minutes, but at least I can be entertained."

I hesitated, but my phone started ringing. It was Turk.

"Damn, what's taking you so long?"

"I already told you."

"And I told you I don't like to be left waiting. It won't take long. I need you to handle something for me. I don't trust anyone else with it."

I blew out a long breath because I knew what "handle something" meant. Kimmie was already leaning through the window softly singing the songs.

She waved her hand at me. "My uncle can be an ass, so just go. He's sitting at his table. I'll be right here when you get back."

I blew out a breath. What difference did it make? The twins weren't likely to wake up again until morning, and even then, it would be a struggle.

"Okay, I'll be right back. If they wake up, just tell them I went to pee and call me, but I doubt seriously they will."

"No problem. I'll call you if I have any problems."

"Okay." I reached for my purse from under the driver's seat, then headed toward the door of the casino. I was walking fast. The sooner I got this shit over with the better. I couldn't wait to say what I wanted to say to Turk, now that I was away from my children.

I hurried inside the casino, hoping to make it to his table and back out in record time, but the second I heard the sound of slot machines my heart started beating heavily and my palms began to itch. Damn, I had to get the fuck out of there fast.

It didn't take long for me to find Turk sitting at his favorite table.

"Yo! Nadine ova here!"

I rolled my eyes because he was so loud and ghetto at times. As I walked over, I saw the stacks of poker chips on the table before him.

Cards were on the table and the dealer had just opened a fresh deck of cards. I stood immobilized and unable to look away. The table was calling my name.

Nadine. Nadine.

My tongue was practically hanging out my mouth as I watched and counted cards. I think I held my breath until Turk's cards came up twenty-one.

He was card counting. He'd been doing it for years and was good at what he did. So, good that according to him several casinos had banned him from playing. Others were happy just as long as he spread the money around. Turk told me he'd learned to lose on occasions just to evade suspicions. In the meantime, I'd learned everything I could until I realized his steadiest flow of income was from distributing cocaine. By then, I was in so deep there was no escaping his reach.

He slid two stacks across the table. Over five-grand.

"Turk, I need to get back to my car."

He didn't even bother to look up as he said, "Why? I heard them youngsters are sleep."

Damn. Was Kimmie reporting back to him?

"Yes, but—"

"Take a seat," he ordered.

The guy sitting beside him had lost the last of his chips and got up. Cheddar, who had run up on my table at the restaurant, pulled out the chair for me. His eyes were telling me to sit my ass down.

Damn, what choice did I have?

I flopped down on the chair and sighed. At least they were asleep.

"Play awhile."

Before I could object, Turk slid over a mountain of chips in front of me. I stared down at them feeling that familiar yearning at my chest that I couldn't fight no matter how much I tried. Before I knew it, I was putting chips on the table and the dealer was placing cards down in front of me. As soon as I saw the face cards, the adrenaline started pumping through my veins.

After that, the cards kept coming and so did the chips. I was on a winning streak. What the hell! I hadn't been that lucky in forever and it felt so good. Shit! It was better than good. It was surreal. Slots machines were dinging behind me. People were laughing, crying out with excitement and I was so caught up in it.

At some point Turk lost over ten thousand dollars in chips. "Ain't this some shit?" he muttered, then pushed his chair back and rose.

"You done?" I asked incredulously. I'm used to seeing him playing for hours.

"Hell yeah. I've played long enough. A nigga is hungry."

I wasn't sure how long he had been at it before he'd called

me. Curious at what he was talking about, I looked down at my watch. The second I spotted the time, I jerked to my feet. "Oh shit!" I had been at the casino almost two hours. "I gotta get back to my kids." I tried to walk away, but Cheddar caught me by the arm.

"Where the hell you think you're going?"

"I gotta go, please!" I was practically pleading.

"Relax," Turk said. "Let me holla at you a sec."

Reluctantly, I followed him over to the side. "Look Turk, I've got to get up out of here." *Finding Nemo* had been long over.

He gave me that look, reminding me he didn't like to be questioned or talked back to. That explained the injuries to his baby mama's head.

"Yeah, no problem." He snapped his fingers and Cheddar came over and slipped the strap of a tote bag over my shoulder.

"What is this?" I asked although I already knew.

"I need you to clean that for me. Then you can hold on to it until I see you at my hearing."

I gave him a long stare and I could see he was daring me to refuse. How was it he had me by the balls? Or in my case, he had me by the nipples? For months, he had been giving me money he wanted me to deposit into my own personal account, because no one would think twice about it, just as long as it was in small increments.

"Can I please go now?"

As soon as he nodded, I dashed toward the door. My heart was practically in my throat I was moving so quickly, but then I remembered I was carrying a bag full of money and decided I better slow down before some off-duty police officer moonlighting as security decided to detain me.

I was passing the cashier's cage when I saw someone who made me stop mid stride and whip around.

"What the hell are you doing in here?"

Kimmie looked up from the slot machine where she was seated and glared over at me. "What are you talking about?"

"What the hell do you mean, what am I talking about?" I was ready to go off. "You're supposed to be watching my kids!"

"I was, until some woman went off on me." She rolled her

eyes like it was my fault she'd had some ghetto run-in.

"What the hell does that have to do with anything? *You just left my kids sleeping in the car?*" I said incredulously.

"Oh." She reached inside her back pocket and plucked my key into my hand. "Here you go. I moved it from handicap to the middle of the lot."

"With my kids sleeping in it? I can't believe you left them out in a parking lot alone!" I was screaming and ready to kick her ass.

She flinched. "What you take me for, some kinda dumb bitch?"

"I don't know. You're the one leaving kids sleeping in the car." I don't know why I was wasting my time. I needed to get out into the parking lot before someone saw them out there alone, unattended and called the police. "I swear to you if anything has happened to my kids I'm going to come back and kick your ass."

"You ain't going to do shit. I watched them just like you asked me to."

"Well if you were watching them, then why the hell are—" I drew a deep breath. "I don't know why I'm even wasting my breath. Let me get my ass outside and check on them." I turned away and had only gotten a few feet when Kimmie called after me.

"They ain't out there."

I whipped around. "What did you just say?"

Now her head was rolling. "I said they ain't out there. If you were listening you would have heard me when I said some woman came and went off."

I walked back over to her. "Hold up. What woman?"

"The woman who'd called your phone."

Quickly I patted my pockets and realized that I had left my phone in the car like a big dummy.

"You answered my phone?" I asked curiously.

"Yes, because I didn't want to disturb the kids."

I guess that made sense.

"She asked where you were and I told her, and when she asked about the kids, I told her, too."

My heart was pounding with panic. Jordan. Jordan must have gotten out of class early, called to find out where I was. I could just imagine Kimmie telling Jordan I was in the casino, while our children were out in the car with a stranger. My wife had wasted no time coming to get them.

I didn't need to hear anything else Kimmie had to say, instead I bolted out the building.

36
Renee

After the week I'd had, I was more than ready for a drink. Danielle sent a text that she and Kayla would be at El Maguey after work and for me to join them. The second Soledad got off and stepped into Quinton's room, I high-tailed it out of there. Only she caught me before I could reach the elevators.

"Renee, can you hold up!"

I swung around and tried my damndest to get rid of the attitude since she had been there for my son. It just wasn't easy when it came to simple-minded women.

"Q keeps asking about his *stuff*. What should I tell him?"

It took me a few seconds to figure out what she was talking about. Once I did, I spat impatiently, "Tell him you got rid of it because you thought the police was gonna come sniffing around."

I could tell she didn't like that answer. "He's going to be pissed."

"So, what? He'll get over it!" I shook my head. "Aren't you a grown-ass woman?"

"What?" I think she had a hard time believing I would talk to her that way.

"Q's still got breast milk on his breath and yet he's controlling yo ass. I just don't get it. Are you just that hard up for a man?" I shook my head at her.

She brought a hand to her hip. "What makes you think he controls me?"

"By that dumb-ass question you just asked me. He's lying in that hospital bed because *his father*, not you, got him here in time. Mario can't stand your ass and I'm too upset with Q to be mad at you. But after that question… I'm gonna be honest, I just don't think you're smart enough to know what was really going on."

Soledad took a deep shaky breath. "Why do you hate me so much?"

"I don't hate you, Soledad. It's women like you that disgust me." My stomach growled and I was dying for a drink. "Flush that shit down the toilet… tell him I did it … make your money if you have. I really don't give a fuck what you do just as long as Q don't get his hands on it." With that I boarded the elevator. I stared at the dumbfounded look on her face until the elevator doors closed.

By the time I made it to the parking garage, I had calmed down enough to drive like I had some sense. The last thing I needed was a speeding ticket.

Parking was almost impossible. I figured it must be due to the happy hour specials. I parked in the lot next door and sauntered over. I had changed into a black cowl neck sweater that hugged my curves and short high heel boots. I never leave home without my heels.

I walked inside and found Kayla sitting facing the door. She waved me over, and I started doing my Beyoncé walk like I owned the place. I was stopped a few times for a brief exchange here and there. That's the shit that happens when you come from a small place where everyone knew somebody you knew. I finally put that shit to an end, because everyone had a drink in their hand except me.

"Hey, girl!" Danielle turned to look up at me as I eased down onto the chair beside her.

"Where's Nadine?" I asked.

Kayla was the first to answer. "Jordan had class tonight, so she's got the twins."

I shook my head and signaled for the waiter. "I don't know how the hell she does it at her age."

"She said if Jordan gets home in time she'd come, but I doubt it." Kayla managed between sips.

"Why's that?" I hadn't had much time to spend with Nadine

since I'd arrived.

She started to answer but a young Mexican man came over to take my order.

"Senorita?" he said and waited, which meant his English was limited.

"*Una lime margarita por favor.*"

"*Pequeno?*" he asked.

"Hell no!" I barked. "Grande."

He nodded and left. My Spanish wasn't that good, but I knew how to speak the international language of alcohol.

"Okay, what were you saying?" I asked.

"I was saying I think there's trouble in paradise," Kayla admitted with concern.

"Why you say that?" I probably sounded like a parrot asking the same questions, but sometimes talking to Kayla was like plucking chin hairs, one painful tug at a time. Damn!

Danielle must have sensed my frustration and decided to move the conversation along. "Didn't you see the way she was acting the last time you were here at the casino?"

"You think she's gambling again?" I asked incredulously. After the shit that went down, I thought that was a distant memory.

"I'm afraid so." Kayla looked ready to cry.

"Damn."

A couple of years ago, Nadine had a habit that had been so bad, Jordan was ready to leave her. Cars repossessed, checks bouncing all over the place. She had practically pawned everything of value. "Now that you mention it, she was behaving a little out of control. But I thought she was in a gambler's support group like alcoholics anonymous?"

"She was, but I think after the twins got older she just stopped going."

Kayla shook her head. "Maybe I'll go and see her tomorrow. Anyway, how's my godson? I hear he's talking."

"And getting on my damn nerves," I muttered and rolled my eyes. "I'm already ready to tell him to 'shut the fuck up.'"

"Praise the Lord! I'm so glad he's back to the living. I'll be by to see for myself."

I reached for the chips and salsa. Like I said, I was hungry.

"He's still Q. I told him I'm going to kick his ass the minute he is up out of that bed," Danielle announced between sips.

"We all are," I told them but I could see they were just as relieved as I was. We had been close for a long time. Our kids growing up together. We went through all the growing pains of being a parent, so when one hurt, we all hurt. That's why our friendship was so solid. "These kids, I just don't fucking get it. They think they can do whatever they want without consequences. You would think after his ass got shot, he would be tryna get his life together. Instead, he's back to talking stupid."

"He'll learn one of these days."

Danielle gave Quinton way too much credit. "Uh-huh. I just hope it's before things get worse."

"I hope he realizes just how blessed he his. God definitely had his eye on him," Kayla said.

I nodded. "I told him next time God's gonna turn his back, but Q thinks he's invincible. Do you know this fool tried to jump out a moving car while tryna dodge that damn bullet?"

"What?" Danielle started laughing.

The waiter returned with my margarita. We ordered dinner and while I sipped and feasted on tortilla chips, I told them about the conversation I'd had with Quinton. "This big dummy jumped out, then walked five blocks. He was so high he had no idea he'd been shot."

Danielle muttered, "Damn, that must have been some good shit."

Kayla was also laughing, so I knew those two had been drinking long before I'd gotten there.

"It's like it's a big game to him."

"That's because that's how kids view life. They just don't realize how serious this shit is because we've made it too easy for them," Kayla commented with a weary sigh.

"He ain't a cat with nine lives," Danielle added with a finger in the air.

"I know that's right." I realized the mood was different than it had been the last few days, and I was happy about that. The heavy burden had been lifted.

"How's Asia holding up?"

Kayla's gray eyes locked with mine. "She's still a little shook, so I let her stay with her girlfriend for the weekend, hoping it would take her mind off what happened."

I leaned back on the chair and shook my head. "I still can't believe that dude is dead."

"What did Q say?" Kayla asked. I had her full attention.

"He said he didn't do it, some other dude set him up. Truck, Trey... or something crazy shit like that! This idiot told his boy Meechie, who hurried out the hospital ready for retaliation." I shook my head again. "When is it going to end?"

"Hopefully you can get Quinton out of here long before then," Kayla said between sips.

"I hope so, but as stupid as he was talking, there was no telling if that was gonna happen." I would give my life to protect my children, but I'll be damn if I'm going to die over stupidity. I was ready to change the subject. "Tell us what happened when Jermaine got home 'cause inquiring minds wanna know."

Kayla shrugged. "We talked. It's a big misunderstanding."

"I'm listening..."

"Uh-huh, we both are," Danielle chimed in. Her elbow was on the table, and she was leaning forward like she was sitting on the edge of her seat, literally.

Kayla looked as if she'd been dying to tell someone. "He has prostate cancer."

"What?" Danielle sucked in a long breath.

"Oh damn. I'm so sorry to hear that."

"He didn't want to tell me, so he lied and slipped off to see a specialist in Kansas City to get a second opinion."

Wow that was not what I had expected to hear. "Damn, that's original. If Jermaine's lying, that truly took a lot of time to come up with."

I felt Danielle's shoe tapping my leg. "Nae-Nae, shut up."

I held up on hands innocently. "I'm just saying that it has to be the truth, because there's no way someone could come up with a lie that good."

"Sometimes you can be so fucking insensitive," she mumbled.

I rolled my eyes at Danielle and steered my attention to Kayla. "What did the specialist say?"

She drew a shaky breath. "He confirmed what he'd already been told. He has cancer."

I shook her head. "I really am sorry to hear that. What's the next step?"

"Well, he can either have the surgery to remove his prostate or do chemo and radiation, but if he keeps his prostate, there's no guarantee it won't come back." Kayla drew a breath and I could see she was trying to hold back tears. "Jermaine is going to take some time and weigh his options."

"I'm so sorry. I'm going to be praying for both of you." I'm not the most affectionate individual, however, I brought a hand over and rubbed Kayla's arm soothingly. "I know cancer is no joke, but everything is going to be okay."

"I'm trying to hold onto hope." Kayla was staring at me with this look on her face, so I knew she was thinking about my big sister, Lisa, and the battle she'd lost with ovarian cancer.

"Don't even allow yourself to go there. Jermaine's gonna be just fine," I told her.

She was blinking away tears and smiled. "I'm just glad I finally know the truth. I just can't believe he tried to hide it from me, but I understand why he did."

Danielle chimed in. "I'm sure. As a man. That's a hard pill to swallow."

Kayla nodded. "Yes, but at least it explains his lack of activity. I thought it was me."

"I told you that man loved your high-yellow ass!"

She smirked at me. "Yes, he does and together we can get through anything with God on our side."

"Amen to that." I said and held up my drink in a toast.

"Just take it one day at a time. You know Calvin is the same way. In my current status, I'm too busy thinking about some thug passion, when I got a man who has been there with me through all the medication trials, throwing up and being sick. He has accepted me and my condition, and I took that shit for granted." Danielle shook her head. "I don't know what the hell is wrong with me?"

"I told your ass. Why mess that up for a side piece?"

Kayla gave Danielle a stern look. "I have no idea what you're talking about, but if it's what I think it is, you better make it right. Calvin is truly a good man."

I agreed. "I've said the same thing to her."

"That's hard to believe," Kayla added with a rude snort, and I couldn't do anything but laugh.

I used to be all about getting all that I could, as much as I liked, but I'd changed. I finally started to grow up. I just prayed it didn't take Quinton quite as long to get his shit together.

"Ooh!" Danielle managed as she swallowed a chip. "Did you see your boss today?"

Kayla shook her head. "No, I decided not to go in."

I was so focused on what she was about to say that I took a long sip. Of course, I got a damn brain freeze.

"Slow yo ass down!" Danielle laughed.

"Damn that shit hurt!" I moaned.

Our waiter arrived with our food when I felt Danielle nudging me on the arm. "Nae-Nae, don't look, but David just walked in."

I waited a moment, then looked over to my right and saw David slip into a booth in back, and he wasn't alone. "Who is that?"

"That's Sheryl, an underwriter at State Farm."

I should have known Kayla would know who she was.

"She's single, no kids."

Okay, I didn't ask for all that. "Hmmm," I guess David found someone."

"You better go get your man." Danielle's eyes were dancing with amusement.

"Girl, puhleeze." I said, however, I swung around on the chair to make sure he saw me. Of course, he did. David's eyes grew large and then he was heading our way. "Here he comes."

"Ugh," Kayla mumbled under her breath.

David looked handsome in a Ralph Lauren long sleeve polo and dark jeans. Timberlands were on his feet. "Good evening, ladies."

"Good evening," we replied in unison. He nodded at all of us, but his focus was on me.

"Renee, how's your son doing?"

"He's awake," I replied as if he didn't already know.

He grinned like he'd just won five dollars on a lottery scratch off. "That's good. I would like to come by tomorrow and speak with him."

I glanced over at Danielle before meeting his gaze again. "About what exactly?"

"C'mon now. About who shot him."

I took a bite of my quesadilla and shrugged. "Q said he doesn't know who shot him."

"And you believed him?" That mothafucka had the nerve to start laughing.

"Why wouldn't I? I don't think he has any reason to lie." I was about to grow a big Pinocchio nose.

I could tell David didn't believe a word of it, but who gave a fuck.

"I'll be up to see him tomorrow." He said it like I should be scared.

"Aren't you off duty?"

Danielle pointed to his table. "Yeah, don't keep your date waiting."

"I'll call you later tonight," he said softly and licked his lips.

"For what?" I wanted to make sure he knew I could care less. That brief stint we had was over. "I'll see you at the hospital."

As soon as he was gone, Kayla leaned in and said, "He needs to go sit down somewhere and leave Q alone."

"I can't believe he thinks we need to talk. I got a fine-ass man waiting at the hotel for me."

Kayla rolled her eyes and then bit into a chip.

"What?"

Even Danielle was shaking her head.

I tossed my hands in the air. "Okay, we all grown here. What's the problem?"

Danielle was the first to speak. "I can't believe you're seeing Clayton."

I shrugged. I didn't have shit to apologize for. "Why we keep having this conversation? He's funny, gorgeous, rich, and even better—he's single."

"Yeah, but he used to have a thing for Kayla." This wench turned up her nose like someone had just farted.

"Yeah, and I used to date Calvin, but that didn't stop you from fucking him, too." That shut her ass up. How you gonna call the kettle black when you're dark as tar?

Kayla wasn't interested in Clayton. I fucked him, not her. I'm still interested in him. "If you also have a problem with it Kayla, I wish you'd speak up."

"I'm happily married and wouldn't trade Jermaine for the world, so it doesn't matter."

"Good, then there shouldn't be a problem," I said with a rude snort. "I'll admit, what I did in Jamaica was wrong, but now... He's nice and I think if nothing else, he and I can be buddies."

"Fuck buddies," Danielle murmured.

"Ha-ha, nothing wrong with being friends with benefits," I replied with a saucy grin.

"Are you ever going to want more?" Danielle eyes said it all.

I shrugged. "Maybe someday." I took another sip through my straw and turned to Kayla. "Kayla seriously, if you have a problem with me and Clayton being friends, I wish you would just say so."

She gave me a smile that was as close to genuine as I was going to get. "No. If that's what you want to do, then I don't have a problem with it. Seriously, I don't. Danielle married your ex, so you never know, maybe you and Clayton might end up being more than friends."

I wasn't much of a betting woman. My experience on the blackjack table was proof of that, but I was a believer that anything was possible.

I hated to admit it to them but I hadn't felt this connected to a man in a long time, and that's what surprised me. I tried to tell myself it was just about sex, but that would have been a lie. There was something deeper going on. The problem was I wasn't in control of my emotions, or the future, if there was a future. And with all the uncertainties, it scared me.

By the time we finished our meal, I had a buzz and was more than ready to see Clayton. I said goodbye to them and called him once I climbed into my rental car. His deep voice instantly came through the phone and made my earlobe tingle.

"Hey, baby, you coming over?"

His words brought a smile to my lips. "I am, if you're up to company."

"I would love to see you. I need to head back home tomorrow, but tonight is all yours."

"That sounds wonderful." I was already shifting the car into Drive.

"Anything special you want to do? Do I need to run out and pick up anything?" he asked. Clayton was so kind and thoughtful.

"Nope. All I want is a pair of big arms holding me while I sleep."

"Baby, you got it." Clayton had me grinning like a damn fool.

"I'm on my way."

* * *

Clayton must have heard my heels crushing the carpet as I walked, because by the time I reached his suite, he had already swung the door open. His cheerful smile warmed my heart. I had forgotten just how good it feels.

"C'mon on in, beautiful."

I had to push the lump from my throat just to say, "Okay." I'd barely put my purse and keys down onto the coffee table when Clayton drew me to him and, hugged me.

"How's it feel, Mama, knowing yo baby is gonna be okay?" he whispered against my cheek.

Tears pushed to the surface that I tried to blink and laugh away. "I have never felt so relieved in my life." I didn't realize that shaky voice was mine.

Clayton took my hand, led me over to the couch and brought me down onto his lap. I lowered my head and rested my cheek against his chest as I told him about Quinton waking up and being able to talk to him again.

"Clay, I had never been so scared in my life, although, to be honest, I never really believed I was coming here to plan a funeral. Q is too selfish for that crap. He's a fighter, just like me, so I knew he would go out kicking and screaming. He's just stupid."

"All men are at that age. Hell, I was a college football star and nobody could tell me nothing. Even the coaches were sick of me, but I was just that good that they had no choice but to tolerate me, and I knew it. By the time I'd gone pro, it had gotten even worse. Drinking, partying, women and bullshit."

I had to give him the side-eye. "That's not the Clayton I met in Jamaica."

"That's because by then I had changed." When he inhaled Ma long breath I knew it was going to be something big. "I was so caught up with that life, I forgot my roots and where I had come from. My grandmother had raised me in the church, and yet I couldn't remember the last time I had been in one." There was another brief pause. "I had promised my grandmother I would come home for Mother's Day and take her to church. My dumb ass went out partying the night before and was so hung over I slept through my alarm. Grams got tired of waiting. She didn't drive, never did. My mom and aunts had already left for church, so she decided to just walk the six blocks. By the time I woke up from my drunken stupor, my coach and the police were at my door. There had been some kinda retaliation, and Grams just happened to walk past a drug house just as it was being shot up in a drive-by."

I sucked in a long breath. "I'm so sorry." My arms tightened around him.

"If I had been there to pick her up, she would still be alive." He sighed. "It took me a long time to get over her death, and that's when I decided I needed to change and became celibate."

"What made you change your mind again?"

"Grams came to me in a dream one night and told me I had punished myself long enough, and it was time to move on with my life. Since then I've been living a life I'm sure she would be proud of."

I snuggled closer to him as I said, "Grandmothers are special like that. I loved mine. She had been the closest thing I'd ever had to a mother, since I haven't seen that crackhead in years."

"Your mom's a crackhead?"

I took a moment to carefully choose my words. I'd been calling her a crackhead for so long, I often forgot that wasn't completely true. "She's bipolar, but when you mix the wrong drugs with mental illness, you end up with a hot mess and that's her. I searched everywhere for my mother and even thought I'd found her a few years back, but after a while I just gave up." I shifted slightly on his lap. "That's why I try to be the best damn parent I can be for my kids. I might not be Joan Cleaver, but Tamara and Q can't ever say I haven't been there for them."

"If they don't know now, they will someday realize just how good they got it."

"I hope so. I try to show my grandson what it's like to have a strong woman in his life, because I wanted him to grow up wanting the same. I did the same with Q, but I just don't know if he gets it."

"I think he does. It's just hard at that age. You want to please your mom, but at the same time you want to prove you're a man who can make his own decisions."

I sucked my teeth. "He's just so stupid."

"We all are, but you can't tell a man that. Calling him stupid all the time cuts deep to the core."

"I know, and I know I shouldn't because it's belittling, but he just does dumb stuff."

"Now *that* sounds a lot better."

We laughed. It felt so good being here with him.

Clayton kissed me and his tongue slipped inside my mouth. He was such a great kisser. There was so much passion and patience, and even better there was confidence. He lay me back on the couch. Somewhere during the kissing on my stomach, he slipped my jeans and panties off with ease. And then his head was between my thighs and kissing and licking me so well, I was cussing and hissing with every stroke. This man was so skilled I just couldn't understand how he had managed to stay single for so long. Just knowing that heightened the moment. His fingers were pumping in and out of my coochie, and I was rocking my hips upward meeting both his tongue and hand. Both were driving me insane and yet it felt so good that I begged him not to stop. When I came, I wailed long and hard and released so much stress I started crying. Hard and long. Poor Clayton looked so stunned and yet he immediately scooped me into his arms and carried me to bed. For the rest of the night, he held me tightly in the circle of his large arms.

There was no doubt about it. Clayton was a keeper.

37
Kayla

I woke up to soft kisses between my thighs.

"Good morning, Mrs. Whitlow."

"Good morning, handsome."

I was still half asleep, but I couldn't think of a better way to be awakened in the morning.

"I was thinking…" Jermaine purposely allowed his voice to trail off which caused me to lift onto my elbows, and I caught the mischievous look on his face. "I was thinking we need to start to explore new ways to find pleasure in the bedroom."

"Really?" I purred. "What do you have in mind?"

It was then I spotted the dildo. It was the battery-powered one that had a clit stimulator on top.

"Where'd you get that?"

He chuckled. "In your supply closet. I also found quite a few other intriguing items." My husband held up a pair of handcuffs.

"You wouldn't?"

"Oh, but I would. Ma'am, you are under arrest." Before I could blink Jermaine had my wrists locked to the headboard and he was spreading my thighs. "Now I'm going to have to search you." He was back to kissing and licking me in ways that made me feel beautiful and loved. How could I have thought this man didn't love me?

I was wiggling around on the bed so much, I didn't even hear him turn the dildo on, but I felt it when he replaced his finger with the head of the device and pushed it slowly inside me.

"Oh," I sighed in pleasure.

"Let me know if I'm hurting you."

I don't think that was even possible. It felt good to be penetrated and licked and teased. He moved the device faster, then slid up on the bed beside me and started talking dirty in my ear.

"That feel good?"

I clutched the sheets. "Oh yes, baby. It's good!" I cried out and I was not lying. I don't know if it's because sex had been lacking or because Jermaine was now sucking my nipples.

"I'm coming! Baby...it's sooo good!" I came so loud and hard I didn't give a damn if my daughter heard us. She would just have to get over it. Mama was happy and in love. There was nothing about that to be ashamed of. By the time I showered and came down to the kitchen, Jermaine had already started breakfast.

"You didn't have to do that," I told him. Not that I was complaining.

"Yes, I did."

I rose on my toes and kissed him on the lips for being so thoughtful.

My husband carried two cups of coffee to the island and eased down onto the barstool. He was quiet and I sensed a changed in him. I could tell by the way Jermaine was avoiding eye contact, he wanted to say something.

I took a sip and swiveled my chair around to face him. "What's wrong?"

"I didn't sleep well last night."

"I couldn't tell," I replied with a saucy grin. Our night had been filled with foreplay. Chuckling, Jermaine pressed his lips against mine, tongues exploring, before he drew back and I noticed how serious he looked.

"What's wrong?" I repeated.

"I was up most of the night, thinking about what I should do."

I was just about to take a sip when I paused with the cup only inches from my lips and asked, "What did you decide?" I was practically holding my breath.

Jermaine took the cup out of my hand and sat it on the island.

"I decided I want you to make the decision."

I looked at him, cockeyed. Last night after I had left the restaurant, we made love, then stayed up late discussing his options. Now he was putting the decision as to how to treat his cancer in my hands. Chemotherapy followed by radiation treatment or removing his prostate, which meant he might never have an erection ever again.

"Sweetheart, you know how I feel. It's really about you, being able to still feel like a man."

Jermaine took my hands in his. "Feeling like a man has everything to do with the way his wife makes him feel."

I searched his eyes. "You're more man than I've ever had in my life, and sex does not define that. It's the way you always make me feel, whole and complete. You have my back and are the epitome of a good man." I shook my head. "Your penis does not define that."

He swallowed. "You mean that?"

I brought a hand up and stroked the side of his face. I've never seen him look so vulnerable before, and I wanted to do whatever I could to reassure him. "I support whatever decision you make. I don't care about erections. I care more about growing old and spending the rest of our lives together."

He released a swift breath as if he'd forgotten to breathe. "I'm glad you feel that way because I would like to have my prostate removed."

Tears filled my eyes and I nodded "Thank you Jesus! That's what I want, too." I wanted to eliminate any chances of his cancer coming back.

"I love you," Jermaine said and we kissed.

* * *

On my way to the medical school, I decided a triple hazel macchiato was in order. I was feeling positive about the future with my husband, but my professional life was still in jeopardy, thanks to Renee's crazy idea to rush over to Dr. Barbie's house. Therefore, I was in no rush to get to work. I placed my order, then moved over to stare out the window.

"Kayla?"

I swung around and drew in a breath. "Clayton. What are you doing here?"

"The same as you. Buying coffee."

"I guess that was a stupid question." He gave me a boyish grin that was so sexy, I immediately felt intimidated. It was one of the reasons why our relationship went no further than deep conversations. I never felt in his league or perfectly yoked the way I do with Jermaine. But back then, the main reason had been because of my low self-esteem and the mental hold Reverend Brown had over me.

Self-consciously, I combed my fingers through my hair. "I want to apologize for Friday night. I'm sure you probably think all of us are crazy."

Clayton shook his head. "No, actually I've never seen friends like the three of you. One was hurting and the others jumped to action." He smiled. "Friends who will drop everything to fight your battles with you... I got mad love for y'all."

I guess I never really thought about it that way. "Thank you. Danny and Renee are crazy, but I wouldn't trade them for anything." I smiled and noticed his beautiful brown eyes grow dark and serious.

"Everything good with you and your dude?"

I nodded. "It was a big misunderstanding."

He nodded and appeared pleased. "I'm glad you found your happiness. I could tell when I met you, you were in love, that's why I bailed out."

"And screwed my best friend." I didn't realize I had said the words aloud until I saw his eyes widen with amusement.

"Yeah... that was not a good look."

I gave a dismissive wave. "No, it wasn't, but it worked out for the best."

"Right. Look at you and dude now married and in love."

I wasn't dating Jermaine when I'd met Clayton but let Renee tell him that because I wasn't. I kicked myself every time I thought about the time I wasted with Reverend Leroy Brown. That bastard almost cost me twenty years to life, if it hadn't been for Renee's quest for revenge. I owed that reckless chick my life.

"A triple hazel macchiato is ready!"

I walked over and retrieved my drink. Clayton walked over to a table near the window and retrieved his drink. Instead of leaving and getting my behind to work, I walked over and asked, "What's up with you and my girl?"

He looked like he needed a moment to collect his thoughts, so I just sipped my drink and waited.

"You're okay talking about Renee?"

I shrugged. "If you're asking if I'm jealous, the answer is yes. Who's to say what would have happened if things had been different back then. You're handsome and successful. Anyone with her head screwed on right would want a gorgeous man like you in their life." I blushed. "But the heart wants what the heart wants, and we can't control who we fall in love with. Otherwise, I could have been interested in you." I winked and realized I was flirting again. Something I never would have done back then.

"Do you have a minute?" Clayton asked and gestured toward the chair beside me.

I looked at my watch. I was already running late, but who cared. I was already in hot water. It would just be one more reason to fire me. "Sure, I have a few minutes."

I eased down onto the chair and Clayton managed to lower his large frame onto the seat across from me.

"I would really like to ask you a few questions about Renee, if you don't mind?"

I took a sip, then nodded. "Sure, what would you like to know?" I folded my arms, suddenly feeling a little less intimidated by him.

"Is she looking for a relationship?"

I must have given him a weird look because he started laughing. "I can tell this is going to be good."

I leaned back and grinned. "Actually, it's not bad. My girl is a hot mess, but when Renee loves, she loves hard."

"I see that in the way she talks about her son."

"The same with her friends and the family she claims." I added with a roll of the eyes. "But when it comes to men, it's a totally different ball game."

He leaned in close. "How so?" Clayton put down his drink and suddenly was all ears.

"Well, she's…" I stopped and realized what I was about to say. Renee might get on my last nerve, but she was my girl and it was not my place to be sharing her personal business, or the tales of her three ex-husbands with every man who asked.

"She's ready to love the right man, when the right one comes along. Whoever that may be, he's going to be lucky to have her."

"That's good to here."

"She's gone through heartache and a lot of BS. Other people it breaks them, but with Renee, it's made her stronger."

Clayton smiled and seemed to appreciate my honesty. "I wish I'd had friends like you ladies."

"Ha-ha! Be careful what you wish for." I winked and then rose. It was time to face whatever was waiting for me at work. Where there's choices, there's consequences and it was time to face mine. "It was good seeing you again, Clayton. I hope to see you even more."

He shook my hand. "Thank you, Kayla. I really appreciate that. Maybe next time I'll get the pleasure of meeting your husband as well."

At the mention, a shiver passed through me as I thought about the road ahead for us. "Yes, you most certainly will."

***

"Lord, please, I don't ask you for much, but please help me get through this day."

I hurried across the parking lot and through the hospital lobby. I caught myself looking over my shoulder every couple of feet, hoping that I didn't run into Dean Fox or Dr. Barbie. I walked into the office using the side door. I was a chicken and decided to avoid the main entrance. I wanted to do everything in my power to evade my boss.

As soon as I was inside my office, I shut the door and was tempted to pull down the shade, but there was just no way of explaining that to anyone and it make sense. Maybe I'd get lucky and the dean had decided to take the day off. *Yeah, right.*

I walked over and removed a bottle of water from my mini-refrigerator. When I turned around, I screamed.

"Sorry, I didn't mean to scare you."

Dr. Barbie was standing inside my office.

"Well, you did." I pressed a shaky hand to my chest. I had hoped to have avoided this homewrecker at least half of the day.

"Again, I'm sorry."

I avoided eye contact and moved over to take a seat behind my desk. Black Barbie just stood there. I decided I might as well get this over with and asked, "Can I help you with something?"

"Mmmm-hmmm. I would like to ask a favor of you." I noticed she was fidgeting nervously with her hands. What in the world did she have to be embarrassed about?

Dr. Barbie closed the door and then walked across the room. Stopping, she leaned over the edge of my desk and this time her eyes were wide. "Dean Fox asked me to speak with you. Can you keep what you saw between the two of us?" I could have sworn she was pleading with me.

"Sure." I shrugged. "It's really none of my business."

Her shoulders relaxed with relief. "I appreciate that. He's doesn't want anyone to know about us yet."

"Yet?" Had I heard her right?

Black Barbie nodded. "Yes, not until after he asks his wife for a divorce."

"*A divorce?*" I'm sorry, but I started laughing. Lord, please forgive me.

"What's so funny?" she asked, clearly confused.

"You, if you really think he's going to leave his wife. They've been married thirty years."

"Why wouldn't he leave her?" She looked perplexed, and I immediately regretted the comment.

"Forget what I said."

She shook her head. "No, I don't want to forget. I want to know why you would say something like that."

She was standing over my desk with her hands on her hips and trying to appear demanding, but I noticed the familiar look of fear in her eyes. I had seen it many times in my mother's eyes after being used and abused by men. I had also seen that same look when staring in the mirror at myself.

"Can I speak freely?" I felt I probably needed to ask permission, just so she couldn't say, "Who asked you" when I was done.

"Yes, of course." There was uncertainty in her voice, but that didn't stop her from taking a seat across from my desk.

I folded my hands on the table and took a deep breath. "I was you once."

"What?" She scrunched her nose up as if to say, "How could you ever be anything like me?"

"I was in love with a man for years. He promised me the moon and the stars. But he also was married. I knew I deserved better, but I hoped that in time he would leave his wife."

She laughed. "He *is* going to leave wife."

I angled my head. "Yeah, so was Leroy and then there was one excuse after another and the months quickly became years."

"My relationship is different," she retorted defensively.

"Is it? How long as he been promising to leave?"

"Uhhh... not long." It was a lie and she knew I knew that.

"Any amount of time is too long. It took me a long time to realize I was getting used and deserved more than my ex could ever offer me."

"I think you're wrong about him."

I studied her expression and shrugged "I doesn't matter to me. I'm not sleeping with him, you are. The question is what does it matter to you? You're the one waiting and hoping. I don't get it. You're so beautiful and educated... don't you feel you deserve more?"

Dr. Barbie fell silent and I waited, sensing she wanted to say more. "I love him," she confessed softly. "And I'm willing to wait, no matter how long it takes."

"Then I wish you the best and hope you are one of the lucky ones." The moment turned silent and awkward. "Don't worry. What's going on between the two of you is your business, not that he'll believe me. I'll probably lose my job when Dean Fox gets here."

"Lose your job?" She frowned. "He isn't going to fire you. He's afraid that you've lost all respect for him and will quit."

I was flabbergasted.

"He knows you're irreplaceable and doesn't want this incident to come between the two of you."

"Wow! I had no idea he thought so highly of me."

"Well he does, and he will continue to as long as you continue to do a good job" Her brow rose. "And keep your mouth shut."

"No problem."

Her smile returned. "Well, I better get out of here. Ooh, before I leave, I would like to order another bottle of O. I sort of used that up." She was referring to the orgasmic lubricant.

"Already?" I laughed, and when I saw the unamused look on her face, I quickly sobered and nodded my head. "I'll put an order in this evening."

"Thank you, Kayla." She turned around and waved a hand over her head. "Have a nice day."

I sunk back in the chair with a sigh of relief. Everything was going to be alright.

Or so it seemed.

38
Danielle

Ever since I decided to end my relationship with Shane, I'd been avoiding his phone calls. But then he started blowing me up with text messages. It had started to get a bit overwhelming, that I decided things were getting out of control. If I didn't answer he'd be calling my phone when my husband was home and that wasn't going to happen. I decided to get it over with. It was time to end things with him before Calvin started to become suspicious.

I ain't gonna lie. My stomach was full of butterflies, especially when I pulled onto his street. I wasn't sure what I was going to say, but I knew there was just no more avoiding that. The problem was the last time I decided to confess what was on my heart to a man, it had been when I had discovered I had contracted HIV. I ended up getting my ass kicked.

I parked at the corner and walked down to his house. Shane worked from home, so he was expecting me. I knocked softly, then tugged on the military green dress I was rocking down over my hips. Just because I was ending the relationship doesn't mean I couldn't look good.

There were heavy footsteps and then the door swung open. "Hey, babe. C'mon in."

Dammit. Shane looked good in a white t-shirt and shorts. Thick, husky with wide shoulders and muscular calves. Images of the two of us having sex pushed through my mind that I quickly kicked to the curb. The same way I was about to do him.

I stepped inside and quickly explained. "I can't stay long. I just wanted to drop by and talk to you about something."

"I'm making lunch. C'mon back." He started toward the kitchen, then stopped, turned around and threw me over his shoulder the way he often did, letting me know he was in control. I couldn't resist laughing as he entered his kitchen.

"Something smells delicious."

He lowered me to my feet. I took a seat at the island and stared over at the wok he had with sautéed veggies and shrimp sizzling inside. Shane was a great cook. He'd made me lunch plenty of times before.

"I'm making stir fry. You want some?"

I met his eyes and he broke my concentration with a big smile. Why was it so easy for my mind to betray me? Shane was gorgeous, but I had to remind myself what I had at home just wasn't worth losing. I hadn't realized that at first. Calvin and I, sure, our relationship hadn't been instant attraction the way Shane's and I had. But all that was happening here was sexual attraction, therefore, I had to put a stop to it quickly. If I need wild kinky sex, I would just have to start flipping Calvin's ass over and riding him the way I needed to feel him.

"Shane, listen…, I have something I need to tell you."

While he poured the food onto a plate, his eyes met mine, dancing with excitement. "I have something to tell you, too. Your membership has skyrocketed."

"No shit?" I said, then cleared my throat. I had to stay focused before I ended up back in bed with him.

"I knew you'd blow up! The concept his hot. Hell, you and I are proof of that."

He was licking his lips and giving me that look. Why did my pussy tingle?

Stay strong bitch.

"By the way, you look sexy as hell today. You wear that outfit just for me?" He had walked around the island carrying a generous plate of food. He sat it down on the granite counter and reached down for my hands. His gaze was hot as it perused my body, heating everything in its path. Damn, why'd he have to be so fucking fine?

But I was not going to fall for his charm. I came here for a reason, and I was about to set things straight.

"Shane, I can't do this anymore."

"Do what?" He had the nerve to pretend like he didn't know what I was talking about.

"You and me. Us."

"What're you saying?" Okay, maybe he wasn't playing.

"I changed my mind. I'm married and I don't want to jeopardize it."

"You wasn't saying that the last few months." He laughed.

My heart lurched. "I know, but I'm saying it now." I lowered my voice softly, hoping it lightened the blow. "I'm sorry."

His eyes, dark and dangerous, locked with mine. "Why you tryna treat me like some random-ass nigga?"

I briskly shook my head. "That's not at all what I'm trying to do."

"Really, because that sure is the fuck what it seems like to me."

I lowered my gaze and couldn't even look him in the eyes because I was embarrassed. I had done a complete ninety degree turn in a week. "I'm sorry. I didn't try to hurt you." I explained and looked at him. "Please believe me."

His lips thinned. "Who said you hurt me?"

Okay, so maybe I really was full of myself to think he would be broken-hearted over me. "Oh, well good! Then we should be able to continue as strictly business partners." Okay, that had sounded ridiculous even to me.

"Business? You got me fucked up." His tone was cold and serious.

"I never said—"

"You don't decide when this relationship is over. I do that. And I'm not done with you yet." His voice was eerily calm.

"Why? I have a husband and want to focus on my marriage. Why can't you just respect that?" A desperate plea came tumbling out of my mouth.

"Respect? Since when have you shown your husband any respect? Not the way you've been rushing off to meet me."

He was standing so close I could see the stubble at his cheek. "Do you know I could leak your members to your site all over the Internet?"

My body stiffened. "You wouldn't dare. That's a security breach!"

"Really? I had no idea," he said with so much sarcasm I wanted to scratch his eyes out.

Bastard.

There was silence. I wanted to say, "Fuck you!" But, I was smart enough to know that was not a good idea, so I stayed quiet. Especially since he had control of my website, which was my livelihood. I didn't have passwords, e-commerce information, dammit, nothing. Shane had complete control, including the personal information of all the members of Positive Connections. If he wanted to, he could turn my life into a circus.

"What is it you want?"

He laughed. "What the fuck you think? You gonna keep bringing that pussy over to me until I say it's over. Otherwise, your site's goin' on blast."

Damn. I was screwed. Literally.

39
Nadine

I parked in the lot across from the courthouse, grabbed my briefcase and jumped out of the car. Drawing a long breath, I pulled the belt tightly around my black trench coat. It had been three days and I still hadn't heard a word from Jordan or seen my babies and I was miserable beyond words. My wife wouldn't return any of my calls. I had even gone by the daycare center hoping to see the kids and got turned away. I couldn't believe this shit. Our account and what money that had been left in the bank had already been wiped out.

What in the world had I done?

After the incident at the casino, I had rushed home with an excuse ready to explain why I'd left the kids in the car. I figured I'd tell her Kimmie was Kayla's cousin, who I knew, so technically I didn't leave them with a stranger while I rushed to see a client, who was in trouble.

Unfortunately, I didn't get a chance to explain, because once I got home the drawers were emptied and Jordan and the children were gone.

For days, she ignored my calls and after the fifth attempt, I called her great aunt's house and she answered.

"Baby, what's going on? Why aren't you at home?" I figured the smartest attempt was to pretend I had no idea why she'd left.

"Why in the world would I be home?" Her voice was so soft and calm, the hairs stood up on my back.

"Because I came home and you weren't there."

"Really? Do you really think I'm that stupid I don't know

what you're doing?"

"What are you talking about? All I know if I came out of the casino and the twins were gone. Why would you do that? They were with Kayla's cousin. One of my clients had a crisis. I had just run in for a moment, that's all."

"Seriously? And what was that exactly? Because when I came into the casino, I found you and that thug from the restaurant, sitting at the table laughing and having a good time."

Damn. I was busted, but still tried to lie my way out of it. "Like I told you, that was my client. He insisted I sit at the table while he explained."

"You must think I'm an idiot!" she seethed.

She had never sound so pissed and it caused me to suddenly feel extremely uneasy.

"Baby, it's the truth."

"No, the truth is I have tried to give you the benefit of the doubt. I got out of class early and called you, and when that chick answered I thought something bad had happened to you. But when she explained who she was, and told me where you were I had a feeling you were in trouble. I couldn't reach your sponsor, so I came rushing inside, intending to drag you away. Instead, I saw you laughing and having such a good time with no thoughts about our children outside with a woman they did not know. I was sickened by the sight."

"Jordan, I'm sorry. I should have refused to come there."

"Damn right! You took my babies to a fucking casino!"

I tried to comment, but she continued. "You left my babies with a stranger they've never seen before. Nadine, you're so addicted you don't give a shit what happens to our kids."

"That's not true. Baby I—"

"Liar!" Jordan screamed into the phone. "You put my children's lives at risk just for a gambling fix. You're no better than a junkie."

I cringed at the comparison. I was so screwed.

"I'm done, Nadine. I've been putting up with your habits for years. Money missing. Repo man. Checks bouncing. All while I made excuses for you. But no more. I am done."

"Jordan please! Just hear me out."

"Leave me the fuck alone. I'm serious, Nadine, otherwise I'm getting a restraining order." The tone of her voice told me to take her word for it.

I finally decided if I wanted a chance at getting my family back, then I needed to give Jordan her space, no matter how much it broke my heart.

I glanced down at my watch. It was almost ten o'clock. I was supposed to meet Turk in the courtyard before we went inside.

I spent the entire night preparing for his hearing, and I can't lie, I was sick to my stomach. The things he had done to his baby mama and then to his son, I just could not in good conscious represent him. And yet, I didn't have a choice. I had already made a deal with the devil that jeopardized my wife and my relationship with my kids. It was like a bad dream I couldn't wake up from, no matter how much I tried.

Realizing I'd wasted more than enough time, I walked across the length of the parking garage and out onto Walnut Street. To the left of the courthouse was a large white gazebo. I walked over and spotted Turk near a tree smoking a cigarette. He had for once listened to me and was dressed impeccably in a dark suit. Unfortunately, his dreadlocks were still a matted mess.

As soon as he spotted me, Turk tossed the cigarette and threw his hands in the air. "You made it."

"Of course, did you think I wasn't coming?"

"You never know with women. Y'all flaky-asses!" He had the nerve to laugh as if he'd just told a joke I would have found funny. "So what's the plan today, counselor? We gonna bring her crackhead past into play and show she's responsible for what happened, not me?"

Just thinking about what I was about to do made me sick to my stomach. "Yes, something like that."

"Good." He slapped his palms together. "And after you get this bullshit thrown out, I want you to file for full custody of my son. That bitch can kick rocks."

I nodded, then turned away in disgust. "I'll meet you inside." I couldn't get away from him fast enough. My legal career had officially gone to shit.

I had just reached the first step of the courthouse when I heard the unthinkable.

POW! POW! POW!

At the sound of gunshots, I stumbled and fell face first onto the pavement and then was scrambling to hide behind a bush. This couldn't be happening! There was screaming, shouting, and the rush of feet. I peeked out between the branches and spotted a man who looked vaguely familiar running away.

Lord, please let me survive this, and I swear I will get myself together.

It wasn't until I heard sirens drawing near and people running out of the building that I crawled out on my hands and knees. I was missing one high heel pump and my pantyhose had a hole in them. That didn't stop me from limping over to join the crowd, gathering near the gazebo. As soon as I managed to push my way through, there he was. Turk lying on the pavement with three holes in his chest. Oh my God! I took a deep breath and fell back to my knees.

By the time the police finished with the questions, my head was spinning. I limped inside to speak with the judge, and once I left his chambers, I made my way home in disbelief. What in the world had happened back there? I didn't know if it was drug-related or if it had been something else. The only thing I knew for sure was that the man I had seen running away, I had seen him before.

On bare feet, I hurried into my house and locked the door behind me. My hands were shaking, I was an emotional mess. I wished Jordan was there to hold and share what had happened. She'd always had a way of making me feel better. Quickly, I armed the security system, because I felt like whoever had murdered Turk was coming back to finish me off. It may be silly, but I decided to stick to the side of caution just to be safe. I went up to my bedroom and removed my clothes. I never did find my other shoe.

I hopped into the shower and felt like that was the only way I could rid myself of what had just happened. Only once under the spray of water, I started crying my ass off and realized I was relieved. He was dead! No longer did I have to deal with Turk and his wicked ways again. As I closed my eyes, I could see his baby mama's face as her attorney informed her he was dead. She turned and looked at me for confirmation. First there had been a look of horror, before relief had been all over her face. She was free of that monster and able to raise her child the way she needed to without him controlling her.

Thank you, Lord.

I'm sorry, but, regardless of how freaked out I was about seeing him lying on the ground with bullet holes in his chest, I did not feel bad about Turk's death. Someone else had done this city a favor.

I got out, dried off, went into the room and turned on the television and within minutes the report of the shooting was on.

This just in. A report of a shooting at the courthouse. The victim has been identified as Donte Marshall, known also as Turk. He had been scheduled to appear in family court for domestic violence. The shooter is still at large.

My heart was beating fast as the camera zoomed in on the area where his body had been lying. And when they shifted to the courthouse, something caught my attention that caused me to grab the remote and hit Rewind. As I moved to stand in front of the television, I hit Pause and leaned in to take a closer look near the steps of the courthouse.

There near the grass was my Vera Wang shoe.

40
Kayla

On my lunch break, I walked next door to the hospital to check on Quinton. He was progressing so well, he was being moved later to a step-down unit. Praise the Lord for hearing all our prayers! Danielle had stopped by Shakespeare's, and for once I decided to cheat my diet. She, Renee and I were all seated in the lobby eating pizza.

"I am so glad you didn't lose your job," Danielle said.

"Me, too," Renee managed between chews. "Although I never thought for a moment you would. If you had, I woulda broadcast that shit all across campus."

"I just bet you would." Danielle gave an exaggerated eye roll.

I licked my fingers and sighed. "I'm just glad things worked out the way they had."

"Hey, listen up!" shouted some tall blonde guy, who was seated in the waiting room, drawing everyone's attention toward the television. We all turned and looked at the screen. I jumped out the chair when I saw there had been a shooting at the courthouse.

This just in… there is a report of a shooting at the courthouse. The victim has been identified as Donte Marshall, known also as Turk. He had been scheduled to appear in family court today for domestic violence. The shooter is still at large.

"What the hell?" Danielle gasped. "You can't go anywhere anymore."

"Wait a minute… didn't Nadine say she was in court this

morning," I said, then noticed Renee was sitting there with her mouth wide open. "What's wrong?"

The pizza box fell to the floor as she grabbed our arms and led us out into the hallway, away from any listening ears.

"What's wrong?" I asked because Renee looked like she was hyperventilating.

"Remember when I told you Q woke up and said Dollar didn't do it?"

We both nodded.

"It was Turk."

I was confused. "Who is that?"

She gave her famous eye roll. "Weren't you listening? That's the guy who just got murdered!"

"What?" My eyes darted in every direction. This couldn't be happening. Not again. "You think his friend…"

Renee nodded and then whispered, "Meechie was there when Quinton told me who shot him."

My stomach started hurting so bad, I hugged myself and paced the hallway. "This has gotta be a bad dream."

"No, it's loud and in living color," Danielle muttered and shook her head.

"I'm calling Nadine right now." I whipped my phone out of my purse and called her number, but got her voicemail. I tried twice more and still the same. "She's not answering."

"She and Jordan are having problems. This is crazy. I'm texting her." Renee removed her phone, pressed a few buttons and spoke into the receiver. "Bitch, ignore us if you want to, but we're on our way over to your house. Don't have me kick the door in." With that she sent the text. "Quinton is resting, and Mario will be up shortly. C'mon. Let's take a ride and check on her."

"I'll drive," Danielle offered and we all hurried to the elevators and out to her car.

By the time we'd arrived at Nadine's house, it looked quiet. Her car wasn't in the driveway which meant she was either not there or it was in the garage. Danielle parked and we all climbed out. Renee walked right up to the door and started ringing the bell like a maniac.

"Renee, calm the fuck down!" Danielle hissed. "Quit acting a damn fool."

"Then she better bring her ass to the door," Renee spat as she continued to push on the bell.

I heard movement inside. The door finally flung open and Nadine glared at us. "Damn, I said I was coming."

"How the hell were we supposed to know that? We've been calling you ever since we left the hospital." Renee sucked her teeth, then pushed past her and we all followed inside. I loved Nadine's house. Bright and cheerful with toys scattered all over the place. I really needed to ask Jordan for some decorating tips.

"What's going on? We saw the news." Danielle looked concerned.

Nadine took a seat on the couch and we did the same.

She was cradling her head with her hand as she spoke. "I can't believe it. He was my client. I had just walked away from my client when he got shot."

"Oh, no!" I cried.

Nadine broke down and started crying. I was the first one up out of my seat and moved beside her to comfort her. Danielle followed. "I can't believe that happened!"

"Neither can I," I murmured soothingly.

"One minute that bastard was boasting about how I was going to help him get off from beating his baby mama, and the next his ass was dead." Nadine had a faraway gaze, as if picturing the incident all over again.

"Damn," Danielle muttered and rubbed her arm soothingly.

"The worst part is I am grateful to whoever did it. I mean I was just thinking if I had a gun I would have shot his ass, and then it's as if someone had read my mind."

"Wow!" I whispered.

The room grew quiet except for Nadine's heavy breathing.

"Turk shot Q," Renee announced breaking the silence.

Nadine's head shot up. "What? When—"

"Q told me Turk gave the order," she explained. I noticed how she was leaned back on the couch without a care in the world.

Nadine looked confused. "But I thought…"

"Dollar didn't have anything to do with it," Danielle interjected as she shook her head.

"Q's friend shot him for nothing?"

"Meechie didn't have anything to do with killing him," Danielle shot back.

Nadine's eyes darkened suspiciously. "And you believe him?"

Renee shrugged and added, "I don't know what to believe, but I bet you Meechie was the one who killed Turk." Her eyes darkened as she leaned forward on the couch and locked gazes with Nadine. "Did you get a chance to see who shot him?"

Nadine hesitated, then nodded. "I told the police no, but I did see someone familiar running away."

Danielle turned on the couch. "Do you know if it was Meechie? He was at the hospital a couple of times. Tall, big guy, dark skin."

"That could have been him, but I'm not sure. I just want to forget this ever happened," she told us with a weary sigh.

"But you saw his face, right?" Renee wasn't letting it go that easy.

"Yes... I guess."

I could tell the whole incident had been very upsetting for Nadine so I changed the subject. "Have you talked to Jordan?"

Nadine sadly shook her head. "No, she won't even let me see my kids."

"Wait a minute. What's going on? How can she stop you from seeing them?" Danielle had straight attitude.

"Because, technically those are *her* kids, not mine. We never signed all the documents to make me their legal guardian."

"You're a lawyer, right?"

Leave it to Renee to have something smart to say. I rolled my eyes at her. "Just leave her alone, you see she's already miserable enough as it is."

"Nadine, what's going on? Did Jordan leave you?" Danielle asked.

"What? What the fuck is really going on?" Renee chimed in.

I guess I was the only one who knew what was going on.

Nadine rose and walked around the room. "I have a

gambling problem."

"How bad a problem?"

She scowled at Danielle. "Bad enough that I've mortgaged our home and practically cleaned out our savings accounts."

"What the fuck?" Renee muttered along with a few obscenities.

"She got tired of it and when I left the kids in the car —"

"Wait, hold up!" Danielle waved her hands in the air. "You left Evan and Ava in the car? Where the fuck you do that at?"

"The casino," she admitted.

"Bitch, you're stuck on stupid!"

I hated to admit it, but for once I had to agree with Renee.

"I actually left them with Kimmie, she's related to you Kayla, right?" She turned to me for help.

I frowned. "Kimmie? She has a baby by my cousin. So *technically* she's not family."

"Damn." Nadine sounded so frustrated. "I know I have to get myself together quickly and get my family back."

"What are you planning on doing?" I asked.

"At this point I am willing to do whatever it takes." Nadine sounded as if her voice was about to break. "I'm planning to take my name off all of our accounts until I can get my habit under control. I just need to get Jordan to trust me. And know I'm sorry."

Renee sucked her teeth all loud and ghetto.

"I'm sure she will in time. That woman loves you," I assured her.

"I sure hope so. I don't know what I would do if I lost her. I have to make things right." She stopped walking and brought her eyes up to meet mine. They welled with tears again. "There's one other thing."

"What?"

Nadine gave us a long look. "I'll be right back." She turned and walked out the room.

41
Nadine

I walked back into the living room and placed the brown briefcase on the coffee table.

"What's that?"

Of course, Renee was the first one to ask. Instead of explaining, I unsnapped the latches and opened it.

"What the…" Renee jumped up from the couch and moved in closer. Danielle, too.

Kayla was the only one too afraid to move as she asked, "Where did you get that much money?"

"Turk gave it to me to clean." I'd never tell them he's given me a briefcase almost every month since I've known him.

"Oh my God! And now his ass is dead." Kayla wailed. She could be a little over the top with the goody-goody-two-shoes bullshit.

"Clean?" Renee sneered.

Danielle wagged her finger at me. "You know that's drug money, right?"

I shrugged. What did it matter now? "Some of it, I'm sure. But most of it is money he won at the casino last night."

"You saw him last night?" Kayla asked incredulously.

I nodded. "I had nothing else to do, so I met him there to discuss his defense."

"Bitch, I thought you said you were staying away from that place?"

"I said I was *trying* to get my shit together, but Turk was part of the problem." I went on to tell them how I got caught up with him in the first place. "The casino is where he liked to do business, which is where Jordan found the girls."

"This is just way too much drama!" Kayla tossed up her hands and I know she was probably about to start praying, which I had a feeling I was going to need some of that to get through the next few weeks. "What if someone comes looking for that money?"

"Didn't you just hear her say that money was won at the casino?" Renee snapped.

"She said *maybe*." Kayla groaned. "I have a bad feeling."

Danielle waved her hand, dismissing her concerns as she lowered back onto the couch. "What are you planning on doing with the money?"

Renee gave a rude snort. "Shit, it's her money! What she needs to do is give some of it to Jordan and make shit right."

Having mixed emotions, I replied, "I've been thinking about it and I'm going to get myself out of this hole I dug and make things right at home, but the rest of it I want to give to his baby's mama."

Danielle folded her arms and nodded. "That's mighty nice of you."

"I think that's exactly what the Lord would want," Kayla said, coming around a little. "Maybe receiving that briefcase was for a reason."

"I agree. I…" I cleared my throat and hesitated. "But I just don't trust myself with the money, so I need one of you to do it for me."

"Why?" Danielle asked.

"I was his lawyer. How would I look showing up with all this money?"

"Like he asked you to hold on to it. And in the event of his death, he wanted you to give it to her."

"Yes, I guess I never thought of it like that."

Renee held up several stacks of cash. "Why are you giving this to her?"

"The way that man beat and abused those two, it's the least he could do."

Kayla blew out a long breath. "Oh my God!"

"She's probably glad that nigga is dead," Renee said and

laughed.

"I know that's right." Danielle snatched the money from her hand and put it back in the case and closed it.

"Seriously, I don't trust myself with this money. I will end up at the casino if someone doesn't take it from me," I emphasized. "Tomorrow, I want to go down to the bank and deposit enough not to draw suspicion into Jordan's account and then send her money every week until all the money I had taken is paid off, including this second mortgage on my house."

Kayla waved her hand. "You sure this money is clean?"

I nodded. "I'm sure. I cleaned it myself."

Renee didn't look convinced. "Tell us how you do that."

"Easy. I cash it in for chips at the casino and then exchange them for cash at the end of the night. Some nights I lose more than I came in with, but it's the cost of doing business."

"Ain't that some shit," Renee muttered, but I could tell she was impressed.

Danielle cocked her head to the right, looking up at me. "How about you go rent a safety deposit box and just give Jordan the key. That way she can make sure the money goes where it needs to go."

"That's a good idea, Danny." I smiled. I knew my friends would come up with something.

"I can take you to the bank in the morning," Kayla suggested.

Renee played on her phone, then hurried over toward me. "Tell me if this is the guy who killed Turk."

I looked down at the screen. It was a Facebook post of Quinton and another guy. "Hmmm, I'm really not sure."

Her eyes narrowed. "Good, keep it that way. It sounds like his death was no loss. He not only had Quinton shot, but he was abusing his family. I say good riddance."

Danielle agreed. "Yeah girl, take that shit to your grave."

"I just hate that Dollar got murdered for nothing," Kayla said.

"Maybe there was some justice there as well," Renee said in a tone a little less indignant.

"Maybe," Kayla said, although she shook her head in shame.

Part of me was starting to feel the same way.

42
Danielle

After we left Nadine's house, I drove back to the hospital and pulled into the parking garage in front of Kayla's car. Renee started to climb out from the passenger's side when I reached out my hand and stopped her.

"Wait. I need to talk to you."

There must have been something in my voice that caused pause because Kayla got back in and stared at me. "What's going on?"

I wasn't ready to say anything to her, not yet. "I just wanna run something by Renee."

Kayla pointed a finger at me. "Uh-huh, I see that look in your eyes. You about to do something stupid."

"No, I'm not." Why couldn't she just get out my car?

"What's up?" Renee asked and was suddenly curious. The car grew quiet and since Kayla refused to get out, I put my vehicle in Park.

"Nae-Nae, I need your help."

"You know I got you. What do you need?"

That's one thing about Renee. She is always ready to come to your rescue. Kayla, on the other hand, had scrunched up her nose.

"If you're asking for Renee's help, then it must be something crazy!" she accused.

I swirled around on the seat so fast, Kayla drew back. "It can't be any crazier than you accusing a doctor of sleeping with your husband!"

That shut her up.

Renee tossed up a hand. "Kayla, either get out or shut the hell up." She looked at me. "Heifer, what is it you need?"

"Shane is ready to fuck me."

"Excuse me? I thought y'all were already fucking?"

"Who's Shane?"

I ignored Kayla and shifted on the seat. "I don't mean sexually. I mean with my website. He's pissed because I wanna end our relationship, so he's threatening to leak the names of my members and their HIV statuses all over the internet."

Kayla sucked in a long breath, but at least she stayed quiet.

Renee looked confused. "Paint me a picture."

"My members joined because membership is anonymous." I quickly explained how it worked because I needed her to clearly understand. If their statuses are leaked, it's gonna ruin me. "I can't allow that to happen! Not to mention it's a violation of their privacy, and even worse it would ruin my company's reputations."

"Oh, this is bad," Kayla moaned.

Renee was shaking her head. "How in the world did you give some mothafucka all that damn power?"

I felt like a child being scolded. Renee was right. I had been so stupid.

"Please, kick my ass later. Right now, I need you to help me come up with a plan. Shane built the site, created the logins and passwords, and did all the updates, even the e-commerce." The more I talked, the stupider I felt. I hadn't learned shit when it came to men.

"Well, for starters you need to get your account information."

"I tried! But he knows I want it, so he won't hand it over."

"Then we'll just have to take them," Renee said and winked.

See that's what I love about her. "How are we gonna do that?"

"Just leave that to me."

"Oh, heck no! Y'all count me out!" Kayla declared from the back seat.

Renee's head whipped around like she was suddenly possessed. "Bitch, didn't I just help you with your problem with your husband? Not to mention all the other shit I've done over the years to save your high-yellow ass."

"Yes." Kayla drew in her bottom lip.

"When I say let's move, you better be locked and fucking loaded!"

I was grinning so hard, I couldn't even look Kayla's way.

Renee's eyes were glossed over, the way they are when her creative mind was working. "I'm gonna have to give this shit some thought, but can you at least get us into his office?"

I groaned as I admitted, "He works from home, but I know where he hides the key."

"Gee...You're smarter than I thought," she replied sarcastically.

Did I tell you I can't stand her ass sometimes?

"What are you planning to do?" Kayla asked. I hope that meant she was finally onboard.

Renee slid down on the seat with a devilish grin. "What do you think? We're gonna break in and get what we need."

I should have known her solution was going to be something illegal. But this was one time it didn't even matter.

"I'll just need you to find out when he's gonna be away from the house, and I'll take care of the rest."

I don't know what was running through her mind, but I was game. Renee was educated, but she could go gangsta in a minute if she thought someone was trying to fuck with one of her girls.

And I was down.

Kayla, on the other hand, had already jumped out the back seat.

* * *

By the time I made it home, I started to feel like things were going to be okay. Being around my girls always helped, especially Renee. I shouldn't always expect her to solve my problems, but this was one situation that required a great deal of assistance. Otherwise, my ass was screwed.

I kicked off my shoes, then moved into the kitchen. I hadn't made dinner for Calvin in a while, and I wanted to surprise him. I found some ground beef in the freezer that I had browned a few weeks ago and decided not to cook. I popped it into the microwave.

"I'm cooking for my husband," I mumbled under my breath as I moved to the food pantry. There was angel hair pasta and spaghetti sauce on the shelf. Today was my lucky day. By the time Calvin walked into the house the pasta was draining and meat sauce was simmering on the stove.

"Hey, Calvin," I cooed and noticed he seemed preoccupied.

"Hey, baby."

I grabbed his hand. That drew his attention. "I made dinner."

A smile finally teased his lips. "It smells delicious. Let me get changed and we can eat." He started to brush past me, but I leaned in close and pressed my lips to his.

What the fuck! Why did his breath smell like pussy?

I drew back and gave him a curious look. "What did you have for lunch?"

"Why?" Calvin looked suspicious.

"I mean your breath smells like you've been eating…tuna." *Or licking someone's funky-ass pussy.*

He started laughing, but I didn't see anything funny.

"Actually, I had a tuna on rye."

It obviously wasn't any tuna I'd ever eaten. But that explained it, or at least to him it did. I wish I could say I felt relieved by his explanation' but instead I was suspicious.

"I guess that means I need a breath mint."

Try a whole damn bottle of Scope.

"Let me go brush my teeth and change. I'll be back in a flash." He kissed me on the cheek and disappeared upstairs.

I stared after him with a hand propped at my waist. Something smelled fishy and I didn't just mean his breath. The feeling of everything going to be alright was long gone and was now replaced with uneasiness. All that eye-shifting and not being able to meet my gaze was so out of the norm. I know my husband, and that funky breath alien who walked through the door was not the man I married. The Calvin I know would have been trying to get me upstairs to join him in the shower.

The timer went off. I pulled the garlic bread out of the oven and turned down the fire under the sauce to simmer. Calvin had left the keys to his Tahoe on the counter. I reached for them and moved out to the garage. I didn't want to risk trying to use the remote. The way he loved that truck, he would have heard the chirp. Instead, I stuck the key in the lock, opened the door and slid onto the seat. In a matter of seconds, I would know if...

My heart practically stopped. Calvin's truck had Bluetooth capability. I turned it on and stared down at the series of calls. There were several to the same familiar number. One even in the last hour.

It was Joiee.

As many times as I called that wench, I had that number practically memorized in my head.

What in the world was my husband doing talking to her? Sure, I could understand the previous calls, but after we talked and I told him to leave that bitch alone, there shouldn't have been anything more for the two of them to discuss. Knowing that they were still connected hurt my heart in ways I couldn't even begin to explain. He was drawn to her. Why else would they still be talking? I got out of his car and slammed the door. Let him hear. I didn't give a fuck. Calvin had betrayed our relationship.

I went back into the kitchen and reached inside the refrigerator for salad fixings. By the time he walked into the room, dinner was served.

"Baby, I'm ready to eat!" he said with a big juicy grin on his lips.

My heart was hurting, and yet, I managed to put a smile on my face. "Go ahead and take a seat."

"You don't have to tell me twice." He slapped his palms together and moved over to his chair, easing down onto it.

I fixed him a plate of spaghetti and carried it over. In my mind, I was tossing the piping hot sauce into his face. I wonder if Joiee would still want Calvin with second degree burns? Of course, I wasn't that stupid.

I dumped it onto his lap instead.

"*What the fuck!*" he shouted and jumped up so fast, you

would have thought his balls were on fire. I guess in a way they were, since he'd come down in a white t-shirt and boxers. The entire crotch was covered in sauce.

"Oops, my bad," I snarled. "It slipped."

While he was screaming and dancing around like some damn fool, I lowered onto my chair and reached for the salad.

"Did you just drop that shit in my lap on purpose?" he shouted.

I pierced a grape tomato with my fork and popped it into my mouth before I raised my eyes from my plate. Calvin was standing there butt naked. He had ripped the clothes off his body. I took a moment to admire his gorgeous smooth skin and his penis. Just thinking about that pink-toe wench riding on his dick caused my eyes to narrow.

"When was the last time you spoke to Joiee?"

"What?" Calvin looked confused. "Yo, I asked your crazy ass a question! Did you just try and burn me?"

"And I asked *you* a question. When was the last time you spoke to that bitch?" I repeated between chews.

"What the…" Calvin came around the table so fast I jumped out of my chair. Rushing around to the other side of the island, I reached for the pan of spaghetti sauce.

"Come a step closer and I swear your dick won't be the only thing on fire."

He shook his head. "I can't believe this bullshit."

He stalked over to the refrigerator and pressed down on the icemaker. A cube dropped into his hand. "You mean to tell me all that is about Joiee?"

I watched as he pressed the ice to the inside of his thigh. His eyes never left mine. "I asked you a question?"

I dropped the pan back onto the stove with a thump. "I saw all the calls. I know you're still talking to her, so don't even try and lie." I brought my hand to my hip and waited for him to try and deny it. Men were good for that.

"Did you ever think for a moment that it may be Joiee who's calling me?"

"What? I told her to never call us again." I wanted to make sure he knew I was no fool.

A strangled laugh came from his throat. "And just because you told her to, she supposed to do it, right?" Calvin was looking at me like I was the one who was ridiculous. "That woman has been blowing up my phone ever since she left my office that day you saw her there."

"So, you're telling me the problem is her, not you?"

"That's exactly what I'm saying."

I gave a rude snort. "And I'm supposed to believe that?"

"I really don't give a fuck what you believe. Both you chicks are crazy."

I watched his tight butt cheeks as he stormed out the kitchen.

"You must think I'm a damn fool," I muttered then cussed under my breath when I saw the mess I now had to clean up.

While I mopped up the sauce, I thought about what Calvin said. What if there was some truth to what he had said. I wanted desperately to believe him.

I put the mop down, then reached over for the cordless house phone. The only reason why we had one was so when Calvin was working at home, he had fax capability. I dialed star sixty-nine and waited for the wench to answer.

"Hello?"

"Didn't I tell you to stay the fuck away from my husband?"

There was a soft giggle. "Danielle, is that you?"

"Bitch don't play dumb! You know who this is. I asked you not to call Calvin anymore. He told me you've been blowing up his phone."

Now she was really laughing. "Is that what he told you? Oh my God! That's so cute. Honey, he's been calling me just as much as I've been calling him. Do I look like I'm that damn desperate?"

"You must be if you're messing with a married man."

"Let's not forget. You opened the door. All I did was step inside." She gave a yawn that was beyond fake. "The problem is once you invited me in, I liked what I saw so much I'm not ready to leave just yet."

"Are you trying to test me?" I was pacing around the kitchen.

"No, I'm just letting you know that I appreciate the

invitation into your home."

I couldn't believe the balls this wench had. "Do you know I will fuck you up? Let me see you anywhere near my husband and see what happens!"

There was a long pause and I was getting ready to hang up, but then I heard her say, "Would you by chance know someone who lives at 237 Stewart Road?"

Her question stopped me cold. That was Shane's address.

"I'll take your silence as a yes."

I cleared my throat. "Okay, what about it?"

"What about it is… I've seen the yummy man coming outta that house. It's also the same house I've seen you go into. I assume he's the same man I caught you talking to on the phone in the ladies' room at CJ's."

I was flabbergasted.

Joiee giggled. "That's what I thought. Now it's my turn to be frank. Stand in my way and I promise you, Danielle, you'll be the one who gets fucked."

With that the phone went dead.

43
Renee

As soon as I felt confident Quinton was doing better, I checked myself into a hotel. Damn, if I was going to spend another night sleeping on that little-ass couch. He wasn't dying and I wasn't one for sitting there waiting on him hand and foot. Besides, Soledad was there by his side. With her needy ass around, that gave me a chance to breathe.

I got up the following morning and spent it in front of my laptop, trying to get some writing done. I was working on a story that had been in my head, dying to be unleashed. I amazed even myself sometimes. People are always asking me where I come up with the shit I write about. Easy, I people watch, listen to the drama, and observe. That shit alone was enough to keep the ideas flowing. Also, my friends knew don't tell me shit because it was liable to show up in a book. That's how I'd ended up airing all of Reese's dirty little secrets. Her fiancé had been running his mouth, while fucking the shit outta me. Every time I thought about my run-in with her and her best friend at the Black & White Ball, I found myself laughing. I guessed she'd never gotten the memo. Don't fuck with me!

I wrote for about two hours and then decided to spend an hour updating my website. I logged on and cussed under my breath. Shit! I had spam all over my pages again. I don't understand that. I spend money every month for a host with firewall protection and yet it never fucking works. If I called, they were going to charge me by the minute for technical assistance. Ugh! I really needed to find myself a bonafide web designer. All my host offered was a temporary fix just so I would keep calling, and they could keep charging my ass. Guess what? I had a trick for those mothafuckas.

I reached over for my cell phone and scrolled through my address book for the number I needed and dialed. As soon as the call connected, I didn't even give her a chance to say, hello.

"Keneshia... where's Jewel?"

My cousin was chewing like a wild animal. "She's in the kitchen."

I knew she would be there. "Put her on the phone," I insisted.

"Hold on. Jewel! Telephone!"

"Damn bitch! All up in my ear."

"Oh shit. Sorry cuz."

Ugh. Ghetto.

I heard her mumble something and then a different voice came over the phone. "Hey, Renee. Whassup?"

Whassup? What's up with these young people today? Not to mention she was calling me by my first name. She better be lucky, I needed her ass. "Jewel, I've got some kinda virus on my website that's spamming like crazy."

"Hmmm. Probably a virus embedded in one of your files."

"Is that something you can fix for me?"

She popped and smacked her gum. "No problem. What's your web address?"

I blurted, "Author Renee Moore dot com."

"Okay, got it." There was that damn smacking again. I took the phone away, looked down at it, then cradled it between my chin and shoulder.

"You need my login and password?"

"Nope. I already got your admin account up on my phone."

Damn. Alright then.

"I'll call you back in a few." She ended the call without saying goodbye.

I don't know what it is with mothafuckas today, but if she could help, then it would be worth dealing with her unprofessional ass.

It was almost lunchtime, so I ordered room service and then jumped into the shower. As soon as I was under the water, I started thinking about Clayton. I couldn't get his sexy ass off my mind. He was back in Kansas City and constantly on the brain. It's nuts, but he made me feel things my crazy ass hadn't felt in a long-ass time. That man made me feel sexy and stirred up so many emotions. It wasn't just about making my coochie tingle. He had my body shivering every single time he called me and I heard his smile through the phone. I found myself smiling and my new and improved titties got hard as shit. Damn, I can't believe it! Feeling like this about a man was just something I didn't do, because it meant setting yourself up for heartache and leaving yourself vulnerable. It was way too dangerous, and yet those feelings were completely out of my control. What was it about Clayton that made him different? I've dated rich before. Even sexy. And yet none of them had me thinking about them the way I was thinking about him. My thoughts kept going over and over the sound of his voice. The feel of his lips against mine and the way he had gone down on me, licking and sucking my pussy, with those gorgeous lips of his. He was so confident and sure about himself that Clayton would have me twisted if I wasn't careful.

By the time I got out the shower, there was a knock at the door and room service was wheeling a cart of food into the room.

"Yum! That smells good."

I saw the way that little boy was smiling at me, standing in front of him in a hotel bathrobe. Made me feel good knowing I still got it. I gave him a nice tip, patted him on the head and sent him on his way.

I was back to editing and sipping black coffee when Jewel was calling me back.

"All done."

"What the fuck?" I reached for my iPad and logged in to confirm. Sure enough, the spam I'd seen was gone. There was my name scrolling across the screen bright and in living color. "How the hell you do that?"

"Easy. I created a virus to kill a virus."

Keneshia was shouting in the background, which meant the call must be on speaker. "Told you cuz she was good!"

And then it hit me. A fucking genius-ass idea.

"How would y'all like to make some money?"

"Hell yeah!" Keneshia exclaimed. "What we gotta do?"

"I'll call you later with the details." I giggled and ended the call. And people wonder where I come up with the shit I write about…

I laughed and made myself another cup of coffee while I put a plan in action.

44
Danielle

"Where's the key?"

"Hold up! I'm looking for it."

I don't why I let Renee talk me into this crazy bullshit because once again here I was doing something that could land my ass in jail. I was down on my knees in the mulch, picking up rocks, looking for the one that hid the spare key to Shane's house. "If you'd hold the flashlight still I might be able to find it," I snapped back. Damn, I wanted to be rid of Shane once and for all, but getting dirt underneath my nails wasn't quite what I'd had in mind. Although, when it came to Renee, nothing was ever ordinary.

"Here comes a car!" Keneshia shouted. So much for whispering.

I made a mad dive into the bushes and got stuck in the kneecap by something pointy. I breathed a sigh of relief when the car passed.

"Oh, good. False alarm." Jewel was shaking and I was sure it had nothing to do with fear, but everything to do with what she'd been smoking when we picked her up. For the life of me, I couldn't understand how Renee was risking everything with a crackhead or whatever this skinny chick was. Shit! I had to remind myself that she was here to help me so I guess I should be thankful even though I knew the only reason why she had agreed was for the money.

I finally found the fake rock that Shane kept under one of the bushes. I knew because he locked his keys in the car once and had to use the spare to get inside. "Here it is."

"About damn time," Renee muttered.

Sometimes I just wished she'd keep her comments to herself. I slid back the panel and removed the key.

"As nice as this house is, you sure this dude doesn't have no alarm?"

Keneshia was a ghetto hot mess. I shook my head and hoped these two weren't coming back to rob Shane later. On second thought, why the fuck did I care. "Make sure nobody is watching while I open the door."

"It's dark, ain't nobody looking over here. Just hurry up," Renee demanded. "And where the hell is Kayla? I thought she was coming."

"I already told you she doesn't want to have anything to do with this drama. She had enough with that whole, *have you seen my dog Riley*, bullshit."

"She should be thankful I have her back, just like you." That heifer is always reminding us of what she's willing to do.

"I am appreciative, even though you'll probably have my ass in jail."

"Yeah, but at least your business will be saved."

I giggled. "You're right. It would be worth the time." Quickly I unlocked the door and we hurried inside. Good thing Shane always left his lights on. "Okay…he's at karate class until nine so we need to hurry and get out of here."

"Where do we look?" Renee asked.

Jewel whistled. "Damn this crib is nice!"

"Hell yeah!" Keneshia agreed.

I just rolled my eyes at the two. All they saw were dollar signs. I'll admit his house was nice with high ceilings, dark wood floors and a great open floor plan.

Renee raised her eyebrows, then said, "Where does he keep his computer?"

I pointed my index finger toward the ceiling. "Shane has an office in the loft upstairs." I started toward the stairs. Everyone followed. "Someone needs to keep watch down here."

"I got it," Keneshia called over my shoulder. "That will give me time to check out his music collection."

Shane did have an impressive collection of albums. He was

into old school rhythm and blues.

"Al Green! My dad would go fucking crazy!"

"Y'all need to keep it the fuck down! We're supposed to be whispering," Renee scolded.

I was hoping she would jump in and handle that.

We made it up to the top of the stairs where the entire loft was his office. There was a massive desk and walls of equipment.

Jewel whistled under her breath again. "He's got some high-tech shit!"

Even Renee looked impressed. "Wow, I don't even know what half this shit is."

"Oh yeah, he's big on website marketing and developing." I don't know why I felt a sense of pride for a man who was trying to screw me.

Jewel wasted no time taking a seat behind his desk. "Like I was telling Renee on the phone, I didn't want to hack into your site until I had a chance to see everything this mothafucka has. And it's a damn good thing I hadn't, because he's got all kinda firewalls and security shit goin' on here," she explained while she tapped away at the keyboard. "He would have known right away I was hacking into your website. And then we woulda been fucked!"

"So you think you can log in?" I asked.

Both of them gave me weird looks.

"Think? Honey do you know who you're talking to?" Jewel asked.

I shook my head. "No, actually I would like to know. You're too talented to be—"

"One Happy Meal away from being homeless?" She gave a sad laugh, but never once stopped typing. "I've been through some shit that you just can't come back from overnight."

I looked to Renee to see if she knew what the hell Jewel was talking about, but she shrugged.

"I'm in," she announced.

"You are lying!" I exclaimed even though I knew she wasn't. When her fingers started going to work I jumped for joy. To hell with being quiet.

"Ima remove his access, change your passwords and wipe everything pertaining to it from his system."

"Thank you so much!" Grinning, I walked over to Renee and leaned in close. "Damn, she's good."

"Fuck yeah. I'm gonna have her start doing some freelance work for me once I get back home."

"Damn, I didn't know you were balling like that?" Jewel hissed. I swung around.

"What are you talking about?"

"Your dating website. I didn't know online dating generated a cool million a year."

If she didn't have my attention before, she had it now. "It doesn't."

"That's not what these reports say. Y'all killing it! In the last three months, you've generated over a quarter of a million dollars. Damn! Can a sistah get a loan, shit!"

Renee and I practically knocked each other over, trying to get a closer look at the computer screen.

"Damn bitch, you're earning more money than me and you were tripping about a first-class ticket!"

Renee was right. There were deposit amounts with more zeros than I'd ever seen in front of me. Was this shit for real?

"What are those?" I asked.

"Account numbers."

I pointed. "That's my account, but I don't recognize this number."

"Well, that there's another bank account." Jewel slid a finger across the screen. "It looks like the bulk of the deposits are going into this second account."

"Hell naw, that nigga was stealing from you!" Renee shook her head. "You gave him too much fucking power."

Like I didn't already know that. She was going to keep rubbing salt in that wound.

"Delete that shit." I was pissed and felt so betrayed. And to think I thought having that man as a side piece was worth the risk. I truly was stuck on stupid.

"Sure, I'll remove it, but I'ma first see how much he's stolen from you."

I rested my hip against the desk and faced Jewel. "Can you get my money back?"

She shrugged. "Yeah, but it's gonna cost you."

"How much?"

Turning, she locked eyes with mine as she said, "Half of what I take from him."

"Damn, she gangsta!" Renee interjected. "I knew there was a reason why I liked you so much."

I waved my hand at her to shut up and focused my attention on Jewel. "Recoup half sounds much better than none. Yes, it's a deal." Hell, it's more than I currently had.

Renee dragged me over near the stairs and began nagging, "Now you happy I had her come?"

"*Oh my God!* Nae-Nae, I can't believe the nigga tried to rob me."

Renee winked. "Just wait until he finds out he's been robbed of a lot more."

I was laughing. I would love to be there when he found out. We were talking back and forth before Jewel interrupted.

"Yo, check this out! Why he got pictures of Prissy on his computer?"

Renee looked confused. "Prissy? Who's that?"

Everyone in Columbia knew who she was. Even me "That's that chick who was found murdered a few months ago." Jewel clicked through a few more photos and I saw her in a cap and gown standing next to Shane.

"Look, there's a caption. *My niece's graduation.*"

I bunched up my nose in confusion. "I don't remember him ever mentioning having a niece, and especially not one who had been murdered." I gave Renee a weird look. She just raised her eyebrow and stared. I was ready to get the hell out of there. "Are you done getting my money?"

"Yeah, I'm just waiting for the transaction to complete. My bad. I was only able to recoup one-hundred-eighty-nine thousand."

"*Only?*" I gave her a hug.

"That's before my cut," Jewel was quick to remind me.

"Hell, that number is still more than I got now!" I couldn't believe it! I was truly a successful business owner.

"I'm almost done here. I routed all the money, deleted the second account and loaded a firewall and security. I also forwarded the files for your website to a drop-box. I'll give you the info later. Let me just finish wiping this computer —"

"Someone's coming!" Keneshia cried out.

The hairs at the back of my neck stood up.

Jewel plugged in a junk drive. "Fuck! I'm not done yet!"

"Then keep working. We'll stall and get you some more time." Renee looked at me and I must have looked like a deer in front of headlights. "You gotta get down there and stall so that we can get out of here."

"How am I gonna do that?" It was too late to get out of there undetected.

"Ho, I don't know! Get naked or something. Pretend you came to surprise him with the pussy!"

She never failed to state the obvious. Quickly, I rushed down the hall and stripped down to my panties and bra. I was going to have to fuck my way out of this.

I heard the garage door open and close and every muscle in my body tightened. I looked down at the music collection. Where the hell was Keneshia?

There were heavy footsteps which meant Shane had walked into the house. Fear and anger raged through my body, but I had to hold it together. All I could think about was him trying to steal all my damn money.

I took a deep breath and got myself together before I started down the stairs. When I reached the bottom, I struck a pose.

"Hey, baby." I watched as Shane walked through the door and smiled.

"Danielle, bae. What are you doing here?" He sounded happy to see me.

"I thought I'd surprise you."

"For real? I thought you was tryna slow this thing down between us."

"I did, but then I realized good dick is hard to find." I sauntered over and kissed his neck and cheek. "I remembered where you hid the key and decided to be here waiting when you got here."

His eyes flashed. "Some stupid mothafucka tried to chop a piece of wood in half with his hand and broke his wrist. Master Seng decided to end our session early."

"That's too bad for him, but good for you and me."

His eyes sparkled the way they always did when he knew he was about to get some pussy. "Let's get this party started."

He had no idea the party had started long before he'd arrived.

45
Renee

"What are we gonna do?"

I put a finger to my lips, warning Jewel to lower her voice. Folks can be so damn ghetto. "You done?" That's the part that was important.

She typed a few additional keystrokes then she nodded. "Yep. All done. Systems wiped and money all transferred." She pulled a junk drive out of the USB port and put it in her pocket.

"Now, let's get the hell out of here," I whispered.

"How we gonna do that?"

"Let's just stay low and wait." I heard Danielle and Shane directly below us. "I wonder where the hell Keneshia is?"

"Hopefully, she's somewhere hiding."

I tried to make sure Danielle and Shane were heading to the rear of the house. I needed to get back to the hospital. Quinton was expecting me and I did not have time to be getting bailed out of jail.

Before we quietly crept down the stairs, I text messaged Keneshia because I didn't have any idea where she was. By the time we reached the bottom step, she came rushing out of a hall closet, knocking over a stack of clutter. I jerked back, knocking Jewel backwards and she landed on her ass. We all froze and waited.

Several seconds passed, and no one came rushing down the hall. I breathed a sigh of relief.

"Damn, be quiet." I scolded and then reached down for some clothes that had fallen out of a black plastic bag. That's when I noticed a green sweatshirt, faded blue jeans and Air Force Ones sneaker that weren't white anymore. There was blood all over everything. After getting shot, I knew what blood splatter looked like. Nevertheless, I needed confirmation.

I glanced nervously over my shoulder before signaling their attention. Keneshia had that Al Green album tucked under her armpit.

"Hey, does this look like blood to you?" I whispered holding the items up with the tips of my fingers so they could see.

Keneshia nodded and whispered. "Hell yeah! Who the fuck he shoot?"

I shrugged. "Beats the hell outta me."

Jewel did the sniff test. "Yep. It's definitely blood."

"It *is* hunting season," I said trying to come up with an explanation since I was about to leave my best friend alone with this guy. "For all we know he's been out hunting deer." Quickly, I pushed the clothes back into the bag and piled everything back in the closet. "Let's get the fuck out of here." I could hear Danielle somewhere laughing. Water was running which meant the two of them were probably getting their freak on in the shower. We made our way to the door and slipped outside and hurried to my rental parked at the corner. I had driven around the block a few times when I received a text from Danielle.

You get it?

I quickly text back. **Yep, outside waiting on you**

Go, I'll call you later

I figured that meant she was going to handle her business and take an Uber back to the hospital where her car was in the parking garage. I would make sure I was there waiting for her.

"Yo Keneshia," Jewel called from the back seat. "That mothafucka was Prissy's uncle."

Her face said she drew a blank. "Prissy who?"

"You know, Prissy Burke, the one they found murdered in the alley earlier this year?"

Her eyes widened dramatically. "Oh shit! I forgot all about her."

"What happened?" A nosy bitch like me needs to know what was going on at all times.

Jewel sucked her teeth. "People still ain't sure how she ended up dead. She was at this party with all of us and her ex showed up. She didn't want to be bothered with that mothafucka, so she and this girl name Dana Whatley left."

"Who was this ex-boyfriend?"

Keneshia snapped her fingers. "Oh shit! It was what's-his-name!"

"Oh damn!" Jewel snapped her finger.

Keneshia was stumbling for her words, the way she always does when she nervous or excited.

I was a second away from strangling her.

Jewel helped her out. "She was Dollar's girl."

I felt like my head was spinning. Dollar! I was always one jumping to conclusions and something just didn't feel right about the entire situation. Especially now that I saw those bloody sneakers. Goodness, it sounded crazy but I guess it was the writer in me.

"Meechie told me he didn't shoot Dollar."

The two of them looked at each other, then at me. There was doubt all over Keneshia's face.

"I don't know, cuz. I saw the two of them having words at the football game and the next thing I know all shit broke out."

Jewel agreed. "Yep, I saw the same thing."

"Did either of you see the gun?"

"No but we sho the fuck heard it," Jewel said and reached over the seat to give Keneshia a fist bump.

She nodded in agreement. "Hell, we all heard it."

I didn't know what to believe. Meechie said he didn't do it. Did that mean he didn't kill Turk either?

"And we all know he killed Turk," Keneshia said as if she could read my mind. "But it's whatever. I ain't mad at him. Both them niggas needed to get gone anyway."

"I know that's right," I replied chiming in and turned the car at the corner.

"I don't give a fuck. I'm 'bout to get the come up!" Jewel started dancing on her seat. "Tomorrow, I'm looking for me a place." She went on to tell Keneshia about the money she'd discovered for Danielle.

My cousin's eyes were wide. "Damn, can I at least get a finder's fee for hooking all this shit up!"

"Girl, you know I got you," Jewel added with a dismissive wave.

While they discussed money, I tried to figure out what was really going on. Unfortunately, I couldn't think of a damn thing to explain it.

46
Nadine

I'd been a wreck since Turk was murdered. My wife left me and my job was suffering so much, the partners called me in to discuss my performance. I just didn't know what else to do or where to turn so I requested the company of my sistahs. We met at Tony's at lunch for a pizza and gyros. I figured they'd be a good sounding board for everything that was going on with me. It had been the right move because by the time our food had arrived I was buckled over with laughter.

"I can't believe y'all crazy asses broke into that man's house!" Nothing Renee ever did surprised me anymore.

"Well believe it," Danielle confirmed with a shake of her head. "That chick had her cousin watching the door like we were some professional burglars."

Some things never changed, and Renee was one of them.

Renee reached for another slice of pizza as she said, "Hey, you know I'm willing to do whatever it takes to get the job done." Tilting her head to the side, she frowned. "This one here decided to play possum."

"What?" Kayla's eyes shifted around the table. "I wasn't getting caught up in that mess."

"It wasn't mess when you had us clowning at Black Barbie's house." Renee was talking with her mouth full.

"Damn! You're spitting across the table," I scowled and wiped my face.

"Oops, my bad."

My eyes shifted to Danielle. "Has he noticed yet?"

Danielle took a sip, then shrugged. "I dunno. I doubt it though, otherwise, he woulda been calling me by now. I hung around long enough to give him some, so he wouldn't get suspicious, then I had him drop me off at the hospital."

"Wasn't he suspicious that you didn't have your car?"

She took a bite. "Nope. I told him I wanted to surprise him, so I took an Uber over."

I shook my head. This chick had an answer for everything.

"So...you're rich now?"

Danielle was blushing. "Nah, but at least I can pay my bills!" Laughing like hyenas, she gave Renee a high five.

Being able to pay bills was a beautiful thing. I had distributed the money just as I had planned, caught up all the past due bills, then went to the bank and deposited nine-grand into Jordan's account. After lunch, I was headed over to Ursula's, Turk's baby mama, to give her the remainder. One-hundred-thousand dollars.

I bit into my gyro and glanced over at Renee who was texting away on her phone.

"How are things with you and Clayton?"

At the mention of his name, she put down her phone and smiled. "Things are good. Really good. We're gonna spend the evening together before I catch my plane in the morning."

"You're really going all the way home and then coming right back?" Kayla had a look on her face that said she thought Renee was crazy. Probably because Kayla never did care for flying.

"Yep, I've got some business to handle. Quinton's probably gonna be discharged in a few days and then he's gonna stay with his father until he gets strong enough to go home with me."

"You really plan on getting him out of here, huh?" I asked between sips.

"Hell yeah, otherwise that knucklehead will be dead before he turns twenty-five. He needs a change of scenery."

"And a job," Danielle added with a grunt.

"That too!" We all laughed.

They always say laughter was the best medicine. I was feeling a whole helluva bit better by the time I was grabbing the last slice.

"What's going on with you Nadine?" Renee asked and slid down on the chair, rubbing her belly. "You and Jordan working things out?"

I shook my head regrettably. "No, in fact, I got home from work yesterday and found she had moved out."

"What the…?" Kayla barked and sat up tall on the seat. "Oh no!"

I nodded my head and probably looked so pathetic to the three of them. "She hired professionals because there's no other way she could have gotten that stuff out the house that fast. Closets cleaned out. The twins' bedroom cleared out."

"Oh damn. Why didn't you call us?" Kayla asked with empathy.

I shook my head. "I was just too miserable. All I wanted to do was ball up on the sofa and cry my ass out. But there was only one problem."

Danielle's brow lifted. "What?"

"Jordan took the sofa, too."

Renee looked at Danielle and then the two busted out laughing. The sound was so contagious even Kayla and I joined in. Like I'd said, sometimes laughter was the best medicine, even if it was at my expense.

"Nadine, I'm so sorry for laughing," Kayla said with an apologetic smile.

"Yeah, me too," Renee chimed in.

Tears welled at my eyes. "No worries. I've cried enough the last few days. It's good to be able to find humor in all of this," I added with a sweep of the hand.

"Have you tried calling her today?" Danielle used a napkin to wipe her mouth.

I gave a dismissive laugh. "Yes, and she doesn't want anything to do with me. She said this is Missouri, the Show-Me state. Until I show her I've kicked my habit and gotten help, she and the children are staying away."

"Then go get your ass some help! Hell, it ain't rocket science."

Danielle frowned as she glared over at Renee. "Damn, Nae-

Nae. You act like it's that damn easy. The way you used to be addicted to dick, I would think if anyone understood it was you."

Renee could be such a bitch when she wanted to. But she was right. I needed to get my shit together fast. I just didn't know where to begin. Without Jordan, I was miserable and depressed. When I'm depressed, I gambled. What the fuck?

"Nadine," Renee began. "I'm willing to do whatever I can to help you, but if you want Jordan back, you've gotta get yourself some help."

Kayla nodded. "As much as I hate to admit it, Renee is right. Actions speak louder than words."

"I agree," Danielle chimed in. "I'll go to counseling with you or whatever else it is you need to kick this habit."

I loved the way they had my back. I looked around the table with tears streaming down my cheeks. We were out in public, so I brushed them away.

Renee smiled. "Damn, it sounds like we are doing an intervention with a crackhead."

I laughed and the others joined me. There were more similarities between the two addictions than I'd ever realized.

"I better get my behind out of here before I get fired." Kayla put her napkin down and rose.

"Chile, please!" Renee snorted. "After catching your dean knocking boots with one of his professors, you could ask for three-hour lunch breaks, and I bet you he won't say shit."

"I know that's right." Danielle gave her a high-five.

Laughing, we all headed outside and onto the sidewalk.

"Well, I'm parked this way." I pointed in the opposite direction.

Renee opened her arms and gave me a big hug. "Hang in there girl. It's gonna work out."

I wish I had her confidence. "I sure hope so. Have a safe trip home. Make sure you call me when you land."

"I will. But don't expect that call until tomorrow. Tonight, I'm hoping to get me some d-i-c-k...d-i-c-k..." She was chanting and gyrating her hips.

"You old freak." I laughed.

Renee winked. "Call me Ms. Nasty."

I waved and was smiling all the way back to my car. I needed that. It had felt good talking to them about my problems. It wasn't necessarily that I needed them to solve it. But sometimes you just needed someone to listen. I climbed behind the wheel of my car and took a deep breath. "Stay focused."

I scrolled through my phone for the address I had saved, then hit Navigate and pulled away. I arrived in a matter of minutes.

I pulled over to the curb and climbed out the car. Bear Creek was one neighborhood I didn't want to be in, but I had to start making things right in my life and this was one of them. I stared up at the duplex in front of me. Dark bricks and dingy siding. Toys on the front porch. Hopefully, this was the right place.

I breathed slowly. In and out. In and out. It took every ounce of strength I had not to jump back in my car, hit the highway and head to the casino. But I wanted my life back. I wanted my wife back. Being strong, letting go, and making things right began now.

I unlocked the trunk, reached inside and removed the briefcase. I don't know why I was looking over my shoulder, but it was as if I'd expected someone to come up from behind and hit me over my head. It probably had something to do with the hundred grand I was carrying in the briefcase.

I made it onto the porch, knocked on the door, and heard footsteps approaching.

"Who is it?" a woman barked.

"It's Nadine Hill. I'm here to see Ursula."

A lock turned and the door swung open. "What can... wait a minute, what are *you* doing here?" Ursula said with attitude. I figured as much once she recognized me. She had seen me in court, time and time again.

I tried to smile and show her I'd come in peace. "Turk wanted me to give you something."

"I don't want shit from him!" She had a hand propped at her wide hip. At five-two she was as short as I was. "The best gift he'd ever given me was dying!" Ursula started to shut the door, but I brought a hand up stopping her.

"I think you'll want this. Take it," I insisted and sat the briefcase down on the porch and took a step back. "He wanted you to have this."

She opened the door and stepped out onto the porch, glaring down at the briefcase like it contained explosives. "Why in the world would he want to give me anything?"

She wasn't a dumb woman, but the look in her eyes told me she wanted to believe there was an ounce of good inside of Turk. It was not my place to tell her people like him were born rotten and died smelling worse than roadkill.

But I knew I had to be careful with a response or she'd never accept it. "He told me to hold onto this in the event anything ever happened to him."

Ursula didn't look like she completely believed me, but I guess it was good enough for her to stop staring down suspiciously at the case. She reached for it.

"I hope that brings you and your son some measure of peace."

"I felt peace the second that nigga was gunned down," she told me with a shaky breath. "You have no idea the hell I went through."

I knew a lot more than she realized. "I'm sorry for everything you went through."

"You didn't look sorry when you were representing his ass in court!" She shook her head and gave me a pitiful look. "I don't know how you sleep at night."

That's the problem. I don't sleep.

"Well, you have a great rest of your day." I twirled around and spotted a man coming up the walkway with a little boy. The boy I recognized as Turk's son. The man, he also looked so familiar. It took me a moment to remember where. The look in his eyes told me he recognized me as well.

"Whassup?" He gave me a head nod, then looked from me to Ursula.

"That there's Turk's lawyer. She came by to bring me a package." She held out the briefcase.

While her son rushed inside, the man took it from her outstretched hand and turned to me, one eyebrow lifted.

"What's this shit?"

I swallowed and stared up at him. He was a big dude. If he was trying to intimidate me, it was working. "When she opens it, she'll understand."

As if he was almost daring me, he popped the latches and looked inside. Ursula rushed over and peered inside. As soon as they discovered what it held, they both looked at each other with grins on their faces.

"Holy shit!" she hissed.

I studied him for a moment, then pointed a finger at him. "Haven't I seen you before?"

He hesitated then nodded his head. "Yeah. I'm Q's boy. Meechie."

And then it hit me. This was the dude in the Facebook post Renee had shown me. It was also the same person I had seen running past the courthouse. The same dude Renee suspected of shooting Turk. The same guy I pretended not to recognize. My heart was pounding. It was time to get the hell out of the projects. "Yes, Q's doing good. I'm going by to see him in a bit."

Meechie closed the briefcase with a loud snap that made me jump. Ursula took it from him and went inside.

"Tell Q I'ma come through later and holla at him."

"Will do." I made a show of looking down at my watch and realized it had stopped. "I'm late for an appointment." With a wave, I slowly backed away. I was not about to turn my back on him. I hurried and climbed into my car and caught myself sliding low on the seat as if I expected bullets to start flying. I don't think I started breathing normal again until I made it onto the main road where there were too many witnesses for anything tragic to happen to me. I pulled into Sonic's.

What in the world was Meechie doing with Turk's baby mama? Especially since Turk was suspected of shooting Quinton. Meechie was suspected of killing Turk and Dollar. Or maybe it was Turk who killed Dollar? I dragged a hand across my low-cropped head as I wondered how I had even gotten connected with any of this ghetto nonsense. It no longer mattered. Turk was dead. Ursula had the money and now my slate was clean.

"Welcome to Sonic's. Can I take your order?" At the sound of the voice on the intercom, I jerked and hit the steering wheel. Damn.

"Uh yes, I'll have a medium lemon-berry slush." My mouth was so dry my tongue felt like sandpaper.

"One lemon-berry slush coming right up."

While I waited, I leaned back on the seat and drew several long breaths. "Stay focused. Everything is going to work out."

By the time the little redhead came zipping over on roller skates, I had totally relaxed. I gave her a tip and pulled away, sipping happily on the iced cold drink. It was just what I needed.

I was headed to the hospital before going back to the office. I made a left onto Broadway and had just passed the high school when my android phone buzzed. I noticed it was a private number.

I tapped my Bluetooth. "Hello?"

"Where the fuck you at?" The voice was so deep and calm, it caused my skin to crawl.

"Who is this?"

"You know damn well who this is. Cheddar. And I wanna know what you did with my man's money."

It was that big Congo gorilla-looking dude that stuck by Turk like a leech on an open wound. How the hell did he know I still had the money?

"I did exactly what Turk instructed me to do with it."

"Which is?"

I cleared my throat. "I'm his attorney, so I'm not at liberty to discuss that information."

He started laughing and the deep sound was like surround sound at a movie theater. I shivered and goosebumps beaded across both my arms and back.

"I saw you today."

I stared blankly out the windshield. "Saw me?"

"At Ursula's... standing outside with that big mothafucka."

How in the world... "I was—"

"You was what? Paying Meechie off for taking my boy out?"

All the slushes in the world couldn't have moistened my

mouth at that moment.

"I'ma tell you what? I better get that money. All of it," he hissed.

I rushed to clear my throat, but still sounded like I was choking. "No, I gave the money to Ursula."

"Then get it back!"

I became one big attitude. "How the hell am I supposed to do that?"

"That's yo fuckin' problem not mine."

I was shaking so bad, I couldn't even speak or drive. I pulled over.

"And you thought Turk was bad," he taunted. I'm in charge now, and I'm gonna be your worst fucking nightmare. Get me that money, otherwise I'm gonna have to pay your family a visit. It's Jordan, right?"

"Don't you—"

"Bitch, you fucked with the wrong mothafucka! Get me that money."

It took a moment for me to realize the phone was dead.

47
Danielle

I was in my office working on my website. Jewel had been by all morning helping me with loading additional security and teaching me basic functions so that I could access information as needed. It was awesome. After handing her a check for her fifty percent, I had hired her to maintain and monitor my website. She had found an apartment and had been talking nonstop about starting her own security and monitoring company. However, after what happened with Shane, I learned I had to always stay in control.

It had been two days since we broke into his house, and I hadn't heard a word from him. I wasn't sure if that was a good or bad thing, but I knew it was just a matter of time. He'd be by to see me…that much I was certain of.

It was almost noon when I heard someone coming down the hall. I looked up to see Portia coming through the door and her daughter was behind her. She came running toward me.

"Hi, Nana!" she said, giggling.

At the sight of my five-year-old granddaughter, my heart warmed. In my eyes Etienne did no wrong. "Hey, baby girl." Swinging around on my chair, I gave her a big hug and a kiss to her high cheekbones.

"What are you two doing here?" I asked, looking up at Portia. She was rocking a form-fitting sweater dress that emphasized all her curves and Chuck Taylor's were on her feet.

"We're on our way to the clinic. Etienne has a rash on her arm. I think it's ringworm." She turned up her nose in disgust.

"Ringworm? I hope she didn't get that crap from daycare." I'd always hated those places.

Portia dropped her shoulder bag to my desk and released a sigh. "Yeah, it seems two other kids are out for the same thing."

Etienne moved over to my computer and clicking the mouse found one of the games I had loaded on my system. It amazed me how smart these kids were nowadays. I had a hard-enough time with logins and passwords. Thank goodness Jewel had helped me come up with a unique way to keep track and store them.

While my granddaughter was preoccupied, I moved over to the small round table near the door and signaled for Portia to take a seat. We had just engaged in a conversation when there was a knock at my door. I saw the curious look on Portia's face and immediately knew who was standing behind me.

I turned on my seat and my stomach lurched up into my throat. "Hello Shane."

"Hey," he said and there was this evil look in his eyes.

He knows.

I rose. "Portia this is my marketing manager, Shane Michaux. Shane, this is my daughter." If anything happened to me at least she would remember the name.

They exchanged head nods. Portia still had a puzzled look. Sensing Shane wanted some privacy, she rose and turned to her daughter. "C'mon, Etienne. Let's go before we're late."

"See you later, sweetheart." I kissed my granddaughter goodbye.

"Later, Nana." She went racing out of my office.

As soon as they were gone, I looked at Shane, glared, then moved to take a seat behind the desk. "What can I do for you?" I asked as if it were another day at the office.

"What the fuck did you do?" Shane hissed at me. He was standing there, fist clenching and unclenching as he waited impatiently for my response.

"What do you mean?" I asked and leaned back on the chair.

Slowly, he moved in close, trying to intimidate me by the evil look in his eyes, but I wasn't going to scare that easy. "Don't play games! We both know the real reason why you were at my house."

"Again, I have no idea what you're talking about," I said

with a raised brow.

"Where the fuck is *my* money?"

"Money? You mean the money generated from my online website. Because if you're talking about my money, it's in my bank account where it belongs."

"I'm the one who designed and runs that website."

"Yes, and I paid you a handsome salary. I even have the cancelled checks to prove it. But working for me does not give you the right to fucking rob me."

He had a look of hatred on his face. "Do you really think your site generated all that money?"

I nodded. "As a matter of fact, I do. I saw the reports."

Shane was now laughing. "You really are dumber than you look."

Now I had attitude. "If I'm dumb, then I guess I'm a dumb rich bitch." That comment knocked the smirk from his lips. "What would make you think you were gonna get away with that?"

"I've got away with it this long, and if you don't give me that money back you're gonna have a problem... and not just with me."

He was so full of shit. I rose and started laughing. "Save that for someone who actually believes what's coming out of your mouth, because that woman isn't me."

"Give me the passwords to the accounts."

"Nope, and don't even try to hack in because it'll activate a virus on your computer. I hired a security manager to handle things, and she was kind enough to revoke all your access."

His eyes darkened with rage and I leaned back slightly with uneasiness.

"See when I told you I was done, I meant that. Now get out of my office."

He was all in my face and pushed me back against the wall. His body pressed up along the length of mine. "That money does not belong to you... or me."

I looked up and noticed the anger in his eyes had shifted to worry. "What are you saying? If it's not my money or yours, then who does it belong to?"

"What the hell is goin' on here?"

It was my worst nightmare to turn around and find my husband standing in the doorway.

"I asked a question. What the hell is going on?" he barked.

Shane slowly moved away from me. "That's a question you need to be asking your wife." His smirk had returned and I knew he was about to make this situation even worse. I tried to plead with my eyes, but I'm sure all he was interested in was payback. I didn't know what to do.

"Who the hell are you?" Calvin asked as he approached us. I tried to grab his arm, but he yanked away from me.

"Danielle, what are you waiting for? Go ahead and tell him who I am," Shane taunted with a sweep of the hand, letting me know I had the floor.

I turned to Calvin, shaking my head. "This is not what it looks like."

"And what is that?" he asked accusingly. "'Cause it looks like something to me."

I pressed a palm against his chest. "Baby, this is my *former* web designer, Shane. He dropped by to pick up his final payment."

"Then I think he needs to hurry and get the hell out of here." Calvin hissed and moved in close. Shane stepped even closer.

"Now is that anyway to speak me?" Shane shook his head amusingly.

This couldn't be happening. No! Not now. Not when I was trying to make everything right!

"Babe," I said softly, hoping to defuse the tension. "Let's go home. He ain't worth it."

Calvin's nostrils were flaring. "I don't even know who the fuck he is."

"Sure, you do. Whenever you kiss your wife, that's my dick you smell on her breath," Shane sneered.

Before I could react, Calvin landed a punch, knocking Shane off his feet and into my table, and then he pounced on him. I screamed, and my assistant came rushing to my office, but by then the two of them were going to blows. There was nothing we could do to stop them. Calvin's fist landed at Shane's jaw, catching him off guard. He quickly recovered and charged at Calvin's midsection. The two landed on the floor. After that they were firing blows that were so hard, I felt my own body flinching in reaction.

"Stop it!" I yelled and jumped between them in time to pull Calvin off Shane, who was gushing blood. I just couldn't tell from where. Calvin yanked free and reared back ready to hit Shane again, when I cried desperately, "Babe, stop! He's HIV positive."

He screeched to a halt, fist in midair. "Get the fuck out of my wife's office!"

Shane got up, nose and lip bleeding heavily, and shook his head. "It's all good. I was growing tired of that old-ass pussy anyway."

I erupted and went straight up to him and slapped him hard across the face. Calvin had to drag me away. Shane was still laughing loudly, even after he walked out my office.

I waited until my assistant left before I turned to Calvin and said gently, "Babe, it's not at all what you think."

"And what's that? You were fucking that dude. That's why you hooked me up with Joiee so you could justify your own actions."

I started to lie, but what was the point because he could already see through it. "I did at first, but once I saw you with Joiee I decided I couldn't do it."

Calvin shook his head with a look of disdain. "I don't even know who you are anymore. I try to give you everything. You mess around with your ex, contract HIV, and yet I still wanted you back, and all you've ever done is shit on me."

"I was wrong and I'm sorry," I said sadly.

"*And that's supposed to make it better*" he gave a strangled laugh "I don't get this shit!"

"Why don't we go home and talk about this?" I suggested, certain we could straighten things out.

"What else is there to talk about? You tried to act like it was about me, when all along it was about you and what you wanted... and it was that nigga there."

"You're right. I should have never got involved with him,

but once I did and felt so guilty, I decided you had a right to have the same free liberties as well," I said, hoping by admitting my mistake he would understand me.

"Is that supposed to make it fucking better?" Calvin asked softly while looking down into my gaze.

"It's a start." I gave a sad smile because he was hurt. I could see it all in his eyes and I wished I could take the pain away. Calvin was right, he had been nothing but good to me. I had gotten greedy and messed up big time.

I pressed my hand against his chest again and felt this breath quicken before he moved away, distancing himself from me. "I need some time to think."

I sighed and threw one hand to my hip. "Think about what?"

"Our marriage." This was like a bad dream. *It can't be happening.* Calvin turned away. "I'll be gone by the time you get home."

I started to stop him, but decided that maybe we both needed time. I made my way to my desk and eased onto my chair. Everything was so out of control. *And Shane got his ass beat.* That was the only thing funny about the situation. The rest of it was so sad. I just hoped Shane finally got the message to stay away from me. I just needed to fix my marriage, but it would take a little time. I had really messed things up. Now I needed to figure out how to make things right again.

My phone vibrated. I reached across my desk and noticed I had a text message from Portia.

I knew that dude looked familiar

There was a video attached. I pressed Play to discover it was the football game at the high school last Friday night. There to the right of the screen was Meechie talking to the dude whose face I'd seen plastered all over the news…Dollar. But it was the man walking up toward them in a green sweatshirt, blue jeans, and Nike Air Force Ones who had my stomach tied up in knots.

Shane.

48
Renee

I loaded my bag into the trunk of my rental and climbed into the car. It was time to say goodbye and get back to the east coast. I was scheduled to speak at a women's empowerment luncheon in Norfolk on Monday, and I had no intentions of disappointing them. Besides, Quinton was doing better. Getting stronger every day. His surgeon had hinted at discharging him next week. Damn insurance companies. If you were breathing and able to take a shit, they couldn't wait to boot your ass out of a hospital bed to keep down costs. Quinton would go home with his father and Rita. After his six-week checkup and a clean bill of health, I would be back to get my son the hell away from this place. I just had this feeling if I didn't, the next time Quinton wouldn't be so lucky. He might get on my last nerve, but at the end of the day he was still my baby.

My Bluetooth beeped and I tapped the button on the side without even looking down to see who was calling. "Hello?"

"You on your way here yet?"

I smiled at the sound of Clayton's soothing voice. "Are you anxious to see me?" I purred.

"Hell, yeah. I'm missing the hell outta you."

"Aww, you sure know how to make a girl feel good about herself."

"That's what I do," he joked. "I was just talking about you with my aunt. She lives there in Boonville."

"Really?" He had mentioned he'd had family here before, but I was so caught up in Quinton's drama, I didn't even bother to ask. One of the first rules of relationships is to ask a man about himself. "Who's your people?"

"The Barton's. You might know her son Chris or her daughter Reese."

His comment caused me to swerve into the other lane. I quickly yanked the car back before I ran into the rear of a parked car. "Oh shit!"

"You okay?" His tone was filled with concern.

"Yeah, or at least I was before you told me who you're related to," I muttered under my breath, only he heard me.

"You know them?"

"Not him, but I know Reese."

There was a long pause. "I'm waiting."

I released a long shaky breath. "Okay, before this goes any further, I have a confession."

"Whassup?"

"I know your cousin *and* her husband Kenny."

He replied in a tone that said it wasn't a big deal. "Around there… I figured as much. Columbia's not that big."

"Okay, let me try this again… Kenny and I were knocking boots while he was engaged to Reese."

"Oh."

"And during the affair I was working on a new novel, and several elements of their personal life somehow got weaved into the story."

"Somehow?" Was that humor I heard in his voice?

"And being that I am such an amazing author, everyone knew who I was talking about, and well your cousin was embarrassed and demanded I remove the book from the shelves which I can't do."

"Of course."

I turned the car into the hospital parking garage. "Anyway, she tried to confront me a few months ago. If you stick around long enough, you'll learn that's not the way to approach me."

"So… let me see if I got this right," Clayton said. "You were fucking her man."

Hearing that word coming from Clayton's mouth, I started laughing. "Did you just say fucking?"

"Quit interrupting."

I zipped my lips.

"You were *screwing* her man and working on a book at the same time. Somehow you started writing about him and my cousin." I heard him swallow before he continued. "The book was released and everyone assumed you were talking about her. Am I right?"

"Completely."

There was another pause. "This reminds me of a movie."

"Exactly." I parked on the first level and just left it running, while I held my breath and waited.

"There's never a dull moment with you," he finally said.

I released a sigh and couldn't tell if he was angry. He was probably sick of all my over-the-top antics. "I really feel bad about the whole thing. I'm a bitch, but I'm not that type of bitch. I don't just set out to hurt people just for the hell of it. I need a purpose."

"I believe that."

"Really?" I breathed.

"Yes, Renee, you have a good heart. And in the time I have spent with you, I've learned that nobody messes with your family or friends. You'll go to battle to protect them. It's certainly a turn-on."

"Turn-on, huh?" I cooed. "How turned on?"

"I guess you'll find out when you get here." He'd lowered his voice to almost a whisper.

"I can't wait." And I meant every word. I turned off the car and strutted across the parking lot. "I'm going to run in and visit with my son a bit, then I'll be on my way."

I ended the call and felt like I was floating. Clayton was amazing! I didn't want to get ahead of myself, but I really wanted a chance to see where things could go from here. That's if he wanted the same.

Danielle had called while Clayton and I were on the phone. As I stepped through the sliding door, I connected the call.

"Hey girl, what's up? I was on the phone with Clayton. You will—"

"Renee, I need to talk to you about something," she said, interrupting me and something in her voice made me frown.

"What's wrong?"

"I rather not say." I could tell she was moving around because the signal was fading in and out.

"I'm at the hospital. You want me to drop by your office before I roll out?" It would delay my time with Clayton, but I'd make it up to him later.

"No. I'm gonna come and meet you at the hospital. I think my office might be bugged." She was whispering.

I thought she was playing, so I started to laugh, but when she didn't join in I realized she was serious.

"Something d-doesn't feel right. But I'll talk to you about it when I get there."

She had me curious about what it could be. "Okay. Call me and I'll come out in the hall, so we can talk in private."

"Okay." She drew a shaky breath. "I have my suspicions about something, but I wanna talk to you in person."

What was I, Grand Central Station? Mario was now calling me.

"Danny, Mario's calling. I gotta go, but I'll see you when you get here." I didn't wait for her response before I clicked over. "Yes?"

"Renee, he's gone!"

I froze at the sound of terror in Mario's voice. "Who's gone?" I asked, even though I already had an idea who he was referring to.

"Q! Q is gone."

"Okay, wait a minute, slow down," I said and started walking fast down the hospital corridor. "Now let's try this again. Tell me what's going on." I don't know how I managed to stay so calm.

"I'm up on the floor, and the nurses said that idiot checked himself out."

"Checked out!" I yelled. "Why the hell would he do that?" I always knew that boy was stupid, but this right here was the icing on the donut.

Mario was breathing hard and so heavy I had to turn down the volume slightly on my Bluetooth. "I can't believe this shit is happening!" he managed between breaths.

"Mario, I'm on my way upstairs. Ask the nurse what time Q left and I will call Soledad and find out if he's with her," I managed in a rush. I was trying to be the voice of reason, even though my heart was beating so hard, I could hear it pounding beneath my chest.

"Renee! I need you to listen!" I heard Mario say. "Have you been watching the news?"

I reached the elevators and punched the button. "The news? No, I didn't even bother this morning. What? What's wrong?" Before he got the words out, I knew it would be bad.

"He's dead!" he cried. "Someone shot and killed him!"

My head began to spin. I stopped walking and asked timidly, "Who's dead?"

"Meechie's dead!"

I heard a scream, and it took a moment to realize it had come from me. "What? When?"

The frustration was heavy in his voice. "I don't know. Sounds like it happened last night."

"I'm on my way up," I said barely in a whisper. I ended the call and just stood there in a daze as I waited for the elevator. This couldn't be happening. No fucking way!

I pressed every button. What was taking so long? I called Soledad and got no answer. "Where you at, girl?" I muttered under my breath impatiently. The elevators were finally moving down. I sent Danielle a quick text.

Meechie's dead

As soon as I hit Send, I decided that maybe that's what she was coming over to the hospital to talk about.

As the elevator arrived at the main floor, I was still fumbling with my phone. When I looked up to board, I stopped dead in my tracks. A small woman was exiting when her eyes met mine.

How the hell was this happening to me?

"Well, if it isn't little Nae-Nae?" she replied as if I should've been happy to see her.

I swallowed the bile that was in my throat and replied, "Hello, Mama."

Other Books by Angie Daniels

Feinin' *Big Spankable Asses Anthology*
Tease
Seduced into Submission: Curious
Seduced into Submission: Serve
Seduced into Submission: Obey
Talk a Good Game
When It Rains
Love Uncovered
When I First Saw You
In the Company of My Sistahs
Trouble Loves Company
Careful of the Company You Keep
Intimate Intentions
Hart & Soul
Time is of the Essence
A Will to Love
Endless Enchantment
Destiny in Disguise
The Second Time Around
The Playboy's Proposition
The Player's Proposal
For You I Do
Before I Let You Go
In Her Neighbor's Bed
Show Me
Wicked Pleasure
Any Man Will Do
Coming for My Baby
Strutting in Red Stilettos
Running to Love in Pink Stilettos
Say My Name
Every Second Counts
A Beau for Christmas
Do Me Baby
Naughty Before Christmas

Curious- Seduced into Submission
Served- Seduced into Submission
Time for Pleasure
For Her Pleasure
Beg for It
Put Your Name on It
Stilettos & Mistletoes
Time for Desire

ABOUT THE AUTHOR

Angie Daniels is a free spirit who isn't afraid to say what's on her mind or even better, write about it. Since strutting onto the literary scene in five-inch heels, she's been capturing her audience's attention with her wild imagination and love for alpha men. The *USA Today* Bestselling Author has written over thirty novels for imprints such as BET Arabesque, Harlequin/ Kimani Romance and Kensington/ Dafina and Kensington/ Aphrodisia Books. For more information about upcoming releases, and to connect with Angie on Facebook, please visit her website at www.angiedaniels.com.

Made in the USA
Middletown, DE
07 June 2019